# HEARTBREAK
# HOUSESHARE

HarperNorth
Windmill Green,
Mount Street,
Manchester, M2 3NX

A division of
HarperCollins*Publishers*
1 London Bridge Street
London SE1 9GF

www.harpercollins.co.uk

HarperCollinsPublishers
1st Floor, Watermarque Building, Ringsend Road
Dublin 4, Ireland

First published by HarperNorth in 2022

1 3 5 7 9 10 8 6 4 2

A catalogue record for this book
is available from the British Library

ISBN: 978-0-00-852293-3

Printed and bound in Great Britain by
CPI Group (UK) Ltd, Croydon

# HEARTBREAK HOUSESHARE

## Emily Merrill

Harper
North

*For Mum and Dad.*

*Thanks for healing all the heartbreaks and moving me into all the houseshares. Love you.*

# 1

I dumped my suitcase onto the bed, blinking fast to avoid another set of tears.

There was something so overwhelming about packing up a bedroom. It wasn't just the boxes, the belongings or even the mega cleaning job once the room was empty. It was remembering the feeling of your first kiss on that particular bed, or the memory of your disappointment at a job rejection at that particular desk. The butterflies when picking a date outfit from the wardrobe or staring into the mirror and feeling ready for your first day at work. Bedrooms are capable of being more than a bed, wardrobe, mirror and a desk. They can be home.

The night before my parents had dropped me off at university in Manchester – almost four and a half years ago now – I'd sat wrapped up in my childhood duvet, already missing a bedroom that I'd come back to every ten weeks. More frequently than that, given that the journey between Manchester and Liverpool was under an hour. I'd dragged my heels massively, trying to convince myself that I didn't need to move out, that I could do university online. Flash forward a year and I felt the same way about leaving halls: desperate not to leave the grubby Jack and Jill bathroom or the giant pinboard covered in random posters. Leaving Manchester for good two years later was even worse, although lessened a tiny bit by the fact that my favourite part of university was coming with me. As much as I hadn't made the most of my overpriced student house, it hadn't made leaving any easier. Manchester had been where I'd first learnt how to cook pasta, and that you should never *ever* 'just risk' mixing your darks with light sheets (even if it was only the odd red sock or pair of knickers). It had been the city I'd stayed up writing essays all night in, and the city where I'd first been drunk. It was the city where I'd met a boy from Reading who studied finance and liked *Misfits* just as much as I did, but only up until season four because after that it got ropey. Moving is always bittersweet. Even if you weren't completely leaving a city behind, just moving halfway across it like I was now.

I stared at the next drawer of clothes I needed to sort through, picking up a ratty pyjama top that I'd got from the freshers' fair in my first year. How could one person possibly own so much *stuff*? For some reason, I'd carried this T-shirt with me from house to house, clinging onto the experience like I was still 18 and could drink five Jägerbombs without breaking a sweat. With a sigh, I placed it in the 'to bin' bag and moved on. I'd met Aaron that week anyway. Definitely didn't need a constant reminder of *that*.

Next up was the little line of snow globes on my dresser, a collection I'd been building for pretty much my entire life. Everyone collects something, right? My gran's fridge was notorious for fridge magnets. First in line was a globe bought at the Blue Planet Aquarium during a primary school trip, and at the other end was one I'd brought home from New York last year with my sister. With almost too many to count, my eyes scanned over the collection, sticking at a teeny tiny globe I'd almost forgotten about. I'd bought that one in a random service station on my way to visit Aaron during one of our dreaded summers away from each other – I stuffed that one in the bin bag without looking. Aside from the one tainted offender that now lay at the bottom of the black bag at my feet, its fate decided, I stared at all twenty-six of them affectionately. Each glass bauble a tiny part of me. Like a patchwork blanket, just significantly more fragile. I grabbed a cardboard box and some bubble wrap and got to work on protecting my precious memories for their travels.

The task was so therapeutic that I almost missed the persistent buzzing of my phone. With a sigh I gave in to it and put down globe number eight.

'Hello?'

In my haste, I hadn't even checked the caller ID. Uncharacteristic. I was more of a weigh up the risks before I jumped into something kind of girl. I checked each box of eggs meticulously before I put them in the trolley, and I *never* left the flat without an umbrella and some hand sanitiser. When Aaron got the job here in London and I'd started looking too, I'd written a pros and cons list the length of my arm. I heard rustling on the other end of the phone, like the caller was in the middle of something else.

'Flick? Is that you?'

I winced. I knew that voice and had to bite back a response of 'Who else is it going to be? You've dialled *my* number.'

I took a deep breath and settled on, 'Yeah, it's me,' instead.

I could hear him breathing down the line. And even though I wanted to reach through the airwaves and slap him, I also found myself cradling the phone. It turned out I really was that pathetic. I had moved to sit on the bed without realising, squished between my still pretty much empty suitcase and a stack of birthday cards from last year that I'd never bothered to sort through. I didn't intend on taking a scribbled birthday card from Aunty Sue to my new place.

'It's good to hear your voice.'

I sucked in a breath and refused to exhale. *Don't ruin this moment. Whatever you do, Flick, don't ruin this moment. Savour it.*

'It is?'

*Damn it, Flick.* Any cool points I'd had, I had just lost in one fell swoop.

'Yeah. So, I'm outside.' Aaron's voice was higher, like it always was when he was saying something that might not be well received. It was a tactic he'd been using for years. Two months ago I'd come home to our flat after work to the whole place smelling of chocolate chip cookies. The plate he thrust in my hands before I'd even taken my coat off was an attempt to sugar-coat (literally) the truth about him spending money from the joint account on a new video game. Why did there need to be a new version of men kicking balls around a field every year that cost half a week's rent? I'd pretended to be mad for a couple of hours, before giving in and biting into one of the cookies, moaning and making him

4

laugh out loud. I slated him now, but Aaron had made the best cookies.

In spite of my best efforts to push our memories to the back of my brain, they ambushed me when I was least expecting it. Even though I'd been there and experienced the breakup in all its technicolour HD glory, my mind betrayed me over and over again, replaying everything with a rose-coloured tint. When I slept, my subconscious brought my relationship – or ex-relationship as it was now – to me in dreams. No one ever spoke about the brutality of post-breakup dreams. I woke up most nights with a damp hairline, searching the empty space beside me whilst on the verge of tears. You didn't just throw away almost four years without it coming back to haunt you. So even after all of that, I was surprised to find that if he were here to apologise, I wanted to hear it. Ached for it, in fact. If he was downstairs with a bunch of flowers, I wanted to know.

'It's kind of cold. Can I come in?'

I practically legged it to the intercom to buzz him up to my flat. Our flat? No one's flat. I had no idea who this little guy belonged to any more. I patted the walls affectionately. Another victim of the events of the past few weeks.

I heard the *ding* of the lift as it paused to drop off someone on the floor below, and then after what felt like an age, another *ding* as it arrived at mine. The footsteps that followed were a sound I knew like the back of my hand. With the imminent arrival of Aaron sinking in, I suddenly had a last minute 'what do I look like' panic and ran to the bathroom, patting down my hair and rearranging my parting, grabbing a tube of lip balm and smearing it over my lips. It was one of those weird tingly peppermint ones. I winced. Anything to make myself look marginally better. Regardless, it could only have been an improvement on the snotty, mascara-streaked mess he'd left behind two weeks ago.

Even though I knew it was coming, I still jumped out of my skin when he finally knocked on the door. I waited, counting out seven seconds before letting myself go and answer it, hopping around from one foot to the other, trying to gift myself some sort of upper hand. By this point, I'd convinced myself that he was here to beg for forgiveness. What level of apology would I accept? A huge bunch of flowers? A love letter? My heart warmed at the thought. And the thought of the make-up sex. He was going to owe me *big* for this past two weeks. I deserved some serious airtime.

I walked over to the door, yanking it open and faking a sort of half-beam. I hoped it didn't look as frantic as I felt. But he knew me, Aaron. He knew my smile, like he knew every other part of me. And he knew when it was fake.

'Hi.' He was standing there in front of me, hands in pockets, looking a bit sheepish.

There were no flowers in hand or hint of a letter, but I decided that it was okay. I could deal with no flowers, as much as I'd already imagined where I would put them (on my desk). None of that mattered as long as he was here to admit that he'd made some sort of mistake.

'Hi.' I rocked back on my heels, suddenly unsure of how to act. Isn't it funny how you can know someone so intrinsically, and then suddenly you don't feel like you do any more? He was a stranger that I knew every part of.

'Can I come in?' Aaron gestured to the hallway, and I stepped back, waving him in awkwardly.

'Yeah, sure. It's technically still your flat too.' *If you want it. If you still want me.*

'Well . . .' He looked around awkwardly. 'It looks weird, empty-ish, doesn't it? What a strange feeling.'

Never mind that all *my* stuff was still here, like the stubborn final layer of grease on a pan. *Look!* I wanted to yell at him. *Look! There's that tea towel that says 'I leaf you' and I thought was really funny when we went to Yosemite. There's that vase that your mum bought for us when we moved here – you from Reading and me from Liverpool. You said you knew I was pretending to like it for your mum's sake, and that it made you love me more. Do you remember? There's the poster for that concert we went to on our third date, when we were still babies and nowhere near ready to take on the world. Look!* I wanted to shake him. *I'm still here. It's not empty yet.*

Instead: 'I know. Weird.'

Aaron put his hands in his pockets again, and it was only then that I noticed the tote bag looped around his elbow. Hopefully, there were some flowers in there. Not enough room in there for sunflowers, my favourite, but definitely room for peonies. Or daisies. If I was honest, I'd probably accept some dandelions that he'd picked out of the cracks between two paving stones.

'So, how are you?' His dimples flickered into sight. There they were.

I tried not to let the dimples throw me off. 'I'm . . .' Heartbroken? Gutted? Having dreams about us? '. . . doing okay. Packing is a little bit boring, though, isn't it?' I laughed it off like it was one big joke. I was one second away from collapsing on the floor.

He grinned. 'Unpacking is even worse.'

Right. Another reminder that he'd already had his backup plan sorted when he'd dropped the bombshell that he was leaving. It had been a scramble for me, a well-calculated adventure for him. My first thought when it had happened had been 'It's a good job this didn't happen when we were still in our eighteen-month contract with the flat', and I'd been wondering ever since if this had been coming for months. When I was oblivious, thinking that everything was fine.

There was another long silence.

'Do you want a cup of tea?' I pointed to the kitchen like he might have forgotten where it was. 'A beer?'

*Please pick beer. Please let it be acceptable for me to also consume alcohol.* I thought of the wine in the fridge, a glass left from the almost full bottle I'd consumed last night whilst crying over reruns of *Friends*. The episode when Ross and Rachel break up, but you know they'll end up together in the end, because that's how it works.

'Nah, I'm alright. I don't have long. I'm meeting some people from work for coffee.'

That's how it was now. I'd gone from being the destination to a stop along the way.

'How are your family? Did they swear as much as they usually do when they helped you move?'

He laughed. 'You know my dad. Swore like a sailor the entire time.' Aaron gestured to the very vase I'd kept to appease his family. 'I left that behind. Mum said it was too ugly to take.'

*Oh, for crying out loud.*

'Dad said to wish you well, Flick.' A small smile, sheepish again.

I pictured Aaron's dad – tall, lanky, a mop of hair. Just like his son. They were a neat family, the kind with fingernails that were always trimmed and that had meat, potatoes and veg most nights. They were also my second family. I was going to miss the Reeds.

It was becoming more and more evident that he was not here to confess his undying love for me. Prior to two weeks ago, I'd never really understood the phrase 'having the rug pulled out from under you'. Now, life felt like a constant conveyor belt of rug pulling. I wasn't sure that there was any rug left in the world to pull.

'So' – I tucked my hair behind my ears – 'what are you doing here, then?'

*If you don't want a drink. If you're just going to stand there awkwardly and pretend like I'm some stranger or friend of a friend, not the girl you swore you'd marry one day.*

He paused, and for a second the facade fell. And then he reached into the tote bag and pulled out a book. A bloody book.

'I found this in one of my boxes. It's yours.'

I didn't even recognise the romcom he held out to me, had no recollection of buying it. He had dropped in to break my heart all over again just for *this*?

'You really didn't have to bring that here. I would have forgotten about it. In fact, I already had.' My tone betrayed my annoyance slightly towards the end.

I didn't take it from his outstretched hand. He placed it on the IKEA table that we'd assembled drunkenly together two Julys ago, high on moving in. We had waited way too long for our takeaway, the pre-dinner drinks going straight to our heads, collapsing on the floor in laughter as we'd attempted to hammer in nails and get the legs to stand straight. We'd put up with things sliding off the table for the last year and a half. I'd assumed we'd be laughing about it forever.

'I also just wanted to see you. It was all a little bit fraught last time, wasn't it? I just wanted to say goodbye.'

*Last time?* Jesus. I resented how flippant he was being. Had one attempt at goodbye not been enough for him? I didn't need a repeat of 'last time', thank you very much. My red, puffy post-break up eyes were only just beginning to fade. And yet a part of me – which I hated right now – was glad for the chance to hug him again. It was like being thankful for a few crumbs when you'd once had the whole biscuit.

Aaron pulled me in, squeezing me tightly to his chest. 'I really am sorry, Flick. Again.'

I didn't speak. If I tried, I would cry, and this whole image of 'fine' that I was trying my best to project would collapse in on itself. I just nodded into his chest.

'This will be for the best in the end. You'll see.' He pulled away and jostled my shoulder like he was my tennis coach.

'Right.' I managed one word.

He turned back to glance at me on his way out of the door, and it occurred to me that I really did have no idea when I'd next see him again, if ever. It was confusing, how you could go from seeing someone every day and then without any warning, see them for no days at all. I'd been annoyed over something stupid, the day before we'd broken up. Something about leaving the cucumber at the back of the fridge to frost over. I wished more than anything that I'd stopped mid-rant to appreciate the little moments of magic that came with Aaron. Not the way he left the cucumber to rot, but the way he wrote messages in the mirror condensation after his shower or put hot water bottles in our bed when I was on my period. It seemed so tragic that one of the last conversations we'd had as a couple had been about vegetables. Not even fresh vegetables.

'Bye, Flick.' All credit to him, he had the heart to look a bit sad as he waved goodbye.

'Bye, Reed.' And then he was gone.

I sighed heavily to avoid crying again and moved back into my bedroom, preparing to continue the painful process of sorting through this flat. I fished around in the bin bag for a minute until I found what I was looking for. Aha. There it was.

I chucked the Aaron-tainted snow globe as hard as I could at the floor in anger, hoping for it to smash. Panic then set in. *Crap*. Had it left a dent?

And then I had my pettiest thought yet, as much as I tried to shake it off. Who cared? The deposit was his anyway.

# 2

In terms of actual distance, the journey from Shepherd's Bush to Acton was not a long one. But with traffic, we were talking twenty-five minutes, worst case scenario.

'I'm wondering how many trips we can realistically do this in.' Dad pointed at the pile of belongings sitting in front of the welcome mat. Now that I'd deep cleaned and got rid of 70 per cent of my life, it didn't look as overwhelming.

'I'm thinking no more than three.' I pointed to the desk. 'How are we going to manage that?'

Dad knotted his arms around his head, squinting and playing car Jenga in his head. 'If we eliminate your legroom, I think we can do it in two. How do you feel about sitting cross-legged?'

'Do what in two?' Mum came in through the front door, laden with bags. 'I've brought supplies for the troops!'

She was holding three sandwich packets from M&S and a selection of organic juices. It was the most 'Mum' purchase I'd ever seen. And I'd seen a lot of 'Mum' purchases in my twenty-two years.

'I thought you were only going for coffee.' I raised my eyebrow.

'I thought I'd be prepared and get lunch whilst I was at it. You should have seen her face when I asked her where the butties were.' She rolled her eyes and started rooting around in her bag. 'Anyway. Egg and cress or cheese and pickle? I think there's some crisps in here somewhere too.'

Dad threw his hands up. 'Lorna. It's 10 a.m. and we still have to cart all of this around London. Can't we eat a little bit later?'

Mum nodded in agreement, opening a mini packet of cashew nuts. Dad stared at her pointedly.

'What? Nuts are brain food.'

Dad sighed. 'So I was just saying to Flick . . .'

'Felicity.' Mum corrected him with my birthname. It was an age-old fight.

'To Felicity, that if she tucks her legs right in, I think we can fit the desk in trip number two. No need for trip number three.'

Dad's stress levels were palpable. London traffic was a nightmare, there was no doubt about it. I knew from Mum that he'd spent days researching the best ways to get around the city. He arrived here every time in a stressed-out state, and it never waned until he'd got from A to B.

'Did you bring the cleaning supplies up from the car? I'll get started on the kitchen.'

I patted her hand. 'Actually, Mum, I've already cleaned it –'

'Two sets of eyes are better than one. Besides' – she grabbed the industrial-sized bottle of CIF – 'you want to make sure Aaron gets his deposit back.'

I thought about the dent in the bedroom floor and just let her get on with it.

***

When Mum had conceded that I wasn't completely incompetent with a toilet brush, and Dad had caved and eaten the M&S sandwiches, it was finally time to start saying goodbye.

'Two minutes until showtime.' Dad gestured to my phone, which was ringing. 'Tell her to keep it brief.'

'When has she ever kept it brief?'

He sighed, leaving me to my sister.

'Hey Flickie baby.' Suze appeared on the screen, her face inches from the camera, beaming at me. 'How goes the move?'

Suze, three years older and the 25 to my 22, had been here all last week, having driven down from Liverpool at the first hint of my meltdown. She'd taken an emergency week off work to piece me back together, spooning Ben & Jerry's into my mouth and even allowing me to pick out all the cookie dough pieces. She was a gem, my big sister, always picking people up when they were on the floor (metaphorically, but also as of last week, literally – I hadn't moved from the living room floor for a solid day).

'It's . . .' I leaned my head out of my bedroom to see Dad huffing over a haphazardly packed box, and Mum flitting around with a dustpan and brush, '. . . going.'

'I'm sorry I can't be there.' Suze pouted. Her red lipstick was perfectly applied, as always.

'Without you, Mum would have found me drunk and stuck to the bathroom floor. Your work here is done and appreciated.' I didn't tell her that I'd sobbed for three hours straight after she'd left. I'd spent the rest of the night horizontal on my bed with cold cotton-wool pads on my eyes, trying to tone down the damage before work the following day. 'Three out of four members of the Sage family isn't bad.'

'True. Although let's be honest, of all the Sage members, I'm the best at spoon-feeding ice cream and scouring Netflix for movies that are *just* weird enough to help you forget all your problems.'

I could see her applying false eyelashes in the mirror she kept next to her desk. It was a Saturday, so that meant that she was probably getting herself dolled up for a gig. Bohemian waves, bold lashes, red lips. She was a bit of a bombshell. Events management during the week, jazz singer by weekend. Suze was a lot of things, never one to be placed in a box. In sixth form she'd woken up one day and decided to film a documentary about the conservation of pine martens (Google it), which won an amateur film-making award. I also remembered her sneaking out in the middle of the night to meet boys, promising to buy me a blue Slush Puppie in return for my silence. Like I said, never one to be placed in a box.

As much as I loved her, I hadn't told her about Aaron dropping by last night. It was a little bit embarrassing how fast my life had hit rock bottom. I'd been so proud when I'd made the move here with Aaron after uni and started working at *Influence* (which, thankfully, was the only pillar of my life left standing). I'd felt like I wasn't the youngest in the family any more; we were all just adults. Now I was moving into a shared house with people I had never even met. Everyone always said that your twenties were guaranteed to be a bit of a mess, but I'd never considered it applying to me. It had been something I'd chuckled at whilst reading the online agony-aunt columns I loved. Never something to relate to, before now.

'Is that Susan?' Mum bounded into the room, waving. 'How are you love?'

Suze waved back without making eye contact, false lashes halfway to her other eye. 'Good, just about to leave for a gig.'

Mum clapped. 'Send us a video on the WhatsApp thingy?'

My sister did finally turn at that, but only to smirk at me. 'Will do, Mum. Just one quick question?'

Mum nodded.

'How many times have you checked that Flick cleaned her kitchen properly?'

I burst out laughing, Mum flapping her duster at the camera. 'Oh, go and sing somewhere will you.'

We all blew kisses at the phone screen until Suze disappeared.

'Right.' Mum perched on the bed next to me. 'You ready kiddo?'

I leaned my head on her shoulder. 'If I say no, will I still have to leave?'

'Unfortunately, yes.'

There was a momentary pause. I knew who we were both thinking about; I'd taken the breakup only slightly harder than Mum, so that was saying something.

'Have you spoken to him at all since he left?'

I thought about the flicker of hope that had settled in my stomach last night. About how I would have taken him back, no questions asked. My skin flushed bright red.

'No, I haven't.'

Mum bit the inside of her cheek. She had loved Aaron like a third child. I'd felt this weird guilt ever since he'd first announced that he was leaving me – a guilt that I'd taken something away from Mum. But when she turned to look at me, cupping my chin and shaking it, I could tell that as much as she'd loved my boyfriend, she loved me more.

She pecked my cheek. 'Right, well no point dwelling on that, then, is there. I lived in a shared house in my twenties and I *loved* it. You will too, you'll see.'

I resisted the urge to shudder. I'd thought that houseshares were something well in my past. I didn't want to go back to a life of sighing when you opened the fridge and your milk was gone, or having to turn your bedroom into a launderette because if there *was* space to hang your washing downstairs, you'd be forced to walk around smelling like everyone's dinner for the rest of the week. Did houseshares get better as you got older, or did they get worse? Did I need a milk padlock like I'd seen on Twitter?

'It's a new adventure. An unexpected one, but still an adventure. Now put on some Chapstick and let's go.'

I took the balm from her outstretched hand. It didn't matter what situation we found ourselves in, Mum always had a Chapstick to hand. It was comforting, in a weird way. I applied it and handed it back to her, checking my eyes in the wardrobe mirror for wayward flecks of mascara. I hadn't worn makeup in over a week – what's the point when the risk of crying it off is so high? But I'd put on the bare minimum today – first impressions and all that.

I didn't know much about the three girls that I was moving in with, other than that their fourth member had left to move in with her partner (a cruel irony). A new fourth inhabitant of 56 Carlisle Avenue had been required, and I'd come across the ad on a spare room website in a stroke of luck. They seemed nice enough from their Facebook photos, but there was only so much information you could gather from various drunken pictures and declarations of love for their friends. I'd lived with girls before – me and Aaron had decided in first year that we'd wait until after uni to live together – but only in the literal sense of the word. It happened gradually; first, you couldn't go for drinks because you'd already said you'd go out for dinner with your boyfriend, and then next time you missed the invitation entirely because you weren't in the living room when the event was planned. Instead, you've moved your toothbrush into a different house, like you prom-ised yourself you wouldn't. When you *are* around, you don't understand the inside jokes any more, which hurts but you know it's your own fault. I'd never been involved in the arguments, but I hadn't been involved in much of the fun stuff either. I thought of the girls in these photos, and the introductory email I'd received, letting me know the where-abouts of the keys and the alarm code. Maybe this didn't have to be the end of the world. Maybe it was a second chance.

I got up to follow Mum, who was being instructed by Dad about which of the boxes needed to go in the boot. They were a force to be reckoned with, my parents. Always had been, ever since I could remember. Mum might have been the one micromanaging, but Dad already had the full quest mapped out in his mind. I smiled at them before grabbing my handbag off the mattress, switching off the light and turning my back on the last year and a half of my life. There was nothing left for me here. It was time to start afresh.

# 3

'Is this it?' Mum craned her neck, looking at the road sign. 'This is it, Felicity!'

I'd been tracking our progress on my phone, trying to help Dad navigate the one-way systems and bus traffic. Without even realising it, we'd crept closer and closer. Mum was right – here we were. Carlisle Avenue. I wiped my clammy palms on my trousers.

'Still half the battle to go.' Dad squinted – his tell-tale concentration face. 'Who knows what the parking situation will be. Bloody nightmare.'

Mum winked at me in the wing mirror, holding back a smirk. I glanced at all my belongings piled up on the seat next to me, spilling behind into the boot. Thinking of the next logical steps – unpacking, trip number two, sorting, cleaning – instead of the emotional turmoil of entering the unknown, calmed me momentarily. Getting from A to B was a lot easier to stomach than introducing myself to three strangers. And then living with them. The journey had passed way too quickly, not nearly enough time to stew over the situation and imagine all the ways that this could go wrong (top three – they immediately hate me on the basic principle that they loved their old housemate; they hate me gradually as a result of who I am as a person; one of these strangers is a murderer who takes me down in the middle of the night). I analysed my clothing choice for approximately the twentieth time. I didn't usually obsess over outfits because I was rarely awake early enough in the morning to afford to care. Today was different; Suze had suggested wearing something that felt the most like 'me'. If it had been her, she'd have waltzed into the new house in a catsuit or something ridiculous. Go big or go home and all that. I'd settled (after five outfit changes) on my favourite pastel pink culottes and a leopard-print bodysuit.

Dad pulled into a space outside the detached house, muttering to himself about the car in front.

'Not as hellish as I thought, Lorna.' He tapped Mum's knee. 'Not as hellish as I thought.'

Mum turned to me. 'Right, how do you want to do this? What's our plan of action?'

Throughout my existential crisis, I hadn't thought too hard about the practicalities. Would they have made sure they were in the house at the time of my arrival, like a welcome party? One of the girls, Katherine, had messaged me on Facebook and asked what time I thought I'd be arriving. What did that mean? Were they giving me space to move in or lingering behind the front door? I felt myself pale. I wasn't entirely sure that I could do this.

'I think you should go in first, hon.' Mum tapped at her phone, probably checking into London on Facebook like she did every time they visited. It would be accompanied by an overly enthusiastic caption, and most likely a photo of me that she'd snapped when I wasn't looking. Within minutes she'd have a stream of comments from colleagues and fellow parents and members of her bridge club. Her social media presence was better than mine by a mile.

She turned her phone off, satisfied with whatever she'd been doing. 'Okay, Felicity. Go in and introduce yourself, and we'll hang around here and follow in a few minutes.'

I was 22, almost 23, and yet I still appreciated the directive. I unbuckled my belt, shaking off the constant feeling of *this is not what I expected my life in London to be like.* I was supposed to be on the sofa in my old flat, watching a David Attenborough documentary with Aaron and putting Celebrations wrappers straight back into the tin.

Smoothing my coat one last time on the way up to the front door, I inhaled. It wasn't that I was scared of these people; I could mingle, I could be civilised. I just didn't enjoy the feeling of putting myself out there, at risk of being rejected all over again. Not by a man this time, but by three girls that I *really* needed to accept me. It felt like the first week of university again, like my parents were dropping me off during freshers' week. This time, though, it was purely operation friendship. No men allowed.

*Pull yourself together, Flick.*

I cleared my throat – nothing is more embarrassing than that sound your voice makes when you haven't used it much – and unlocked the door using the key I'd picked up yesterday. It felt weird unlocking a door and walking into a house that I'd only seen once. None of the girls had been

there the first time I'd viewed it, so I was going in totally
blind. It felt a bit like walking into a random house on a
random street and asking to be part of the family.

I wasn't sure what I'd been expecting when I twisted the
key and pushed open the door – maybe the sound of the
kettle or several pairs of feet wandering around upstairs. Instead,
you could have heard a pin drop. There was a long hallway
leading into the open plan kitchen slash living room, and one
bedroom on the ground floor, along with one of the two
shared bathrooms. The bedroom on this floor wasn't mine, so
I bypassed it and went straight to the kitchen.

'Hello?' I said it relatively loudly, announcing myself so that
no one panicked and thought I was an intruder. Was I over-
thinking this? Probably.

A girl with pink hair in French braids was dancing in the
middle of the kitchen, huge headphones covering her ears as
she chopped up some strawberries. She hadn't heard me, so
I stole the unexpected moment of peace to glance around
the room. It was almost . . . clean. A far cry from some of
the houses I'd seen at uni. I'd imagined piled up dishes, splat-
ters of sauce on the walls, crumbs all over the worktops. It
had kept me up last night, thinking about it.

'*Shit.*'

I jumped out of my skin at the sound of the girl turning
around. She had her hand clasped to her chest.

'Sorry, I didn't mean to swear. But you did scare the *shit*
out of me.'

Her eyes were kind, so I knew she was kidding.

'I did shout, but –'

She waved me off. 'I know how I can get when I'm listening to my Saturday morning playlist. It's a serious issue. I'm literally unable to stop dancing.'

I refrained from checking the time on my phone. Saturday morning playlist? It was around 3 p.m.

I stuck out my hand. 'I'm Felicity. Everyone calls me Flick, though.'

The pink haired girl squinted at me before breaking into a beam. She shook my hand. 'I'm Katherine, but everyone calls me Kitty. See? We were clearly destined to be housemates.' She looked me up and down, and I held my breath. 'I *love* that outfit by the way. I've been looking everywhere for a pair of trousers like that.'

I liked her; I'd already made up my mind. Kitty had an ease to her that was infectious. She chatted to me about the logistics of the house – who was where (Stacey was at work, and Maia was out for a run), where everyone kept their shoes, how the bin rota worked. All of the things I'd been anxious about discovering. It was like she was working through my worry list, conscious of how it felt to be the new, fourth member of an already established club. I loved her for it.

'So, where are your parents? I assume that you didn't walk here with all of your stuff.' She was munching on the bowl of strawberries I'd caught her preparing, offering me some and shrugging when I declined.

'They're unpacking the car.'

She nodded. 'Thought it would be better if you went in first, did they?' Kitty obviously saw the stricken look on my face. 'Don't worry, you aren't that predictable. My mum just did the exact same thing when I moved in eight months ago. Except I don't even think she was cool enough to wait outside. I'm pretty sure she just hovered in the hallway, listening to me meet everyone. She's proper nosy, my mum. Peels the curtain back every time she hears voices on her street. Do you want me to show you your bedroom?'

I was pretty sure I knew which one mine was, but again, I didn't want to risk walking into someone else's and making a faux pas on day one of the new adventure. I followed Kitty up the stairs, which she took two at a time, practically leaping from step to step. I didn't imitate the weightlessness. Knowing me, I'd have tripped and landed at the bottom with an audible splat. There were photos stuck randomly on the wall next to the banister, of a group of girls on nights out, at restaurants, and even one with them all piled on the sofa downstairs. None of them looked as terrifying as I'd imagined.

She passed by one of the bedrooms on the second floor, rapping on the door. 'This is my room. I'm not weird about it. If you want to come in, I'm almost always fine with it.' She wiggled her eyebrows. 'Unless there's a sock on the handle. Obviously.'

Why would there be . . . *Oh.* I was glad I hadn't asked.

She gestured to another door. 'This one is Maia's. She likes her space, so you'd probably be best waiting until you see her downstairs. We're all different here, but I promise it works.' She turned back and smiled at me again.

*Please God, let me fit in here. I will never ask for another thing again. Except maybe a promotion at the end of the work year, but even that I am willing to forego for this.*

We headed up another flight. That was the thing about the houses here – they were extremely narrow, but tall. I tried not to think about the precarity of the stairs as we headed up. How on earth were you meant to navigate them after a glass of wine? Again, I had visions of an audible splat.

'And this is your room – ta-da!' She twirled like a magician, pushing open the door into the smaller attic room that somehow qualified as a fourth bedroom. 'It's small, but there's a lot you can do with it. Tara had lights strung up here' – Kitty pointed to an exposed beam – 'and a clothing rail here by the window, because of the size of the wardrobe.'

I bit my lip, trying not to think about the free space I'd had when me and Aaron moved in, and how much fun I'd had making the place ours. I breathed in deeply. I could do that here too. I could.

'Are you okay?' I opened my eyes to see Kitty staring at me, concerned. Her headphones were hanging around her neck, still blasting out her 'Saturday morning' playlist. I could hear Shakira's 'Hips Don't Lie' faintly echoing from them.

'Yeah, I'm fine.' I smiled tightly, fighting the prickle at the corner of my eyelids. 'Moving day is always weird.'

'Eugh. Tell me about it. So overwhelming. And packing and unpacking is enough to tip anybody over the edge. I bet you need to do at least another five trips, right?'

I grinned. There was at least one person here who I seemed to click with on an entirely superficial level. I could do this. 'My Dad is optimistic that we'll get it done in two.'

Kitty raised her brow. 'Ambitious. Anyway, I'll leave you to get settled in. I'll probably be in my room most of this afternoon working on a mix for my next gig, but if you need anything, I'll leave my door open a smidge. See you downstairs later?' Her headphones were halfway to her head again, just waiting on a response.

I nodded and she disappeared down the stairs of doom. Moments later I heard Mum introducing herself, before appearing in the doorway with the first box of clothes. Her eyes swept over the room, taking in my living situation. She paused on the wardrobe.

'I think we might need to order a clothes rail, Felicity.'

I closed my eyes once more and took a deep breath. It was just a house.

# 4

I reorganised my small shelf of books for the third time; I'd tried authors by alphabetical order, titles by alphabetical order, and now I was creating a rainbow with the spines. In reality, all three ways had looked fine. I was killing time, delaying the inevitable. I jumped when my phone vibrated. Caught red-handed by Suze.

You haven't been downstairs yet have you?

I pictured my sister's eyes doing that scary thing they did when she wanted you to follow her instructions, something I'd done religiously when we were children. I'd been doing what I was told my whole life, but I was dragging my heels now, unwilling to take her advice. There was nothing wrong with hiding out up here until everyone else had gone to bed. I hoped they weren't night owls; my stomach was rumbling.

Mum and Dad had left in a hurry a few hours ago, not fazed by leaving me behind in a foreign place. When Mum had left me at university for the first time, she had cried the whole way home (or so I'd been told). Today she had left me with a kiss on the cheek and a promise to send a care package in the post, and now I was sat on my bed wondering how I was supposed to do this next bit on my own. For four and a half years I'd almost never been alone, as sad as that sounded. My snow globes were lined up on my windowsill (albeit a sill to a very small, not very bright-looking window in the corner of my room, but a windowsill all the same), and I'd ordered a clothes rail from Argos to come urgently. I'd even paid for next-day delivery. Suze had sent down a box of scented candles as a housewarming gift, so I'd popped one of those on my dresser. It had occurred to me that if a candle lighting experience went wrong up here in the tiny box room, I didn't stand much of a chance. The scent was 'Fresh Cotton', but Suze had scribbled out that name and written 'Fresh Start' on the glass jar in permanent marker instead. She wasn't one for nuance.

*Come on, Flick. Pull yourself together.* I stared at the small pile of trainers that I'd gathered to put on the communal shoe rack downstairs. A valid reason for entering the shared living space. They'd been sitting there for half an hour whilst I'd weighed up the benefits of going downstairs (food, and maybe some friendship) against the negatives (feeling like an outsider, the potential of tripping over . . . it was also possible that I might have misunderstood Kitty when she'd said it was a communal shoe rack, and therefore look like an idiot carrying a handful of shoes).

My phone buzzed again.

I know you're ignoring me. You're just
delaying the inevitable. Go say hi.

'Alright, alright.' I held up my hands even though she couldn't see me. 'You win.'

I picked up the trainers by their laces and headed downstairs, wistfully glancing back at my laptop, which had been playing reruns of *Schitt's Creek*.

Kitty was coming out of her room when I reached the second floor, and I tried not to make my relief obvious. She had wireless earbuds in this time, and didn't jump out of her skin when she saw me.

'Oh, hey!' She closed her door behind her. 'I was just on my way down. I'm *starving*. I'm pretty sure everyone is in the kitchen – are you going to come and meet the others?'

When I nodded, she ploughed on. 'I don't know whether you have plans for dinner or anything, but Maia and I thought it might be nice to get a housemate arrival dinner.'

'A housemate arrival dinner?'

Kitty fiddled with one of her braids as she paused on the top step. 'One thing to know about us is that we like to find any excuse to order food. And yes, I know that due to extortionate rent and the price of avocados and sourdough that we are very much broke and will never enter the property market, but there's nothing like a bonding experience over food. I'm a firm believer in that. So, you in?' She blinked at me expectantly.

I panicked. 'I like food.'

*Good lord what was wrong with me? I like food?* I tried to claw my dignity back. 'My mum brought all kinds of snacks with her from back home, and I swear nothing compares – just wait till I introduce you to a sausage and bean melt.'

'You northerners and your weird baked goods. One of the girls I tutor practically spontaneously combusts every time I pronounce the word "scone". You'll have to teach me your ways.' Kitty laughed as she bounced down the stairs. 'Come on, then. A dinner is being planned in your honour.'

I followed her, stopping to find the shoe rack that – thankfully – had an empty row and a Post-it note reading 'Felicity' on it. I thought momentarily of the condensation shower notes that Aaron used to leave for me. After swallowing the lump in my throat, I took a deep breath and carried on walking.

Kitty was already in the kitchen, leaning on the breakfast bar and pouring herself a glass of wine. Something red; I wasn't really into wine. She was chatting under her breath to another girl, who was already drinking a glass and checking for dirt under her nails with her free hand, a pencil tucked behind her ear. She was tall – the kind of willowy reserved for people who walked runways – and her dark hair ran way past her shoulders. They were leaning into each other with the familiarity of two people who'd known each other a long time. I sent another silent prayer to the gods, asking to fit in.

The girl I didn't recognise held out her hand. 'Hi. Nice to meet you. I'm Maia. I live upstairs next to Kitty.'

With her attention turned to me I realised that I had seen her on Facebook during my pre-move stalk. She was the lawyer.

'Hi.' I panicked. 'What are you drinking?'

She laughed. 'I have no idea. I've had to teach myself to like wine, never mind understand it. Stacey bought this. For someone who will drink Lambrini in a park, she knows a lot about wine.'

Stacey was the only member of the house that I had left to meet. I listened out for signs that she might be coming to join us, but the hallway was empty.

I twisted my fingers nervously. 'I definitely don't understand wine either. I just said that to fit in.'

Maia laughed and then tilted her head. 'Your accent reminds me of uni. I like it. Where do you work again? I did read the email, I promise. I'm just stuck reading textbook after textbook at the moment and I swear nothing sticks up here.' She pointed at her head.

'I'll let you off. I work at a magazine in Bloomsbury.'

'That is so cool! What kind of magazine?'

I reeled off my standard synopsis of *Influence,* the lifestyle magazine I'd been working at since the September after I graduated. The whole thing had been kind of a fluke; they'd never recruited for a grad scheme before. With magazines being a dying breed, they'd decided that they needed to inject some youth into the operations. Instead of it being a grad scheme that renewed every year, I'd have been there for two years in September – eight months' time. Then, they'd review the scheme and its success. I knew I was lucky to have landed my job, and I tried never to take it for granted, even when my alarm went off at 6 a.m. and when strangers invaded my personal space on the Tube.

Kitty handed me a glass of wine that I accepted out of politeness, and I sucked in through my teeth. Gross. It tasted like vinegar. I gestured to her. 'Never mind *my* job seeming cool. I didn't even know that DJs actually existed.'

That earned me a laugh from both of them.

'One of my exes called us the unicorns of London. Although when you meet one DJ, you get introduced to all of their DJ friends and suddenly the spell is broken. Also, *technically* it doesn't pay enough yet to earn full-time job status. One day maybe.'

Maia nudged her. 'She's being modest. She's the coolest girl in West London. Literally the only person I know that could pull off pink French braids.'

Kitty patted them affectionately. 'It adds to the unicorn vibe.'

Watching them converse like this with ease, I found myself wanting to be a part of it. For a second, I forgot the reason why I was here in the first place.

'Why are you reading textbook after textbook?' I turned my attention to Maia whilst Kitty poured herself another glass. I knew she was in law, but I hadn't the faintest idea how any of that worked.

She braced her hands on the corner of the counter. 'I'm in a prison of my own making. I'm studying for the bar at the moment.'

'Ha, get it?' Kitty snorted. 'Prison of her own making?'

Maia smirked. 'That was unintentional.'

As she spoke about her current legal training, I watched her, quietly inspired by her determination. You could tell how passionate she was about her job. Maia was 25, working as a paralegal in Mayfair. I wondered if she got the Piccadilly Line in the morning like me (I'd been googling my route to work like a madwoman – I might have lived in London for a while, but the Tube still freaked me out).

The front door slammed. 'And that'll be the mystery house member.' Kitty nodded towards the door. 'I don't think she's ever managed to close that door lightly. Guarantee you'll always hear her before you see her.'

'Hey guys.' The girl, who I assumed was Stacey, flounced into the room and put her bag on the worktop that separated the kitchen from the living room. 'The traffic is mad out there. Oh, hey.' She shot me a small smile before going to the cupboard to get herself a glass.

'I did tell you it would have been quicker to walk to the salon today.' Kitty shook her head.

'I know, I know, but when have I ever taken advice?' Stacey sighed. 'I let Claire' – she turned to me – 'my boss, try out this new curling technique to help me wait out the traffic, but in the end I had to just go for it. Never again.'

Now that she mentioned it, her hair was looking very bouncy, like she'd wandered out of a TRESemmé advert.

'Never again until tomorrow.' Maia was flipping through the post that was piled up on the worktop.

'Quite possibly. It's like the trauma of giving birth; you forget about traffic and risk it all over again. Hi, by the way.' She smiled at me. 'If they haven't already filled you in, I'm Stacey.'

'The only one of us brave enough to risk the ground-floor bedroom.' Kitty swallowed.

'It really isn't that bad, once you get used to the idea that you'd be first to be murdered. Plus, it's easily the biggest bedroom. I was the first out of us three to move into Carlisle Avenue' – Stacey grabbed a packet of digestives out of the cupboard and starting eating, then continued with her mouth full – 'and the girls I was living with then made us draw straws. I'm proud to say I've stuck it out.'

'Just to add, though' – Maia pointed in the direction of the front door – 'the chances of us being murdered are slim. They're being dramatic.'

'You can remain calm from your first-floor safety net.'

Maia rolled her eyes at Stacey.

Kitty clapped her hands. 'And now that the introductions are over with, I'm starving. What are we getting?'

'Oh yeah, I'm actually not staying.'

'Oh, for crying out loud. After all that. I could have been eating spring rolls by now.'

'Sorry.' Stacey shrugged. 'I promised one of the girls at the salon that I'd go out for their birthday drinks in Soho.'

'I thought we'd discussed tonight, though.' Maia raised her eyebrows, jutting her chin in my direction slightly in an attempt to be subtle. I was way too paranoid about what these women thought of me to not pick up on such discreet mannerisms.

'Yeah, I know, sorry about that. But I've got to go. I'll see you around, Felicity!' She spun around and walked out of the room before I had the chance to say anything. The sound of her bedroom door slamming behind her made us all flinch.

'Why do I let that scare me every time?' Kitty clocked the expression on my face. 'Don't take it personally, she has more friends than everyone I know put together. She was definitely one of those kids who had a flock in primary school.'

I tried to not let on that it bothered me. I knew it had been going almost *too* well.

'She's finding it weird now that Tara doesn't live here any more. They were really close. Give her a day or two and she'll be fine.' Maia looked me dead in the eyes. 'Now. This is your one and only test.'

I swallowed.

'Don't look so scared. What's your takeaway of choice?' She handed me her phone, which had a food delivery website already loaded. 'We get a lot of options round here.'

Thank God. *Surely* I could pick a takeaway.

I scrolled through the list, feeling more nervous by the second. I knew they were kidding about it being a test, but still. I didn't even know what my preference was. Aaron had liked pizza, so that's what we'd always ordered. When Suze stayed over she usually picked Lebanese, and my housemates at university had always gone to the local chippy on a Friday. Had I *never* had total autonomy when it came to a takeaway? The more I thought about the past few years of my life as I gawked at the variety of menus, the surer I was that 1) I was incapable of making this decision, and 2) I was going to cry.

'You okay, Flick?' When I glanced up both of them were staring at me, even though Kitty was the one speaking. 'Because it really isn't a big deal. We can just pick. We're game for anything.'

'Other than sushi.' Maia shuddered.

'Other than sushi. Didn't I tell you that the takeaway decision was too much to force on someone?' Kitty nudged Maia.

'No, no, it's not that.' I tried to smile at them, not wanting them to regret my arrival as the newest member of this shared house. 'It's just been a rough couple of weeks.'

Maia, in particular, softened and took the phone from me. 'When I moved here, I'd just been dumped by my first girlfriend.'

Kitty jumped in. 'I left uni and had a quarter-life crisis. We get it.'

My chest warmed with unexpected feeling towards these two practical strangers.

'We always joke that this house is a home for girls in a crisis. There's no pressure here, just healing.'

Maia rolled her eyes. 'Christ, Kit, you sound like a self-help book.'

I thought about the restaurants I'd just seen listed on Maia's phone and picked the first thing that sounded good to me. Not to Aaron, not to Suze, just me. 'How does Thai food sound?'

Kitty smirked. 'I *knew* I liked you.'

★★★

I pushed the plate of pad thai away from me. 'I think my stomach might be about to burst.'

Kitty took the plate from me, scraping the rest onto hers. She paused when she caught us both staring at her. 'What? We're all one financial crisis away from being broke; we can't have waste.'

We weren't in the living room; Kitty had assured me that the amount of food we were about to consume required the space to sprawl out and really lean into the food coma. Instead, we were crowded into Kitty's bedroom, which was a lot bigger than mine. Maia was sat slightly away from us, intermittently glancing at the giant textbook on her lap. The commitment was real.

'Get used to that.' Kitty pointed her fork in Maia's direction. 'Very stressed the majority of the time.'

'How about you? What are your hours like?'

'Most of my gigs tend to be in the evening, but I tutor kids online during the daytime on weekdays and dabble in social media freelancing when I can. It all works out.'

'That makes me feel tired just listening to it.'

She shrugged. 'It's how I function.'

Maia looked up. 'It's how society has taught us to function.'

'And what's that? Healthy?' Kitty stared at the textbook.

'Fair point, but don't shoot the messenger.' Maia got back to her studying, taking a bite out of a sweetcorn fritter on the way.

Kitty carried on talking about the kids that she was tutoring, and the ratty emails that she got from parents on a daily basis. I knew the hustle culture all too well; I couldn't count the times I'd barely seen daylight either side of entering and leaving the office. It didn't help that most of us were on grad schemes that held a question mark at the end, or worked freelance with no set hours. It had pained me to take a day of annual leave to move house.

'So, why "Flick"?' Kitty asked, making me jump.

Maia's head came up from behind the textbook. 'I also want to know this.'

I was pretty used to this question coming up within the first hour of meeting people, so the fact that these two had made it all evening without asking was quite impressive. I prepared to reel off the same story I'd been telling for years.

'I've played tennis forever. It started out as after school clubs, and then at weekends, and when I went to uni I played for the team there. I became known for this move that I did' – I acted out the movement with my wrist – 'which completely threw my opponents off. After one of my first matches, the coach called me Flick as a joke, and it stuck.'

My whole life I'd wanted a nickname. My sister was effortlessly cool, an obvious Suze instead of Susan. Felicity was too long, too 'fairy princess', and I'd ached to have a shorter, sassier name like my older sister did. I had tried to instigate my own nicknames, with things like Liss or Licity. I'd even tried Fliss at one point, but nothing had ever stuck. Not until I'd picked up the tennis racket. Flick was not quite effortless or cool, but it was me, much to my mother's dismay. She'd spent endless hours during her pregnancies scouring baby name books. It irked her that both of us had rejected our birth names. All our birthday cards were addressed to Felicity and Susan, even though my dad had adopted our nicknames too. She was holding onto our names for dear life.

'I like that.' Kitty nodded in appreciation. 'Everyone always asks me if I like cats.'

'Do you?'

'I mean I'm not a psychopath. But I'm also not obsessed to the point of changing my name for them. Kitty just sounded a lot nicer than Katherine.'

'And there aren't many nicknames associated with Maia.'

Kitty scoffed. 'As if you need a nickname with a name like that. You don't understand the plight of having a boring name.'

I smiled at their back and forth, the relief at tonight's events almost overwhelming. Two out of three housemates wasn't bad. Yes, it was only night one, and maybe in a month we would be arguing over whose turn it was to clean the toilet and who had nicked whose eggs, but right now, it felt like things might be alright. A houseshare do-over and a change of scenery to help me forget how London had wronged me. It didn't feel like I was heartbroken and desperate for house-mates. It felt like an adventure.

# 5

I swiped my phone to pay as I exited Holborn, hoisting my satchel further up onto my shoulder. Last week on my commute I'd have huffed at the Londoners pushing past me, at the general hustle and bustle of the city. I'd let myself fall out of love with London when I'd realised that Aaron had fallen out of love with me. But for the first time in two weeks, when I looked around at my fellow commuters, I smiled.

It was only a nine-minute walk to the office after I left the train, but I liked to gift myself an extra five minutes in the morning. This was partly a safety net – I'd grown up with a fifteen-minute wait between trains. The number of mornings I'd missed the train to school as a teenager, running down the road with my blazer flying behind me, had scarred me. Here you had to wait five minutes for another Tube – and that was if you were unlucky. I lived in fear of only making the Tube by a fraction of a second; a couple of weeks into living here I'd witnessed a man's satchel getting stuck in the doors, and I'd had visions of that being one of my limbs ever since. Aside from the whole Tube scenario, I loved the walk into Bloomsbury. It was never boring. Yes, this city could easily be misunderstood for its heavy footfall, traffic and the number of people that avoided eye contact on the streets. But when I was feeling warmth towards London – I still couldn't quite bear to call it home yet – I could deal with these small frustrations. I could cope with the chewing gum on my heels and the restaurant queues as long as I could have all the good parts too. The good parts that, this morning, I was starting to notice again. During my first two years at university I hadn't really considered London as my next destination. I always assumed I'd stick up north, but then Aaron had got his job here, and it felt like if I didn't move, I'd be missing out. Sometimes it might have felt like I'd followed him (and in part I guess I had), but I loved my job. It had been a culture shock but it had felt like something I *had* to at least try. A lot of my classmates were either going home to London or moving here from the north too, and it was hard not to get swept up in the idea of commuting and working in the capital. Even if there were lots of things I did miss about home.

Bloomsbury was quite a literary rich district of London, so I often spent my lunch hour in bookshops, perusing the titles and working my way through my reading list. There was an online book club at *Influence* that they were still trying to lift off the ground, and I considered it my duty to read along. My favourite lunch-break haunt was a tiny bookshop dedicated entirely to female authors. It wasn't just the bookshops I loved – the farmers' market outside Birkbeck College every Thursday, with slices of pizza oozing with cheese, and doughnuts so sugary that they made my teeth hurt, was another draw to the area. Bloomsbury felt like a moment of peace.

I stopped off at the coffee shop on the corner of Sicilian Avenue, nipping in to grab a pastry. It was still January (why was January the longest month of the year?), so I handed over my reusable cup for a cinnamon latte, which I cradled between my freezing hands in between bites of the flaky almond croissant. I didn't even let myself wince at the price of it. As far as I was concerned, this morning was the first morning in a while when I hadn't woken up and immediately remembered the breakup. Instead, when I'd woken up and gone to make myself some coffee this morning, I'd bumped into Kitty, who was already at the kitchen table on Skype with one of her students. The kitchen was already *alive*; it didn't need my sadness to inhabit it. I'd resented London for what it had done to me, when really it wasn't to blame.

I pushed on the glass doors of the office block, after wiping my hands on my trench coat to make sure they didn't leave greasy croissant fingerprints on the surface.

'Felicity!' As soon as I made it inside, Cecilia accosted me. I grabbed my lanyard from my pocket, struggling to keep up with my boss as she strode to the stairs, already taking them two at a time. *What was it with people taking stairs two at a time in this city? How was everyone not breaking their neck?*

Cecilia Evans wasn't the scary Editor-in-Chief that I'd pictured the night before my first day here, but she wasn't far off. Being the graduate, I did the most assistant-y work out of anyone here, so I tended to get the brunt of it. The more I got to know her, though, the more I realised that it had very little to do with me, and a lot to do with her never-ending to-do list. Like some bosses that my friends talked about, Cecilia didn't fob everything off onto us, and she stayed just as late as everyone else.

Cecilia instructed me, glancing behind to check I was still following. 'I've got a meeting with finance at eleven, and we need to make sure we have all of our figures in order for then.' I checked my phone, which read 8.57. Cecilia's heels clicked on the tiled floor as she went through her mental checklist.

She wasn't even out of breath. I held the air in my lungs to hide my panting. I hadn't changed my emergency contact here yet – would Aaron be the one they called if I passed out on these stairs?

'And can you look over that Garfield piece? The one about making the best of a box room in London? I've pushed it back to the April issue – it needs some work.' She stopped suddenly, turning around, glasses halfway down her nose.

'Is everything okay?' I resisted the urge to flatten my hair and check my parting.

'Yes. I just remembered that the piece about wardrobe space is due in today.' Her eyes narrowed. One of our freelance writers was known for her late submissions.

'Already on it.' I added another point to the Post-it note I was scribbling on. I'd learnt on my second day here to keep a stack of Post-it notes and a pen in my coat pocket, ready to jump into my role as soon as I entered the building. 'I chased her ahead of time and it landed in your inbox last night.'

Finally, Cecilia broke into a smile. She tucked her short blonde hair behind her ears.

'That's great work, Felicity.' She nodded. 'Great work. See you in the meeting at eleven?'

I resisted the urge to squeal. I'd earned a place at the finance meeting. 'Of course.'

'And would it be alright if you —'

I stopped her. 'Skinny mocha, no cream, extra sprinkles?'

My boss's smile widened. 'What would I do without you?'

She went into her office and shut the door, and I let out an exhale. The morning ambush was the most stressful part of my job. All you had to do was survive the first ten minutes.

I plopped down at my desk, where Felix was already sitting at his booth next to me, tapping away.

'You handled that like a G.' He didn't look up from his keyboard.

'I thought so too.' I took the last sip of my latte before popping the cup away and turning the desktop on. 'Gets easier every time.'

'I remember when you were just a little baby grad' — Felix pretended to dab at his eyes — 'jumping every time she raised her voice. Remember when you got the coffee order wrong?'

'I shudder at the thought.'

'Never forget the extra sprinkles.' He looked over sharply. 'Never.'

I laughed along with him. It had been almost a year and a half since I'd stepped into the *Influence* office, or rather, accidentally found the offices on my fifth walk around the second floor of the building. I was due an evaluation in the next couple of weeks, to decide where I would fit into the team going forward. At the moment, I was doing a little bit of everything — editing, admin, being Cecilia's PA — but after the next year I hoped to have a little more of a niche place.

I was really hoping that they decided to rerun the grad scheme so I could pass off some of the admin tasks. I wanted to be able to commission pieces for the magazine, like Felix. Although technically it was Cecilia who managed me, Felix had been my honorary mentor right from the first day.

'And how are we doing this week?' Felix didn't look over this time, instead giving me just enough dignity so that we could both pretend he hadn't heard me sobbing in the staffroom last week. He hadn't said much in the moment, but cups of tea had steadily appeared on the edge of my desk throughout the rest of the day.

'I'm a bit better.' I typed my password into the computer. 'Moved into my houseshare on Friday.'

He sent over a sympathetic look that said it all. Houseshares were the norm in London, but Felix knew how much I'd loved my old flat. He reached into the drawer under his desk and pulled out a packet of custard creams, offering them to me without a word.

I took one, letting the crumbs fall on my keyboard. 'Thanks, but it really isn't that bad.'

I could tell he was sceptical. 'Housesharing is always that bad. Wait for it to settle in. When I was 22, I lived with a man who never washed up the entire time I lived there. And what was worse, he just ate from his crusty crockery.'

I gagged. 'Ew. Don't put me off my custard cream.'

From behind us, Fiona, a middle-aged mother of two, joined in. 'When I first moved to the city I lived with a girl who played the saxophone.'

'That sounds like it could be –'

'At 3 a.m,' she finished. 'Every morning.'

'Ah.' I clasped my hands in front of me. 'The thing is, they don't really seem like that.'

Felix smirked. 'Give it time. Everyone seems at least partially normal when you first meet them. Wait until one of you forgets to put the bins out or leaves their washing on the drier for too long.'

'They've all been living together for months; they've probably got their routine down.'

He looked over at me seriously. 'You could be the problem Flick. We've seen how long it takes you to wash a teaspoon in the staffroom.'

I kicked the wheels on his computer chair so that he slid away from me a few inches, but I was laughing. I loved the office camaraderie. We were a small team, our jobs intersecting in order to make *Influence* run its issues on time. Print journalism was dying out; in a world where almost everything was online, fewer and fewer people wanted to carry around a physical magazine in their backpack. Ten years ago a larger team might have been justified, but as it was the small number of us ran like clockwork. There were only a handful of people – tech staff, the finance people – that I didn't know by name, but most of the office staff I knew more than I sometimes cared to know about. Felix was 29, living in Camden with his boyfriend of two years, and a cat that they'd snuck into their strictly monitored flat. He kept a photo of Noodles (the cat) on his desk, and I swear it watched me. I'd had to cat-sit for Felix at my flat a few months ago when his landlord only gave a few hours' notice for a surprise inspection. Noodles had sat on the armchair, staring me and Aaron down until we fed him.

Fiona's desk was right behind us, and she spent the majority of her time here constantly trying to keep up with the ever-changing nature of the internet. She'd been an editor for a long time, and she kept us all in check. Sadie was the social media guru and her desk was right beside Cecilia's office. She was easily the favourite. Social media was the saving grace for journalism; you could share articles online and reach thousands more readers in the blink of an eye. Of the twelve of us in the office, I could rattle off facts about most people. If you worked for a year on a small publication against tight dead-lines, you got to know the team.

'Flick?' Sadie called at me from the end of the line. She had a pixie cut and giant hoop earrings that I swore got larger every time I looked at them. 'Did you get the email I sent over with our Twitter figures? Could you add them to the monthly spreadsheet?'

I shot her back a thumbs-up and got to work. And for a whole harmonious forty-seven minutes, I only thought of *Influence* and Carlisle Avenue.

# 6

How are you doing? How did the move go?

I continued to stare at the message from Aaron in horror. I was alone in my new living room, folded onto the tiny ratty love seat like a pretzel with my phone balanced on the arm of the chair. I was pretty sure that I was the only one in the house. Kitty always went for a run at this time of day, and Maia was almost definitely still at work. I knew from the group chat – something I hadn't been a part of since university – that Stacey was out with some friends for a drink. Of all the girls at Carlisle Avenue, her social life seemed by far the most vibrant. Kitty was in a close second, and Maia and I trailed at the back, although Maia seemed content to be there. I'd met Sophie now – her girlfriend – and seeing them laughing at the kitchen table, so at ease in each other's presence, was a stark reminder of what I'd lost. That one person who lit you up when you were with them. Thank God Kitty and Stacey were single too; they were consistently raving to each other about the benefits of being a single woman in London. It dulled the ache a bit.

I'd been living at Carlisle for just under a week now, and I was starting to find my groove, not listening to the movements downstairs before leaving my bedroom and walking into the kitchen with a bit more confidence. I still hadn't quite clicked with Stacey, but we'd started talking more when we crossed paths in the kitchen at night. She wasn't cruel – there just wasn't the same instant connection I'd had with Kitty, or the mutual respect from my budding friendship with Maia. Mum had assured me that if I gave it time, she'd come around. Enough had been happening in my life that I hadn't paused to dwell on it too much – we were fast approaching our February issue release at work, and it was all hands on deck. Everyone was so frantic that I'd ended up doing all kinds of things that didn't come under my usual umbrella – yesterday I'd stepped into a design meeting to cover Felix, and it had been refreshing to do something brand new. Life felt so full that I had barely stopped to think about Aaron (either that, or I was deliberately refusing to think about him). I was also planning on playing tennis again this week. Since that soul-crushing night in my old flat, I'd struggled to commit to my usual routine. The memories were still too raw. Aaron had never missed one of my matches, meeting me afterwards for a drink at the pub nearby. Him, a pint of lager. Me, a Malibu and coke (I might have graduated, but my alcohol preferences hadn't). To fight the inevitable nostalgia, I'd switched my membership to an indoor court near work; I didn't need a constant reminder of the past, things had to be about moving forward now. I was making a conscious effort to not let all my memories of London become tainted. This didn't have to be our city; I could make it mine again. Being far away from Shepherd's Bush was doing a world of good, since I didn't pass our local Italian deli or Bush Theatre or any of the other places that we met after work for spontaneous dates. I'd thrown whatever energy I had left at the end of the day into making my box room at the top of the house feel less like a prison cell and more like a tiny – but cosy – space. I'd ordered a selection of throw pillows (something Aaron had always put up a fight against), and I was waiting for some art prints to arrive. One was an illustration of Manchester, and the other one of Liverpool. I could bring all my homes together in one space, so that they were all rooting for me to thrive in this one. Between work, getting to know my housemates, and interior designing, I'd barely had time to grieve my relationship. Until now. At 7.30 p.m. on a Wednesday, sat on a ratty love seat. Oh, the irony.

When there was no contact with Aaron, it was easier to resume total denial and pretend none of it had happened. No relationship, no Shepherd's Bush flat, no breakup. Potentially an unhealthy way to approach it, but I'd reclaim tiny fragments of the experience when I was ready. I'd even ignored a couple of Mum's phone calls, sick of the phrase 'How are you doing, *really*?' I didn't want to dwell on my actual feelings; no one wanted to be friends with the girl that lived in permanent wallow-mode. I was selfishly only replying to texts when it was a non-Aaron-related question. Phone calls with Suze weren't an issue. She knew exactly how I felt from her own breakups over the years (there had been significantly more for her than there had been for me – Aaron had been my first and only boyfriend), and she could talk for England about irrelevant things. When we were younger, the gap between us had felt huge. How could I relate to her sneaking off in the middle of the night when all I cared about was getting my English homework done? Why did I expect her to care about tennis trials when she was miles ahead of me, navigating the world of work? The older we became, the closer we became. Our experiences, once almost identical during the time of Play-Doh and party rings, had diverged during our teenage years and then moved closer together again once I'd left university. Now, she was my first call. Always.

'What are you staring at?'

I jumped, startled by her voice. Maia was standing in the doorway, a carton of oat milk in one hand and her laptop case in the other. She had a huge indent mark on the bridge of her nose from her glasses, and several tendrils of hair had fallen from her ponytail.

'Oh, it's nothing.' I clicked the lock button on my phone.

Maia shrugged in acceptance. Kitty had been exactly right when she'd said that whilst everyone in the house was different, it seemed to work. Maia was less pushy than my other house-mates, a quiet observer who dipped in with wisdom when you needed it most. Where Kitty was bubbly and vibrant almost 100 per cent of the time, Maia was more introverted, but she cared deeply. I could tell. Granted, I'd only been living in the house for a handful of days, but it was enough time to make my own observations. It had been so long since I'd felt the opportunity to make real friends like this, and I wanted it. I watched Maia walk through the living room to the kitchen, pulling food out of her tote bag and setting it on the side. Three red peppers, a pot of hummus, some cheese. It was like a Mary Poppins bag; there was no way the food items that kept appearing had managed to fit in there in the first place. Some tortillas, a bag of apples, and moisturising hand soap that she placed next to the sink. I watched in fascination for a moment before making conversation.

'How was work?'

She shrugged. 'Tough, but I'll get there. It's what I signed up for. There's a clause I'm struggling with at the moment, so it's a lot of extra work. Nothing I'm not used to, though. You?'

I told her about the articles I was editing at the moment for Cecilia; one was an in-depth look at infertility, the other a comparison of all the bakeries in Mayfair. Working for a lifestyle publication offered constant whiplash, but the free pastries were a definite perk.

'That sounds interesting. I promise I'm going to pick up a copy when it comes out.' She pushed her glasses on top of her head, rolling her shoulders.

'Oh, I get a free stack whenever we publish. I'll grab you one.'

Her facial features broke their silence and burst into a smile. 'That would be great. Thanks. So, any big plans for this fine Wednesday evening?'

I'd been planning on devouring a family-sized bar of Dairy Milk and continuing my re-watch of *Schitt's Creek*. I said as much, not needing to appear cool. It wasn't that type of house.

'A respectable set of plans.' Maia laughed and opened the fridge to put away her purchases. 'I'm beginning to wish I'd bought a bar now you've said that.'

'I'm open to sharing.' *Ah, the things you'll do to earn companionship.* 'How about you?'

'I think I'll probably head over to Sophie's for a bit. It's already late, and I wanted to go to the gym, but alas, a woman can't conquer the world all in one day.'

'The gym does pale in comparison to a date.'

'Exactly.' Maia nodded. 'I just kind of want to be cooked for and given some TLC.'

I felt my shoulders drop. Hearing about Maia's plans, I couldn't help but mourn over the ease of nights sat on the sofa next to Aaron. We'd had a Wednesday tradition of making the most random meal out of whatever we could find in the fridge. It was a stupid game, but I missed it. Maia must have been able to read the sadness on my face because she abandoned the bell peppers that were in her hands and came to sit opposite me.

'Want to talk about it?'

Of all the people that I'd imagined opening up to in the house about a breakup, it wasn't Maia. Maybe that was exactly the reason why I should.

'I moved here because I moved out of a flatshare with my ex.' I fiddled with one of the cushions on the love seat. 'It's all I've known for a long time. I'm finding it difficult to be on my own.'

Maia nodded. 'I did think it might have been a breakup. No offence to this house, but people tend to arrive here in crisis mode.'

'What gave it away?'

I had thought I'd been doing so fine. I'd even turned up the pressure in the shower the other morning so that they couldn't hear me crying.

Maia was staring at me sympathetically. 'The huge tub of Phish Food in the freezer was a giveaway. Or maybe the fact that you have, like, no photos up in your room. Or, you know, the shower.' She looked a bit sheepish after admitting to that last one.

I grimaced. 'Oh.'

Maia leaned back on the sofa. 'Breakups are the worst. It's a fact.'

From an obviously highly intelligent woman, this simple statement made me feel better. Validated. 'Yep.'

'How long had you been together?'

'Almost four years officially. It would have been our anniversary next week.'

Twelfth of February. Two days before Valentine's. I had big plans to order a pizza with extra cheese and cocoon myself inside my dressing gown, only leaving to get more alcohol.

Maia grimaced. 'You know, it's scientifically proven that the loss of a relationship is similar to actual grieving. You lost something huge, and it was unexpected. You have to let it happen. Trust me, I've seen Stace and Kit cry over *plenty* of people.'

I thought about what she'd said. I guess it did feel like I'd lost someone. Even though he was still walking around out there, he was far from walking anywhere towards me.

'I was so late to the dating thing.' Maia pulled a nail file out of her back pocket (who keeps something so entirely *practical* in their back pocket? I thought about my own back pocket, which only contained the wrapper from a Penguin bar) and started to file her nails, pushing down the nail beds. 'But I've been around those two for a while now and they've gone through their fair share of crying in the shower and sitting at the kitchen table looking like death warmed up.'

She smiled at me. 'It's okay to be upset about it. And it's okay that you'll probably think you're fine, and then be upset about it all over again. Whatever it is you're feeling, it's almost definitely okay to be feeling it.'

'If you don't end up a barrister, you'd have very reasonable career prospects as a therapist.'

Maia laughed. 'We all jump on board when we're needed. Last time Kitty's dating life went kaput she went into total rage-girl mode and tore up her bedroom. It took me *weeks* to help her get everything back to normal. You try and get iced coffee off a white wall. Next time she gets heartbroken, I'm plastic-wrapping her bedroom in advance.'

I liked the sound of this. A house where girls put each other back together again. I showed Maia the text Aaron had sent out of the blue.

'That's . . . weird. It was his choice, I assume?'

I swallowed down the lump in my throat. 'Definitely wasn't mine.'

'He should leave you alone. It isn't healthy to drag out communication like that.' It wasn't just her nails that she was practical with, it seemed.

We sat in silence for a moment. I didn't think I was going to get anything more, and to be honest, I wasn't looking for sympathy. It was a really shitty thing that had happened, but I wasn't the first person it had happened to. I knew that.

Maia got up to leave. 'For what it's worth, I'm glad that it happened. You're a really cool person to have around, Flick. I like the way you organise the fridge when you think no one is looking. See you later. Text me if you need anything.'

She grabbed her keys from the worktop and left the room. I couldn't stop smiling.

★★★

It was only a temporary distraction. An hour later and I was under the covers, muffling the occasional sob that forced its way through. It was almost comical how quickly a day could crumble. This morning at the office had been my most productive day in weeks. I'd climbed onto the Tube feeling *good* about today. And then the text happened. I thought about Aaron, and what he was probably doing right now. It was 9 p.m. on a Wednesday. He was probably in front of the Xbox, doing nothing particularly thrilling. Momentarily, thinking about that made me feel better. I looked down at the chocolate stain on my white duvet, and the message from the streaming service I was using that read 'Are you still watching?' I needed to get off my horse, it was way too high.

I sat up and shifted the laptop from my knee, grabbing my notes from work with the intent of distraction. The last time Suze had gone through a breakup – she was now, as she liked to call it, a permanently on purpose single woman – she'd thrown herself into work to the point where we were all a bit worried about her. She'd leave family dinners early to get back to her email account, and she'd even passed on her own birthday celebrations in favour of an evening in the office. I didn't want that to be me, but I did have some emails to reply to, and the article about the cafés in Mayfair to proofread for Cecilia by tomorrow. And to be fair, reading about all the different types of pastry, cake, and coffee available in London, a space which was now completely my own, Aaron-Reed-free haven, didn't sound too awful. I spent a good twenty minutes checking over the grammar (woe betide anyone who didn't notice the improper use of the Oxford comma) and jotting down all of the places I was going to try at the weekend, before giving up and unpausing the TV show.

My phone buzzed again – a message from Stacey to the group chat. My heart cinched at the sight of the still unopened message from Aaron. Maia hadn't advised to reply, Suze *definitely* would have stolen the phone and pressed delete, and although I knew deep down my mum would have wanted to know how he was, even she would have suggested that I don't reply. What good would it do to text him back? I didn't think I could ever be his friend. How could you be just friends with a person when you'd spent four years thinking about their last name attached to the end of your first? I'd always liked the name Felicity Reed. Flick Reed.

I deleted the message. It was time to be Felicity Sage again.

# 7

If there was one thing that I'd learnt early on during my childhood, it was that if you wanted to grow up a Sage, you had to at least try to love tennis as much as my dad did. He'd camp out in the living room during Wimbledon, jumping up and shouting at the screen in the same way that my friends' parents screamed at the TV when a football match was on. Each year during the US Open, he'd hold a celebratory barbecue in the back garden, complete with US flag tablecloths and the special burger buns with the sesame seeds on. There was no room to be half-hearted when it came to the sport my dad loved most; I'd been given a racket for my fourth birthday, and then that was it. Of the two of us – Suze and I – it had been obvious from the off who his best bet was. My sister was vocal about what she couldn't be bothered to do, whereas I was a people pleaser through and through. Even if I hadn't fallen in love with the sport, I'd probably still be playing, if only to please my dad. But I *had* fallen in love with it, spending countless summers playing with him on the outdoor courts in our village whilst Suze sat on the wall and texted her friends. Tennis had become a source of relief – which is why I was whacking tennis balls at a wall on a Thursday night.

'I usually try to get it over the net, but this works well too.'

I turned to find a man laughing at me from a few metres away. He was wearing sweatbands on his wrists (a definite beginner) and had eyelashes long enough for me to dislike him on principle. I tried to place his accent, which stuck out like a sore thumb just like mine did. Definitely Northern. I resisted the urge to scoff at his comment and carried on hitting the ball. I liked to think that I was quite an approach-able person, but this man had chosen the wrong day. I'd woken up fifteen minutes late this morning because I'd stayed up late reading over some pages for the magazine, and had ended up on the 8.11 a.m. super-packed Tube, squished next to someone's potent lunchbox. It had a knock-on effect throughout the day, making me late to submit the finished pages to Cecilia. In my frustration (I was your classic teacher's pet – being late for anything made my blood run cold) I'd tripped in the staffroom and spilled a mug of tea all over my jeans. It was my own fault; I hadn't been able to shake Aaron's message all week. No amount of chatting in the kitchen to Kitty or burying my head in work had helped. And it was about to get so much worse. Tomorrow was looming ahead of me – we'd spent our last anniversary in Spitalfields Market, taking turns to buy food from the vendors and ranking them on our own personal scoreboard. I turned back to my tennis racket, squeezing the handle tight. Tomorrow was going to be the worst.

'Sorry if I offended you. I was only joking.' I'd almost forgotten about the man standing slightly to the side of me, who was now scratching his head in panic. Attempting to make the situation less awkward, he started pelting tennis balls at the wall with me. His shots were nowhere near as good as mine.

The courts were basically empty tonight – apparently most people were starting Valentine's weekend extra early – and yet here was this stranger, adamant to remain in my corner of the tennis court. I watched him out of the corner of my eye, facing the wall with a gritted look of determination. He was tall and lean, with dirty blonde hair that was so well groomed it was clearly not long out from a haircut. His racket looked almost brand new. I put him out of his misery and replied.

'Some days you play matches, other days you just need to hit something really hard with no consequences.' I shrugged and continued.

He nodded, not looking at me. 'Bad week?'

I stopped what I was doing, finally feeling a bit guilty for my cold welcome. This wasn't one of those men who liked to pester women in a public place. He didn't even seem like one of the men who asked you to rally with them and then wouldn't stop grunting and flexing every time they hit a shot. This stranger seemed relatively normal. 'You could say that. Bad month.'

'Ah.' He swung his racket again. 'One of those. Last week I had a really bad day. I could probably have made a hole in this wall.'

I was sceptical. 'With one of these?' I held up the tennis ball, which, whilst not very nice if it hit you in the face at full speed, was still after all just a ball.

'Well, maybe not a hole. More of a dent.' He held up his hands in defeat. 'Okay. No walls would have been harmed during the process. But if I could have, I would have.'

'Okay, I'll bite. How bad was the day?'

He winced at the memory. 'Since I moved to London, I have been terrified of one thing and one thing only. So, I was getting on the Tube in the morning –'

I stopped him in his tracks. '*No.*'

'Yes. Yes, it is what you think it is. A girl jumped on the train at the last minute and I lost my footing. I got stuck in the door. I was that guy.'

I'd abandoned my racket to cover my face. 'That's literally my worst London nightmare. Either that or forgetting to swipe my card on the way out of the station and waking up the next morning with an astronomical bill.'

'Can that even happen?'

'Probably not, but I like to catastrophize. I'll give it to you – getting stuck in the doors is a very reasonable excuse to attack the walls. Justification granted.'

He bowed. 'Thank you. I thought so too.'

By this point I was smiling at the conversation, as much as I'd tried to fight it. It was extremely easy to talk to him.

'So, man who interrupted my agenda against this wall' – he smirked at my comment – 'do you have a name?'

'Teddy.' He crossed his arms over his (admittedly rather nice) chest and smiled at me.

'Like the bear?'

The smile disappeared and he reached down to grab his bottle from the floor. 'First time I've ever heard that one.

Okay, girl who made fun of my name and appears to hate this wall, what's your name?'

I gritted my teeth. This was a war I should not have started. 'Flick.'

Teddy choked on his water. 'Touché.'

'No, I'm serious.'

'*Flick?* Your name is *Flick* and you just criticised mine?'

'Fair enough, I didn't think that one all the way through.'

He grinned. 'Indeed. Well, Flick' – a pause, clearly to check that I wasn't about to reveal that it had been, in fact, a joke – 'it's nice to meet you.'

I eyed his hand like it was poisonous. Shaking hands was weird on the best of days, never mind clammy tennis hands. I took it anyway, not wanting to offend.

'Nice to meet you too, Teddy Bear.'

'Only my family gets to call me that.' He pouted.

Okay, so clearly I'd misjudged Teddy. He wasn't a tennis court creep or anyone trying to invade my space. He was just someone who'd arrived at a tennis court, on his own on a Thursday night. That said a lot. London, like most cities that were loud in appearance, could be the loneliest place in the world.

'So, Teddy.' I twirled my racket around in my hands. 'Since you clearly aren't going to let me get back to my wall –'

He half-smiled. 'I'm sorry about that. I wasn't –'

'Would you like to rally with me?'

He blinked. He really did have nice eyes. Kind of blue, kind of green. 'Oh. I thought you were about to tell me to piss off.'

I snorted. 'Do I look that intimidating?'

'Hitting a ball with the fury of a women scorned?' He shrugged. 'Yes, yes you do.'

'I'll take it.' I grabbed the ball from where I'd let it roll close to the edge of the courts, throwing it to him just in time for him to react and catch it in his fist. 'Let's rally.'

***

If anything good had come out of the evening's events, it was that my tennis encounter had broken Stacey's resolve to not connect with the new housemate.

'Okay, let me get this straight.' She pointed her fork at me accusingly. It was an hour and a half later and I was sat at the breakfast bar, trying to eat a bowl of teriyaki noodles in peace. 'You had a rally, conversationally and tennis-ly –'

'That's not a word.' Kitty pointed out, looking up from her laptop. When Stacey had come into the room and joined in our conversation with gusto, Kitty had given me a knowing look. I clearly wasn't the only one that had noticed the cold front.

'Not the point. Flick had a rally with an attractive man, and just up and left without making sure she had any point of contact? Abominable.'

'Again, you never really hear that word either.'

'Kitty, I swear to God . . .'

After we'd played a few games (he wasn't a bad rally buddy, I had to admit) I'd made my excuses and left the courts, wanting to be home with plenty of time to go over some email admin before work tomorrow. And really, there was no space in my life for a Teddy. Man *or* stuffed animal. The bedroom was small enough as it was.

'I don't want a man's number. I'm still very much getting over my last emotional turmoil at the hands of one of those.'

I saw them exchange a look.

Kitty stood up to put her dishes in the sink. 'Fair point. I take it back, I'm in full support of the rally and dash.'

'Rally and dash? It sounds like some sort of dirty game.' Stacey shrugged when we turned – disgusted – to her, and continued eating her dinner. She was eating a salad with tiny potato waffles immaculately positioned around the edge of the plate. From our kitchen encounters, I knew Stacey could incorporate some form of potato into any meal. It was a talent. The other day I'd watched her eat mashed potatoes with her stir-fry. She looked up from her food. 'So clearly you're part of the single girls' club. Welcome to the dark side. But you know, you don't have to have a relationship with this guy.'

I considered it. Could I do a fling? How *did* you have a fling? I was pretty sure I'd make a complete idiot of myself and start crying during sex. Plus, the thought of having sex with anyone else still made me feel physically sick.

'I just don't think I'm there yet.'

'When Oprah said "the best way to get over someone is to get under someone else", she was totally right. Just saying.' Stacey stuffed another waffle in her mouth.

'*Did* Oprah say that?' Kitty shook her head behind Stacey's back. I tried not to laugh.

'Well, someone said it. The point is, flings are good for the soul. Friends with benefits are good for the soul. A good shag is good for the soul.'

Kitty's pink head popped up from where she was crouched under the sink, looking for the fairy liquid. 'Amen to that.'

Clearly, the way to crack Stacey's cool outer shell had been to bring up men, and sex. I noted the achievement. *Thank you, Teddy. You did more for me than you know.*

'What are we Amen-ing?' Maia walked through the kitchen door, one headphone pulled out to listen to us.

'A good shag.'

'Right. Should have known it would be something like that.' She ignored the face Kitty was pulling at her. 'Who is having sex?'

'Not tennis boy, that's for sure.' Stacey sighed. 'Or at least if he *is* having it, it isn't with Flick.'

'Who is tennis boy?' Maia grabbed the pen from the magnetic list on the fridge. 'We need bin bags by the way.'

Stacey pulled her phone out from her back pocket. 'Let me just – oh wait – I can't show you who tennis boy is, because *Flick didn't even get his last name.* Never mind his phone number. Not even a measly email address.'

'Is this going to haunt me until the day I die?' I looked from Kitty to Maia.

Kitty nodded. 'And probably into the afterlife.'

# 8

'For God's sake, Felicity, this is only going to make you feel worse.'

I'd finally caved and called Mum. I was pretty sure that she'd have preferred my continued silence over the current situation.

'Please tell me you've stopped reading them.'

I let my silence speak for me, my thumb still scrolling through my message history with Aaron.

'Oh, *Felicity*. Do you want me to get your dad on the phone as well?'

A tear fell onto my laptop keys. 'No, don't. It's embarrassing.'

'Oh, love, it's definitely not embarrassing. It's okay. Everyone has cried at something a bit ridiculous at some point or other.'

'Ridiculous? Thanks very much.'

I could picture her flapping her hands. 'Oh, you know what I mean. In two years' time you'll look back and you *will* think it was ridiculous to cry this much over a few texts about picking up chopped tomatoes on the way home. That's how time passing works.'

I'd been doing so well. All day at work I'd kept my head down, devouring two of the brownies from the stall outside the office building and inducing myself into a sugar coma of distraction. I'd called Suze on my way home, who had convinced me to organise a brunch date with her next week and distracted me further with stories about her new intern. Apparently, they had accidentally ordered twenty thousand napkins for an event instead of two thousand. If I thought my day was bad, that intern's day was infinitely worse. I'd even stuck around in the kitchen for a few minutes when I'd arrived back at Carlisle, talking to the girls as they planned their evening. Kitty was playing a gig in Shoreditch, Stacey was going with her, and Maia had a date with her textbooks, something she seemed *way* too happy about.

'Flick' – I knew it was bad if my Mother was calling me by my nickname – 'I know you're still scrolling. Stop it.'

I obliged, feeling instantly a little bit better. I resolved to delete our message history after tonight.

'Okay . . . and breathe.' Mum took an exaggerated breath down the other end of the line. 'I've started going to Wendy's yoga classes in the church hall on a Wednesday. I'm getting very good at breathing exercises.'

I hiccupped. 'I don't think downward dog is going to help right now, Mum.'

'Shut up and breathe will you.'

I listened to her, closing my eyes and focusing on inhaling and exhaling.

'Would it help if I told you to picture a beach?'

'No, it wouldn't.' I bit back a laugh. Slowly, my sobs softened until I was just sniffling now and again. Heartbreak *was* a bit like grief, I'd come to realise. Distractions could only work most of the time.

'I'm going to tell Wendy how well that worked.' Mum sounded pleased with herself. She couldn't see me, but I raised my eyebrows anyway. 'How are you doing in general, though, Felicity? I feel like you've dropped off the face of the earth.'

I considered the question for a second. 'I'd say a solid six out of ten.'

'A six out of ten is not bad. Not bad at all. Lionel, come here.' I heard her whispering something about me having a minor blip. 'Felicity is here.'

'Hi Flick.' Dad always spoke so loudly that I had to turn the volume down a notch. It was endearing. 'What are you up to tonight?'

'*Lionel.*' The line sounded scratchy, like Mum had covered the microphone. When she moved her hand and the sound became clear again, Dad sounded more upbeat than usual.

'Nothing wrong with a night under the duvet, love. Order yourself a pizza. I'll give you ten pounds next time I see you.'

'As nice as that sounds,' Mum interrupted, 'what is everyone in the house doing tonight? Can't you shift yourself and do something with them?'

I hesitated. Technically, they were going to Kitty's gig, and I could definitely ask to join them. It was either that or pester Maia whilst she worked, which sounded a bit like entering a lion's den. I said as much to Mum, whose face brightened.

'Oh, that's perfect. Just ask if you can go too. God, I used to love a gig. When I was your age, I used to crimp my hair and go out on the town with . . .'

I let her go on, already worrying about going downstairs and asking if I could go with them. I hadn't been offered a direct invite; was it rude to ask if I could tag along?

'What if they'd rather it was just them?'

Mum paused mid-tale and tutted. 'Flick, you spent the entirety of university feeling on the outskirts. *This is your chance.* We all know that this is a sad day for you, and I'll be honest, Felicity, I still remember the date of my anniversary with the man I dated before your dad. You have to keep moving. You could even get the crimpers out.'

'Mum, it's the new roaring twenties. Crimpers aren't a thing.'

She made a face. 'You're being petulant. Going out will make you feel better. You know I'm right.'

'I do?'

'I'm a mum. Being right is what we do.' I heard Dad snort in the background.

'Ignore him. Now put on a tight skirt and some eyeliner and *go join them.*'

I hung up, sincerely hoping that my dad hadn't still been in the background to hear that last part. I looked at my clothes rack, pulling a tiger-print skirt from a hanger and grabbing a black bodysuit. My motto in life was always to dress more confidently than I felt; it never failed me. Ten minutes later and I appeared almost presentable, my blotchy cheeks and slightly blocked sinuses the only sign I'd been sobbing for an hour straight since I got home from work.

'Oh shit.' I poked myself in the eye with my mascara wand, making my eyes water.

'Are you okay up there?' Kitty shouted up from her room. When I didn't respond straight away, I heard her trot up the stairs. 'Christ, what happened to you? You look like you have conjunctivitis.'

I sighed.

'No, but seriously, are you okay? Mascara-related injury aside, that is. I could, erm . . .'

Credit to her, she was trying to avoid my embarrassment.

'You could hear me sobbing?' I laughed when she nodded. 'It's my anniversary today. Or rather, it was.'

Kitty perched on the bed, one braid in, one braid out. 'We could tell that you were a bit down.'

Finishing off my lip gloss, I gestured to my appearance. 'Fancy letting me tag along tonight? I can't fester in here with my own thoughts any longer.'

My housemate beamed. 'Do you even have to ask? I wanted to invite you earlier, but I didn't know if you were counting on ice cream in bed or watching *The Notebook* over and over until you fell asleep.'

The tightness in my chest relaxed.

'We're a package deal in this house, right from the off. You never have to ask.' Kitty smiled. 'I know what it's like to feel like this city might swallow you whole if you let it. Let me just go and finish applying glitter to 60 per cent of my body

71

and then I'll be good to go. When you go down, hurry Stace up. If you don't round her up like a sheep then she'll never leave the house.'

***

It was always weird when you saw one of your friends doing their job outside of the familiar environment that you knew them in. Like, *Hey, this person that I associate with hairbrush dance parties and cleaning rotas exists in an entirely different, professional capacity.* When I'd first seen Suze at one of her events a couple of years ago, watching her with a clipboard and a serious look on her face, I'd almost spat out the lemonade I was drinking from a tiny plastic cup. The first time I'd seen Mum behind the counter at the dentist when Dad had taken us to get our teeth checked, I'd felt personally victimised when she'd shushed us for being too loud in the waiting room. But standing here in this bar/basement hybrid, of which London had so many, had to take the cake. Kitty was up on stage with huge head-phones covering her ears, real mixing decks under her fingers. There were people standing near the front of the room, cheering Kitty on, and she had an intense, thoughtful look on her face. She was clearly very good at this.

'Cool, right?' Stacey handed me a Desperado.

'Yep. Very cool.'

We'd stood in line at the bar for an unreasonably long time waiting to be served, and then paid an unreasonable price for the first round of drinks. But such was London, and such was life. The unreasonable had become the normal in this city.

And my mum had been right – the moment I'd decided to make something of my night, rather than wailing down the phone to her and wallowing, I'd instantly felt better.

'Sorry about your shitty day.' Stacey smiled at me sympathetically. 'No number of Desperados will make it not shit, but it might help a bit.' She clinked her glass against mine and took a breath. 'And I'm sorry that I haven't been the most hospitable.'

I didn't know what to say.

'I just . . . well, I found it really hard when Tara told us that she was leaving. Like I said, I've been in the house the longest, and when I watch people come and go, it's just a constant reminder that I feel like I'm not moving forward. You know?'

And everything suddenly made sense. It was never about me. 'I've never felt more like I'm moving backwards than I have in the last month.'

'It's a weird one, isn't it? I love the house, and I love those girls to bits, but I can't help feeling like I'm 27 years old with no direction. When I was younger I kind of assumed that I might have been engaged by now, or have my own place.'

I'd forgotten that Stacey was older than me by five years. It was impossible not to think about your twenties (and probably your thirties too) as a bit of a race. Social media didn't help; I was constantly comparing myself to other people when I checked Instagram on my commute.

'And it's not like I'm not happy for everyone. I am. I just struggle with it sometimes, the feeling that I'm this Carlisle Avenue artefact that never changes. I'll be in the history books when they find a fossil of me drinking wine in that same ground-floor bedroom.'

I smiled. 'If it helps, you seem like the core of Carlisle. Far from a fossil. And I don't know what the hell I'm doing right now either.'

'Thanks Flick.' She held up her Desperado, which I clinked again.

'Here's to not knowing what's going on half the time.'

Stacey cheered. 'And to a new friendship. I might have dragged my heels, but I'm here now.'

I beamed. Annoyingly, my mum *was* always right.

'Does Maia ever come to these gigs?' I thought of her retreating to her room, taking a black coffee and a stack of textbooks with her.

'Sometimes. She comes to the occasional gig to make sure that she has a leg to stand on when she drags us to Comic Con.'

'I've always wanted to go to that!' Given that Aaron was obsessed with gaming and all things Marvel, it had never made sense that he wouldn't dress up and go to the convention with me. Who didn't want to dress like a superhero for a day? I'd tried to convince Cecilia to send me there for an article, but it hadn't gone down too well. Something about not aligning with the vibe of the magazine.

'Oh, believe me, she'll drag you along too. We always go with her friends from university. It's a testament to how much we love her that we're all prepared to dress in spandex.'

Kitty started a new track at that moment, igniting an enthusiastic roar from the crowd in front of us, who were already gyrating and drunk enough to not care about personal space. I knocked back the Desperado, needing it to get on the right level. I hadn't been clubbing much since moving to London, aside from the one time Sadie had managed to convince the office to go wild after some post-work drinks. Even at uni I'd pretty much always chosen to stay in with Aaron instead of going out with my housemates. I was beginning to think that maybe putting all my eggs in one basket when I was in Manchester hadn't been the best idea I'd ever had. I looked at Kitty, glitter lining her parting between the fiery pink French braids, wearing nothing but a sequined halter neck and denim shorts. And then to Stace, who was wearing leopard-print flares and a white bandeau, already moving into the crowd and beckoning for me to follow her. Maybe it wasn't too late. Maybe this was my chance.

# 9

I groaned and reached for the paracetamol in Suze's outstretched hand. She wiggled it out of sight for a second, laughing at me.

'If I was running on anything more than two hours sleep, I might have found that amusing. Why are you always so prepared?'

She shrugged. 'It's a life skill I've acquired through multiple situations like this' – she gestured to my head – 'when I didn't have painkillers to hand. You learn fast.'

I managed a grunt in response whilst I gulped down a glass of water. 'You're Mum thirty years ago.'

'Going to take that as a compliment. I hope you're still going to be able to consume your body weight in pancakes. I chose this brunch place for a reason.' The look of genuine concern was definitely more for the pancakes than it was for me and my hangover.

'I will give it my most valiant attempt.'

She *hmph*ed at me, opening the front camera on her phone and reapplying her mauve lipstick. Saturday morning brunch had been a tradition when I was in high school and she was in sixth form, although back then it was strawberry jam crumpets and cups of tea in the café down the road, not the trendy places she chose nowadays. Brunch with my big sister had always felt like a privilege – I knew plenty of sisters that didn't get along, the younger constantly vying for the older one's attention. Whilst that might have been true for us when I was in primary school and she was miles ahead in high school, it hadn't been true since.

'What?' I noticed that she was staring at me, one eyebrow slightly raised. *Had I even remembered to brush my hair this morning?* I checked. 'Oops. I might have been going for a bohemian look, you never know.'

She snorted. 'This is all very amusing to me. I'm enjoying it. And for the record, I'm pretty sure anyone with actual bohemian style might be offended by that.'

'Way to kick a girl when she's down.' I checked my reflection in my spoon, clumps of last night's mascara still hugging my lashes. 'It isn't my finest moment, I know.'

It had been a week since my heart-to-heart with Stace, and I'd gone out with them again last night to another of Kitty's weekend gigs. We'd stumbled in when it was starting to get light outside, Stace promptly collapsing on the sofa whilst I made us a stack of toast, the soggier with butter the better. Both of us had fallen asleep downstairs, barely touching my lovingly made snack, only to be woken by Kitty starting her day and making homemade granola a couple of hours later. Kitty, who'd still been out with some friends when we'd left the bar. She'd waved me off with a blasé 'I'm used to it', but in my eyes it was nothing short of magic. I felt like I'd been knocked on the head with a frying pan.

Suze waved her menu in front of my face, grinning. 'Look alive. I cannot have been this bad during my wilder days.'

'Sorry. And yes, you were.' I had vivid memories of holding her hair over the toilet when she was in sixth form. I read through the menu, trying not to gag at chocolate-covered waffles and blueberry pancake stacks.

'I wish I'd been there.' She looked wounded. 'I've been asking you to come with me to gigs for years.'

'If it helps, this' – I gestured to myself – 'was born out of desperation to fit in. I have no shame in admitting that.'

'And how is that going for you? Fitting in?'

I filled her in on the houseshare, something I'd really started getting into the swing of. Particularly since Stacey was no longer avoiding me; I think she found solace in the idea that I too had no clue whatsoever what I was doing half the time. Maia was at Sophie's most nights since she lived closer to the library, and Kitty's sleeping schedule had been erratic whilst she juggled all of her jobs. It had lumped the two of us together, sharing fajitas and pasta bakes whilst watching reruns of old sitcoms on TV. It was the kind of companionship I realised I'd been missing for the last few years.

Suze was resting her head in her hands, listening intently. 'I was worried about you moving in there on your own. I know Mum and Dad were too, even if they didn't say it. I'm glad it's working out. Stacey sounds like my kind of woman. Pasta bakes and single life? I want that.'

Suze lived on her own in a flat in Liverpool city centre, away from my parents in a nearby village with our family dog, Kernel. Suze had named our golden retriever when she was in her early teens – apparently he'd been the exact same shade as a popcorn kernel. As much as it had pained her (like it had pained me) to leave Kernel behind and move out of our childhood home, Suze had always been the most independent person that I knew. I could never understand how she sat at the dining-room table during high school and did all her homework herself, whilst I needed Dad – who spent my school years frantically googling equations to figure out how to do it himself – to try and explain every step. When she'd moved out without looking back, I'd been in awe.

'I thought you liked living alone.' I folded the napkin next to me into something that resembled nothing like a swan.

'I do. If I had to share my kitchen with other people I'd scream. But coming home to dinner and gossip doesn't sound too bad. I come home and pop on Heart FM for company. It's a little bit different.'

The waitress came over and delivered our smoothies, and I thanked her, guzzling it down.

Suze sipped hers at a much more normal pace. 'It's just so strange, my little sister going out at all hours of the night.'

'When you think about it, I'm just making up for lost time.'

'True. Don't get me wrong, we liked Aaron just fine, but maybe he . . .' She paused.

I waved her on. 'Do your worst.'

'Well . . . maybe he held you back. He definitely wouldn't have gone to a gig in Shoreditch one weekend and then one in Clapham the next.'

'I think that's all the more reason to do it now.'

She grinned. 'Who are you and what have you done with my rule-following little sister?'

I shrugged, secretly happy with her evaluation. I *did* want to try something new on for size.

'I have to say, I'm impressed at how quickly you've made new roots. I'd have been shitting it moving into that house.'

'Thanks for telling me that now.'

'Well, it's all worked out, hasn't it?' She laughed. 'If I'm ever feeling like I need a boost, I imagine that you actually pulled out that milk padlock in front of everyone.'

'Don't. That appears frequently in my nightmares.' I scrunched up my nose. 'I dreamt about getting back together with Aaron again last night. He came to the new house and everything.'

Suze patted my hand. 'It's crazy how your brain turns against you in these situations. I still dream about my ex-boyfriends. It's completely normal. Ask any of the girls in your house, I bet they'd back me up.'

For a second she'd sounded almost jealous. 'Are you sure you aren't about to tell me that you want to move into Carlisle too? I'm not sure my attic room can squeeze two human beings in there. There's barely enough room for me and the spiders.'

Suze laughed. 'No, I really do mean it when I say I love my own flat. I do miss the old days of living with another girl, though. It's an experience everyone should tick off their list at some point.'

'Their list?'

She nodded and sipped again from her glass. A green juice. Totally Suze. I'd opted for something pinker and generally less scary looking. 'You know, a list of things you want to accomplish or experience. Like living in a house with your friends.' She pointed at me. 'Tick.'

I'd never really thought about what would be on my list. Moving to London was a big one. Get a grad job, tick. Move in with Aaron (did you still tick it if you moved out less than two years later?), tick. What else?

'Are you trying to come up with a list?'

'M–hmm.' I tapped my chin. Did I want to skydive? I imagined plummeting to my death. Nope. That one wasn't on my list. No life–gambling activities for me.

'Don't overthink it, Flick. It's meant to be fun. Your twenties are the ideal time for experiments and adventures and things that go bump in the night.'

I gave her a questioning look.

'I stand by that statement. When I was 22, I wanted to do *all of the things.*'

'You're 25. It's hardly as if your time has been and gone.'

She nodded in agreement. 'Oh, absolutely. I don't plan on accepting responsible adult life for at least another five years. I just think that post–breakup is the ideal time to step back and think about what you actually want for yourself, rather than having to consider anyone else.'

She had a point. It was like choosing a takeaway that first night in the houseshare; what would my life look like if I only had myself to think about? I mulled it over for a second. Definitely a lot less Formula 1. And probably a lot more of cooking things that I'd never tried before. More time to think about my job.

'Oh, I hear you.' Suze raised her glass in salute when I thought that last part aloud. 'I would never have got that promotion at work if I'd stayed with James.'

'How is work?' She'd been working for Out of Your Hands, an events management company that spanned across the UK, ever since she'd moved out five years ago. When she'd first started working there she'd been in admin, but now she was one of the main events coordinators. She worked from home a lot, but most months she was in London for a couple of days, meeting with clients. I was always glad when she needed to travel here for work. Kitty, Stace and Maia were good, but they weren't Suze. No one was.

'It's hectic, to say the least. We're still recovering from the drought of money coming in following the Christmas period. Not many people think about events for a good couple of months after all of the December parties.'

'Any events coming up?'

Last year she'd been one of the coordinators for a multi-charity fundraiser that had taken place in Hyde Park, and it had been epic. She had a knack for drawing people into an event. All of her business cards were on seeded paper; plant them once you were finished and they'd bloom into a handful of wildflowers.

'I'm working on a summer event for some high-profile clients, and I'm organising a big dinner in April. After that, there's a bit of a gap, but I'm sure people will start deciding that they want events again soon. There was talk of opening ourselves up to the wedding side of events. Not sure how I feel about dealing with meringue-shaped brides, and grooms disappearing just before the big moment.'

The waitress arrived with our breakfast.

'Oh my *God*.' Suze stared at the huge stack of pancakes that had just been placed in front of her, oozing Nutella and sliced banana.

If you wanted pancakes in London, you were never too far from a place that was willing to serve them to you. I tried not to let my stomach curl at the sight of the sweetness. My own breakfast – eggs and bacon – was much more manageable right now, although the chances of my hangover letting me clean the plate were slim.

'Mum told me I needed to check you were alive and well. I think you freaked her out big time last Friday when you had that meltdown about the texts.' She said it matter-of-factly before spearing a mouthful and devouring it. 'These are *heaven*. Literal *heaven*.'

I hated the idea of Mum worrying too much about me. I had my moments, but most of the time things were on the up. I'd been a bad daughter.

'How mad is Mum?'

Suze thought about it for a second. 'She's pissed off that you keep dropping off the grid. Not to scare you, but she did call you "Felicity Alice Sage".'

I groaned. 'Oops.'

It was normal in our family to get called by your full first name, but your middle name too? I was in trouble.

'Oops indeed. You'll have to make it up to her.'

'I just feel like I open up a huge crack in my heart when I talk to Mum.' I mimed spearing my chest and letting its contents ooze onto the table. 'I can't joke around with her like I do with you, it's a full-on therapy session.'

'I hope you're not avoiding your feelings, Felicity Alice Sage.' Suze smirked at her joke, but there was a touch of concern mixed in there too. That was the nature of our relationship – she could make me laugh like no one else, but there was also no one I'd rather have as an agony aunt. Even if she had forced me to get dressed when all I'd wanted was to live in pyjamas forever.

'I'm not avoiding them, per se.' I shovelled eggs into my mouth, thinking. 'I just have a lot of other things I can focus on right now. When someone gets four years of your life, it doesn't seem fair that they get much more than that.'

'Granted, I see your point. But I raise you four more years of repressed feelings.'

'I'm not repressing my feelings. I've cried in the shower more times than I can count on my fingers, okay?'

Suze nodded, placated. 'It's not that I want to see you upset.'

'Yeah, yeah, I know. You sound like my housemates.'

She looked wounded.

'Not that they could ever replace you,' I interjected quickly before carrying on. 'I just don't see the point in constantly crying and pining for him to come back. I did that for two weeks, and then he showed up on my doorstep and –'

'*Wait.*'

Crap. I still hadn't brought that up yet. It was embarrassing that he'd turned up to reiterate that he didn't want to be with me. The rom com he'd returned sat on my bookshelf like a constant kick in the teeth. I relayed the story to Suze.

She slapped her palm against her forehead. 'God, that boy. Hadn't he driven the knife in far enough by moving out?' She noticed my pained expression. 'Sorry, too far.'

'No, you're right. It was a really weird moment. I thought he might have been coming back to tell me that he'd changed his mind.'

Her facial features softened. 'Oh *Flick*.'

I waved her off. 'If I think about it, I'll cry. So I'm just trying not to think about it.'

'Fair enough. I wish you'd told me at the time.'

I moved my food around my plate. 'I didn't want to tell anyone about it. It's too humiliating.'

She reached across the table and slapped my arm. 'You're an idiot sometimes, did you know that? The amount of embarrassing shit I've done after breakups would be enough to paper my bedroom walls. When I broke up with Eric that time —'

'Karma for dating someone called Eric.' I pointed my fork at her.

'Shut up, I thought it was sexy. When I broke up with him, I wore his hoodie for like a month straight afterwards without washing it. It began to smell so bad that I didn't really leave the house.'

'Ew.'

'Exactly. Now *that* is embarrassing. The only thing about your situation that's embarrassing is that *he* turned up to say goodbye at all. What a weirdo. Are you going to finish that bacon?' She eyed up my food, changing the conversation abruptly.

I let her have it even though my hangover was waning, thinking about what she'd said. There wasn't much that I wouldn't take from my sister's lips as gospel. I thought about how I'd spent the last few weeks feeling ashamed of how everything had turned out. The more time I spent around the women in my life – Suze, my mum, the girls at Carlisle Avenue – the more I realised that it wasn't like that. It didn't have to be something that I'd failed at.

'You know what?'

Suze looked up from my plate. 'M-hmm?'

'I think I'm going to write my twenties list.'

I was already planning it in my mind. What *did* I want from my twenties?

'Oh, I am *so* on board with this.' Suze got up to pay. 'Let's start with something crazy.'

# 10

'So let me get this straight.' Kitty undid one of her braids, looking at me sceptically from the reflection in the mirror on her windowsill. 'You've started a breakup list.'

'No.' I held up my hands. 'No, I'm removing the breakup from the narrative. This is a *twenties* list.'

So far, since my brunch with Suze yesterday morning, I'd managed to come up with eleven ideas. Things I'd always wanted to do, and some things that Suze had helped me think up on the spot. She'd shown me the list that she had made when she was 22, and the majority of the items on that list were too wild to repeat. Mine was much (*much*) tamer.

Kitty ran her fingers through her now wavy hair. 'Come on, then, let's see it.'

I handed over the A4 refill pad.

### *Flick's Twenties List That is ABSOLUTELY NOT a Breakup List*

1. *Start playing tennis matches in London again*
2. *Learn how to make sourdough*

3. *Dye my hair*
4. *Live in a houseshare*
5. *Start playing the piano again (and learn because I want to, not because I was told to)*
6. *Travel around Italy*
7. *Buy a Polaroid camera and take 100 photos*
8. *Have a go on Kitty's mixing decks*
9. *Visit every café in the Mayfair article*
10. *Work one of Suze's events*
11. *Go on enough nights out to make up for lost uni years*

Kitty nodded a couple of times, murmuring to herself as she got deeper into her analysis of my list. I lay back on her bed, counting the number of houseplants hidden in every corner. My favourite discovery so far whilst living at Carlisle had been how every one of my new friends packed as much personality into their rooms as they possibly could. In a rented houseshare, there was limited space to make it your own, but they'd managed it.

Stacey's room was the most chaotic: a clutter of makeup brushes and hair tools all over the floor, with photos stuck to every surface and a chair covered in clothes, which she had deemed 'the dumping ground'. Ironically, there was no laundry basket in sight. Despite the fact that she was 27, her room reminded me of my friends' rooms when we'd lived in halls in my first year of university. It felt like the kind of room that you could make yourself at home in, or go to if you really needed a hug.

On the one occasion that I'd been inside to borrow a hole punch, I'd learnt that Maia's room was practically a library, with neat book towers along one side of her wall, as well as a tall oak bookcase as the main feature. Most of the titles she seemed to read for pleasure were sci-fi, but the odd piece of literary fiction was dotted around. There was a quiet confidence in the layout of her bedroom. A desk covered in academic articles and case files, a clean white bedspread, a handful of photos on her bedside table. One was of her and Sophie leaning in towards each other with vanilla ice cream cones in their hands. They were grinning, the beach behind them, cheeks flushed from the wind. Another photo was of her and a woman who must have been her mum, considering the likeness between them. It was Christmas in the photo, a glittering tree behind them. Not a tree that would have looked at home in the Sage household (think homemade decorations from when we were 5, and enough tinsel to sink a ship), but an elegant, colour-coordinated masterpiece. The last photo was of everyone at Comic Con, Kitty dressed as Black Widow and Stacey pulling a face but still posing with a hand on her hip, an excellent Superwoman. Maia was effortlessly cool as the Scarlet Witch. Instead of the hundreds of photos in Stacey's room, each choice felt purposeful and selected especially.

Kitty's room was cluttered in a different, more organised way to Stacey's. There was a set of mixing decks next to her bed, and assorted rock vinyl hung like a gallery on one of her walls. Houseplants of varying sizes lurked in every free space; there must have been over twenty. How she had any time left in her day after watering them all was a mystery to me. I'd noticed that her collection was beginning to take over the house; there was a new spider plant in the bathroom, and ivy hung in the kitchen. Her windowsill was covered in all the pots of glitter she used for gigs, and she had a small selection of books stacked on her bedside table – mostly memoirs and contemporary fiction compared to Stacey's romance novels and Maia's sci-fi.

I had no idea what my room said about me – it was a work in progress. I had visions of bright colours and a beautiful rug at the foot of my bed. That would have to wait until payday. At least I had somewhere to hang up my clothes now.

'Well, a lot of these things are easily doable.' Kitty gestured to the item on the list that referred to her decks. 'Decks, Flick. Flick, decks.' She introduced me to her pride and joy. 'Have at it!'

'As tempting as that is, I want to have a go and actually feel like I know what I'm doing. Have my main character DJ moment.'

She laughed. 'We'll make it into a group activity. Decks and pizza night.'

One of the things you learnt pretty quickly in this house was that *everything* revolved in some way around food. A couple of nights ago Stacey had organised a whole evening of card games and reality TV around a lasagne that she'd made. Food was at the heart of these friendships, and I wasn't complaining. It was comforting.

'And number four you can already tick off, thanks to us.' She grabbed a metallic gel pen from the pot on her bedside table, ticking the item off the list. 'I feel like these are all things that could realistically happen.'

'That's the point. If I put things on there that won't happen in a million years, or things that I have very little control over, then I won't feel motivated to do them.'

She fiddled with the end of one of her braids. 'How would you feel if we ticked one of them off this afternoon?'

'As in right now?' I grabbed the list from her, trying to decipher which one of the goals she was talking about.

'Like, *right now* right now.'

Given that we'd already established that the mixing decks would be a formal event, there was only really one of two goals that she could have been referring to. She pulled open her wardrobe door, revealing a selection of brightly coloured boxes on the lowest level.

'Ta-da!' She pointed to the array of hair dyes. 'You didn't think I'd always been Barbie pink, did you?'

I stared at her, a bit in awe. Every hair colour you could think of, she had a dye for. Platinum blonde, bright red, auburn, blue.

'Your hair has been *all* of these colours?'

'Me and Tara combined. We had a bit of a reputation for convincing not only each other but all sorts of people who came in this house to change their hair. We almost convinced Sophie to go green.'

I tried to imagine Maia's face if her girlfriend came out of Kitty's room with green hair.

'Yeah.' Kitty spotted my expression. 'That's why it was an almost. So, are you in?'

Even though I'd written it on my list, I hadn't expected it to be fulfilled straight away. My hair was nothing special; it hung halfway down my back, was midway between blonde and brown, and lacked any real hairstyle. I had no idea what I was going to do with it. People's hair said a lot about them. Kitty's said confident and bold; Stacey's bouncy waves said *I always look this fabulous*; Suze's artfully messy top knot said that she had her style all figured out. What did I want my hair to say about me? I looked at the assortment of box dyes and pointed to one that stood out straight away. One that felt like me.

'I'm in.'

***

It wasn't long before Stacey joined us in the second-floor bathroom, chiming in now and then to make sure Kitty was applying the dye right (which, she claimed, she definitely was). Maia had briefly looked in at the chaos, shaking her head and laughing at me bent over the bath before she headed out in her running gear. It was such a contrast, Stacey shouting instructions from her perch on the toilet seat and Maia looking focused as she headed out in her running shoes, that it was almost laughable.

'I promise, this is going to look amazing.' Kitty used the shower head to rinse off the dye. 'You might have a little staining on your hairline, but that will go.'

I groaned. 'Will it have disappeared by 9 a.m. tomorrow by any chance?'

Stacey nodded, but she was biting her lip. 'Oh yeah, sure it will.'

'OW!' I blinked quickly, my eye sore from the sudden blast of water.

'Sorry, sorry. Lost control of the shower for a second.' Kitty was trying not to laugh as she turned the stream of water off, grabbing an old towel and wrapping it around my hair. I was instructed not to look at the almost finished product, but to face the wall and sit on the desk chair they'd borrowed from Maia's room.

'Okay, so I let you take the reins with this dye mission' – Stacey pulled the towel from my hair as she directed the statement at Kitty – 'but the next step is my forte. I want to cut and style it.'

There were definite perks to living with a hairdresser in London. Last year I'd sat for three hours in one of the salons that Sadie had recommended, and I'd walked out two inches of hair and over a hundred quid lighter. It had *not* been a pleasurable experience.

'Work your magic.' Kitty gestured to my head. 'Honestly, Flick, you made the right move coming here. A cut and colour, completely free of charge. We should put that on room advertisements!'

'Hey!' I flicked her, true to my name. 'I'm not going anywhere anytime soon.'

I was surprised at how adamantly I felt about it.

Kitty's face softened. 'I know, I know. We've got our claws in you now, Flick.'

We both looked at Stacey, who was snipping at my hair, tongue hanging slightly out of her mouth as she concentrated.

Kitty laughed. 'Stace, please tell me this concentration face is specific to this house, and not the salon.'

'Oh, shut up. Head still, Flick.'

I did as she asked. 'At least let me pay you guys some sort of discounted –'

Stacey interrupted. 'It's a rite of passage to dye your hair after heartbreak. Those kind of hair jobs should always be free, in my opinion.'

'Yeah.' Kitty nodded. 'And that box of dye wasn't going near my hair anytime soon. I'm enjoying living the pink life. So technically you did me a favour. And now we get to take pride in the fact that we helped you tick another item off the list.'

'What list?'

Kitty explained the idea of my twenties list whilst Stacey finished cutting my hair, moving us to Kitty's bedroom halfway through so that she had access to a hairdryer.

'I feel like Carlisle is the perfect place for a list like that.' She spoke between a mouthful of hair slides that she'd been using to section my hair.

Like with Kitty and the basement gig, I was struck again by that feeling of admiration at seeing one of my friends doing what they did best. It was one thing to see Stacey lounging in the living room scrolling on her phone for hours on end – impressive in a completely different sense of the word – but quite another to see her focused and at work on my hair.

'Okay.' She grabbed the mirror from Kitty's windowsill and prepared to hold it up in front of me. 'The big reveal.'

Kitty was practically bouncing on the spot. 'I have to say Stace, I think we've outdone ourselves here.'

'Couldn't agree more.'

They counted down from ten, growing more excited by the second. Honestly, whatever it looked like, it was worth it to be a part of this experience.

'Voila!' Stacey put the mirror in front of my face with a dramatic flourish. 'What do you think?'

I gasped. It was me, Felicity Sage, but at the same time, it wasn't. It was someone completely different. Which was exactly how I felt lately, and not in a bad way.

Stacey had styled it in big waves and cut shorter pieces to frame my face. The colour that I'd chosen – a bright auburn copper shade – complimented my skin tone in a way that the dirty blonde colour never had. I beamed.

'*Guys.*'

'Do you love it?' Kitty looked worried for a second.

'Of course she loves it, Kit.' Stacey waved her off. 'How could she not? She looks amazing.'

I grabbed one of each of their hands and squeezed. 'It's exactly what I wanted. Pass me the list?'

I used the same gel pen and ticked off the second item. Another thing checked off my twenties list. Suze had been right; this *did* feel good.

# 11

A brown paper bag landed in front of my face, a few crumbs spilling out onto my keyboard.

'Don't say I never give you anything, Flickster.' Felix plopped down next to me. '*Holy shit.*'

I pretended I didn't know what he was talking about. 'Holy shit what?'

'*Your hair.*'

Sadie piped up from the end of the line. 'I almost didn't recognise you when you came in a few minutes ago. I was like, "who have we hired now?" I have some hoops that would look *amazing* with that copper by the way.'

Felix sighed. 'If you start wearing hoops as well as being an auburn-haired beauty, it'll be too much for me. I'll have to move desks.'

'Oh, stop it, you're making me blush.' I opened the paper bag that I'd momentarily forgotten about. 'And now you're making me happy too.' I took a bite of the salted caramel brownie.

Usually I was the baked-goods fairy, but today it appeared that my good deeds were being returned. The brownies outside the office were legendary; if you didn't get them quick, you'd be left with a selection of lemon drizzle bars and granola flapjacks. Which were good, but they weren't salted caramel brownies. Obviously.

'You're welcome, kiddo.' Felix started up his computer, taking out his planner. 'What's the mood like this morning?'

I didn't have to look in his direction to know that he was gesturing to Cecilia's office. She'd been in relatively good spirits when I'd arrived at work fifteen minutes early, complimenting my hair before going into her office and flipping the little sign on her door to read 'open'. If her stress levels were high, it always read 'closed'.

'Suspiciously optimistic,' I reported.

'Oh God. Calm before the storm. Better get cracking.' Felix started typing furiously. It was like he was trying to hammer in the words, as if bashing the keyboard might make them appear faster. Although it never felt like there was a hierarchy (other than Cecilia) within the team, Felix was our content coordinator, so he had a lot of responsibility. He sourced our writers, and collaborated with them to get hold of the content that he then passed on to our editorial team. After that, when all of the writers had been found, he worked with design to make sure the chronology of the whole magazine made sense. He didn't give himself anywhere near enough credit for the part he had to play in the finished product. We were only just approaching March, but things were already heating up for our next print issue in April. The deadline for the issue to go to print was looming.

'How are we doing with the article about period poverty?' Felix glanced at me expectantly, launching immediately from joking around to getting down to business.

'The second draft is with Fiona.' I checked the item off my own list and forwarded the email to Felix.

'Excellent. And the Garfield piece?'

'It should be almost ready. It's with Cecilia; for some reason she wanted to check that one over.'

Felix nodded. 'It's because of the backlash from estate agents last time we wrote about box rooms in London. That's why it got pushed from this month's print. Right, I'll just check in with design.'

He got up and went over to the other side of the room, already chatting to the design team before he'd even reached their desks.

Fiona shook her head, opening the brownie bag that Felix had left on her desk too. 'He tires me out just watching him.'

'Me too. He's the Influence glue.'

When I'd started working at *Influence,* it had taken precisely one month for me to realise that things were always hectic around here. As soon as one issue went to print, people started fretting about the next. The constant action and buzz – I loved it.

One of the editors, Carmen, stumbled into the office late, her glasses halfway down her nose. Little beads of sweat tracked her hairline. She rested her palms on her knees and bent over to catch her breath. 'The Tube was rammed, I had to get the next one. Am I in trouble?'

The last half of the sentence was hushed, and we all knew what it meant. My eyes darted to the office, where it looked like Cecilia was on the phone.

'No, you're safe for now. Just sit down quick!' Felix called out from the other side of the room. 'Your secret is safe with the rest of us.'

I stifled a laugh. We knuckled down for an hour or so, only pausing when Sadie went into the staffroom to do a hot drink order. I knew it by heart from my first couple of months here: Felix was a tea three sugars (blasphemy), Fiona was a black instant coffee, Sadie was a chamomile tea, and I flitted between tea with one sugar and the caramel latte sachets I always got if they were on offer at Tesco. The other half of the office tended to do their own tea-break runs, just for ease. There were only so many runs to and from the staffroom that a person could do.

'Here you go.' Sadie put my latte down in front of me, her hands cradling her own mug. I noticed a couple of new gold rings weighing down her index finger and thumb. 'Have you *seen* the dishy guy from IT? I'm considering dropping my laptop on the floor just so he can fix it.'

I tried to subtly glance in the direction that she was pointing to, where Cecilia was talking to a guy who had his back to me. He looked tall-*ish*, but aside from that, there were no distinguishing characteristics on show. To be honest, I was only looking for Sadie's sake – one week mindlessly swiping on Hinge and I was 100 per cent over it.

'I can't see him.'

Sadie tapped her acrylics on her mug. 'Just you wait until he comes out of that office, Flick. Just you wait.'

'Aren't you in a long-term relationship?'

She scoffed. 'Do you see Patrick in here?' She pretended to check the room out. 'Nope. I don't see him either. It's called window shopping, Flick,' she said with a wink.

'Okay, well, when he turns around I'll email you my thoughts.'

Sadie laughed and strode back to her desk, where she pulled up our Instagram account. We were hosting a staff Q&A this week; I'd always assumed that social media was pretty self-explanatory, but for all of her crazy ideas, Sadie knew exactly what she was talking about. Her whole strategy was about making the reading experience more human, and more inter-active. It was one of the ideas that had landed her the job six months ago. I craned my neck to get a good look at the man in Cecilia's office, who was now pointing to something hanging out of the back of Cecilia's desktop. We rarely got a good look at the tech and finance teams, since they worked for a few of the businesses in the building. He was still completely out of view. Just as I turned back to my desk to admit defeat, Felix spotted me staring as he came back to his seat.

'What are you trying to look at?' He glanced at the office. 'Oh, I *see*.' I noticed him checking out the Tech guy too.

'What is it with all the taken members of this workforce admiring the single staff?' I shot him a look and he held up his hands. 'Leave some for the rest of us.'

'Hey, I have a cat with my man. I cooked *ramen* last night for him when I got home, and I don't even really like it. Last week I went to watch football at the pub, Flick.' He clocked my expression. 'I know, check my temperature. So, it's not like I'm about to jump ship, but I can still admire pretty things.'

Sadie piped up. 'That's what I said!'

We all got back to work, managing ten minutes of undisputed concentration before I noticed the office door open out of the corner of my eye.

*Finally.*

I tried to be covert, pretending to be engrossed with the final proofs of an article about leg-hair activism. The guy turned in my direction, his gaze settling on me.

*Shit.*

It was Teddy. His eyes widened in recognition. Almost nine million people in London, and *this* had to be the Tech guy. Stacey would have been lapping this up.

'What are you doing?' Felix poked my seat, watching me slide further and further down. I was slumped so far that I was sheer moments away from slithering below my desk.

'Felicity?' Cecilia called me from her open office door. 'Can I have a moment?'

*Double shit.*

One, because it just drew more attention to me. Teddy was already staring at my seat slump, looking bemused. And two, because I hadn't told him that my name was actually Felicity. His head was tilted like Kernel's did when he couldn't quite work out what we were trying to communicate to him. Now that I considered it, Teddy *did* have golden retriever energy. I resisted the urge to smack my palm against my forehead.

'Sage?' Cecilia threw up her hands. 'Sometime today please?'

I got out of my seat, feeling my cheeks flush. Did that woman have to keep throwing new names into the mix? I passed Teddy on my way to the office, giving him a small smile before moving past him, closing the door behind me.

★★★

'Have you got the latest figures from sales yet for last publication?' Cecilia gestured in the direction of the door. 'Something is wrong with the logging system. I just spoke with Theodore from IT. We need to send them over to Michael manually via email for now.'

Michael was our big boss. I only knew him from mixing events and the odd occasion when he dropped into the office. He got my name wrong every time. How hard was Felicity to remember? I'd had Florence, Francesca, Flora. And every time, he seemed to manage the name Felix.

'Earth to Felicity.' Cecilia waved her hand in front of my face. 'Got the figures? I sent them over in an email.'

'Yep, they just came through.' I took the paper copy from her outstretched hand and tried not to panic at the influx of new admin work.

'Okay, great. If you could get that done by end of day that'd be great.' She paused, staring at my hair. 'What inspired this change by the way?' Cecilia pointed to my head. 'I'm assuming it was a boy?'

I was pretty sure everyone in the office had seen me crying at my desk back in January, but I hadn't thought that Cecilia had noticed. Now, looking at the almost sympathetic expression on her face, I could tell she had.

'Yes, but also no. I feel like I missed out on a lot of the years where people do crazy things. So I'm doing them all now.'

Her interest was piqued, and she waved me in the direction of the chair opposite her so I could sit down. 'Oh, that *is* interesting. Sort of like a pilgrimage?'

I tried not to laugh. 'I mean, I guess. Like a quest to make the most of my twenties.'

Cecilia peppered me with questions for a few minutes, wanting to know what else was on the list. She smiled at the salute to the Mayfair article.

'When I was 24 my boyfriend broke up with me in Costa. Totally didn't see it coming; had to move back in with my parents.'

I was a bit taken aback by this information. Not only because I had no idea how old Cecilia was (Felix thought maybe early fifties; I was lingering more in the mid-forties), but because in all the time I'd worked here, she'd never offered up any personal information. In the main office, secrets were traded like Panini stickers in the school playground, but in here, the boss's office? Information was treated like solid gold.

'A list like yours might have helped me back then. Very relatable.' Cecilia nodded to herself and made a few notes on the sheet in front of her. 'Remind me, how much writing have you done with us this past year, Felicity?'

I blanched. It wasn't like I couldn't write at all; I mean, I proofread enough of it to know what good writing looked like. But my degree had been in management and marketing, not creative writing. I didn't say anything.

'Don't look so scared. Writing is easy if you're writing about something you're interested in. I've seen some of the notes you send through – you're acting like you're incompetent, but you're actually pretty good.'

I mean, I had filled in for a couple of writers once or twice on the *Influence* website, when we were short on content. It hadn't been anything ground-breaking, but it had been a nice change from typing numbers into a spreadsheet or checking for incorrect grammar all day.

'I've written bits and pieces.' I shrugged. 'You know I'll do pretty much anything.'

I was also very aware of the fact that my grad review was almost due. Would it look good to hesitate when asked to step up? Probably not.

Cecilia's face broke into a smile. 'I want you to start writing a column.'

I paused. Had I heard that right? 'Sorry, what did you say?'

'A column. Documenting your progress with the list, and life in your twenties as a single young woman in London. I think it could be fascinating. The whole reason we started this grad scheme was to try and engage a younger audience. Sadie is working with the team on our social media presence. Why settle for a short Q&A when you could document your whole life online?'

'I think you're vastly overestimating how interesting my day-to-day life is.'

Cecilia wasn't backing down. 'Well, isn't that the point of the list in the first place?'

My mind was whirring. An Instagram Q&A with the rest of the team I could manage. I knew how to talk about my favourite smoothie and what animal I would be if I had to choose one (chameleon). But my own column? I wasn't sure I was up to that. The website to accompany *Influence* in print was an addition that they'd been working on ever since I'd started here, so I knew they were still looking to expand its contents. And granted, if I were scrolling through the internet, or if Kitty and Stacey were, I think they would probably click on a column like that. Suze definitely would. But did it not deserve someone a bit more qualified? Working for the student newspaper and quickly writing the occasional article here was as far as I'd gone. Then again, they'd be less likely to make me redundant if I had my own column.

'Felicity?'

I jumped at the mention of my name.

'I know it's a big jump, but I think this will be great for the magazine. Can I count you in? All you have to do to begin with is write a couple of updates. It doesn't have to be pristine; Fiona or one of the editorial team can go over it with a fresh set of eyes. I'll even ask Felix for his input. We're trying to make *Influence* appeal to people in their twenties. What better way to do that than to get our graduate to write something every week? Plus' – she narrowed her eyes, going in for the kill – 'there couldn't be a better motivator for you to actually do the things on your list.'

She had me there, and she knew it.

'You make a good point.'

A smile. 'Can you have your introductory piece in by Thursday? If it goes down well, we could culminate the column in an article in the June print issue. People in your life bracket are constantly scrolling or flipping through the pages to find someone that they can actually relate to, to prove to them that *they can do it too.* I don't see why that can't be you.'

As much as one half of my personality was screaming *red alert, red alert, everyone in position because this is a panic situation,* the other, more rational, part of me knew that this was a big opportunity. I thought of Suze, who would jump at the chance to try something new. Or Kitty, who would already be halfway through writing her first piece. And I thought of Aaron, who would never expect me to say yes to something like this.

I fiddled with the belt hook on my jeans, finally looking up. 'I'm in. I'll have the first instalment in by Wednesday evening.'

Cecilia clapped. 'Brilliant. This, Felicity, could be the making of you. Your life begins when you start chasing the things *you* want.'

I left her office feeling slightly flustered. Felix was mouthing 'is everything okay?' to me from his desk, tapping his wrist where a watch would be. Usually, an impromptu visit to the boss's office – and especially one that lasted as long as mine had – never meant good news. I waved him off and mimed drinking from a mug. He nodded back. This kind of life-altering opportunity required extra-sugary hot drinks (think Malteser hot chocolate sachet, the likes of which were *treasured* in my corner of the staffroom cupboard) and a full debrief. I was rounding the corner into the staffroom when I bumped straight into Teddy.

# 12

*Shit.* I'd forgotten all about him. The showdown with Cecilia had momentarily wiped my brain, but Teddy was definitely here and very real in front of me. I winced at the accidental jab of his elbow into my side.

'Well, that was not how I wanted to say hi.' Teddy scratched his head awkwardly. 'I thought that was you in there, so I waited. Didn't actually intend on accosting you as soon as you came out, despite how it might look.'

*Leeds. That's his accent.*

'Don't worry, I was flagging. I probably needed a collision to wake me up.' I didn't; that meeting with Cecilia had left me wide awake.

'Right.' He didn't look convinced.

I gestured for him to follow me into the staffroom, where he made himself at home, leaning against the counter. 'Drink?'

'Go on, then. But only if it's Yorkshire tea. So, how have you been? Since you, er, left our match quite abruptly.'

My cheeks flushed. 'Sorry about that. That was weird.'

He shrugged. 'No problem.' Teddy gestured between us and said, 'Clearly we were supposed to meet again. So, the elephant in the room . . .'

My mouth turned up against my better judgement. 'Go on.'

'Flick, Felicity, Sage . . .'

'Huge misunderstanding.' I put my hands to my face. 'And highly embarrassing. Felicity Sage is my actual name, but no one ever uses it except Cecilia and my mum. Most people just call me Flick.'

'And it's Flick because . . .'

'Tennis nickname.'

Teddy grinned 'And so we come full circle. Flick – she who darts away from a tennis rally when she knows she's the weaker player.'

'Whatever helps you sleep at night.' I held out my hand. 'Flick – she who would crush you like a grape in a singles match.'

I'd always been told that I was mild until it came to tennis.

Teddy took my outstretched hand and shook it. 'Déjà vu. Are we ever going to get past the introductory stage?'

I tried not to notice how green his eyes were, but ultimately failed. He had a small scar above his left eyebrow, and it became more apparent when he was smiling, like now. 'Maybe we're destined to repeat our intro over and over.' I bit my lip. 'Theodore.'

'Oh Christ.' Now he was the one who looked embarrassed. 'I didn't realise you knew about that. Names are given, not chosen.'

'Cecilia dropped you in it too and I just couldn't let it slide, sorry. The ammunition was too valuable.'

'I completely agree. I'd have thought less of you if you hadn't made fun of me for it. I might be the only man born in Leeds called Theodore.'

*Leeds. Knew it.*

'Oh, and another thing.' Teddy was relaxed now. 'I *have* been told in the past that I lack observational skills, but your hair was definitely a different colour when I first met you. If you didn't want to play tennis with me again, you didn't have to change your whole identity.'

My cheeks heated. 'Complete coincidences, I promise. Even more so if you count the fact that I had no idea you worked in this building. God, you try your best to shake a guy off . . .'

'I swear I was completely under the impression that this was a Flick-free zone. Be honest, do you even work here? Or were you just trying to bump into me again? If so' – he gestured to the office – 'this is impressive, I have to admit. All your fake colleagues played along very well. In fact, a couple of them are staring at us still.'

I didn't have to turn around to know it was Sadie and Felix.

'Have you been working in the building for a long time?'

Teddy shrugged. 'It depends what you class as a long time. I'd say this has been an incredibly long six months.' He didn't elaborate on why. 'I moved up to London six months ago and I tend to rotate between the businesses in the building, which is probably why I haven't been up here before. One of the other tech guys has a crush on one of your colleagues, so the rest of us don't usually get a look in. If the word *Influence* is uttered, he's up here like a flash.'

'I hope you realise that I'm going to need more details. I thrive on office gossip.'

He looked solemn. 'I've been sworn to secrecy, but I can tell you who it is he likes.' Teddy leaned in. 'The guy that's currently staring at us. I don't think he's blinked the entire time we've been stood here – it's quite unnerving. Is that a picture of a cat on his desk?'

I looked behind him to confirm what I already knew (Noodles had been the final nail in the coffin). I smiled in amusement as Felix tried to look busy when I turned to watch him too.

'He's taken, sadly. As is the other girl staring at us.' I signalled with my chin to Sadie, who was now pretending to be engrossed in the label on her Diet Coke. 'How do you take your tea?'

'Very important question. Splash of milk, one sugar.'

I didn't point out that our tea order was identical – I was sure millions of people in London were sitting at their desks right now cradling a mug of the same. I passed him his tea in a slightly chipped but well-loved Eeyore mug. I took Piglet. We stood for a minute in silence, both doing that predictable thing where you try to take a sip straight away and end up scalding your lip.

'I really am sorry about leaving so quickly last week. If it helps, my housemates haven't let me forget it.'

Teddy grinned. 'You told your housemates about me, then?'

Oh shit. I didn't want him to think I'd gone all googly eyed over him. In fact, I didn't want him to think that I'd been thinking about him at all. Now was *not* the time to start flirting with random men I'd found in tennis courts. I had a list to complete.

He shifted from one foot to the other. 'On that note, I do actually think it's weird that we bumped into each other again. I realise that if you'd wanted my number on Friday, you would have stuck around, so absolutely feel free to decline. But here I am, and here you are.' He shuffled again. 'What I'm trying to say is, how about dinner sometime?'

I winced. He noticed.

'And now that I've said that and witnessed your reaction, I realise I might have got the wrong end of the stick. Don't worry, I can just send Carl up here to ogle your friend. I never have to come up here again.'

Despite the awkwardness of the situation, I smirked. 'Thought you were sworn to secrecy.'

Teddy put his mug down. 'All oaths go out the window when you want the ground to swallow you up.'

'It's not that I don't want to go out with you, Theodore.'

He mimed being stabbed in the chest. 'Kick a man whilst he's down, why don't you.'

'It's just that things are a bit . . .' I searched for the right words, '. . . up in the air at the moment. I recently came out

112

of a long-term relationship and moved in with a bunch of strangers. And I'm about to take on a massive project here at the magazine – Cecilia wants me to start writing my own column.'

Teddy whistled. 'Wow.'

'Yeah.'

I hadn't intended on divulging my life story; he'd made me feel at ease to the point where really, I could have just said no. But I got the sense that Teddy didn't *do* this much, and I didn't want him to think he wasn't dateable. He was. Just not by me.

'You know, that really softened the blow. Sometimes you just need to know it was a them problem.' He smiled. 'I'm kidding. It's fine. I really am sorry to hear about your partner, though. Nothing worse than having your life turned completely upside down. Been there, bought the T-shirt.'

My interest was piqued, but he didn't elaborate.

'But the column, wow. That's highly impressive. I feel like I need to also give myself a pat on the back for just giving it a shot asking out the most up-and-coming magazine journalist.'

I resisted the urge to shove him. 'I wouldn't quite go that far.'

'Second most up-and-coming magazine journalist?'

'Yeah, sounds about right. Get in your league, Teddy. I'm going places.'

We laughed for a moment and stood in comfortable silence. I didn't want to turn around and clock the expressions on my colleagues' faces.

'Well, Flick Felicity Sage. I can't say making friends in London has been going particularly well for me so far, but this feels like a step in the right direction.' He stuck out his hand. 'Hi, I'm Teddy. How do you feel about a completely innocent, platonic bite to eat some time?'

I shook his hand. 'You just wanted an introduction do-over where I didn't call you Teddy Bear, didn't you?'

'Am I that transparent?'

'Unfortunately, yes. But you know what? You got me. A completely innocent, platonic bite to eat sounds perfect.'

'I probably got it wrong anyway. Maybe the real reason we keep bumping into each other is because we're destined to be mates.'

I bit my lip, feeling a sudden pang of guilt, but shook it off. Yeah, he was right.

'I might even spice up your column, you never know. I'm a *great* agony aunt for my mum and all her friends.'

'You'll regret offering that. I seem to require a lot of advice these days.' I grinned at him as he saluted me and put his mug in the sink.

'See you around, Flick.'

I left him with my number, and we waved as we parted in the hallway, him to go back down to IT, and me to my desk. I handed Felix a coffee from the kitchen. He was sitting ramrod-straight in his seat, wide eyed. He was going to *love* this.

★★★

EMILY MERRILL

## The Twenties List: Welcome!

*Hi everyone, I'm Flick.*

*(And by everyone, I'm under no illusions that it means more than five people, including both of my parents. Hi Mum and Dad.)*

*For anyone who isn't related to me by blood, let's start with some introductions. I'm Felicity, otherwise known as Flick, graduate magazine assistant here at* Influence. *I'm 22 and live in West London with three brand-new housemates (who probably make up the other three readers). I studied Management and Marketing at the University of Manchester, grew up by the sea surrounded by Scousers, and gained my nickname from a signature tennis move. I'm very much an average twenty-something. I'm sure I'm not the only person in London who moved down here from the North, or who moved into a house with complete strangers all in the name of being able to afford life in this city. Which means that, quite predictably, I'm also definitely not the only one currently experiencing the aftermath of a pretty sudden breakup.*

*Original, I know. Who hasn't been dumped? There's something completely universal about the experience, whilst at the same time it feels like no one else could possibly have been through the same things as you and lived to tell the tale. We cry in the shower and eat ice cream for breakfast, leave the house without brushing our hair, and spend our entire evenings scrolling through our iCloud photo memories. It's*

115

*not a glamorous life, but it's ours. It's occasionally fine – some days when you wake up it feels like a new, crazy adventure, and a takeaway latte can help you to romanticise pretty much anything. But most of the time, life in your twenties is terrifying. And yet, we're all still here. Surviving (sometimes thriving) in a city – or maybe more accurately, a world – that makes us feel like we're walking on a treadmill that keeps speeding up, ready to fling us off. This might seem pretty dramatic, and yes, there are so many other, more important issues to be typing about at 3 p.m., but I know I'm not the only one who's stress-eaten a pack of Hobnobs on the Tube or opened a Help to Buy ISA and left a fiver sitting in there for three years. If anything, it's a comfort for me to be writing this. Even if no one is actually reading it. But for the sake of my job, let's pretend that some of you are.*

*I was sitting at brunch the other morning with my sister – Suze, here you go, full credit where it's due – and she suggested that I write down a list of things that I want to do now that I'm single, in a relatively new city, and in my twenties. Kind of like reclaiming my life, although I refuse to call it a breakup list. Now, the list thing seems to have stuck. They've aptly coined it 'Flick's twenties list' in my houseshare, and whilst my goals are still relatively tame, they're enough to keep me going for a while. How could I possibly be sitting in my bedroom crying when I need to learn how to play piano again and take 100 Polaroid photos for my wall? Who knows, maybe I won't complete everything on the list. But the thought that I might is enough to keep me moving. And moving feels like a step in the right direction (no pun intended).*

*I want to dye my hair crazy colours and learn to make bread just because I can. I want to figure out my place in this city that isn't really my home yet, and bounce back from heartbreak in style (maybe bounce was the wrong word – it's currently more of a dragging motion). Most of all, I want to document it, so that if I ever go through this again (pray for me that I don't though, please), I'll know that I can do it. And if you're reading, you'll know that you can do it too. After all, like I said, what I'm experiencing is universal. Maybe, if we all pull through together, we'll make some sense of this crazy decade where nothing ever turns out like you expect it to. Whatever you choose to take from this column, I'm glad that you're here. Whoever you are. Wherever you are.*

*Signing off from my first week on duty,*

*Flick x*

# 13

I pushed my knuckles into the dough, blowing away the hair that was stuck to my clammy forehead. This took *effort*.

'So you're telling me that you get to live out your perfect twenties, and you're going to get *paid* to do it?' Stacey watched me kneading the bread from across the room whilst she flicked through my first column. I'd submitted the piece as Cecilia had requested by Wednesday evening, and she'd been weirdly thrilled. I looked over at Stacey, who was still scrolling.

'Yeah, that's about right. My job is strange. Does this look fluffy enough to you?' I tilted the bowl to show her.

She shrugged, spooning some chocolate cereal into her mouth and talking through it. 'I mean, I have no idea. I'm not the best candidate for this. Ask Maia when she gets back from the supermarket; I'm sure she's made bread before.'

*Of course she has.* I made a mental note to ask her opinion before baking the loaf. It was Saturday morning, and I'd had my 'sourdough starter' resting throughout the week, ever since Cecilia had roped me into the column. I was starting with the easier tasks on my list, the most mundane. It wasn't feasible just yet to take off and tour Italy, as much as I'd like it to be.

Leaving a flat in London so abruptly was *not* cheap. I wondered if it would be cheeky to ask Cecilia to put a tour of Italy on expenses.

'You know what, Flick? This is really good. I would read the shit out of this column. Let me see the official list again?' Stacey flapped her hands in the direction of my list, which was laid out in front of me alongside the BBC sourdough recipe that I had pulled up on her iPad.

'Shouldn't you be keeping this original list in pristine condition or something?' Stacey wiped some flour off the front. 'You've clearly been using this as a coaster for your cups of tea. What if the column really takes off? This could be worth something someday.'

'Unlikely.'

'Where is your optimism?' She went back to reading. I read the list along with her, even though I must have proof-read it about twenty times before I'd submitted it with my introductory column. The first post had received minor bits of interest from our readers, including several comments and strings of heartbreak emojis. In our day and age, that spoke volumes.

1. *Start playing tennis matches in London again*
2. *Learn how to make sourdough*
3. *Dye my hair*
4. *Live in a houseshare*
5. *Start playing the piano again (and learn because I want to, not because I was told to)*
6. *Travel around Italy*

7. *Buy a Polaroid camera and take 100 photos*
8. *Have a go on Kitty's mixing decks*
9. *Visit every café in the Mayfair article*
10. *Work one of Suze's events*
11. *Go on enough nights out to make up for lost uni years*
12. *Read five memoirs and learn how to be a proper adult from people who have already done it*
13. *Train myself to drink black coffee so I am sophisticated*
14. *Start writing a magazine column*

I'd added on a couple of new items since it was now being considered an actual paid project. Felix and Sadie had been ecstatic, to say the least, for me to start writing the column, and my parents had jumped up and down on FaceTime when I'd told them about the opportunity. Mum had rushed off the phone to go next door and tell her friend, and Dad had just smiled, telling me that he thought I was doing great. It was at least 100 times better to hear that than the sympathy votes I'd been getting over the past month. The list was a time-consuming enough project that, aside from a momentary meltdown over fajita spice mix in the supermarket (fajita Friday was a sore spot now), I hadn't crumbled since our anniversary. I had also spotted recently that Aaron had checked into a gig on Facebook with a girl I didn't recognise – who, for the record, looked perfectly lovely – but Maia had calmly removed the phone from my death grip, hiding it for the night and diverting the crisis. The three of them had distracted me with a game of shag, marry, kill, and to be fair, it had worked. You only needed to hear that one of your friends would kill Chris Hemsworth and they completely had your attention. Even if, in Kitty's defence, it had been a tricky line-up. The four of us were slowly becoming more of a four than a three-plus-one, I hadn't checked Aaron's Facebook profile for at least ten hours, *and* I was making bread. Progress. Although to be honest, looking at the sad lump of dough in front of me, that was a bit of a stretch.

'This is a very good list.' Stacey tapped her spoon against her lip and finished reading. 'It makes me wish I could go back five years and be 22 again.'

'I'd much rather be 27 and have my life a bit more together.'

Stacey burst out laughing. 'Life together? You're funny. I'm in the exact same position I was in three years ago when I moved into this house, I just have a mediocre savings account and my first smile line now. Twenty-two is the best age.'

'I only have three and a half months of it left.'

Stacey leaned in to see the list, reading some notes I'd jotted on the side, tilting her head to understand my scrawl. 'Turning 23 in a handful of months is just more of a reason to make the most of this. Also, isn't that perfect for the column? Everything is more exciting with some sort of deadline.'

It was true. With Cecilia wanting the column to culminate in an article for the June print issue anyway, the last dying months of my twenty-second year fit perfectly into the magazine schedule.

'It's almost like it was meant to be.' Stace read my mind.

I stared at the dough in front of me, which still looked kind of flat. 'It's a roaring success so far.'

We both turned at the sound of a key in the front door.

'Place your bets.' Stace wiggled her eyebrows.

I said 'Maia' at the same time as she yelled 'Kitty'.

'Not Kitty, just me.' Maia walked into the kitchen and I punched the air. 'Wow, I don't usually get that kind of reception. Are you making sourdough?'

I held out the bowl to her. 'Show me your ways, *please*.'

She considered my plea. 'Only if I get formal recognition in the column.' She was only kidding, already tying up her long hair, but it made me smile to hear my friends so readily accepting my twenties list. I'd worried it might sound stupid, especially to Stace and Maia who were years older than I was, but they'd welcomed the quest with open arms.

There was nothing that this house wouldn't embrace, it seemed. Aside from socks with sandals. Stacey had made her position on that *very* clear when Kitty had taken out the bins wearing a pair of Crocs and fluffy socks.

Maia had her sleeves rolled up and was patting flour onto her palms, careful not to spill any onto her clothes. I glanced down at myself, covered in white.

'Pass it to me, Flick.' She gestured for me to pass her the bowl. 'Come to mama, little dough, I'll make you *aaall* better. Did that nasty lady hurt you?'

Stacey snorted. 'Quote this word-for-word in the column, please.' She paused, putting down her phone. 'Hey, isn't your date tonight?'

I threw my tea towel at her. 'It's not a date.'

'You have a date?' Maia glanced up in surprise, bread momentarily forgotten.

I groaned. 'Not a date. It's a "mate date". Can't a girl go out with a man and it not be automatically romantic?'

'Of course she can.' Maia shrugged. 'I just thought you might be getting back on the horse.'

'I'm not liking the visuals I'm getting from that.' Stacey's face was scrunched up. 'But hey, at least now we can actually stalk tennis boy.'

'Wait.' Maia paused, hands folding the dough. 'This is *tennis boy*? Didn't you rally and dash this guy? God, I can't believe I just said that out loud.'

I opened my mouth to fill in the blanks but Stacey explained for me. It was hard to believe there'd ever been any kind of frostiness between us now.

'She did rally and dash him. Turns out he's the tech guy at her office.'

'No way.' Maia's eyes were wide. 'What a small world. I won't pry into whether this is or isn't a date with tennis boy, I respect your privacy. Where are you guys going?'

'Wow. Imagine that. Respecting privacy.' I stuck my finger up at Stacey, who stuck her tongue out at me. 'We're meeting at St James's. He lives in Stratford, so we tried to pick some sort of middle ground. Suze has been recommending one of the food trucks near there for ages, so now feels as good a time as any.'

'Aren't you going to be cold?'

Stacey butted in. 'They can keep each other warm. Besides, it's weirdly not chilly for the end of February. I had to shed several layers on my walk to the post office this morning.'

'It's actually not that weird. It's climate change.' Maia turned to me, smiling softly, and pointed to the dough again. 'I think what you were doing wrong is kneading too hard.'

Stacey piped up. 'Lord knows that's the mistake I make in pretty much all of my relationships.'

Maia frowned and gave Stacey the side eye. 'I thought you were afraid of commitment.'

'You see' – she closed her magazine and joined us at the breakfast bar – 'that's my issue. I'm the worst bits of both flaws. I crave attention, and then when I get it, the *ick* hits me hard. It's a treacherous cycle.'

'I thought you were the main voice of the "single girls in London" movement anyway?' Maia put down the bowl she was holding.

'Don't point that wooden spoon at me, Maia.' Stacey held up her hands. 'I very much am at the spearhead of that movement. It doesn't mean I don't want to acknowledge my emotional hang-ups so that I'm ready if something comes along, though. Like I said to Flick the other day, a fling is good for the soul.' She pointed to me. 'Felicity here has inspired me. Getting back on it, not moping around about that finance nerd forever.'

'I'm not moping.' I watched Maia carefully turn my lumpy excuse for dough into something resembling the photo in the article. 'Nor am I "getting back on it". Teddy is a friend. Besides, I still need time. I still get sad.'

Maia shot a look in my direction. 'We saw you with the fajita spice.'

*Was there anything that these girls didn't spot?* I threw my hands up. 'Can a girl not cry in the shower and in the Mexican-food aisle of Tesco in peace?'

'That's why we didn't mention it at the time. Seemed a sore spot.' Stace shrugged. 'Do you know what's better than feeling sad about spices? Feeling great after a date, and the good sex after it.'

'I'm tuning you out now. I'm 100 per cent not having sex with Teddy. Or anyone for that matter. I'm trying to make sourdough over here.'

Maia was looking at my list on the table. She was the only member of the house who hadn't taken a good look at it yet. I was a little nervous.

'Hey, if this is the path to life-togetherness, I have it cracked. Making sourdough, drinking black coffee . . .' She paused, looking serious. 'Flick, do you just want to be me?'

I threw a handful of flour in her direction and she laughed. 'For God's sake, I was trying not to get any of that on my clothes.'

'Anyway,' Stace got up, putting her bowl in the sink, 'I need to get ready for work. Lots of women going on actual dates that want their hair blown out. I could –'

I stopped her before she started. 'No. It's a *park*. Potentially a food truck. With a *friend*.'

'I think she would eat out of a bin just to prove that this is not a date. Don't you think, Maia?'

I almost stomped my feet, something I hadn't done since I was about 5. '*Stace*. It *isn't* a date.'

Maia grinned. 'Someone is nervous.'

'Am not. Also, traitor.'

Stacey left the room laughing, already on her phone again.

'I'm only kidding. For what it's worth, single-woman empowerment aside, I always need time to heal after a breakup.' Maia continued to knead.

'Yeah?'

'Always. Plus, I like not having to bounce from one to the next. Sometimes you don't need someone else to fill the gaps for a while. Sometimes, there are no gaps.'

'Any chance you've written a memoir?' I gestured to my list. 'I'd quite like to read it.'

'A memoir that consists entirely of work, home, work, home, repeat? Thrilling.' She laughed, consistently humble, and then paused to sniff. 'Can you smell that?'

I couldn't.

'Hairspray. I can always tell when Stacey is about to leave the house. You should see the preparation when she goes on dates. Last time I almost bought an inhaler.'

'You did not.'

'It was close. I could taste hibiscus whenever I ate in the kitchen for at least a week after. I'd like to give the girls who let her have the ground-floor room a piece of my mind.'

I knew that Stacey had been living at Carlisle the longest – three years – and when she'd moved in, she'd been with a completely different set of housemates. I liked the way that the girls spoke of all the different people that had rotated in and out of the house. Like no one was ever forgotten. Stacey had moved in first, followed by Maia a couple of months later, and Kitty just a little over two years after that. They reminisced about Tara and the other girls of Carlisle with love and respect, and it was a concept that I adored. It didn't matter where you went or how you got there, part of your legacy would always stay stuck in the Carlisle house. I looked again at Maia with her face scrunched in concentration as she prepared my loaf for the oven.

'Do you want to try a pattern on top?'

I could think of worse places to have your legacy rooted in.

# 14

'I didn't even know food could *be* this good.' Teddy groaned from his end of the bench, taking a huge bite from the carton in front of him.

We'd found a good spot in St James's Park, with a great vantage point over the many dogs that came through with their owners. We'd been playing a game of 'what is that dog thinking' whilst we'd been sitting here. Teddy was a great dog-voice actor, surprisingly. I pocketed my phone, saving the photo I'd just taken of the street food for my column. Cecilia had emailed to suggest that I provide 'visual evidence' for *The Twenties List*; that my audience (like I actually had one) would connect to me more if I provided aesthetically pleasing content. I thought of my Instagram grid, which had been sorely neglected in the past few months. Was I more likely to be invested in someone's life if I could see the pretty pictures to match? Probably. Cecilia was like my mum – annoyingly always right. The best I could do for now was a photo of my pulled pork waffle in the middle of the park. She was probably hoping for something a bit classier, but what did she expect? I was a graduate living in

London. If it was relatively cheap, I was all over it. I shovelled a mouthful of food into my mouth, speaking through it.

'My sister, Suze, has been telling me about this truck ever since I moved here. I can't believe I ignored her for this long. Sad, really.'

Teddy sighed. 'If I had a pound for every time my siblings have ignored me, I wouldn't have to do that god-awful commute every morning. Last week, someone actually sneezed on my arm. You could see the particles and everything.'

I scrunched up my nose. 'If I thought about the proximity of all those people and germs before I got on the Tube, I wouldn't get on at all. It does have its merits though. I saw a Metro article yesterday about a lost dog that had jumped on the Central line without his owner realising.'

Teddy motioned for me to carry on. 'There better be a happy ending to this.'

'Oh there was. The people of London got him home. The Tube has its benefits if you look hard enough. My friend at work – the one your colleague fancies – met his boyfriend on the Tube.'

'Shit, really?'

It was true, and my favourite story to tell. Felix had met Sebastian on the Northern line, where they'd made eyes at each other every day at 7.30 a.m., until one day Sebastian sat down right next to Felix and said he knew a great place for breakfast. They'd both got off the Tube at Tottenham Court Road, had eggs Florentine and cappuccinos at Salt & Pepper, and the rest is history.

Teddy had been listening intently, smiling to himself. 'Wow, my guy really doesn't have a chance, does he?'

'Not at all. Break his heart slowly, though.' I took another big bite of the food. 'So, how many siblings do you have?'

He answered nonchalantly. 'Four.'

'*Four?* Christ.' I took another forkful of the waffle, closing my eyes in bliss when I hit a pomegranate seed. 'My sister and I fought for our parents' attention enough, and there were only two of us. We used to climb all over their bed in the morning to win their love.'

Teddy laughed. 'Be honest, that was last week, wasn't it?'

I held my hands up. 'Guilty as charged.'

'It's weird, though.' He turned his head to watch a golden retriever chasing a frisbee. 'My younger brothers are both as needy as humanly possible, which makes sense given our upbringing. The other three of us – me, my older brother, and my sister – just kind of cruised along. It was a mutual understanding that we just had to get on with it. There isn't much of an age gap between us three – we're all in our mid to late twenties. My younger brothers are very much still in their early twenties, and they absolutely never let us forget it. It's alright for me – 25 is still young enough to laugh it off. My sister absolutely hates it.'

The golden retriever caught the frisbee in its mouth, earning a round of applause from several passers-by. Whoever said Londoners weren't friendly was lying.

'Does your sister live in London too, then?' Teddy looked over at me expectantly.

'Nope, she lives in Liverpool. A lot more central than my parents, but close enough to pester them when she needs to.'

'Is her accent stronger than yours?'

When he spoke about accents his own became stronger, almost as if he were more conscious of it.

'I think so. She's definitely lived there longer than I have. Hers is the strongest in our family, Mum probably comes in at a close second.'

'You must find it weird here then, so many southerners.'

I thought about it for a second. 'To be honest, I barely notice it any more. Work is a complete mishmash of accents, and Aaron had a southern accent anyway so —' I cut myself off, remembering how we used to sit next to each other in the beginning, asking each other to say certain words and laughing at the difference in how they sounded. A wave of nausea came over me, and I set the waffle on the bench beside me.

'Hey.'

I glanced up to see Teddy's face, concerned.

'You know, I don't mind if you want to talk about it. It might even help.'

Was it rude to talk about Aaron when Teddy had asked me out and I'd said no? I wasn't sure.

He read my mind. 'It's not going to break my heart to hear about you with another man, Sage, if that's what you're thinking.'

I flinched in surprise at the nickname, although not because I hated it. It was kind of nice.

'I just didn't see it coming. At all. I'd been thinking about what might happen next, now that we were living together. We'd spent our first Christmas with each other, doing that thing where you have to see both families in a time crunch, but you do it regardless because all that really matters is that you spend most of it together. I thought we were moving forward, but it turns out we were grinding to a halt.'

Teddy was a good listener, I was learning. He nodded. 'You know, it's rough, but it might turn out to be the best thing that ever happened to you. I went through a similar thing a few months before I moved here – in fact, that's *why* I moved here, and I thought I would never get over it. I used to spend hours every day typing and un-typing messages to her on WhatsApp, desperate to repair what we'd broken. Then this job came up, and I thought "what have I got to lose?" It turns out, sometimes all you need is a change to make you realise that, deep down, you didn't want things to stay the same.'

I gave the man in front of me a more thorough once-over, clearly having not given him enough credit.

'Even though right now I don't agree with you, I think it's highly possible that in the end you might be right.'

He grinned. 'Oh, I often am.'

I nudged his shoulder, having moved up the bench a little to hear him over the sounds of a busy London park on a Saturday afternoon. He was wearing a faded pair of black jeans and an olive-green jumper, a bit of a contrast to the shirt and tie that I'd seen him in last. And even more radically different to his tennis gear.

'So, how is the houseshare going? You should know that our staffroom chat the other day prompted a list of topics that I'm ready to bombard you with,' he said.

'My life cannot be that interesting.'

'No, I'm serious. We haven't even got onto your infamous magazine column yet.'

'If by infamous you mean "read by about ten people, one of which is probably my mother" then yes. As for the house-share, I'm . . . cautiously optimistic.'

'You mean no one has stolen your last square of chocolate yet? Or used the last of the toilet roll and forgotten to replace it?'

There had been a minor incident with Stacey and one of Maia's coffee filters, but even that had been an anomaly. Apparently, the day before Maia sits an exam is not the best day to use the last of her coffee supply. I'd written it down in my iPhone notes, like I'd been doing with all of the things I considered to be important in the house (how many sugars everyone liked in their tea, and when people tended to use the shower in the morning).

'No, nothing like that. We had a bit of a transition period where I was the new girl, but now I just feel really safe there. It's this space where girls support girls, nothing untoward or competitive. Do you know how rare it is for society to let us have that?'

Teddy choked on a bite of his food. 'Consider me impressed. The last time I shared a flat, other than with my ex, was with a guy who couldn't figure out how to flush the toilet.'

I wrinkled my nose.

'I'm not even sorry for telling you that. If I had to see it every day, you have to visualise it too.'

'I'm going to remember that on the day my housemates finally do something unreasonable. *Especially* if it's hygiene related.'

He tapped his chin. 'Just a heads up – the readers of your column probably won't want to know about that. As gritty and honest as I assume you want to be, that's definitely too far.'

'What do you take me for, an amateur?' He laughed and I continued. 'You'd probably be correct. I have no idea what I'm doing.'

I leaned away from him and dropped my abandoned carton of food in the bin, which was overflowing with cider cans and cigarette butts from the night before. I should probably put an asterisk next to the photo I'd taken of the waffle for my column: *Hardly ate any of this due to post-breakup nausea. RIP £8.*

'So, what exactly prompted the London move? Considering I spilled my guts to you in the staffroom, it's only fair.'

Teddy laughed, but it didn't detract from the slight frown. 'Like I said, the last time I shared a living space, it was with my ex-girlfriend. We broke up, she moved out, and I realised that all my friends had moved on with their lives whilst I'd been playing house. I didn't have a lot to show for my early twenties and I wanted to mix it up. Flash forward seven months and here I am.' He gestured to the park around us. 'London in general that is. Not St James's specifically.'

'How are you finding it so far? I haven't been to Leeds that much, but it must be quite the culture shock.'

He nodded. 'Yes and no. I've been living the city life for a while now – I didn't go to uni, it wasn't for me. Jumped straight into an apprenticeship after sixth form and spent a lot of time working for companies in the middle of Leeds. London and Leeds are both cities in their own right, but they have some similarities. The one thing I'm struggling to get used to is the social scene. For a city with nine million people, it's hard to find friends.'

I was taken aback by his honesty. For the most part, living in this city, I'd been pretty lucky. I'd moved here with a built-in best friend, and the people at work were social enough. And now, without even meaning to, I'd moved into Carlisle, with a group of people I could feel would be friends for a long time. City loneliness was something I knew that existed, but fortunately it wasn't something I'd experienced first-hand.

'I guess that's why I've taken to stalking people in their offices in exchange for friendship.' He shrugged, and I laughed.

'Is that why you've been playing tennis?' I knew from the first time I'd met him that he'd only been playing casually for a couple of months.

He nodded. 'I figured I needed to be a bit more active considering the nature of my job, but an evening spent at the gym wouldn't get me anywhere, connections-wise.'

A lot of people that I'd met at my previous courts near Shepherd's Bush had been in it for the social aspect. I said as much.

'It's been good so far. Although you do meet some right freaks. There was this one girl that repeatedly whacked tennis balls straight at the wall. Threw me right off my game.'

I scoffed. 'Yeah, right. Can you be thrown off your game if you've got no game in the first place?'

'Fighting talk, Flick. I like it.'

We laughed again, settling into comfortable silence as we watched the passers-by in the park. I wasn't sure why I'd been nervous about this. Teddy, like so many of us here, was just trying to find his people.

'So, you said you wanted to shake things up. Of all the places to find a new job, what made you pick London?'

I was fascinated by the reasons people chose to come and live in this huge, sprawling city. Felix had moved his entire life cross country after seeing one particular flat in Camden and falling in love with it. Kitty came here for the music scene. Maia knew which firm she wanted to work for and had followed that dream all the way here. Stacey had lived here her entire life. Looking across the bench at my newest friend in this city, I wanted to know his reasons too.

He scratched his head nervously. 'My life was stagnant. I was living in the place I'd known my whole life, seeing the same people and spending every weekend the same way. How long do you keep making excuses before you make the decision to kick-start your life?'

I *loved* his answer.

'It's a city that never, ever rests. I like that. I'm an insomniac, so I love that I can go out in the middle of the night and there will always be something to do. Have you been to that board game café in Central?'

I'd never been but I knew it.

'And the diner in Stratford' — I knew this was where his one-bed flat was — 'it's open twenty-four hours. Do you know how many twenty-four-hour diners there are where I'm from?' He didn't wait for my answer. 'None. That's how many. I never sleep, and neither does London. We're meant to be. Well, in theory. We haven't quite found our rhythm yet. Are you ready to go? It might be warm for this time of year but I'm beginning to lose the sensation in my toes.'

I nodded and he threw his own rubbish away, gesturing for me to lead the way. We continued talking as we walked the length of the park, never missing a beat. I thought of my twenties list, stuck on the mirror in my box-bedroom. Would I have said yes to this friend date if I hadn't been on this mission? I wasn't so sure. That list was the best thing to happen to me in quite some time.

★★★

**The Twenties List: The First Proper Check-in**

*Dear Reader,*

*So, it's been a week since I started my experiment and seriously committed myself to the list. As it turns out, tackling a project like this requires a lot of stepping outside of your comfort zone. Not my strongest suit. It also requires a lot of yeast; unsurprisingly, I am not a natural sourdough chef. You won't be seeing me on the* Bake Off *anytime soon.*

*My first lesson in adulthood, tame as it is, is to never, ever, over-knead your dough. It will come out kind of sad-looking and taste like Play-Doh. Not that I know what Play-Doh tastes like, but I can imagine. Now that I've semi-successfully made a loaf of bread, (I even added a little leaf pattern on top for decoration), I can't deny that I feel a little bit more equipped to take on the world. First, the loaf. Then, the rest of my life.*

*After the bread, I got a bit stuck. The twenties list is great, but some of the things on there actually take a bit of umph. My housemate suggested that I might feel more ready to take on the list (and my life) if I visited her salon for some spa treatments. Self-care and all that. I wasn't about to say no to a free treatment, but I absolutely should have done; she'd booked me in for a wax, not a facial like she'd promised. And not just any wax – a bloody Brazilian. This is the same housemate that keeps swiping for me on dating apps. Safe to say I don't feel any more ready to take on the list, but I do feel less ready to ever enter her salon again. I'm pretty sure I've still got a bit of the wax-goop mixture stuck to my inner thigh, but I'm too scared to have a proper look and sort it out. It's a good job I'm single, that's all I'm saying.*

*One thing I can wholeheartedly say I've ticked off the list is the houseshare. I spent so many hours looking on spare-room websites, stressing myself out about where to live and who to live with. It turns out, all you need to move into the ideal houseshare is a dangerous habit of getting takeaways three times a week, and an acceptance that no one will ever hoover the stairs. Since university, I'd always assumed that my opportunity to have a vibrant group of friends was over,*

EMILY MERRILL

*aside from the odd pint after work with colleagues. It turns out it's never too late. Houseshares really aren't as terrifying as they seem. Unless you steal the coffee supply of a stressed-out paralegal.*

*And speaking of friends, I've managed to make another one. It's almost like my relationship was holding me back. I went on a friend date this weekend. Life begins when you start chasing cool food spots around London, let me tell you. If you want a relatively cheap spot for lunch with friends, with a side helping of freezing your toes off, I'd highly recommend the pulled pork waffles in St James's Park. Past Flick is cursing herself for not trying it sooner. And the whole friend thing too. Photos to follow.*

*Flick x*

# 15

'You have *got* to be kidding me.' I stared at the laptop that was sitting on Cecilia's desk. Usually, I would have tried to refrain from using that phrase in response to the woman who essentially paid my rent, but these were extenuating circumstances.

She clapped her hands together, joyful. 'I had no idea this was what you'd intended with the column, but it's genius.'

I pinched the bridge of my nose. I'd arrived at the office this morning with a spring in my step, spurred on by the fact that no one had cancelled the column yet, and by my new friendship with Teddy, which was blossoming. I felt like I had a purpose at *Influence* now that I'd never had before. Cecilia was acting like my new best friend; I hadn't even had time to sip my chai latte before I'd been summoned in here. When I'd sat down, Cecilia had immediately turned her laptop screen to face me without saying anything, showing me the series of comments on my second column. With a little help from Sadie and her social media skills, instead of just a handful of comments, we now had about thirty. It seemed to be mostly young women in their twenties (or 'kindred spirits' as Sadie

140

had coined them), but there were some comments from people in their thirties cheering me on too, living their twenties all over again through me. We had the odd troll, including a comment that asked why on *earth* the public were supposed to care about a random 22-year-old – to be fair, I was inclined to agree there – and then there was *the comment*.

'This is *gold*. Literal gold.' Cecilia was rubbing her hands together.

'But it's nonsense.' I shrugged. 'This isn't a dating column.'

Cecilia pointed to the comment in question. 'Read it aloud to me.'

'The comment says "Did you go on a food-truck date?! I am living for this column." This means nothing,' I pointed out. 'She's got the wrong end of the stick. I said in the column that I went with a friend. I've reiterated multiple times how single I am. It's my whole thing.'

'It *was* your whole thing.' Cecilia smirked. 'I've had a better idea.'

I groaned. 'Seriously, one comment means nothing. People need me to be single. What's the point without it?'

'Now read aloud the comments below it.'

I turned my attention back to the screen. 'This feels a bit like digging my own grave.'

'Felicity.'

'Okay.' I held my hands up. 'One says "If I wasn't hooked before, I am now!" and then there's one that says "I LOVE this Felicity girl, this is the best post-breakup column. It makes me feel like I could do it too".' I glanced up. 'This is really lovely, and I'm glad it helped. But we need to correct them.'

Cecilia grinned. 'Most of the other comments fall into the same category. People love a dating column, Felicity. Especially one that covers dating in recovery from a breakup.'

I could see where this was going, so I decided to disappoint her before she got too carried away. 'He's my friend. Literally zero going on. In fact, I've already rejected the idea of a date, right here in this office, last week.'

'Really?'

'Yes! Isn't the whole point of this column that I'm a single role model figuring it all out?'

Cecilia tilted her head 'Yes, originally. But why can't a woman have it all?'

She did make a valid point, not that I was about to tell her that.

'Gone are the days when a woman has to choose just one thing. This isn't a dating column, a career column, or a foodie column. This is a life in London series. This is *everything*. It can be a multitude of things, like the modern woman. No woman falls into just one box.'

As much as I enjoyed the sentiment, the direction in which this chat was clearly going did not add up to me.

'Okay, but slight issue. Everything you said is true, but I'm *not* dating him. Teddy is just my friend.'

Cecilia sighed. 'You're a vibrant young woman, what's not to like? I'm sure you can bring him round to the idea again.'

I resisted the urge to fire off a sarcastic retort. 'Why does it have to be about him not liking me? I'm a hoot. It's because I don't want to date him. I'm *enjoying* single life. I've realised that life begins when you can eat a ready meal for two all to yourself.'

'I'm not going to lie to you, Felicity — that's a bit sad.'

'How about the fact that every evening is my own? Or that there's no one around to criticise the books I'm reading, or the trash TV I'm watching? Plus, I've never had so much time to spend with my friends.'

Cecilia pondered what I'd said. 'I'm not asking you to change that. But aren't all columns a little slice of fiction these days anyway? Fragments of reality in between the most notorious storytelling?'

I thought about the agony-aunt columns I referred to religiously. I bloody hoped not. It would be a bit like finding out that Father Christmas wasn't real. The adult version.

I pondered it all for a minute, trying to slot it all together in my mind. 'Are you saying what I think you're saying?'

She'd better not have been saying what I thought she was saying.

'I am.' My boss tapped her acrylics on her desk, a huge smile forming. It was a little bit off-putting, the number of smiles that Cecilia was dishing out these days. 'You can just fictionalise a few dates with this guy. Spice up the column. That way you can keep your ready meals for one and your nights out, and the readers of the column will be satisfied. No one ever has to know that in reality you're comfortably single.'

'Is that not just lying?'

She scoffed. 'We're a lifestyle magazine. Dating is a huge part of modern life. We're not lying, we're embellishing. Trying to give the people what they want.'

It sounded the same as lying to me, but Cecilia was right – the column *had* tripled in its readership since the comments about my 'date' in the park. We'd even had a mention in an influencer's Instagram stories as she talked about the realities of being a young professional in London. It made logical sense. But did it make *emotional* sense?

'You do realise I'm going to have to convince Teddy to pretend to date me, right? There's a huge likelihood that he'll laugh me off the face of the earth.'

Never mind the crippling humiliation of it all. *Sorry, Teddy, I don't want to go on a date with you. But how about a fake date?*

Cecilia hushed me. 'He's the guy from IT, isn't he?'

I was surprised she remembered him.

'Yeah, he was in here last week.'

She nodded. 'Even easier, then. He understands business. It won't take much to get him invested.'

I admired her positivity whilst I bulldozed through the concept with my scepticism. She talked me through the finer details, giving me deadlines until I felt way in over my head. Why couldn't I have just kept the list to myself? Why had I even made it in the first place?

After twenty minutes of her reasoning, I caved. If only to make it stop. This wasn't ideal, but it seemed like I didn't really have a choice. When people got something in their brain about someone online, it was hard to convince them otherwise. Even if I tried to write into the column that Teddy was a friend, nothing more, would they believe me? People believed what they wanted to believe.

On my way out of the office, Cecilia stopped me. 'Felicity?'

'Yeah?'

'I think it'll all be more believable if they believe it too.' She nodded towards the rest of the office, where I could see Felix flicking paper clips over to Fiona, trying to get her attention. 'It's for the good of the column. See you tomorrow.'

*Crap.* I closed the door behind me, gulping at the thought of lying to my colleagues. If my life hadn't been a hot mess before, it was now.

***

'Excuse me.' I pushed past a sweaty man on the Tube, dodging his underarm patches and grabbing one of the empty seats.

The Piccadilly line was hell on an evening like this one, when everyone was clearly desperate to get home. I took out my phone, drafting a few thoughts I'd had for the column in my notes. Over the course of the day, I'd decided that the dating side of everything could be as small as I wanted it to be. Surely the young women of London were more interested in the Carlisle girls and my quest to complete my list than they were about a boy? I almost groaned at the thought of having to explain this to him. One pulled pork waffle on a park bench did not a fully-fledged friendship make. I knew Teddy enough to ask to borrow his phone charger, and maybe even to grab me a brownie on his way to get his own. I did *not* know him well enough to ask him to pretend to date me. I was sweating at the idea. We were playing tennis on Thursday again after work, so I guessed I could casually drop it into conversation over a warm-up. Anything to delay the experience by a few days. I pulled up the column, staring at the comment that had sent my life into complete disarray. Reread it a few times. *Hang on.*

> @StaceFace14: Did you go on a food truck date?! I am living for this column.

The comment was accompanied by a teddy bear emoji. I hadn't mentioned Teddy's name in the column for the sake of privacy, and there was really no other relevant reason to use the emoji. This coincidence and the username 'StaceFace' were too obvious. Subtlety really wasn't her strong suit. I let the reality of the writer's identity sink in. I was going to kill her.

***

'Guys?' I shut the door, leaving my keys on the little hooks in the hall. I'd spent the rest of my train journey stewing. Stacey was in for it.

'In here!' Kitty called out from the kitchen.

When I got in, I was faced with all three of them sitting at the worktop, chatting and sharing a pizza. Kitty was already in her pyjamas even though it was only 6.30 p.m. – a true benefit of working from home. Maia had clearly only been a few minutes ahead of me, her jacket still on and her briefcase on the counter. And it might just have been my imagination but Stacey's expression, from where she sat on one of the bar stools, could have been described as sheepish. Yeah, StaceFace was living among us. I was sure of it.

'So, Stacey,' I kept my voice low, unassuming as I grabbed a can of lemonade from the fridge, 'leave any comments on any articles yesterday?'

She paused, slice of pepperoni halfway to her mouth. 'Erm . . . so the thing is –'

'I knew it!' I cut her off, throwing my hands up in the air, exasperated. 'You have *no* idea how much more complicated my life has just become because of that comment.'

Stacey winced. 'Oops? It was funny, you have to admit.'

'Wait.' Kitty glanced between us like she was watching a tennis match. '*What* comment? What's going on?'

Maia swallowed before speaking. 'I second this line of enquiry. We need more details.'

'Care to explain, *StaceFace*?'

Stacey got out her phone and showed the girls the column and the stream of comments below it. I took the time to grab a slice of the huge pizza – a takeout from one of the pizzerias down the road. I was mad, but I wasn't mad enough to forget about my stomach. That was a whole different level of mad. Maia had her hand over her mouth, trying not to laugh.

Kitty looked up from reading the screen. 'I don't understand. You aren't dating him. Why does it matter? Can't you just set them straight?'

I nodded. 'That was what I was planning on doing. Until my boss latched onto the idea and decided that it would be a great idea for me to fake-date Teddy.'

Maia's eyes widened, and she bit back a smile. 'Oh shit.'

Stacey was pale. 'And now, I second Maia. Oh *shit*. I really did not see that coming.'

Kitty was the only one of them not acting like this was a bad thing. In fact, she was laughing her head off.

'Kit, this isn't funny!'

She put her slice of pizza down, wiping the grease from her fingers onto some kitchen roll and hiccupping between laughs. 'It's just so *Flick*. I swear I live my life vicariously through you.'

Maia nodded. 'Agreed. My days always seem so boring when we hear about yours. First the rally and dash, then the column, and now a fake relationship. We did not need to pay for a TV licence, this is entertaining enough on its own.'

'It's not entertaining, it's humiliating.' Even I was trying not to smile now. Their reaction was infectious.

Stacey tilted her head. 'Okay, I take full responsibility for this mishap. But this *could* be kind of fun.'

I sat down at the table with them, taking another slice of pizza and resting my head on the cool worktop. 'How? *How* am I going to ask Teddy if he'll fake-date me? I like us as friends. We're *good* as friends. This will only ruin things.'

Stace shrugged. 'I mean, it's basically just carrying on as you are. No one has to know that you both go back to your separate flats and sleep sweet dreams alone.'

'I don't usually agree with her, but she's right on this one.' Maia frowned. 'As long as you're both on the same page, nothing really has to change. You just have to act like you're dating. It doesn't even have to be the main focus of the column; your list is the focus. Dating is just part of it.'

'As long as he doesn't care that you're fabricating it, does it really matter? He sounds pretty cool.' Kitty dipped her crust in a pot of garlic dip. 'This is literal holy water.'

'I really am sorry, though.' Stacey pouted. 'Forgive me? I got excited by the cute waffle photo.'

'She really does get carried away too easily.' Kitty sighed. 'We've all been left in awkward situations because of it. One time, she told her 15-year-old – and may I just add here, completely tone-deaf – cousin that I'd give her free mixing lessons. I think I nearly lost an eardrum that day.'

'Oh yeah.' Maia grinned. 'And do you remember that time you accidentally set Tara up on a blind date with one of her exes?'

Stacey pouted even harder. 'Those disasters were all born from good intentions. Flick?'

She was still staring at me, looking like butter wouldn't melt.

'Fine, but you're all coming with me when I have to explain this to Teddy. I was going to do it when we were playing tennis, but I just don't think I can handle it one-on-one.'

Stacey stuck her hand out. 'Deal. I wouldn't miss this for the world.'

'What do we prefer?' Maia held out both her hands. 'Sweet or salty popcorn?'

Kitty laughed again. 'This house got way more interesting when you walked into it, Flick. What did we do with our evenings before we had your twenties list?'

# 16

I stared down into my cider, talking way too fast to get it all out.

'Wait.' Teddy stared at me, a smirk tugging at the corner of his lips. 'You're telling me that your readers think we're dating? And now we have to go along with it?'

We were at a pub in Ealing and I was counting on the girls arriving any second now to ease the tension of this very moment. In fact – I glanced at my watch – they were already late. Typical. I could imagine that the very person who was holding them up was the very person who was responsible for this whole mess in the first place.

'I mean, you could say no. I wouldn't blame you in the slightest. In fact, I'm almost swaying towards actively encouraging it.'

'How did this even happen?' He turned the bottle of beer he was holding round in his hands, slowly peeling off the sticker. 'Were you going on and on about the colour of my eyes?'

I laughed at him batting his eyelashes at me. 'No, one reader commented that she thought we might have been on a date, and the idea was born. People will latch onto anything.' It was too humiliating to admit that the 'reader' was one of my housemates.

'God, you're like the new Bridget Jones. Diary and all.'

When I furrowed my brows, he shrugged. 'I have an older sister. Whenever she got dumped, we used to sit in the living room and watch that movie on repeat. Either that or one of the other many romcoms of the noughties. If I really put my mind to it, I could probably quote *How to Lose a Guy in 10 Days* word for word.'

I smiled, imagining four boys sitting with their older sister in the living room watching a romcom, arriving purely to console her but staying because it was an absolute classic. It reminded me of all the dance parties I'd had with Suze to help her boogie out her heartbreak. Singing Kelly Clarkson with our hairbrushes, sliding on the kitchen floor in our slipper socks.

'So, how do you feel about fake dating yours truly?'

I didn't know if I was hoping he'd shut down this idea or say yes.

Teddy rocked the beer bottle in front of him back and forth between his palms. 'I know I work elsewhere in the building, but on the odd occasion that I *do* have to come into your office, Cecilia would know that I'd said no to her master plan. To be frank with you, she scares the living daylights out of me. If you're game, then I am too. What's a fake relationship if not a friendship with a few added stunts?'

My cheeks heated. 'I mean, technically, you're right. It's just whether you want the readership of *Influence* to believe we're dating.'

He set his glass down on the table. 'You do realise this whole friendship began because you turned me down, right? You and me, in the staffroom, remember that?'

I pulled a face at him.

'You know, here I was a few weeks ago, thinking about how boring and anti-climactic my life in the big smoke was turning out to be.' I watched Teddy as a slow smile lit up his face. He had the kind of smile that could transform a face. Kind of goofy, too much teeth. But at the same time, just the right amount. He continued. 'And now, I've got a new friend, a fake relationship, and a tennis buddy all rolled into one. I am so glad I decided to come and annoy you that day.'

I was still sceptical. 'You're reacting to this a little too well. I thought I'd at least meet some resistance. I'm going to have to write about this.'

Teddy's expression turned serious for a second. 'Flick, I'm being 100 per cent serious. My life involves working and sleeping. And sometimes cooking, but mostly tortellini from the supermarket so that definitely doesn't count. I need to feel like I'm living here, and right now I don't.'

I sighed. 'But I'd do that anyway – be your friend. This isn't an either or.'

'Look, I can imagine that this has put you in a bit of a predicament at work, hasn't it?' Teddy nudged me. 'What are friends for? Besides, when this column takes off and you're a celebrity, I can give up the day job and be a trophy boyfriend.'

'We're going to have to be really convincing. I don't want anyone to find out that I'm lying; it would jeopardise the column and be *highly* embarrassing.'

Teddy shrugged off his jacket and took another swig from the bottle. 'So really, what this comes down to is a lack of belief in my acting skills. I took drama GCSE, Sage, have some faith. It's easy, see?'

He tapped on the shoulder of a random guy (probably a student, by the looks of it).

'What are you doing?' I hissed.

The man turned around (definitely a student, way too much hair gel), smiling awkwardly at Teddy, who was beaming.

'Hi mate. Just a quick question. Isn't my girlfriend beautiful?'

The stranger burst out laughing. 'Is this a joke?'

Teddy's face dropped. 'She just really needs to hear it today.'

I wanted to bang my head against the table.

'I mean, yeah, sure.' The guy looked at me. 'You're beautiful. I like your earrings, they're cool.' He gestured to my hoops, which were made from rainbow resin. It *did* feel good to get a compliment, I had to admit.

Teddy turned to me as the stranger walked off, shaking his head. 'See? Easy. Welcome to life as my girlfriend. Your ego will never dwindle.'

'Your execution was a little off. He looked terrified.'

He nodded. 'Agreed. Luckily, we have time. I got this. Hang on, how did this become me convincing you?'

'No idea, but I think we've got a plan.' I opened up my phone. 'In fact, let's start off on the right foot.'

Teddy watched as I added a heart to the end of his name in my phone.

'Do people still do that?'

I panicked. 'Do they not? God, I am so out of the swing of dating. We're never going to pull this off.'

'Relax. It's going to work out, I promise. We'll get you that bestselling column.'

That wasn't how columns worked, but I didn't have the heart to tell him that. How did I feel so reassured by a friend I'd only technically just met?

'Just so you know, I'm a pretty high-maintenance boyfriend.'

I could tell he was kidding by the promise of a smile, but I played along. 'Yeah? How so?'

'I leave towels all over the floor, I never pick up my socks . . . I'm basically the boyfriend from hell.'

'Who's the boyfriend from hell?' We whipped around to see Maia leaning against our booth, the others behind her. I could see Kitty at the bar, ordering a round of drinks.

'Ooh, does that mean you asked him already?' Stacey slipped in next to me, holding her hand out to Teddy. 'Stacey O'Sullivan. I'm the reason you're in this situation. Sorry.'

*Oh, for God's sake.* 'I hadn't actually told him that, but thanks.'

Stacey winced. 'I don't think I should ever be allowed to talk again.'

Teddy shrugged, taking it all in his stride even though he didn't know what was going on. 'No reason to be sorry. Dating Sage won't be too awful, I'm sure. I'm Teddy by the way.'

He shook her hand, but she wasn't even looking at him any more. She was staring bug-eyed at me, mouthing '*Sage?*'

Maia, all credit to her, played it cool like I knew she would. Sophie was hovering behind her, and I waved her into the booth. I didn't know her as well as the others yet, but she was clearly the perfect fit for Maia. Quiet, thoughtful, and sweet. And her one-liners cracked me up. She had shiny red hair, which she often styled into twists and braids so intricate that I couldn't even figure out where they'd started. When she came over, she always arrived with bags of sour sweets and a horror movie recommendation – something the rest of us were all unified in hating, but no one could bear to say no. Especially Maia, who had her hand on the small of Sophie's back now, making sure she had a spot in the booth. I watched as they both introduced themselves to Teddy, who took them in one by one, giving them his full attention.

'You did not mention how cute he is,' Stacey whispered in my ear.

'And you did not turn up on time,' I whispered back.

She flushed, batting me away. 'It turned out for the best, didn't it? It sounds like he's fully on board with fake-dating you. Ah, how I love being a matchmaker.'

Kitty arrived at the table, balancing six pints in her arms.

Teddy's eyes widened. 'I have to say that this is the most impressive first impression yet. Won it by a landslide.'

She balanced the glasses on the table and bowed. 'I was a bartender for three years. I know my way around pint glasses. And if you ever need someone to change a keg, I'm your girl. I'm Kitty.'

Teddy took her outstretched hand. 'Teddy. I'm the boyfriend.'

I nudged him. 'You do realise all of them are in on it, right?'

He nudged back. 'You need to get in character. The moment we lose it is the moment it's all over. The jig will be up. The lie will collapse.'

'I think I like you.' Stacey clinked her pint glass against his. 'Some might say that I, also, am a tad dramatic.'

Maia scoffed. 'You can say that again.'

Kitty tilted her head. 'If you're going to commit to all of this' – she pointed between me and Teddy – 'the timelines need to add up. Flick, I know you've been out of the game for a while, but Teddy wouldn't be your boyfriend yet. You need to keep dating and work up to a big reveal.'

I hit my head against the table and groaned. 'Big reveal? I wanted to make this as small of a part of the column as possible.'

'You are right, though.' Teddy blanched. 'I'm going to have to think of a way to pop the question.'

'This is so weird.' Sophie was laughing.

'Welcome to Flick's life.' Kitty rubbed my shoulder, gesturing for Sophie to scoot up to make room for her in the booth, and the six of us settled into easy conversation. It didn't escape my attention that I hadn't had this – a group of people, bouncing off each other and buying rounds of beer – the entire time I'd been in my relationship. Certainly not since living in London. Not for the first time, it occurred to me that maybe Teddy had been right about my heartbreak. Maybe this was a good thing.

'Where's your head at?' He whispered in my ear, half with me and half watching Sophie try to down a pint in thirty seconds. The others were cheering her on, even Maia, her girlfriend bringing out a side to her that the rest of us sometimes couldn't. It really was magic. Stacey had a dating app up, letting Kitty swipe for her. They kept wrinkling their noses whenever they saw a man holding a fish, both intensely playing a game where you had to drink every time one appeared on the screen. They'd nearly finished their drinks.

'It's wandering, I'll admit.' I traced my initials into the condensation on my glass. 'But to good places, I promise.'

He nodded, smiling. 'I'm really grateful to you, you know.'

'I'm trying to sense the sarcasm in there. What in particular are you grateful for? The fake dating, or the sweaty pint?'

'No sarcasm.' Teddy stared at the table for a moment. 'It's refreshing to not be sitting in my flat, trying to come up with ways of getting out of the house. Last month I played a solo game of supermarket sweep. I'm seeing this city in a whole new light now.'

I beamed. 'That's what fake dating is for.'

Teddy laughed. 'Exactly.'

***

Three hours later I was sitting on my bed, twirling my laptop cable in my hands as I listened to the phone on speaker.

'You've started doing what now?'

I couldn't see Suze, but I could hear her surprise as if she were right there beside me. As well as the whir of her dishwasher in the background, a mundane reminder that normal life existed.

'I know. My life has gone from the tragic to the straight up bizarre.'

'You're making my life seem boring.' I could hear her laughing, the metal clink of spoon against mug as she made her tea. Suze only ever drank peppermint tea – a beverage I thought tasted like muddy water.

'Susan Sage, I never want to hear you say that your life is boring again. You're my cool older sister. I bet you're wearing hoops and red lipstick even though it's 10 p.m., aren't you?'

'Have to stay on brand. So, who is this random guy anyway?'

I explained. She already knew about the column, but I hadn't told her about Teddy. Before I'd run into him at *Influence,* our original meeting hadn't seemed significant enough. I filled her in now.

'Oh God, you were angry-racketing?'

'I didn't even realise it had a name.'

I heard Suze blow on her tea. 'Are you kidding? Dad used to warn us all when you guys got home from tennis. If you'd been angry-racketing, we steered clear of you for the night.' She paused. 'So, would I approve?'

'Of what?'

'This new boy.'

'I think you're missing the point.'

She laughed. 'I understand the concept, but I would place a pretty high bet that the majority of fake relationships turn out to be real in the end.'

I had to be honest, fake dating wasn't something I had much knowledge about. I settled for silence, neither agreeing nor disagreeing.

'Just be careful, okay?'

This was the curse of having an older sister. Suze was the master of advice, solicited and unsolicited. There was no reason to be careful. Teddy was just, well, Teddy.

'I think I'll be alright.'

I imagined Suze sat in her bedroom (for the record, Suze's bedroom said a lot about her too: leopard-print rug, wall tapestry, a trendy stack of books, multiple clothes rails and plant pots), biting her lip to avoid giving me an earful.

'I just think it's a bit weird. That's all.'

'I'm not disagreeing with you. But it's for the sake of the column.'

She changed the subject. 'When's your next deadline anyway?'

'Why are you changing the subject?'

I heard her sigh over the line. 'I'm not. I just don't know what to say. I have zero experience in this kind of thing, and I'm just worried it's going to end in tears. I want you to realise how great being single is.'

'I'm realising that just fine. I *am* single.'

'I know, but now no one else will know that. I thought the whole point of the column and your list was to embrace this new space you'd found yourself in.'

'It was.' I paused. 'You know what a job can be like, Suze.'

The number of times that Suze's job had taken priority was too many to count. I really thought she would understand.

The silence stretched on. Just a few hours ago I'd been so content. We'd ended up renting one of the pub's air hockey tables and hosting a mini tournament. Teddy had been surprisingly good and we'd thrashed the others, coming in first place with Sophie and Maia not far behind. It had been the perfect evening. Now I felt a bit deflated.

'Flick? You still there?'

Every time Suze had come home from a night out when I'd been in high school, I'd waited on her bed with a bag of Doritos whilst she took her makeup off, desperate to hear every single detail. If she got with someone, I passed no judgement. I just wanted to be part of it. And although we weren't 15 and 18 any more, I was disappointed that she didn't feel the same way about my escapades now. I took my hand out of the bag of Doritos on my duvet.

'I'm not stupid, I've got this. It's just a bit of fun.'

I heard her sigh. 'I didn't mean to ruin your evening. I'm really glad you're making the most of London, and that you're making friends. I just worry that if you don't give your heart time to heal –'

What wasn't she getting? I *was* giving my heart the space it needed to heal. I'd turned down the chance for an actual date, this was just work. I huffed, knowing the signs of a fight that only sisters can have. 'You're the one who encouraged me to make the list. None of this would have happened without it.'

'I encouraged you to complete it with your new housemates. Not some random man that you picked up in a tennis court.'

I threw my hands up to the ceiling, aware that she wouldn't be able to see me.

'You know as well as I do that sometimes, when things are expected of you at work, it's incredibly hard to say no. I want to succeed at the magazine, and to do that I need to take a few risks.'

She was breathing hard. I knew she was mad, but I couldn't stop this whole thing just because my sister didn't approve. 'Do you know what? It really isn't my business.'

*Thank you.*

I wondered for a second if she might just hang up. And then: 'Do you want to hear about the gig I did yesterday? A woman tried to offer me money to sing at her husband's stag do.'

As much as I wanted to teleport to her flat and have it out with her, I still wanted to hear this. It didn't matter if it was scandalous or mundane, I'd always been enticed by the idea of knowing my older sister's secrets. Suze knew that. She was offering an olive branch. In high school we could have been tearing each other's hair out one minute, and then the next I'd be lying across her bed flipping through a magazine. That was just how we operated.

'And the best part was that she thought a twenty-pound note would cut it.' Suze laughed down the phone and it was instantly infectious.

In the same way she felt sadness when I did, crying with me on the bathroom floor after Aaron left, I couldn't not laugh along when she was amused by something. We were tied by an invisible thread, spun by years of family parties and camping trips.

'Are you eating Doritos? I can hear you crunching.' Suze said it with a hint of a smile.

I felt momentarily embarrassed by my naive assumption that we would have giggled about my strange life over the phone, debriefing over snacks like old times. I didn't want to lose that closeness, even if she was in Liverpool and I was here. A ping came through on my phone.

'Why are you texting me?'

She laughed softly. 'Just look, you idiot.'

I opened up the message to see a bag of the same tortilla chips lying at her feet where she was curled up on the couch. I couldn't recall ever apologising to Suze, or her to me. It was always an unspoken apology – like when I was 10 and she had been 13, and she'd bounced too hard on the trampoline when I was playing egg in the centre. I'd had a red mark on my forehead for weeks after, but that night, when I'd gone to sleep, there was a tiny pile of M&Ms on my pillow. Over time, tortilla chips had become the new M&Ms.

'Night, Flick.'

I hung up, telling her to call me tomorrow night. I grabbed my list from the bedside table, thinking through what she'd said. I took the lid off my gel pen with my teeth, adding a secret item to the twenties list, directly under number fourteen.

### 15. Enjoy being single

I wouldn't publish this one for *Influence*, but I'd know it was there. I might be pretending to date, but I knew when my sister was right. I wasn't ready to do it for real yet.

# 17

'Oi, Flick. Come and look at this.' As soon as I sat down in my desk chair, lunch break over, Sadie beckoned me to her end of the line.

It was Friday afternoon, and everyone in the office was borderline cranky, anxious for the weekend to arrive. Fiona had been huffing over HTML for a solid hour, and Felix kept accidentally deleting files, swearing under his breath every time. The team were beyond custard cream cheering-up territory. Sadie was still gesturing for me to wheel my chair over in her direction, so I did as she asked, prepared for her to show me another troll comment. My fourth column had gone up yesterday – we'd decided on weekly Thursday instalments – and she had a fascination with the collection of trolls that had descended on my comment section. She kept encouraging me to 'use them for motivation', but I couldn't help but feel a pang of sadness every time I saw 'Jerry6870', or 'Bloglover23109' take a stab at my writing, or the photos I'd begun to attach to the updates. Jerry6870 had said something quite nasty about my legs in the last comment section. Instinctively, I glanced down at them. They weren't chicken-y, were they?

'Are you looking at your legs again?' Sadie tutted at me. 'Troll comments come from a place of insecurity. It has nothing to do with you, babe.'

From across the room, Felix wolf whistled. 'You have the prettiest legs in the office.'

'I'm pretty sure you can't say that,' Sadie said, frowning.

I shrugged. 'Rather a compliment from Felix than a stab from Jerry.'

'Who *is* this Jerry?' Fiona threw her hands up, really not understanding the whole troll thing.

'Anyway, Flick. *Look.*' I approached Sadie's laptop and saw that she wasn't actually pointing to a new troll, but to a series of requests on the *Influence* Instagram asking for a livestream with me. 'You're required.'

'I don't get paid enough for this,' I wailed.

This wasn't the first time I'd considered asking Cecilia for a raise, although to be fair, the column was pretty central to the best parts of my life right now. It was bringing Carlisle even closer together – we'd had our long-awaited mixing decks tutorial last night over beer and ice cream. Unsurprisingly, I'd been shockingly bad at it. Teddy and I had played our first doubles match on Tuesday, and I had to admit, it felt nice to have a partner again. Aaron had always groaned at the idea of actually playing with me in a match. I smiled at the memory of us winning, Teddy doing a victory lap that ended in a forward roll. He'd texted this morning to report that he was convinced he'd slipped a disc.

'I'm thinking we use one of the meeting rooms and set up a cute backdrop for this live Q&A.' Sadie closed her eyes, envisioning the finished product. 'There's some leftover glitter paper from when I was taking some flat lays. That should work.'

I must have looked slightly terrified because she waved me off. 'Look, it'll be fine. You'll only be asked random Instagram things like "if you could live in anywhere in the world, where would you live" and things like that.'

'I don't even think I know the answer to that question.' Would I pick Tuscany? The idea of pasta every day of my life sounded ideal. Or New York? I'd always imagined that the journalism scene there would be extremely cool.

'Stop pondering it – they're meant to be quick-fire answers! I'm also going to need your favourite flavour of ice cream.' She scrolled through the comments. 'Oh! And I need to know what your advice is for aspiring journalists.'

'I just don't get it.' I gestured to the website, which was open on her desktop. 'Why are people this interested in me after only three instalments of the column? Why do people care this much?'

Sadie clucked, fluffing up her hair. 'It's not about you.'

Right.

'What I mean is, it's not about you. It's about what you represent. Flick, you're dipping your toe into adulthood and showcasing it for the world –'

'The *world*?' I was sceptical.

'Okay, a small portion of the world. People relate to you. Do you know how many people have been dumped and left blindsided? Or started living with strangers? Or tried to make finances work as a graduate in a new city? You're having the same kind of mundane experiences that people stress about, and you're documenting it along the way. How many times do you think people have typed these questions into Google? Now they get a human response. People care about Flick because at the end of the day, Flick is everyone.' She created a circle with her hands. On the other side of the room, Felix snickered.

'Can we get that on a T-shirt?' He too made the circular gesture. 'Flick is everyone.'

Fiona piped up. 'Can Flick be me? I have a pile of ironing at home that she can do.'

'I noticed Noodles' litter tray needs emptying too. Flick can be me if she wants.'

I sent Felix a stormy look. 'Har har. You won't be laughing when they ask to interview my colleagues on Instagram live.'

'I would thrive in that environment. Do you know how many times I lie awake at night and think about my responses to those questions?' He shot me a serious look. 'FYI, if I was a vegetable, I'd be an aubergine.'

'People.' Sadie's face was solemn. 'I know you don't understand my role here, but this is a huge moment. We're finally engaging readers online. This is exclusive content, and besides, I just messaged Cecilia. She thinks it's a great idea.'

I groaned. Of course she'd get Cecilia on board as a form of blackmail; there was no getting out of it now.

'Come on, Flick. Let's head into the meeting room to film this. It should only take thirty minutes.'

Felix snickered again. 'Good luck. And remember, Flick. *You are everyone.*'

Sadie paused, one hand pushing the meeting-room door, awkwardly carrying the backdrop under her other arm. 'Oh, and Cecilia also said to hand over Flick's afternoon schedule to you Felix, since you're the most clued in on it all.'

He threw his hands up in the air, not laughing any more.

★★★

I returned to the office an hour later, frazzled. When I'd started on the grad scheme here at *Influence*, I'd had to do a lot of tasks I hadn't expected. I'd never been responsible for liaising with writers, and as much as I'd said in my CV that I'd used Excel, I really hadn't been equipped for the monthly spreadsheets. But the need to answer rapid-fire questions about my perfect first date and my favourite pancake topping had tipped me over the edge. What ice cream flavour would I be? Was I a gin and lemonade or a gin and tonic kind of woman? Did I know what my five-year plan was? That last one had hit a nerve. The whole point of my column was that I had no clue what I was doing. A five-year plan? Absolutely beyond my realms of thought.

'You know, I did *not* have you pegged as a gin and lemonade girl.' Sadie shook her head, tapping away at her phone as she responded to some of the comments on our livestream. 'And from these comments, none of these people did either.'

'I'm not surprised they didn't know that, considering they also don't really know me.' I picked at a hangnail, accidentally making it bleed. That whole thing had stressed me out.

'They feel like they know you, which is exactly what we wanted. This column is going down well. Even better than the Mayfair article. People lapped that shit *up.*'

I sat back down at my desk, leaving Sadie to chatter absent-mindedly about how she would definitely be a strawberry soft scoop.

'How's my little superstar?' Felix turned to me from where he was staring at his email. 'And more than that, I've just been catching up with the column itself.'

I interjected. 'You mean, you haven't been hanging off my every word for the past three weeks?'

'Hey, I'm literally in my final year of the dreaded twenties. I don't have to hark back to the disaster that was my own life at 22. Anyway, I was reading the column, and it got very, *very* interesting.'

All of a sudden, I felt the need to become completely absorbed in my computer screen, pulling up my own emails.

'Who is this young man I spotted you sharing food truck delights with?' He raised an eyebrow. 'I cannot believe you told the column that you were dating someone before you told me.'

It was true. I'd followed the plan in yesterday's column, slotting in a minor detail about playing air hockey on our next date. It had been surprisingly easy to make it up as I went along. I was almost sad that I couldn't be honest about our friendship, which was becoming incredibly solid. He was just one of those people you felt like you could be totally yourself with. I'd had to send an explanatory email to my parents before the column went live, and Mum had just replied with a flurry of exclamation points and a promise to discuss it at length when they came to visit next weekend.

'Yeah, it was kind of unexpected. It's still in the early stages, though – nothing serious.' I remembered what Kitty had said at the pub. We couldn't jump in all guns blazing.

Felix huffed. 'I would have thought, as primary office-mate –'

'SSH. You can't let anyone else know that.' I knew the way to his forgiveness was flattery.

He already seemed placated, whispering now. 'Well yes, as primary office-mate, I would have considered myself privy to that kind of information. Don't you think?' He started getting carried away. 'Maybe we can double date. Sebastian has been wanting to try this weird fusion restaurant and I need moral support. *Oh.*' He grabbed my arm. 'We bought the London version of Monopoly last week when we were in Waterstones. I could make some cocktails, we could play the game . . .'

I felt guilty already. And the web of lies had barely even begun.

'That sounds nice.'

Cecilia chose that moment to open the door to her office, so I was momentarily saved. Felix hummed the *Jaws* theme tune under his breath, making Fiona snort.

'Everyone? Attention please. Thanks. So, I know it's been a stressful month in the office. With our new column launching, a more cohesive social media strategy, and getting things sorted for our April issue.'

She gestured to a cardboard box, pulling out several glossy copies of our latest issue.

'It's *stunning*.' Sadie took one of the copies that Cecilia was holding, outstretched for anyone who wanted to take a look. 'I need to make a reel flicking through this ASAP.'

It never got old, that feeling of grasping a shiny team effort in your hands. When I was little, our parents had let Suze and me both choose a magazine subscription, and every month we'd waited by the letterbox, desperate to hold the glossy pages in our hands. Now, that same feeling was amplified, knowing that I'd actually played a part in making it. It was even stranger to think that if all went well, I'd have an actual print article in there next time. I'd come a long way since those days of waiting by the front door in my pyjamas for my princess comic to arrive.

'Lovely, isn't it?' Cecilia stroked the issue. 'One of our best yet, I think. A true collaborative effort.'

We had all slowly crowded round, passing the magazine around and cooing over our favourite parts.

'I wanted to thank you for the hard work, and for jumping on board with all the new additions to our schedule here in the office.' She pointed at Felix. 'I know you can't have been too thrilled to have to cover an extra workload today whilst we filmed for Instagram.'

Beside me, Felix shrugged, but his eyes were wide. Cecilia wasn't always free with her praise.

'We've all stepped up to make this magazine the best it can be, on and offline. So I ordered some bubbly on expenses!' Cecilia smiled as a couple of the staff cheered. 'I thought we could take the last couple of hours off and celebrate what a fabulous issue we've created here. It's something truly special, and with all of you on board, I believe that it's only going to get better with time.'

She opened the door to her office a bit wider, revealing a tray of long-stemmed glasses, prosecco bubbling to the top. *What in the world was going on?*

'Oh, and I invited some of the external staff up to share the glory. We wouldn't get very far without the other teams that help us.' Cecilia shot me a funny look and wiggled her eyebrows.

Oh God. I got it now.

The noise of the lift reaching our floor sounded out. A few of the finance and tech teams meandered in, including a man that made a beeline for Felix, who paled. And right at the back, grinning mischievously at me, was Teddy.

# 18

It took approximately five seconds after he'd ditched his admirer for Felix to clock Teddy, recognition setting in.

'*Oh*. I knew I had seen your face somewhere other than that food-truck photo.' He nudged me. 'You sneaky devil, fraternising with the other teams.'

Felix was staring at both of us expectantly. I felt Teddy stiffen beside me – we both knew that this was our first real test.

'Yeah, that's me. Computer guy by day, Sage's date by night.' Hearing him say that out loud, in front of people we actually had to try and convince, was startling.

Felix looked impressed. 'You do realise she's precious cargo?'

Teddy smiled softly. 'I do realise that, yes. I have every intention of handling the cargo with care.' I blushed.

'That's what I like to hear. So, Teddy, how do you feel about fusion restaurants . . .'

I listened to them chatter in amusement, imagining what it would be like to *actually* introduce Felix to someone that I was dating. I felt awful that this whole interaction wasn't quite real.

Cecilia clocked our cluster and strode over, handing out glasses of prosecco. Teddy took a massive swig. His fear of my boss cracked me up.

'And here's the man who's garnered quite the interest with our readers.' Cecilia was looking down her nose through her glasses at him, but there was definitely a hint of a smile playing on her lips. She was loving every second of this.

'Is it me they're interested in, or is it just that I'm dating your hotshot columnist?' Teddy, all credit to him, held his own. He did wipe his palms on his trousers after he spoke, though.

'It's probably that too. You should tell them that you met at work – they'd lap it up. Everyone loves a good meet-cute.'

I resisted from telling her that we hadn't *actually* met in the office. I didn't want the tennis story in the column; the more we mixed the lies with the reality, the more complex the web would get. We had to at least try not to blur the lines.

Teddy smiled at Felix. 'From what I've heard, our meet-cute doesn't even come close to yours.'

*Good effort, Teddy. Nice deflection.*

Felix put his hand to his chest. 'I'm flattered. And you're right. It was a good story, but don't tell Cecilia that. She'll make me write an agony-aunt column next.'

'Somehow, I don't think endless photos of your cat would have the same readership,' Cecilia said, smirking. She turned to offer her tray of prosecco to the other new arrivals, leaving Felix looking put out.

'Wow, that hurt. Writing one of those is my worst nightmare, but now that I know she thinks it wouldn't be up to scratch . . .'

'Ha.' I hiccupped over the prosecco. 'Cat pun.'

'Unintentional.' Felix still looked sad. 'I can't believe Cecilia doesn't think Noodles would make good content.'

Teddy held up his glass. 'I'd read it, mate.'

'Thanks. How did you two manage to keep your meet-cute in the office private anyway?' Felix stroked his stubble. 'I don't understand how I missed this, I'm usually so observant. When anyone gets up to go and make a coffee, I'm all over that – so *how* did I not see this happening? I want all the details.' He sent me a stormy look.

I panicked, knowing that we were going to have to fabricate something on the spot. I was not a practiced storyteller.

'It was funny really, we –' My brain froze. I couldn't think of a single thing to say. My loyal subscription to Netflix romantic comedies was failing me. There was no way we were going to pull this off. And if I couldn't pull it off to Felix, how was I going to do it online to hundreds of people?

Teddy interjected. 'We were getting lunch at the sandwich shop. You know, the one on the corner by the offices?'

Felix's gaze flitted between us, eyes narrowed. 'I know the one.'

'I got to the front of the counter and ordered the goats cheese and chorizo –'

'Respectable choice.'

'Thanks. So I ordered, and then after I paid I heard Sage order the exact same thing. Mine had been the last one.'

I saw where he was going with this, and chipped in for plausibility. 'And I must have seemed irritated, because he said I could have it.'

Teddy smiled. 'We ended up splitting the sandwich over Diet Cokes on our lunch break. We started getting lunch together almost every day after that.'

Little did he know that his story was actually very believable. I'd spent a lot of lunch breaks in the toilet, crying, in the immediate aftermath of the breakup. No one knew I hadn't been sharing a romantic sandwich elsewhere.

Felix was fully invested now, eyes no longer narrowed. 'You know, that might just be about a sandwich, but my heart is well and truly warmed. It's no Tube story, but it'll definitely do.'

Teddy shot me a glance that said 'Thank me later'.

Sadie and Fiona had made a beeline for us at some point during the story and were now listening too. Not even Sadie, who was leading the social media side of things, knew that Teddy was just my friend. I was quite impressed that we'd managed this; all three of them were staring at us, looking touched by the sentiment of a sandwich.

'You know, I thought you might let this column flop.' Sadie shrugged when Felix nudged her. She'd clearly accepted a second glass of fizz. 'Sorry, my parents are always telling me I need to keep my thoughts to myself. But now that I've started, I might as well continue.'

Felix snorted. 'Yeah, might as well.'

'I thought you might crumble under the pressure, with all your other responsibilities I mean.' Sadie glugged from the glass again. 'But this dating side to the column really does just

175

elevate the whole thing to new heights. With the right social media buzz, we'll have hit the market right on the nose.'

In a lot of ways, Sadie reminded me of an office Stace.

Everyone started flicking through a nearby copy of the issue, pointing out the parts that they'd had a hand in. Felix seemed so happy that I wanted to squeeze him, but that was probably the free drinks.

'So.' Next to me, Teddy ran his hands through his hair. 'How did I do?'

'Do you know what?' I held out my glass for a clink, which he reciprocated. 'I think we might actually be able to do this.'

'Thank God.' He picked up a copy of the magazine. 'I have to say, Flick, this is very impressive.'

I pointed out a few of the columns, showing him the articles I'd helped to edit. This was the first issue that I'd had a considerable amount of responsibility for; for the first year of my post-grad role, I'd done a lot of helping around the office, general admin, and making cups of tea. I'd felt like a part of the team from day one (on my first day, Felix had showed me all of his favourite restaurants on Google Maps, and Fiona had bought me a brownie to split whilst she told me about her own daughters that were my age), but it had taken a while for Cecilia to trust me with more than just menial tasks. Now I was seeing it in print, the little spaces I'd helped with, I felt a bit emotional.

'You okay?' Teddy nudged me. 'Is this article meant to have this kind of impact?'

We were staring at a page entitled '10 ways to make your wardrobe more sustainable.'

'I mean, I care about the future of the planet a lot, but no, I'm not getting emotional over that. It's just . . .' I gestured to the office and the people in it. 'This is something I probably would have told myself I could never do. And I'm doing it.'

His expression was warm. 'Your ambition is impressive. Anyone that doesn't appreciate that isn't worth having around.' We both knew what he meant.

Even though I knew that Cecilia inviting the external teams up to celebrate with us was just to integrate Teddy and the column, it felt *right* to have him standing here.

'And you know, the magazine would flounder if our computers didn't work.'

'Now you're just trying to butter me up. What is it that you want?'

'That depends. What does Teddy Stewart usually give to his women?'

His expression turned sad for a second, his frown lines showing. It was only a moment before his face broke into his usual smile. 'Whatever you want, your wish is my command. Although you only get three, and then I'm returning to whatever lamp you found me in.'

'My first wish is another glass from that tray.' I pointed behind him, and he grabbed me another drink.

'You're easy to please. So . . . what's the situation with, you know, contact?' A faint flush appeared in his cheeks.

I had to really control the urge to spit out the prosecco (which actually, second glass in, I was beginning to think was the cheap cava from Tesco Express). 'Contact?'

'I mean, it's going to look a bit weird if we're dating but we never show affection. What's the plan?'

To be fair, I hadn't even thought about that. God, the politics of faux-romance. It hadn't mattered when I was with my friends, who all knew, or when I was taking a photo for my column. But here, with a group of people who thought 'Teddy and Flick' was an actual thing?

'I mean, just act like you would if we were actually seeing each other.' I said this quietly, aware that Felix had impeccable hearing skills and was only four feet away.

'Okay, mission received.' Teddy saluted me, and I pushed him, laughing.

'Flick?' Sadie had appeared. 'We're all going to the pub for another one.' She leaned in to whisper, '*Even Cecilia*. Are you two coming?'

I looked at Teddy, who nodded. 'Yeah, we're coming. Let me just grab my coat and we'll meet you guys outside.'

Sadie skipped off, linking arms with another girl who worked on the opposite side of the office to me. I grabbed my coat off my chair.

'Are you sure you don't mind giving up your evening for this?'

Teddy was leaning against the desks, waiting for me and checking his phone. 'It's all part of the deal, right?'

'Well yes, but –'

'My plans involved watching a true-crime documentary and defrosting a bolognese from last week. This is a considerable improvement, promise.'

He reached out his hand, wiggling his fingers to entice me. Was this weird? Was I out of my mind to do all of this? Suze definitely thought so. She'd been dodging my calls ever since that night. The girls at Carlisle were on board, but I got the sense that they would be on board with most things if they were fun. This was the wildest thing I'd ever done, by a considerable amount. But wasn't that the point of my twenties list? If Suze had been here in person to see it unfold, I was sure she'd have understood.

'Sage?' Teddy was staring at me, hand still outstretched.

I looked at him, so open and ready for this unexpected adventure. Trying to find his own place in this vibrant city too. Someone who was fast becoming a person that I could depend on.

'Let's go.' I took his hand, feeling his fingers curl around mine as he tugged me in the direction of the office door.

We were almost out when I spotted Cecilia grabbing her bag from her office. She saw me and winked.

★★★

**The Twenties List: Let's Get Down to Business**

*Dear Reader,*

*I hope you're having the best week so far. We're about to launch a new issue of our magazine here at* Influence, *so we're all feeling particularly high spirited. We even had fizz in the office (should I be saying that on the internet?)*

*In a complete plot twist, someone submitted a question to me on our Instagram, so I'll be starting today's column with a bit of an agony-aunt take. Not that I would consider myself to be in any sort of position to start handing out advice, but it makes me feel better that one of you thinks I give off that impression. Rosie from Greenwich wrote in and said:*

**'I moved to London last month, and I'm really struggling to make friends. What would you suggest?'**

*First of all, Rosie, if you're struggling to make friends in a new city, you're probably in the same position as about 90 per cent of the people living there. When I imagined moving, I imagined a city where every young person is constantly milling around, waiting to be scooped up for friendship. Anyone that's moved to London will tell you that unless you're lucky, that's rarely the case. London is a city full of young people, but for some reason, it's so difficult to actually meet them.*

*Moving into a houseshare was a huge turning point for me. It's a bit of a gamble – I've heard horror stories – but it's the best way to get stuck in with new people. I was lucky that I ended up with non-weirdos, although there's still time. I'll report back. There's something really comforting about coming home from a long day at work and spending time in the kitchen with people, instead of retreating upstairs. I'm also a firm believer that London is a city made up from friends-of-friends. If you get invited out for a drink after work, do it. You never know who else will turn up: your friend's housemate, or their friend of a friend, or their old pal from university. Friends-through-friends are a valuable resource. I think we all know someone who's had a meet-cute like this.*

*I recently started getting back into sport again, and it's such a good way to let off steam after work and meet like-minded people at the same time. Joining some kind of club that regularly meets means a constant opportunity to make connections in the city.*

*London is a city where perseverance pays off, and I imagine it's the same wherever you are in the world. If it helps, I can almost definitely promise that the people you're looking for are looking for you too. Good luck, Rosie!*

*Do you have a burning question that you want me to try and answer? I had a lot of fun with it this week, so feel free to email us using the links below!*

*Speaking of the twenties list, this week has been a good'un. I'm now over a month into my new living situation, and if you'd told me then that I would love it now, I wouldn't have believed you. It's a whirlwind of alcohol, music and gossip, but it feels so good to be part of something. I haven't been part of a group like this since high school. The girls tried to create a food budgeting chart this week, which, I have to say, I'm sceptical about. I've never known any of my housemates to skimp on food, ever. It's how we communicate.*

*Reaching the six-week mark means that I've reached the one-month dating mark with Teddy. Who knew that office meet-cutes actually happened? I was terrified to let anyone in again, but it gets easier with every date. I used to look back on my past relationship with a pang of wistfulness; now I'm questioning how happy I actually was.*

*The rest of this week has consisted of fights in the office over the last blueberry muffin (scandalous, no one warns you about the diplomacy skills you'll need for the world of work), and trying another five black coffees in an attempt to tick something else off my list (nope, it's just not for me. WHY does it taste like tar?) I also managed to find a shortcut to the office, so I have a little bit of extra time in the morning. It's the little things.*

*What have you been up to this week?*

*Flick x*

# 19

I bit into the sweet crêpe, groaning.

'You know you have Nutella running down your chin, right?' Kitty snapped a photo of me on her phone. 'Sorry, I needed it for the birthday photos. We're going to ruin you in June, no regrets.'

'I don't even care right now.' I took another bite, resisting a second groan. 'This, *this,* is the kind of thing that you move to London for. Right next to "get a job in journalism" was "always be in close proximity to Nutella crêpes".'

Kitty wrinkled her nose; she hadn't been impressed. 'Sometimes you think you know who you live with, and then you realise you don't know them at all.' She bit into her own crêpe. 'Yeah, lemon and sugar, that's the stuff. Once, I saw Maia order a *savoury* crêpe. If I was Sophie, I'd have had to leave in the dead of night.'

Kitty had only been teaching one online class this morning, so we'd headed into Camden as soon as she was done. Camden Market was one of my favourite places in London – a vibrant, eclectic mix of the many cultures and cuisines that existed under this one big umbrella. I lived for the stilton, bacon and pear toasties or the fluffy pittas filled with falafel and hummus. And clearly, I could never say no to a crêpe. Food brought Londoners together.

Kitty perched on a bench, finishing off her crêpe and rolling the cardboard sleeve into a cone. 'So, what are we waiting for? I want to capture this moment.'

The next item on my list was to pick up a Polaroid camera and start capturing all of the pocket-sized photos for my bedroom walls at Carlisle (there was no way I was going to get my deposit for that room back – I'd already scuffed the walls when I'd done some late-night furniture reorganising). I loved the idea of an instant moment captured on film. When Suze and I were little, my dad had taught us both how to use his old cameras, sitting us on his lap and flipping through our family albums. There were hundreds of photos of my parents, whether it was on safari in Tanzania for their honeymoon, or standing in front of the cot they'd spent a whole day building in preparation for Suze's arrival. Mum didn't love tennis, so the thing that they'd always shared had been documenting their life together. My dad was ruthless with a camera – you were captured as you were, no second chances given – and I kind of liked that one-chance approach to photography. I'd popped some new film and batteries into the bright yellow camera that I'd chosen this morning. After passing it to Kitty I picked up my food again to pose so she could take a photo of us.

'Make sure you really get the Nutella.' I spoke around a final bite.

'Oh, believe me, Flick, I will. There's no missing that splodge on your chin.'

The snap of the camera confirmed that my first Polaroid had been a success, and we placed it between us, waiting for the image to develop. Slowly but surely, a tiny photo appeared: Kitty beaming, me holding up the remains of my crêpe. It was the small moments of my new life that I'd always want to remember. This one included, where I was living for me.

I held it between my fingers. 'Sometimes I still feel down. But mostly, I'm just glad that this year is turning out like it is. If only for making memories like this.'

Kitty smiled. 'I know what you mean. I was in a relationship when I first moved here two years ago, and whilst I loved them, I got over it pretty quickly in the end. When you're living in this city, you realise how much there is to live *for*.'

I thought about living in Carlisle – a house where there was always someone around, always something going on. I was learning more about myself than I ever had at university, or during my first year in London.

Kitty picked up the photo from where I'd placed it back on the bench, squinting to see the details that time hadn't yet revealed. 'I've been thinking a lot about what I would put on my own list.'

'You have?'

In my mind, Kitty already had her life together. There was no one else I knew that would be up at the crack of dawn to do yoga (even after a late-night gig), or who would be able to manage her hectic schedule. When she wasn't DJing or tutoring online, she was working behind the scenes of a sustainable fashion brand. She wasn't exactly what I thought of when I pictured a 23-year-old in crisis.

'Yeah. It made me realise that moving to London really did mean that I started ticking things off a list, even if it was subconscious. Before moving in with the girls, I hadn't even considered trying to make money from my gigs. And I would *never* have got my nipple pierced without Stace holding my hand.'

I snorted. 'Carlisle Avenue, the best place to turn to for *any* kind of support. What else would be on your list?'

'Well, I definitely want to go skydiving at some point. And you know those flash mob dances? I'd love to dance in one of those,' she said as she twirled one of her braids.

'You make my bread and Polaroids look pretty tame.'

She burst out laughing. 'Those are just the really rogue choices. I've wanted to join a choir ever since I moved here. One of those choirs where no one can really sing, but they're there because they love to do it and it means that they're part of a community. I also think it's about time that I got my driving licence. *That* is going to come back and bite me at some point.'

Back home where I'd grown up, it had seemed like a fatal flaw if someone couldn't drive a car. When you lived in a city like this, you often had no idea who could drive and who couldn't.

'Oh! And I want to work my way through the Kama Sutra.' She wiggled her eyebrows.

A man walking in front of us shot us a panicked expression.

'Yeah, you're definitely making the bread and the Polaroids look tame. Oh my God . . .' I blinked at the situation unfolding in front of me, swiping at my mouth, trying to get the Nutella.

'What's going on?' Kitty whipped her head around, trying to glimpse what I'd seen.

I pointed her in the general direction of a dumpling cart, where I could still see the bright blue T-shirt with the words 'Game On' emblazoned across it. I'd know that T-shirt anywhere – I'd put it in the darks wash enough times.

'Aaron alert. Over there. *Quick,* do I still have it all over my mouth?'

In an instant, Kitty jumped on board. 'Christ, okay. No, it's all gone. I'd redo the ponytail if I were you.' And then, 'Really, though? From what I can see over here, he looks like a loser.'

'Doesn't everyone look like a loser when they've dumped your friend?' I spoke through the hair tie between my teeth.

'Fair point, but no. I see my ex on Instagram and know that I absolutely still would if I could. That looks better, no frizz going on now.'

I breathed for what felt like the first time in two long minutes, happy that if Aaron noticed me, I would look semi-decent. He was still partially obscured by the cart, but I could tell he was sitting at a bench like us, eating. I let myself feel it for a second, the loss. It was heavy, like something sinking inside from my chest to the pit of my stomach.

'Weird, isn't it? I think the first time I saw my ex was in a Sainsbury's Local. I had panty liners in my hand, so you're doing better than me. Panty liners and cranberry juice for a UTI, if I remember right. Not a good look.'

'I kind of thought, since Teddy and the column and you guys, that it wouldn't affect me that much. But I'm not sure I can stand up right now.'

'Looks like you won't have to.' Kitty winced, her eyes still on him. I tried to look inconspicuous but failed miserably, twisting around to see Aaron getting up and walking over here with purpose. We locked eyes. I thought I might vomit onto the pavement in front of us. I didn't think the crêpe would taste as nice when it made a reappearance.

'I'm guessing you don't want a photo of this.' Kitty put the camera inside her tote.

'Flick?' Aaron was about three feet away now, squinting. 'I was sitting over there eating dumplings and I thought, *I know that girl.*'

That was putting it mildly.

'Yeah, it's me.' I tried to smile but it came out all funny. I probably had chocolate in my teeth, too. Next to me, Kitty very lightly put her pinkie finger on mine for a second, an act of solidarity.

Aaron was laughing, waving his arms around. 'This is crazy. Of all the spots in London and we bump into each other today. I haven't been to Camden since . . .' he trailed off. 'Anyway. How are you?'

The more he spoke, the more detached I felt from the whole situation. Like I was in one of the alternative reality video games that he used to spend hours playing after work. 'I'm great. This is Kitty, my housemate.'

Kitty didn't hold out her hand like she'd done when I'd introduced her to Teddy. 'Katherine. Nice to meet you. Thanks for giving us Flick, she's ace.'

Aaron winced for a second but pushed through. 'No problem. I'm glad it's all working out for you guys. I'm guessing everything is still ticking along at the magazine?'

I nodded. Had he not checked my LinkedIn? It hurt that he hadn't mentioned the column, and it hurt even more that it was probably because he didn't know. I knew all about his change in job role, which he was chattering on about now.

'What made you decide to do that?' I released my fingernails, which were cutting crescent-shaped marks into my palms. The whole time I'd known him, he'd been dead set on which company he wanted to work for. It had been the whole reason for us planning our move here. 'Were you planning on leaving your old job?'

He coughed into his hand. 'Well, I wasn't. But then, everything was changing . . .' he had the sense to look a bit sheepish, '. . . and I realised that if everything else was changing, why not change that too? A fresh start.'

'A fresh start.' I'd been about to repeat it sardonically, but Kitty had got there first, staring at him with her eyes narrowed. 'Sounds nice.'

I let his words mull over on my tongue. A fresh start. They tasted bitter.

'Yeah.' He'd started doing this antsy thing with his feet. We all stayed silent for a minute – me and Aaron out of awkwardness, Kitty I assume to make it more awkward for him. I loved her, I really did.

'Aaron?' A tall, pretty woman was walking over. I gulped. As she got closer I realised I recognised her from his social media posts about that concert he'd been to. 'I came back from the loo and you were gone.' She looked really surprised

189

to see him talking to us. 'Did you leave the food unattended? I think they threw it in the bin because you left.'

Aaron ignored the question, still speaking to me. 'This, this is Sara. She's . . .'

Sara held out her hand, turning her full attention to me. 'We work together.' She was beaming at me. Could she not read a room? 'And you are?'

Aaron was watching us warily. 'This is Flick.'

'Oh. *Oh. Hi.*' The grip she had on my hand intensified. Or was that just in my imagination? Of all the ways that I'd imagined bumping into Aaron again, this was not one of them. Sara had said they worked together, but I wasn't an idiot. I could see the way that, now the introductions were out of the way, his gaze was lingering on her. And she had really great hair. I'd want to date that hair. I didn't begrudge him his happiness, but I definitely didn't want to stick around and watch it happen.

Kitty read my mind. 'We're meeting our other housemates on Primrose Hill in fifteen minutes, so it was good to meet you both.' She stood up, swinging her bag over her shoulder.

'Oh, right.' Aaron stared at her for a second, unblinking. 'Well, it was great to bump into you, Flick. I'm glad things are working out.'

Sara had stepped back and was checking her phone.

'Good luck with your new job, and your new –' I gestured to her, then realised I'd put my foot in it. 'Good luck with your fresh start.'

We left, Kitty rubbing my arm as we walked. 'Killer last line. Left it on a strong note.'

It happened precisely ten seconds after we'd turned the corner. I burst into tears.

'Oh Flick, come here.' Kitty pulled me in tight for a hug. 'It was always going to happen. The city is big, but it isn't big enough to avoid someone forever. At least it's out of the way. Shall we go home?' She had her phone out. 'I'll rally the troops. I can text Teddy too, if you want?' I nodded, still crying. This wasn't the slow ache of grief, the kind of pain that snuck up on you throughout the day. This was the kind of shock I thought I'd left behind in the shower the week that I couldn't stop sobbing. How could someone that I'd loved so unconditionally just be leaving me behind?

I wiped my eyes, mascara streaking my fingers and letting me know that I'd gone full panda mode in the middle of Camden. 'Yeah, let's go home.'

# 20

'Oh *love*. That must have been hard.' Mum twisted her fork into her carbonara, spearing a piece of bacon and accidentally spilling sauce on her sleeve. She had a reputation for never leaving a restaurant without some remnants of food stuck to her. 'I've experienced a lot of things in my life, but I maintain that nothing is quite as bad as seeing a partner when you've split up.'

'I agree.' Dad chimed in, and Mum's head whipped up simultaneously to mine. 'I remember when me and your Mum had a fight so bad that we tried to call it off. We bumped into each other in the queue for popcorn at the cinema and I thought my stomach had dropped out of my arse.'

Mum patted his arm. 'For a second there, Lionel, what you said was almost profound.'

I broke off a piece of the same slice of bruschetta I'd been working on for the last ten minutes. It had been a full twenty-four hours, but I still couldn't get the image of Aaron and Sara out of my mind. I honestly felt nauseous every time I considered them going home together after; no one went out for random dumplings with their colleague on a Saturday afternoon. As much as Stacey had tried to tempt me with jam doughnuts and cups of tea last night, my appetite showed no signs of imminent return. I'd almost cancelled my evening with my parents, who were visiting the city overnight (or, probably more accurately, making sure I was okay). Our table at Emilia's had been booked for a good couple of weeks, and I'd known how badly my dad was looking forward to his huge bowl of pasta. There are some things you just can't take away from someone. And I also really missed them, even more so after yesterday.

I tried to take my mind off things. 'I don't think you've ever told me and Suze that you broke up for a while. You're ruining your image.'

Mum tutted. 'We hardly split up. Your dad is being dramatic. We had a brief wobble because we were deciding where we were going to go after university. Your dad wanted to stay in Liverpool, and I thought that I wanted to move down south. It turned out that all it took was seeing him in the cinema a week later to know my plan was never going to stick. The rest is history. We couldn't keep away from each other. Sorry.' She winced at my facial expression. 'Too much information. You're so grown up now that sometimes I forget.'

'It was a good job we bumped into each other.' Dad spoke through a mouthful, and I caught Mum nudging him. 'Your mum couldn't sleep for weeks after watching *Misery* at the cinema that night.'

I was getting that weird sensation you get when you realise that your parents had whole lives before you. 'Let me take a photo of you both.'

'Wait! Let me fix my lippy.' Mum swiped on some of her signature Bobbi Brown, leaning into my dad as I clicked the button on the front of the camera, waiting a second to make sure the photo wouldn't be blurry.

'That takes me right back.' Mum pointed to the Polaroid, which was appearing now out of the top of the camera. 'Doesn't it take you back, Lionel?'

I stared at the small white photo as it developed, smiling at the sight of my parents. For as long as I could remember, they'd been a team. Now, I had it captured forever. Just like with the photo I'd taken yesterday with Kitty, I planned to scan all of them onto the office computer to pair with the weekly column.

'Let me see that other one.' Mum grabbed for the Polaroid of Kitty and her crêpe.

'Don't get pasta sauce on it.'

She scoffed. 'Charming. Kitty seems lovely. Knowing you're in that house brings back such fond memories of my house-share. I think I have a Polaroid from our first house Christmas. Your Dad burnt the turkey completely.'

Mum and Dad had met in their houseshare at university, breaking one of the cardinal rules of sharing: *never* date your housemate. Although to be fair to them, thirty-three years later they were still very much best friends. I guess it didn't hurt to break the rules sometimes.

'Are you happier now, then?' Dad asked me the question through a mouthful.

'If you're asking if I'm wallowing less, then yes, I am happy.'

194

'Even with this fake boyfriend? I've got to say, I don't understand all of that.'

'*Lionel.*' Mum shook her head. 'If it makes you happy honey, we're happy.'

'But he's nice to you, this man? He's a good friend?' Dad looked mildly concerned, and it made my heart pang. I thought of Teddy, who I knew was organising his record collection tonight and watching the latest series of *Top Gear*. I was pretty sure I was in safe hands. I imagined him on his own in his flat, and almost wished I'd invited him here tonight to meet them.

'You'd like him. He plays tennis.'

Dad's eyes lit up, and he went off on a tangent about his own matches with his friends at the local tennis courts. He'd had to stop playing a couple of years ago due to a knee injury, but now he was slowly getting back into it, playing a few friendly matches every now and then. Teddy and I were playing our first doubles match next week; the thought of Dad and I enjoying the thing we had most in common, even with one hundred and eighty miles between us, made me smile.

'Ooh.' Mum shoved her screen towards me. 'I'm a bit obsessed with checking the comments on this website. I think I've shown your column to half the village.'

Dad took his glasses, which were tucked between the buttons of his shirt, and perched them on the bridge of his nose. 'Sixty-two comments. Who are all of these people?'

I sipped the elderflower spritzer in front of me. 'To be honest, Dad, I'm beginning to question that myself.'

'Did you forward the latest one to Suze?' Mum clicked something on her phone between bites of pasta. 'I tried to do it, but I don't know if I did it right. Probably better if you do it. Last time I tried to forward her something, it ended up being a video of two cats talking to one another. Happy accident, but an accident nonetheless.'

'Speaking of Suze, have you heard from her much lately?' I dropped it nonchalantly into the conversation because I knew my parents would panic if they knew Suze had gone MIA, but I hadn't heard back from her in two days. For anyone else, that would be an acceptable reply window. Suze, however? An extremely long reply window. She was always attached to her phone.

Mum glanced at Dad before speaking. 'She didn't want to make a fuss after everything that has happened to you this year, but she's having a bit of a rough time of it at the moment. I think the column might cheer her up.'

'She's having a tough time? She hasn't mentioned anything to me about it.' I pulled out my own phone, checking to see if there was anything I'd missed. We were two sides of the same coin; if there was something wrong with one of us, we were the first person each other turned to. How did my parents know this, and not me?

Dad coughed. 'She lost a few gigs she was looking forward to. Got pulled up at work for a deadline she missed. Called us in a panic the other night, wanted to come and stay with us for a couple of days.'

This was news to me. Suze never missed deadlines – ever. She was the one I moaned to on the phone when I was

196

struggling to get everything done. The one I called when I didn't know whether to put my new T-shirt in the dark wash, and the one I asked when I had no idea how to change a bulb. The three years had always been the difference between put together and clinging on. Staying with my parents? Her independence was Suze's favourite thing in the *world*.

'I'm surprised she didn't tell you, Felicity.' Mum sipped from her glass, no idea that she was rubbing salt in the wound.

'I . . . maybe she left a voicemail that I didn't get.' I knew it wasn't true, but I was almost embarrassed that I didn't know this snippet of Suze's life.

'I'm sure it's nothing that a glass of wine and a hot bath won't fix. Don't worry about her, I've been making cups of tea on demand.' Mum patted my hand. 'Just give her a call.'

# 21

I put my phone back in my locker, frustrated at the same dial tone I'd been getting every time I'd tried to ring my sister in the last week.

'Suze? Where *are you*?'

Now that I knew she was having a rough week, my failed attempts to reach her felt more significant. I imagined her sitting on my parents' sofa in front of the fireplace, snuggled up to Kernel like we always did when we felt crap. If she was ignoring my calls, it wasn't because of our argument; we didn't hold grudges. She hadn't posted anything on her Instagram stories (a sad but effective way of monitoring someone's mood in the twenty-first century) for the past two weeks, and she hadn't been online on Facebook for days. I'd refreshed the messenger app, hoping to see the green circle that let me know when she was online. I knew that Mum had this covered, but it felt unnatural to not know the ins and outs of my sister's life.

'Seriously, where are you?'

'You talking to yourself again, Sage? Is this how you get pumped up for a game?' Teddy put his hands on my shoulders, jostling me. I felt the contact all the way down my spine.

'Is this the kind of wit you were using to make friends before you met me? I can almost see how it was so unsuccessful.'

He squeezed his water bottle so that a spray of water hit me square in the face. 'Touché. Please use that venom on the court, I need a win today. I couldn't open a can of beans this morning and it set the tone for the whole day. I need to feel victorious.'

I checked my phone for messages one last time before Teddy shut the locker. He paused, noticing my hesitation to leave my phone behind. 'You good?'

I sighed. I knew my sister. When she wanted to get in contact, she would.

'Yeah, I'm good. Let's win this thing.'

★★★

'Break point!' One of our opponents called out the score, letting us know that we were one serve away from losing the match.

Teddy smirked and looked at me. 'If our story had a narrator, they would say "Flick and Teddy did *not*, in fact, win this thing".'

I'd been naive in thinking I wouldn't be a bit rusty after taking a couple of months off from tennis. That, paired with the fact that Teddy hadn't been kidding when he'd said he was a beginner, meant that we were facing quite the defeat. I wasn't playing competitively – it was more about creating a community – but it still hurt. As soon as Teddy had seen the twenties list he'd mocked up an action plan, Post-it notes included. Right at the top had been 'start a tennis tournament'. It was going to be impossible for me to really start playing tennis again if it wasn't with other people, and Teddy wanted to find a way to introduce himself to some of the other people who frequently spent their weekday evenings here, so we'd posted a note on the pinboard at reception. A plea for doubles teams to play with us, whatever their ability. Slowly we'd mapped out a mini tournament for the next few weeks. As it turned out, there were a lot of people here that were looking for ways to fill their time. For a city that supposedly was always moving, there seemed to be a significant number of inhabitants that felt stagnant.

'Here goes nothing.' Teddy served the final shot.

I held my breath. 'Shit.'

The ball hit the net before it could gain any speed. Hitting the net was Teddy's signature move, I was learning.

'And . . . match.' The guy on the other side of the net gave his partner a high five.

'Don't take a photo of this for the column.' Teddy braced his hands on his knees. 'It's too humiliating. The net is my greatest nemesis.'

I smiled to myself. 'Everybody has to start somewhere.'

'That's what people say when someone is horrifically bad at something.'

Laughing, I shrugged. 'What do you want me to do, lie?'

'He's not that bad.' The shorter of the two men that we'd been playing (I was pretty sure his name was Nathan) jogged over. 'And without both of you, this whole thing wouldn't exist. Do you want me to log the scores?'

He was talking about the whiteboard we'd set up in the changing rooms, a makeshift way of tracking the tournament.

Everyone was getting quite into it; there'd even been a scuffle last week when someone contested the results.

'Do we have to record this one?' Teddy winced.

'Yes, we do. Three more wins and it's straight to the top for us.' Another high five between our opponents. I didn't have to look over at Teddy to know that he was trying not to react.

'Are you going to post another email with next week's schedule?' The question was directed at me. All three men looked at me expectantly, including Teddy. The admin associated with the twenties list was starting to feel like another full-time job. If nothing else, I slept really well at night now.

'Yep, I'll send around an email.'

Nathan grinned. 'Thanks. You're doing a great job with this. My weeknights were beyond boring until this doubles thing got started.'

We packed up our stuff to take back to the lockers, Teddy smirking from behind his water bottle. 'Did you hear that? You're doing a great job.'

I fought with a smile and lost. 'What's your point, Theodore?'

He laughed. 'You really are doing a great job with this, and the list in general. It makes me want to make the most of my time in London too.' I must have been smiling because he reached out and touched the corner of my mouth. 'Happy with that?'

I grabbed my work clothes from the locker. 'Ecstatic. Just what I needed to get through the evening.'

'I thought as much.' He swung his backpack over his shoulders. 'Split a pizza with me?'

201

This was swiftly becoming a Tuesday routine. Finish work and head to the courts together, and then share a 50–50 pizza after – half veggie deluxe for him, half chicken and pepperoni for me, and a large raspberry Fanta, two straws. I liked our Tuesday set-up.

'Yeah, I'm in.'

'Perfect.' Teddy was looking at the photo I'd taken of him prior to the match, adopting a ridiculous position with his racket. When I posted about this in the column, I'd probably say that the pizza outing was an actual date, and I'd probably say something gross about having a teammate on and off the court. Whatever it took to make Cecilia happy. At least the tennis tournament and pizza part of the story was real. It made the whole thing feel like less of a sham. However I decided to spin it for the column, tonight just felt like two friends splitting dinner after completely bombing a tennis match. And I loved it.

★★★

The house was unusually silent when I walked through the door an hour later. It crossed my mind that maybe the house invasion had finally happened. *What did you do in this situation?* I tried to think of what I'd seen on TV as I hung my scarf up. The house was never silent. Ever.

'Anyone home?'

No answer. Weighing up the danger, I went into the kitchen and flicked the switch on the kettle. I desperately wanted a hot bath and a cup of tea, and I did not want to sit on the curb in the cold outside. I was willing to take the risk that the house was being invaded. My muscles wouldn't be able to take it if I didn't get straight into a bath that was borderline-boiling, with just the right amount of Epsom salts.

Whilst I waited for the kettle to boil, I pulled up the BuzzFeed article I'd been reading on the Tube. Kitty had sent it to all of us following a conversation we'd had last night about the actual validity of horoscopes (I was firmly on the side of 'not valid'). This was the kind of scintillating conversation you had in a houseshare.

Suze: Sorry, been completely MIA I know. Been a weird few days. How are you?

It popped up on my screen whilst I was reading about the position of the moon. Thank God she was alright.

Me: I've missed you! Things are good, saw Mum and Dad at the weekend.

I missed out that I knew she'd been at their house. I didn't want her to think we'd all been speaking about her; she had a tendency to get very defensive very quickly.

Suze: They mentioned :) I'm incredibly jealous that you took Dad to that pasta place before you took me, he's been going on about it all week. Fancy a trip to Liverpool soon?

She didn't have to ask me twice. I made a mental note to book tickets tonight. I was already looking forward to walking along the Albert Dock with Suze; the fresh air was the best medicine. And hopefully, I'd be able to get to the bottom of what exactly was going on.

The kettle popped and I poured water into my favourite chipped mug from the Manchester Christmas markets, watching the water darken and swirl as I poured the milk in. It was oddly satisfying to make a cup of tea without the various sounds that accompanied a busy group of women. I was halfway to the stairs when I heard a sniff from Stacey's room. *Shit.* Was our house invader crying? I heard another mini sniffle. I knew that sound well; I was usually the one making it.

'Stacey?' I knocked lightly on her door and was met with silence on the other side of the wood. 'I thought no one was home. Are you alright?'

After waiting another few moments, I backtracked, giving her space. I had just turned away when the door opened, revealing a very sad looking housemate. The skin around her eyes was red. She gestured for me to come in, and I perched on the edge of her unmade bed, putting my mug on her bedside table. Stacey plopped herself on the comforter next to me, immediately starting to sniff again. It was such a contrast to her usual demeanour – always positive, bubbly – that I was momentarily stunned.

'Has something happened?'

She started bawling again. *Oops.* I racked my brain, trying to think if she'd had anything significant going on today. I came up empty.

EMILY MERRILL

'It's just –' She wiped her nose. 'I've got this family meal tomorrow, and I really don't want to go.'

Of course. She was meeting her parents and her younger siblings in Soho tomorrow for dinner; a rare occasion when they were all going to be in the same place at the same time. I wasn't sure why she was hesitant about going, so I just waited. Most of the time, if you gave people the space to speak, they would.

'We're hardly ever in the same room if it isn't Christmas Day. Both of my siblings went away for university, and they don't really come back. I'm the only one of us that stayed here.'

Stacey was a Londoner through and through. I tried and failed to picture her in Manchester, or Liverpool.

'Are you not looking forward to it? Actually, stupid question. Obviously you're not.'

A smile broke through the sniffs. 'Not the best at this, are you?'

'No, but I did just make a cup of tea.' I passed her my mug. 'Mind the chip on the left-hand side.' As much as I wanted it, it was clear that Stace needed it more than I did right now.

She took it. 'Thanks. I don't usually go for the dirty water the rest of you seem to like so much, but these are desperate times.'

Stace was one of those weird people who didn't like a cup of tea. We all tried not to hold it against her, but it was hard.

'In theory, I always look forward to meeting up with my family. We've always been close, especially since my grandparents passed away. It's made us more of a unit. But recently –'

She hiccupped. I waited.

205

'Recently I've just been feeling like such a *failure*. Toby, my brother, has just bought a house with his girlfriend, and Boo is smashing it at uni. Just came top of her class in one of the assignments.'

I knew better than to ask about the name Boo. I was no stranger to weird nicknames.

'I never went to university, I've never left London apart from to go on girls' holidays to Ibiza, and I'm not even in the realm of thinking about buying a house. How am I the oldest, and yet the most stuck?' She passed me the mug back. 'I thought I was sad enough to stomach that, but I just can't do it. Sorry, Flick.'

It made me really sad to think of Stace alone in her bedroom, comparing herself to her siblings because she couldn't afford a house yet. Stacey was beautiful; she was the kind of woman that you immediately wanted to be friends with, who walked into situations with the kind of hope that most people lost after childhood. She was a lot more than the daughter and sibling who couldn't afford a house deposit.

I gave her a side hug. 'You know, you remind me a lot of my sister. The kind of person you can always depend on. You can't learn that at university or buy it with a deposit.'

It was true; Stacey might be all over the place, but she had compassion in abundance. She didn't seem convinced, so I tried again.

'I watched you redo the silicon in our bathroom with ease last week. I can't even change a bulb without shorting the fuse. We don't like to go on about it in case it goes to your head, but you're a bit of a legend.'

Finally, the hint of a smile. 'That's a big statement for a girl who can't seem to move out of this house. When Tara left, I couldn't believe that I was behind *again*. That's why I was so weird about everything. I feel like I'm a dusty frame on the wall of the living room, or the weird lime that's been in the fridge forever that everyone refuses to touch.'

That lime had seen things. I shuddered. 'Well, I for one am glad that you were here when I moved in.'

'This is true,' she mused, 'you would never have become friends with Teddy if it wasn't for my meddling.'

I nodded. 'I have to admit, it was actually one of your finer moves. Even if I do have to live a lie now. I've gained four friends since moving into Carlisle, and two of them have been your doing. Adulthood is weird, and it makes you feel like you're a failure when you aren't. It should be about finding your own timeline, not comparing yours to anyone else's.'

Stacey was fiddling with a magazine that was discarded on her bed, and she was smirking now. 'I don't know if it's because you've become an agony aunt, but I swear you weren't this wise when you moved in.'

I laughed. 'God, I know.'

'A small selfish part of me was relieved to see that someone else was a bit of a mess too. Shame you managed to clear that up.'

I poked her. 'I've got a fake relationship and I'm living in a room the size of a utility cupboard. Most nights when I get in from work I make instant noodles and eat an apple afterwards for balance. I saw my ex-boyfriend in the middle of Camden and bawled on the Tube for twenty minutes afterwards.'

'You're right, total mess.' Stacey laid her head on my shoulder. 'Thanks for the dirty water, even if I didn't drink it. Still appreciated.'

'You're welcome. Do you want the bath that I was about to run?'

She grinned. 'Wow, I must be in a state if you're offering up your post-tennis-match bath.'

'What can I say? You were all there for me during the shower weeping phase.'

Stace winced. 'Don't, it's too soon to joke.'

'Tragedy plus time equals comedy.'

'Not yet.' She shuddered. 'Not yet. Well, I think I'll take you up on your offer. I've been eyeing up those bath salts all week.'

I ran a bath for Stace, sprinkling in extra bath salts, then headed back down to her room. I stayed there for a minute after she went upstairs, folding some of the clothes on the floor and tidying up. I always felt better when things were in order in my room. As soon as Suze had arrived at my flat after the dumping, she'd sat me down, cracked open a bottle of wine, and started tidying my kitchen for me. This, now, made me think of my sister even more. Seeing Stace so unsure of herself had shocked me. Maybe, even when you acted as though you had everything figured out, you still had those moments of panic. Maybe Suze was having one of those moments right now. I pulled up the train app on my phone and booked tickets to go and see my sister.

# 22

I stepped off the train at Lime Street Station, already searching for my sister in the crowd even though there were so many heads bobbing in front of me under the big glass ceiling. London crowds still caused my chest to tighten sometimes, but the crowds here never did. The accents around me tilted upwards at the end of their sentences; it felt like home.

I spotted my sister's messy bun, her face brightening at the sight of me. This was technically her city now, but growing up it had always been ours. Some of our best memories were here.

'Flick!' Suze gestured for me to squeeze through the crowd to a corner of the station where the footfall was less hectic, right in front of the arrivals and departures board. She wrapped me in a giant hug, squeezing for just a second longer than usual.

'Hi Suze.' I hugged her back, closing my eyes and relishing the feeling of complete security. We'd never needed a comfort blanket growing up – we had each other. 'How are you?'

'Oh, you know.' She flapped her hands around a bit. 'Busy with work. Shall we go get a coffee? It feels like it's been too long.'

She pulled me to the entrance of the station, walking quickly. It was a running joke that if you walked with Suze, you had to be prepared to take some painkillers at the end of the day.

'That's because it *has* been too long.' In reality it had only been a few weeks since brunch. But that was an age for us.

'I've put my fancy bedding on the spare bed for you. It's leopard print.'

'Leopard print? That's so unlike you.'

She nudged me. 'I'm surprised you could spare a weekend with such short notice. Life sounds so hectic in London now.'

In all honesty, it hadn't been easy to get here. I'd been writing my next column on the train, all about feeling the pressure to get on the property ladder, and the pressure put on people in their twenties in general. Teddy, Sophie and all of my housemates were going out to the pub tonight; I could see from the group chat that they were discussing when to congregate. None of that really mattered though, not now I was here.

I linked my arm through my sister's and hiked my weekend bag further up on my shoulder. 'Never too busy for you. Shall we go to Leaf?'

Suze smiled. 'Classic.'

★★★

We sank back into the wide sofas at our favourite coffee shop in Liverpool. We'd spent so many evenings here when I was in sixth form; in fact, this was where Suze had played one of her first professional gigs. Fairy lights were strung around each corner of the large open space, and there were plants everywhere. It reminded me a lot of Kitty's room.

'Okay, so give me the latest Flick run-down.' Suze cradled her matcha (I had a much tamer breakfast tea in my hands). 'Are you fake-married yet? I feel really bad about how I reacted to the whole thing.'

'Hilarious, but no. Still happily fake-dating.' I poured some milk from the tiny jug on the table. 'It doesn't matter, it's forgotten. I promise. It *does* sound kind of ridiculous.'

She laughed. 'We've all done crazy things for work. I think I was just worried that your life was way more interesting than mine. Do you remember the time that I didn't sleep for forty-eight hours just to fold hundreds of origami swans? That experience shaved a good five years off my life.'

'Not only do I remember *you* not sleeping for forty-eight hours, but I remember all four of us staying up until 3 a.m. together doing it. I don't think I've ever received payment.'

'Your payment is my presence in your life. So, Mum showed me a picture of this Teddy guy that she'd found on Facebook.'

I scowled. 'Of course she did.'

'Yep. I think their whole street is reading your column now. I wouldn't be surprised if she prints them out and posts them through letterboxes like a cold caller.'

'So *that's* where all the troll comments must come from. I knew Colin next door never liked me.'

Suze choked on a sip of coffee. 'Yep. Our tennis ball went over the fence *one time* and he's never forgotten it. I read about your successful sourdough loaf. How is the rest of the list going?'

I filled her in on some of the other items I'd ticked off, pulling the Polaroids out of my bag to show her. I now had about ten, including some new photos featuring me with panda eyes on the Tube (Kitty said that we needed to remember it, so that we could track my progress), Felix hugging the outside of the brownie cart, and Maia sitting candid on the sofa, a rare moment of relaxing in front of *SAS: Who Dares Wins*. That girl was an enigma.

Suze held them up between her fingers. 'I love these. They have such a retro feel to them.' Suze lifted one to the light to get a better look. 'Is this him?'

The photo was all of us sat around the breakfast bar at Carlisle, playing gin rummy. Teddy had one arm slung around my shoulders, halfway through a burst of laughter. We had all been smashed at that point in the evening.

'He looks kind.' She shook her head. 'I can't believe you convinced him to go along with the whole thing. You'd better be getting a pay rise for this, Flick.'

My sister wasn't the first person to ask me that. Maia had also made quite the face when I'd informed them all that no, I was just in it for the potential of a promotion at the end.

'To be honest, I'm just enjoying the experience. How often do you get to write a column?'

'True. Well, I guess that's the whole point. You can definitely tick that one off your list. Not many of us get to *actually* be an agony aunt. Even if I feel like yours sometimes.' She smirked. 'Shall we split these?'

We'd ordered a slice of coffee and walnut cake and a salted caramel brownie to share. I cut into them both with a knife and stuck my half of the brownie straight in my mouth. 'London has some cool coffee shops, but does anything really beat this?'

'No, it does not. I haven't been here in so long.'

That was a red flag. Whether it was to watch other people sing or to perform herself, or even just to work with a coffee, Suze was always in here. She was fiddling with a loose thread on her cardigan whilst she glanced around, looking a bit melancholy.

I changed tack. 'Played any cool gigs lately?'

Suze didn't know that our parents had told me about a few of her gigs getting cancelled. I hoped it was beginning to pick up again; this was Liverpool – there was never a time of year when music wasn't a big part of the city.

'It's a bit too sporadic for my liking.' She didn't elaborate immediately. 'It's such a big part of my life. I don't like it when the work is slow. I guess I'm lucky to have two jobs. Shouldn't be complaining.'

Her eyes seemed tired, and I noticed she looked a bit paler without the lipstick that was usually her trademark. I watched the thread from her cardigan get longer and longer.

'You're going to have none of that left.'

'It's thrifted. It was probably on its way out.' She used the knife to cut through the cotton. 'Fixed it.'

I took a bite of the coffee and walnut. 'You know, it's okay to be sad about not getting gigs. That's your passion project.'

Suze shook her head. 'You're here for the weekend to have *fun*. I don't want to be sad about anything.'

'May I remind you that the last couple of times you've visited me, I've either been sobbing my heart out to the *Les Mis* soundtrack, or hungover.'

I did feel bad about the quality of my hosting skills during Suze's last couple of trips to London. I needed to rectify that and bring her along to one of Kitty's sets, or take her to the pasta restaurant that Dad had liked so much. Maybe she could meet Teddy. I wanted to know what she thought.

'Looking after each other is what we do.' Her smile didn't quite reach her eyes.

*Let me, then.*

Next to us, a young couple were sharing some kind of smoothie, two straws dipping into the same drink. They looked like students, and for a split second I was overcome with a wave of my own grief. I batted it away, focusing on the task at hand.

'So,' I changed the subject, sensing that this was a no-go, 'any gossip?'

When I had first arrived at uni, sitting on my bed in halls and working up the courage to use the Jack and Jill bathroom, I used to call Suze every night. I'd lived for the tales of her and her friends back home here in Liverpool. Suze hadn't gone to university, instead moving straight into the city and getting a job to pay the rent. Out of the two of us, she'd always been the sister bursting to break free. And the stories of the friends she'd made when she got here were iconic.

'I actually haven't seen the girls much lately. I've been really busy with work . . .' She stared out of the window.

Worry hit me like a strike to the gut. 'Not even Codie?'

Codie was her best friend, the girl that she'd lived with in her first flat. Me and my sister were as close as sisters could be, but we were strikingly different. She and Codie, however, were peas in a pod. Their first flat together had been a bohemian wonderland.

'No, Codie got a new boyfriend. They moved in together last month.'

I didn't know that. 'What's he like?'

Suze shrugged. 'He's alright. Not good enough for Codie, although I'm not sure anyone would be.'

That sounded more like my sister.

'I have to say, I didn't see it coming. Her moving on without me.' She necked back the last of her matcha. 'Ready to go?'

I was more than a little confused, but I nodded, grabbing my bag.

★★★

When I'd been living in my student house in my final year, I'd been insanely jealous of Suze's flat. She had been 'curating her space' for years, picking up bits and bobs at markets and antique stores. There was a cool print of the docks on the wall in her hallway, the first striking piece of art that you saw when you came in through the front door. She had one of those retro record players – lime green – and everywhere you turned there were recipe books and memoirs and vinyl records. It was so incredibly *Suze*. Right now, though, it left little to be desired. There were dishes stacked up by the sink, and a layer of dust coated the giant mirror in her living room. Clothes were in random piles on the floor; her favourite red jacket slung haphazardly over the radiator. I had to say, I was a bit taken aback.

'I know it's messy right now.' She must have sensed I was about to comment. 'But I just don't have time. I'll pick everything up in the next week or two.'

*The next week or two?* Stacey, I would expect that from. I'd be worried if she said the opposite. But Suze? This was not my big sister.

'Shall we get Indian or Lebanese tonight?' She had an app up on her phone, scrolling through the choices. 'The Chinese we always get isn't very good any more. They changed hands and the veggie curry is literally just a handful of mushrooms in watery sauce.'

'You're really selling it.' We'd just eaten those huge slices of cake; I could barely stomach the thought of eating anything else (and that was saying something). Suze's energy was frantic, like she was trying to distract me from the state of the flat.

She made a face at me. 'I just really want fatteh. *Please* let me have fatteh.'

She looked a bit like she was about to cry. She was blinking, hard.

'Lebanese it is. Are you sure that you're –'

'Tabbouleh?' She interrupted me. 'If you don't get your orders in here early, you completely miss the boat.'

She was skirting past the issue. Her flat, her inability to disclose almost anything about her life . . . I was concerned.

216

It felt foreign. Suze wasn't someone you often needed to feel concerned about. I felt the dynamic shift, sitting down on her sofa and pulling a random pair of jeans out from under me.

'Suze?'

She glanced up from where she was pouring wine. 'Yeah?'

'Is everything . . . alright?' In my head, I'd planned it more eloquently.

'What do you mean?' Again, that false smile was back. A little too wide. Held a little too long.

'You seem . . .' I searched for the word.

'Seem what?' She laughed. 'Come on, Flick, it's just me. I seem what?'

'Sad.' I gestured to the dishes. 'You seem sad.'

She paused for a moment before pouring more wine into both glasses. 'I'm not.'

'But when we were in that café, and I brought up Codie –'

Suze snapped. 'I said I'm not sad, Flick.'

There was an awkward pause, not unlike the one from our phone call a few weeks ago. Suze hardly ever snapped at me; it wasn't her style.

'Did you come here to pester me about this? Is that why you wanted to come and see me?'

I bit my lip. 'Well, it's just that Mum and Dad said –'

'You were talking about me behind my back?'

*Shit.* I hadn't meant to let that slip. I wasn't used to needing to tread so carefully.

'No, it just came up.'

For a moment, she looked like she might burst into tears again. And then she snapped out of it, rushing around the room and picking things up. She moved to the sink next, running the hot water tap and squeezing a third of a bottle of Fairy Liquid into the bowl.

'The flat being a mess doesn't mean anything, Flick. It's just me being lazy. I'm fine, okay? *Fuck.*' She yanked her hand away from the hot tap, cradling her palm. She was panicking, her hair out of its bun, tendrils flying around her face. The T-shirt under her dungarees looked creased.

I backed off, trying to tiptoe around her. 'Okay, let me do that. Please go and run that under some cold water.' I walked to the sink. 'I didn't mean to offend you.'

She took a deep breath. 'I know. I just –'

The sentence trailed off, and she disappeared to the bathroom. The flat was silent for a few minutes. The stack of dirty dishes in front of me dwindled, replaced slowly with a clean pile on the other side of the sink. When I was done, I picked up her red jacket from the radiator, lighting her incense to make the room smell more like home. When I'd done as much as I could, I peeked in her cupboards. A can of beans, a couple of Pot Noodles. A packet of crumpets that had seen better days. I made a mental note to suggest going to the fruit and veg market in Clayton Square tomorrow morning. After I was done snooping (when you're worried about someone, anything goes) I sat on the sofa and waited. When she re-entered a few minutes later, looking decidedly less like she might bolt out of the front door, she sat next to me, placing her hand on top of mine.

'I'm sorry, Flick.'

I wasn't exactly sure what the apology was for, but I didn't press.

'Work is just manic right now. It's been a lot.' She passed me the glass of wine she'd originally been pouring for me. 'Olive branch?'

She seemed much more like herself now, her smile genuine for the first time all day. She'd clearly gone and splashed her face with cold water. I took the wine. 'There's no need for an olive branch. I will take the wine though, since you're offering.'

I clinked my glass against hers, fighting against the concern that was still bubbling underneath the surface.

# 23

'Have you got everything? Your ticket? Your phone charger?'

I patted my pockets. 'Sorted.'

My sister pulled me in, hugging me tight. 'I'm sorry about Friday night. You really cheered me up by coming here. I needed a dose of Flick.'

Before this moment, she hadn't admitted that she'd needed cheering up. The whole of the weekend had been spent pretending that Friday night hadn't happened. Yesterday had been a typical Suze blur, packing as much as we could into the one full day we had. This city was never boring, whether we were walking along the river, hot chocolates in hand, or stuffing our faces at the Baltic Market. It was now Sunday morning, and I was blinking away the effects of the bottle of wine we'd stayed up to drink last night. It had been 2 a.m. when we'd finally admitted defeat, halfway through watching *John Tucker Must Die*. She'd seemed alright yesterday, miles better than the previous day. I'd thought that this trip would leave me with some clarity – either she was okay, and our parents were worrying too much, or she'd have told me what was going on. I'd been left with an uncomfortable sort of middle ground.

She caught me wincing at the bright lights in the station. 'Lightweight.'

'It was that cheap wine.'

She shrugged. 'Needs must. So, what are your plans when you get back?'

I was actually going to Teddy's flat for the first time, for dinner. That is, if he texted me back. I think the gang were all feeling a bit fragile after last night, because it was almost lunchtime and I hadn't heard from anyone back home in London. It was nice to imagine Teddy and the Carlisle girls spending time together without me; I knew that having a group of friends was something he'd been trying to find for quite some time.

'I'm probably going to cram in some work. The column takes a lot of time away from the other work Cecilia piles into my inbox.' *Why hadn't I mentioned going to Teddy's?*

She frowned. 'You aren't working yourself too hard, are you?'

'Suze, I'm the grad. I live and breathe working myself too hard.'

Her face fell. 'Sorry, I guess I wouldn't know.'

Our different pathways at 18 had never been a sore spot before. In fact, Suze had always prided herself on her decision not to go to university.

'You were wise to go straight into work. I wouldn't still be making cups of tea for people if I had. Mum says that you're going to theirs tonight? For a roast?'

I panicked for a second that she might have latched on to the idea of us talking about her again but she didn't notice, just picked at a hangnail.

'Yeah. I've missed Dad's roast potatoes. What can I say?'

She clearly didn't know that I knew she'd been going every week for the past month.

'Right.' I glanced up at the departures board. 'Platform five.' I tucked my phone into my back pocket. 'Are you sure you're going to be okay?'

Suze nodded, her smile tight. 'I'm fine, seriously. I've just had my coil fitted and it's probably sending me loopy. Fill me in on anything else that happens in London, nightmare run-ins with the ex-boyfriend included. I still can't believe that even happened.'

'C'est la vie.' I hoisted my overnight bag further up on my shoulder. 'It made the column way better anyway.'

'That column makes you *wild*. Aside from the sourdough. That mundane update was actually very useful.'

'That was all Maia. No credit due here.'

'Well, you can thank her from me. I ate a slice as soon as it came out of the oven. Lathered it with butter.' She made a sex noise. 'Anyway, the point I was making is that the column is very cool. I'm proud of you.'

'The twenties list was *your* idea.'

Suze shrugged. 'Yeah, but I don't think my list was quite in the same league. It's making me want to pick mine up again and add a few more things.'

I listened to her talk about learning to cross stitch and make croissants for a minute, glancing anxiously at the departures board. Usually, when I came to visit Suze she had a busy Sunday planned, running off to meet Codie or her friends from work, barely able to wait with me until my train arrived. It was like an alternative reality, and I felt bad leaving her behind.

She suddenly squeezed me tight. 'Call me this week?'

'Of course.'

As I walked away to find my platform, I glanced back at my sister, getting smaller and smaller in the distance. She didn't know I was looking; she was staring at the floor and biting her lip. I didn't know what to report back to my parents, I had no idea what was going on.

★★★

Teddy met me outside Stratford Tube station. He'd offered to meet me off my train from Liverpool when it arrived at Euston, but I'd declined. I didn't want him to have to go out of his way for me, despite how nice it might have been to hand my bag over. I'd spent the whole journey crushed up against three other people. I rolled my shoulders out, relaxing my body again.

'I hope you're ready to try the world's *best* pierogi.' He wrapped his arm around my shoulder, giving me a squeeze. Somewhere along the way, the affection he'd shown me when we snapped a photo for the column or when he came to the office had seeped into our quieter, more platonic moments. The first time it had happened he'd frozen, overly apologetic. But it was nice, in a way. To feel completely comfortable with someone, without the risk that they might break your heart.

I jostled his side. 'That's a bold statement. I've been to Kraków. I've tasted some delicious pierogi in my time.'

'Only a scaredy cat backtracks. And I, for one, am not a scaredy cat.'

'Didn't you ask me to catch a spider for you in your office the other day?' He'd sent me a text, asking me to hotfoot it to the third floor to catch a (tiny) eight-legged creature. I'd finally seen the other offices – they didn't have a patch on *Influence*. No custard creams in sight.

Teddy looked wounded. 'You promised never to speak of that again.'

'My lips are sealed from now on. You have my word.'

'Much appreciated.' He gestured to the block of flats we'd arrived outside, pulling open the door. 'After you. Also, don't be expecting much from this place. It's no Carlisle.'

It was funny. Our little four bed in Acton wasn't really anything special, but people seemed to hold it to a higher standard. Proof that it was never really about the place, but the people in it. With Kitty's incense or the smell of Maia's cooking, our house always felt like a home.

'Nowhere is like Carlisle.'

Teddy nodded. 'Granted. Even so, my London life is a work in progress. It really isn't anything magical to look at. I know how you like to look at London through a gaze of wonder, but you'll struggle with this one.'

I smiled at his words. 'A gaze of wonder?'

'Yeah,' he pushed open a door after we'd climbed a flight of stairs, 'it's one of the things I like most about you. You never complain about the chewing gum on the streets, or the commuters, or the noise. You just moved to a city and slowly fell in love with it. I like that.'

'I'm not sure I was overjoyed with being here when I met you.'

He considered what I'd said. 'That was a blip. You can romanticise anything, I'm convinced. But this is the ultimate test, because this flat is a shithole. Okay, here goes.'

When he'd finally fished out his key, he waved me in first. It wasn't as bad as I'd been expecting, just small. There wasn't a lot of separation between the living room and the bedroom, just a single bed with a sofa three feet away from it, and a worn coffee table covered in printed coding.

'Am I privy to confidential information here?'

He pretended to freak out, and then grinned. 'Nah. I'm a pro, Sage, you don't see anything I don't want you to see.'

My eyes must have widened slightly because he flushed, moving on to show me the kitchen.

'It's tiny, but it's mine.'

I could see plates piled up ready to be stacked in the dish-washer; clearly, a lot of preparation had gone into this meal. The more I got to know Teddy, the more I realised how thoughtful he was. He picked places to meet with an easy route home for me, and when he'd been on his lunch break last week (knowing I was having a rough day in the office) he'd offered to bring me half of his sandwich.

'What are you smiling at? It isn't that impressive.' He was staring at my expression.

'Oh sorry, no. I like it. It's cosy.'

'If by cosy you mean incredibly cramped, then yes, I know exactly what you mean. Very, *very* cosy.'

I took my faux-fur jacket off, getting comfy on his sofa. 'I think people who live on their own always have places that give off this lived-in, safe vibe. Suze's flat is the same way. It's like, when you have to get used to your own company, you create the right place to do it.'

Teddy nodded. 'Huh. It turns out you can bring your gaze of wonder here too. Let me show you the mould in the bathroom, see what you can do with that. Drink?' He held up a mishmash of ingredients. 'I read on your column that you like an espresso martini, so I thought we could try it out.'

My cheeks warmed at the thought of him reading what felt like my diary entries, even if bits of it had been doctored. It was embarrassing to know that he'd read the false accounts of our dates, even though he was completely in on it and sometimes gave me ideas for the lies himself. I shook off the feeling. It was just Teddy.

'Sage? Espresso martini?'

I rolled up my sleeves. 'Let's do it.'

# 24

I had to admit, the food was delicious.

'Hats off to you, Theodore.' He pulled a face. 'This is some good stuff.'

He bowed from where he was sitting opposite me at the tiny dining table. 'It only took four tries to get it right. I'm kind of sick of eating pierogi for dinner, I have to say.'

'Just so you know, my cooking is sub-par in comparison. I don't have the commitment to eating the same thing all week in preparation.'

'You can pay me back with a brownie delivered to my office.' He smirked. It had become a routine; if either of us was making a trip to the cart, they had to buy two (three since last week when Felix got in on the deal).

'Be honest, the only reason you did all this' – I gestured to our almost empty plates – 'was so I'd incur brownie debt, wasn't it?'

'I'm offended that you would think that.' He paused. 'But you aren't totally wrong. Plus, when you and Felix visit my office my colleagues think I have a life for once. It's a win-win.'

I stabbed another pierogi with my fork, moaning as I bit into it. Teddy hid a smug smile behind his cocktail glass, clearly pleased with himself. He'd lit candles and balanced them on his bookshelves. If I wasn't crystal clear on the situation, I could definitely convince myself that this was a date.

'How is work going at the moment? Nosy colleagues aside.'

He shrugged. 'Same old, same old. I'm beginning to think that instead of being on the tech team for a whole office building, I should go into something more specialised. I've been playing around with computers since I left school, and I feel a bit past the point of telling people that they need to try turning their computer on and off again.'

'God, that wasn't anyone at *Influence,* was it?'

'No, it was someone from the events company on the floor below you. In all fairness, they were very thankful.'

Cecilia sometimes used the events company (much to Suze's horror) when she needed to throw a launch event. That had always been something that fascinated me about London, how transient the offices were. We were on floor six, and then below us was the events management start-up, a make-up brand, and an office that was always changing function as businesses were rolled in and out. At one point it had been a dog food company; it hadn't lasted too long.

'Speaking of events, how was your sister?' He got up to start clearing everything away.

I carried over our plates, moving on autopilot and loading them into his dishwasher. He complained about this flat, but I could count on one hand the amount of people I knew renting in London who had dishwashers.

'She's not great. Completely flipped out when I suggested that everything wasn't alright. I don't know what to do. I checked in with my parents yesterday – apparently when she's there she just curls up on the couch, she isn't her usual self at all. I know she normally helps Mum in the kitchen, or takes the dog for a walk with Dad. She doesn't seem to be interested in doing much. I want to help, but she isn't letting me in.'

'You know,' Teddy rinsed a bowl before handing it to me, 'she's probably defensive because she doesn't understand it either. It can be really hard to accept that you're struggling with your mental health.'

I bit my lip. It hadn't even occurred to me that something deeper might be going on. *Did that make me an awful sister?* I wanted to turn around and get on the train back to Liverpool, despite being three espresso martinis down. I was used to me and Suze talking *too much,* fighting to get all of our stories out before we parted ways. This silence between us was harder to interpret, but she'd been with me throughout all my hardest moments. I wanted to be there for hers.

Teddy rubbed my shoulder. 'Whatever it is that your sister is struggling with, you care enough to keep an eye on it. That counts for a lot. When one of my brothers, Greg, was in sixth form, he really struggled. My parents didn't know what to do, but in the end all that mattered was that we were there for him, and we listened.'

It was really sweet to hear Teddy talk about his family – something he rarely opened up about. Hearing him talk like this gave me a sneaking suspicion that he was homesick.

'How is your brother now?'

He smiled at the thought. 'Oh, Greg is doing really well for himself. He works in graphic design; he's actually very good. I fix the computers, but I have no idea how to do anything creative with them.'

'What do your other siblings do?'

Teddy grinned. 'Well, my parents own a little café, back in Leeds. Good coffee, good sandwiches, good cake. That kind of thing. My older sister, Mika, is manager there. Greg is next, and then me right in the middle. My younger brothers – Otis and Max, they're twins – help out in the café when they can. They've just graduated, and from what I can tell they're still figuring it all out. That's all five of us.'

'God, I still can't believe how many siblings you have. And everyone in their twenties! Your mum must have had her hands full with you all.'

'Tell me about it. The fun never ends. Mum and Dad are the OG agony aunts. It amuses everyone that there are so many of us. I was the middle child so school was bearable, but by the time the twins got there the teachers were having a field day with it. And don't even get me started on when it comes to Christmas. I'd rather avoid the whole thing altogether than have to buy presents for that many people.'

'Scrooge.'

He lifted his eyebrows. 'You try living in London and having a family that big at Christmas. I was eating pesto pasta for a solid month. God help us when people start having kids. Another martini?'

I could get used to coming here. The service was impeccable. 'Do you even have to ask?' I held out my glass.

Teddy focused on the task at hand for a moment, adding the ingredients to the cocktail shaker. He had one of those cool barista machines in the corner of his kitchen (more living proof that no matter how tiny a flat was, you could make it your own), and he carefully levelled out the coffee in the grinder before making the espresso shot. How had I never noticed how nice his hands were? *Woah there, Flick, stop creeping.*

I sipped the martini when he passed it over. 'So, let's play a game.'

Teddy grinned. 'Random, but okay. Hit me with it.'

'It's the alcohol, I automatically resort to games. Although no Ring of Fire, I promise. Me and Suze used to play this one in the back of the car when we went on family holidays. Three words to describe each other.'

'That game must have been over quickly.'

'Funny. We used to do it for anyone – three words to describe the Queen, three words to describe our dog, three words to describe our dad. I'm just personalising it to make it interesting.'

'Interesting is a stretch.'

I huffed. 'Fine. You come up with a game.'

'No, I'll bite. I'm no famous writer like you, though, so give me a minute.'

He tapped his fingers on his knees, thinking.

We'd played this game the other night, Stacey getting annoyed when Maia described her as 'dramatic', and Kitty laughing so hard she almost cried when I used the word 'practical' for Maia. To be fair, she'd seemed quite pleased with the description, saying she'd add it to her CV. They'd used the word 'spontaneous' for me, which was a first. Until the twenties list, no one ever would have associated that label with me. I was intrigued as to how Teddy would describe me. He was beginning to look a bit stressed.

'I'll go first, since it was my idea.' I thought of my friend, who'd been practising his pierogi all week. 'So, first: considerate.'

Teddy smiled. 'Are you just trying to make my head bigger?'

'Of course.'

'Carry on, then. Second word?'

I closed my eyes, picturing Teddy in the pub that night, agreeing to be my fake date. 'Second word for you is adaptable.'

'How so?'

'Well, I met you playing tennis, and then the next day you showed up at work in a suit. You agreed to be my fake boyfriend, and now you're serving me pierogi. Who knows what you'll do next, Teddy Stewart.' I leaned forward on my hands. 'And third: fortuitous. Because you're the happiest accident I've encountered in a long while.'

'You are good at this game. I need to cook for you more often.'

'It's always a good plan to butter me up with food.' I shrugged.

'Can hungry be one of your words?'

I shot him a look.

'Kidding, kidding. After much consideration, your first word is honest.'

'That's rich. From one liar to another.'

Teddy choked back a laugh. 'These are special circumstances – we're attempting London media domination. But in general, I feel like you're completely transparent with the world about what you want from it, and how you're feeling. It's a rare thing, Sage.'

I thought about it. I guess I was pretty open about what I wanted, especially lately. For four years I'd gone along with someone else's plans. I refused to do that any more.

'I'll accept that. Feel free to continue to shower me with praise.'

'Lord, my fake girlfriend is hard to please.' He rubbed his hands together. 'Okay, second word is fearless.'

'You should see me if a moth flies into my bedroom.'

Teddy sighed. 'I might change my second word to idiot. Moths aside, I could never have moved here and gone for it the way you have when I was 21. Let alone face the challenges you have over the past few months. I've lived here for six and I was really struggling until I met you. And I've got three years more life experience.'

He continued. 'And even though I know first-hand how hard it is to put yourself out there and do all of the things that being a young person in this city requires, you just do it. You just take it all in your stride. You're kind of inspiring, Felicity.'

My cheeks warmed, both at his use of my first name – I just couldn't bring myself to hate it in this context – and the compliment. I wondered if he'd have called me fearless if he'd seen me that first day at Carlisle. It seemed funny to me now that I'd once been so scared of the three girls that had turned my London experience around.

'So, is inspiring your final word?' I could feel my skin was still flushed, but I didn't want to let him know how much his words had touched me.

He shook his head. 'Don't cheat me out of my final expla-nation. My final word is vibrant. I've never met someone as alive as you are.'

I blushed even harder. 'You know, this game was a brilliant idea. I don't think I'm going to get my head through your front door.'

'Well, I know you don't like to talk about it, but I can tell that you started these last few months feeling decidedly un-vibrant.'

It was funny. Until this conversation I hadn't even thought about Aaron tonight. I could imagine how he might have scoffed at the game, reeling off three random words just so he could get back to his computer. Obviously, four years into a relationship, things were different, but I didn't think he'd ever have put that much thought into his answers.

'I think the readers are going to have a field day with this game.' He spoke through a mouthful of leftover pierogi that he'd snagged off the counter. 'This will earn me brownie points. Did you know that one of the comments last week coined us 'Fleddy'? It's official. We have a ship name.'

'We do? Wow.'

He nodded. 'Yep. And we need to get our heads back in the game. We both called this a fake relationship, but we aren't supposed to be official yet. There's meant to be a big moment, right? In fact' – he clapped his hands together – 'why not make it tonight?'

He stood up and cleared his throat. 'Felicity Sage, will you be my fake girlfriend?'

I burst out laughing. 'I don't think you actually have to ask me. I can just make it up. No one will ever know.'

'Webs of lies are easier to spin when you've lived the lie, Flick. I thought you were meant to be a pro by now.'

I glanced around the room again at the effort he'd gone to tonight. The candles, the tidy flat, the food he'd been practising all week. The game. I didn't want to lie about this. 'You know what, I think I might pretend you asked me at our favourite Italian restaurant.'

Teddy was taken aback. 'After all this effort? I think your readers would be impressed.'

'I just don't feel like giving them this.' I watched him get up to carry on tidying the aftermath of his cooking. The actual food might have been pretty, but he clearly didn't clean up as he went along. Maia would have had a heart attack at the amount of washing up there was to do.

'Fair enough. But I did it on the walk home *after* the meal, okay? Nothing says cheesy like asking someone to be your girlfriend in an Italian restaurant.'

'Literally, cheesy.'

His head fell back as he groaned. 'Walked right into that one. Do I have something on my face? You keep looking at me weird and it's freaking me out.'

I startled. Had I been staring? 'No, you don't. Sorry.'

'Okay, weirdo. You just keep staring, then. How do you feel about ice cream? One tub, two spoons? There's a new conspiracy-theory documentary on YouTube that I think you're going to *love*.'

I watched him potter about, setting a tub of ice cream to melt whilst he loaded a tablet into the dishwasher. I had been staring. I was definitely in trouble.

★★★

## The Twenties List: The 'You Won't Believe This Update' Update

*Dear Reader,*

*I'm writing this week's column from underneath my duvet (insert a special, dedicated apology to my boss here), and I have BIG NEWS. Capital-letter-worthy news.*

*After bumping into my ex, which was not ideal – we won't harp on about that again – I now have an actual boyfriend. It still feels a bit weird to say it out loud, like I'm in the playground at primary school. If you'd told me a couple of months ago that I'd be writing this, I'd never have believed you, but it just feels right. Dating at 22 feels a lot different to dating at 18; back in my first year of uni it all felt more straightforward. I met my ex at an awkward halls mixer during freshers' week, and then we not so subtly hung out as 'friends' for a couple of months before we slept together, and the rest is history. Well, it's all history now. Dating as a 22-year-old is a complete trip. What is the difference between exclusive and official? Surely, if you aren't seeing anyone else, you're in a relationship. My housemates tell me I'm dead wrong, and they have the list of situationships to prove it.*

*Anyway, onto the juicy details. Me and Teddy went out for dinner last night at the cutest little Italian restaurant in Stratford (he got an olive linguini, I got the lasagne – you know the drill) and when he walked me home from the Tube, he asked me at my front door if I wanted to be his girlfriend. It was very sweet, very classic. He knows how much I love a movie moment and it felt just like we'd landed in one of my favourite romcoms. So, what happens now? Do I introduce him to my family? The tables have turned – I'm asking you for advice. Send us your thoughts using the usual links!*

*I've been thinking a lot about timelines this week, I think in part because I'm realising how different mine has turned out in comparison to what I'd expected from my twenties. For the first eighteen (and depending on whether you go to university or not, twenty-one-ish) years of your life, there's a somewhat clear structure set out in front of you. Finish GCSEs, finish A levels, go to uni. It's comforting in a way. Your twenties aren't like that, and it creates this whole realm of comparison. Who is buying a house first? Did that acquaintance I barely know on Instagram get a promotion before I even found my first job? It opens up this sad, competitive culture. Holly, from Newcastle, sent in a question this week that perfectly ties into what I'm about to say:*

**'Ever since we graduated, I've found it hard not to compare myself to my friends. We went to university at the same time, graduated simultaneously, so why do our lives seem so different now?'**

*Well, to quote Theodore Roosevelt (not my favourite Theodore of all time, don't worry, Teddy) 'Comparison is the thief of joy.' And it's true. I think we so often get caught up in the lives of everyone around us that we forget to focus on our own. It's like those wind-up toys that you get in Christmas crackers – all the toys are moving along at the same rate, and then all of a sudden a couple of the racers shoot ahead. Some people are gloating all over LinkedIn about their promotion, or posting photos of their new house keys on social media. I even saw someone I know from school post a baby scan last week. Our twenties feel like the first decade where literally anything is possible. No two paths are exactly the same, and it can be really hard to make peace with that. The night of my breakup, when my ex left our flat – bags packed and ready to flee – I'd stared at someone's engagement photo for twenty minutes straight. The grief I felt for that lost version of my future was immense.*

*Most of the time, all we see is a status update, or a tweet. We only get a tiny fraction of the story. That person who boasted about their promotion might be struggling to cope with the workload, and that colleague who has the picture-perfect weekends might be doubting their decision to move in with their partner. We don't see the arguments, or the job rejections, or the moments where things aren't going to plan (of which I'm sure there are so many).*

*If there's anything I've learnt so far from this year, this column, and living with a group of young women who have such varying goals, it's that your twenties really aren't up for comparison. Pacing is everything; you just have to find yours.*

*I hope that helps, Holly!*
*Flick x*

# 25

I read over the column before submitting it to Cecilia, biting my fingernails. This was the most dramatic lie yet, and I was starting to feel like a complete fraud. Did I back out now and pretend the Teddy thing hadn't worked out? It would be completely plausible. My finger hovered over the button.

'Felicity?' I jumped out of my skin, accidentally hitting send anyway. *For fuck's sake.* Once Cecilia caught sight of the development, she'd be all over it like a rash.

She came up behind me now, unaware that I was shooting her daggers. 'Sorry if I scared you. You're in the office early.'

It was before 8.30 a.m., but I was juggling two roles, and the agony aunt side of things was getting a bit demanding. 'Yeah, I just submitted the next column.'

Given that the damage was done, there was no risk with driving the nail into the coffin a little further.

'I look forward to reading it with my morning coffee. Carmen offered to get that this morning.' *Wow.* That was new.

'We need to run through the schedule today, Felicity. I don't want anything going wrong, this needs to be a tight procedure.'

240

*What?* 'Schedule?' My blood ran cold. Had I forgotten to do something? I'd thrown myself into work this week, so the idea that I might have missed something was a bit crushing.

'Yes. Alexis Lastbury is coming in today to interview you for her podcast. Did Sadie not tell you? It's a pretty big deal.'

I shot Sadie a look through the glass that separated our desks, even though she wasn't paying attention. She seemed to be eating a McDonald's hash brown at her desk. 'She did fail to mention that.'

Cecilia's expression blanched for a moment before she smoothed it out. 'Well, not to worry. It'll be relatively easy. Just remember to really exaggerate the modern dating thing.'

'How am I supposed to do that any more than I already am? A fake proposal?' I immediately regretted the sarcasm, stress clearly getting the better of me. 'Which, for the record, is definitely off the table.' I refused to give her any more wild ideas.

Cecilia scoffed at me. 'Don't act like you aren't loving that part of your assignment. You look at that young man like he hung the stars.'

'Pfft. I do *not*.'

She had to be joking at this point. Seriously.

'Anyway, Alexis is coming in at around 2 p.m. Fiona is happy to cover the admin for this afternoon, so it should all work out nicely. Ask Sadie to run you through the outline email that Alexis sent over yesterday morning. I asked Sadie to CC you in the conversation.'

Sadie and I were going to be having some serious words. 'Podcast, outline, got it.'

'And Flick?'

I smiled at my boss's use of my nickname.

'Yeah?'

Cecilia wrapped her knuckles on my desk. 'Brilliant work. You're a natural writer, and we're lucky to have you here.'

She turned around fast enough that I couldn't catch her expression. Probably on purpose. Cecilia didn't do affection if she could help it. Sadie finally spotted me through the glass.

'What's got you so happy?' She spoke through a mouthful, slurping her orange juice. The hash brown wrapper had been swiftly removed, but I could see it poking out of the bin.

'Well, it definitely isn't the email I was supposed to receive.'

Her eyes went wide. 'Oops. Yeah, that completely slipped my mind. I'll forward it to you now. I think you'll like Alexis. She's cool. I've considered emailing her back and asking if she wants to go for coffee with me.'

I let Sadie get back to stalking our client list and got my gel pens out of my bag, setting them up beside my planner and pulling up the email. I was not going to let the thought of a podcast interview scare me half to death. I was Felicity Sage and I'd done much scarier things. I could handle this.

The email was pretty straightforward, just an outline of the questions she'd be asking. Some were about my breakup and the origins of the column, and others were simple, like my go-to places for dinner and drinks in London, or my top five essentials for being a graduate in the city (one, don't get roped into a massive lie that your whole career depends on).

'Getting prepped for Alexis?' Felix sat down beside me, placing some sort of to-go box in front of him. I peeked into the parcel and saw an acai bowl.

'You'd better not be smirking over there. Me and Sebastian are doing a health kick this week.'

'Right. So did everyone know about this interview other than me?'

He shrugged. 'Likely. Alexis is a major catch. She's got a *lot* of followers.'

'Is that meant to make me feel more at ease?'

'Sorry. I saw Cecilia do a happy dance when she thought no one was looking after Sadie told her about the interview. The excitement was infectious.'

I tried to picture our boss doing a happy dance. I was struggling.

'Yeah, I know. Hard to imagine. Scout's honour though Flick. She did the worm and everything.'

'She did *not*.' I refrained from whacking him with a gel pen. 'I'm young, but I'm not stupid.'

'Speaking of young' – Felix brought up the website on his computer – 'have you seen how much you've rallied the twenty-somethings of London?'

In all honesty, I'd stopped checking on the engagement with the column last week, aware that if I knew I was writing for a large number of people, I'd become too bogged down by the pressure. 'No, I have not.'

He whistled. 'It's gone up even more since yesterday. Your comments section is in the triple digits now.'

I felt the blood drain from my face. 'Seriously?'

'Yep. You're definitely getting that spot in the June issue.'

The print issue. The light at the end of the tunnel. 'And then I can sink back into anonymity.'

'Yeah.' Felix laughed. 'Like that's going to happen. My bet is on a regular feature. I'm expecting a marriage proposal announcement in *OK!* magazine by the time the year is out.'

This time I didn't hold back, whacking him with the gel pen.

★★★

I heard the lift doors open, but I was so engrossed in the article about co-parenting I was proofreading that I didn't bother to look up until a sandwich landed on the keyboard in front of me.

'Delivery,' Teddy murmured, kissing me on the cheek.

Felix cleared his throat. 'Do we all get one?'

Teddy straightened up. 'It's a big sandwich. She can split it.'

'Speak for yourself.' I unwrapped the wax packaging, revealing one of the goat's cheese and chorizo combinations from the bakery down the street. The bakery from our supposed meet-cute. 'Yeah, this baby is *aaall* mine. Smell it and weep.'

Felix shuddered. 'What a horrible, *horrible* phrase.'

Cecilia must have clocked Teddy's arrival, because she came out of her office. 'Just the people I wanted to see.'

'Oh Christ,' said Teddy.

'I've just read the new column.' She stopped just in front of us. 'Excellent news.'

She seemed so excited that for a second I forgot she was in on the plan.

'Make sure you mention this in the podcast.' Cecilia gestured between us and strode back to her office.

Felix motioned for me to explain. 'Go on, then. What's the scandal now? I knew I should have brought popcorn for lunch today.'

Teddy jumped into action. 'I asked Sage to be my girlfriend.'

'You mean it's *official?*' Felix smirked. 'Big news. Congratulations. Let the road to the death of the honeymoon period commence.'

I was pretty sure a bead of sweat was dripping down my spine. I felt Teddy's hand squeeze mine under the desk.

He turned to me. 'Do you have fifteen minutes for us to eat these outside?'

'I do indeed.' I saved the edits I was making. A break was probably due anyway, before I had an actual existential crisis. 'Let's go.'

We made our way outside, lucky that we were only a five-minute walk from Bloomsbury Square Gardens. Teddy chose a bench away from everyone else.

'Your hand was so clammy in there. I almost dropped it.'

He must have seen the stricken look on my face because his expression softened. 'I assume this whole fake relationship thing is stressing you out?'

'Is it that obvious?' I took a huge bite of the sandwich, comfort eating.

'Only to me.' He gently bumped my shoulder with his. 'It's all going to be okay you know.'

'But what's the end goal of this?' I swallowed. 'How far does it go? I mean I've got to go on a bloody podcast in an hour and spin even more lies.'

He shrugged. 'If your column is still running in a few months then we'll just stage a breakup. Let's make it messy, break up over something stupid. You never made the bed, and I always ate tuna for lunch and it grossed you out in the end.'

I was laughing, but the idea of a fake breakup actually made me sad for some reason. Where would we be now if I'd just said yes when Teddy asked me out in the first place? I changed the subject.

'How is the saga with the events team going? Had to ask them to turn their computers on and off again this week?'

Teddy groaned. 'As soon as this week is over, the better. I've been jazzing up my LinkedIn profile ready to start looking for something else.'

The thought of staging a breakup and Teddy *actually* leaving our office block made me feel even worse. I knew we'd still see each other, but I liked being able to eat lunch together and grab a drink at one of the bars nearby after work. Naturally, we'd see each other less when we didn't work in the same building.

'So, how many followers does this Alexis person have, anyway? We can handle a couple of hundred.'

'I think about two hundred thousand on Instagram.'

I patted him on the back when he started coughing.

'Christ, just a few, then. I do sometimes forget that you're famous.'

'I'm not –'

'I think I have thirty-seven followers, and my family make up the majority of them. Look, you'll smash it, I know you will.'

We sat in silence for a moment, eating. A woman across the park from us was sitting on a bench, phone clutched in her hand. Her cheeks were red, and I noticed her swiping underneath her eyes. I thought back to January, in the days after the breakup. That had been me. I rooted silently for the woman on the bench.

'So' – Teddy balled up his wrapper, throwing it directly into the bin and looking pleased with himself – 'I've got a surprise for you.'

I whipped my head around. 'Good surprise or bad surprise?'

'What's it like being such a cynic? I want the normal Flick back – this podcast ordeal has changed you. Of course it's a good surprise.'

I badgered him to tell me for the rest of our break but he wouldn't budge. Apparently he'd reveal everything tomorrow when he came over for dinner. The girls had instructed me to invite him; he'd fully won them over whilst I'd been in Liverpool. I watched him now, refusing to give anything away. I'd always thought I was able to read Teddy like a book, but he was getting more cryptic by the day.

★★★

When I returned to the office, our guest had arrived. Sadie looked like she was about to keel over with nervous energy.

I knew how much it was killing her not to ask for a photo. Alexis sat opposite me in the meeting room now, her acrylics tapping against the keys on her iPhone and snapping a photo of our microphone set up.

'Sorry, got to check in on my Instagram stories. I've been getting a lot of requests to have you on the show. People are going to be *excited*.'

I still couldn't quite get my head around that. 'I can't begin to imagine why.'

'You're London's graduate sweetheart. People are invested. You're an inspiration to all of the heartbroken people who find themselves scrolling through old text messages before they go to bed. And the fact that you met because of a traditional meet-cute, and not on a dating app? It's unheard of, and people lap that shit up.' She put a hand over her mouth. 'Sorry, not the most professional.'

'Go crazy.' I waved her off. 'We swear like sailors in this office.'

'Good to know.' She retreated into her own little bubble, adjusting her equipment and setting up for our interview.

Alexis was what I imagined when I heard the term 'influencer'. She wore relatively high heels (the chances of me doing that in the middle of a city, or anywhere, were slim), and her eyeliner was immaculate. The saying 'sisters not twins' when it came to eyeliner wings did not apply here. They were on point. She was short, but she instantly commanded a room. And she was constantly checking her phone, replying to comments and uploading snapshots of her day. She definitely would have made a better Flick Sage for the column, no doubt about it.

'Lean a little bit into the microphone? Yeah, yeah that's it. And if you could refrain from tapping on the table – I know it's easy to want to fidget – that would be great. The microphone picks up everything.'

I gulped, trying not to breathe too loudly.

'You don't need to look so afraid either, it's a podcast – we can cut out anything that you decide you don't want to be in there. First time?'

I nodded, biting my lip. 'Yeah. I'm usually the one on the other side of the interview. Well, not even that to be honest. I'm the one who gets the coffee and proofreads the pieces.'

Alexis laughed. 'You clearly underestimated the power of a good old agony-aunt column. They were starting to die out and needed a revival. Right, we'll do a sound check and then we'll be good to go. Are you ready?' Alexis beamed at me.

I took a deep breath, comforted by her relaxed attitude to the whole thing. 'Ready.'

***

**Transcript of interview with Felicity (Flick) Sage for**
**The Sunday Podcast**

*Alexis: Hi guys! Welcome to the latest episode of* The Sunday Podcast. *You asked, and I listened. I've got a very special guest on the podcast for you today. Before I start chatting with her, let me give her a fitting introduction. You may have heard of* Influence *magazine, the up-and-coming lifestyle publication with its office located in Bloomsbury. Today I'm joined by graduate magazine journalist-turned-major-columnist Felicity Sage, writer of* The Twenties List. *After bouncing back from a breakup and taking the internet by storm, Flick is showing us all how life in London as a young person is done. So, let's meet Flick.*

*Felicity: Hi everyone! I'm so pleased to be here. Thank you for having me.*

*A: Thank you for coming on. There's nothing I love to discuss more than how different people figure things out, in your case 'the twenties'! Although I'm nearing the end of mine, I still don't have a clue what's going on half the time. It's kind of our thing on this podcast. Life, love, and everything in between. I'm extremely excited to have you on the show today. You've become every girl's post-breakup dream.*

*F: \*laughs\* I'm not sure I'd go that far.*

*A: You know what they say, when a girl changes up her hair colour, she means business. So, let's start off with the gritty bits. How did* The Twenties List *come about?*

*F: Okay, so it stemmed from a conversation I had with my sister over brunch. I was coming out of a really tough breakup and wondering what to do next, and she was telling me about the list of goals that she made at the beginning of her twenties. All the wild and wonderful things she'd wanted to do. It seemed like the ideal distraction from heartbreak, so I made my own list. And then Cecilia – my boss – heard about it, and, well, the rest is history.*

*A: I LOVE that. Your sister sounds like my type of person. So, for any listeners who haven't yet had a read of your list, what type of things are on there?*

*F: It started off small, with things like reading memoirs and baking sourdough –*

*A: Very adult. I respect that.*

*F: I'm tame by nature, so it made more sense to begin with things that felt doable. So, I have a few of those smaller goals, and then, obviously, I played breakup bingo and dyed my hair. There are a few larger things on the list too. Living in a houseshare was definitely one of the most nerve-wracking items.*

*A: And how is it going? I know that for a lot of people post-breakup, finding a new place to live is the most important practical step, and sometimes the hardest to do. It's difficult to go into a new situation when you aren't feeling your strongest.*

251

*F: Honestly? I'm loving every second. The girls I live with make most things bearable. The four of us make a good team. I know that one of my housemates in particular will kill me if I don't say hi to her on here. She listens to your podcast every weekend.*

*A: Really? What's her name? Let's give her a shout out.*

*F: Stacey.*

*A: Hi Stacey! Thanks for listening. I live for a good houseshare story. I lived with a group of strangers when I first moved here six years ago, and it had its moments, but in general it was one of my most valued experiences. You grow so much in that kind of environment.*

*F: In so many ways, it feels like a major silver lining. Living in a house with people who cheer you on and lift you up is so important. And I feel like, in this day and age, society pushes us to be intimidated by a group of strong-willed women. But those women are the kindest and most welcoming people I know. I mean yes, sometimes we forget to hoover, and yes, if anyone touches my housemate's coffee then we have our issues, but in general it's such a safe place to be.*

*A: I love that. It shouldn't be the norm to instantly feel wary of strong women. It sounds like you've lucked out with your housemates. Hearing about them in your column cracks me up. I imagine they've had a lot to say about recent events, have they not?*

*F: \*laughs\* I don't know what you mean.*

*A: You had to know I'd pounce on it. Tell us about your accidental sandwich shop slash office meet-cute. You don't hear many of those nowadays, in the world of modern dating. You're a beacon of hope to us all.*

*F: \*long pause\* Well, I was absolutely open to trialling dating apps. I think it could have been interesting. But Teddy came into my life totally unexpectedly. I never expected to meet someone like him – and during my lunch break, too.*

*A: Productive lunch break.*

*F: I think that might be the only time I've ever been productive during my lunch hour. We just instantly clicked. I definitely wasn't my friendliest self when we met, either. It's a good job he's patient. I'd like to think I'm more fun to be around now.*

*A: Oh, I so get that. I'm such a grump when I'm newly single. If you're new to Flick's column, you can follow along with not only her list, but her experiences with modern dating too. It's scandalous. So, tell us about Teddy.*

*F: Well, he's three years older than me, and he moved to London just a little over six months ago. We both play tennis,* and he has the biggest record collection out of everyone I know. He's great. Really sweet. If I'd planned things, I probably would have actively said that I didn't want to start dating again as soon as I did. But you can't choose life, right?

A: Absolutely. Part of life is realising that it's completely out of your hands. Well, I for one am rooting for you all the way. And I'm sure that I won't be alone in that. In a world where dating is tough, Felicity Sage is doing the hard work for us. If you have any questions that you'd like her to answer, she's now combining her updates for The Twenties List with an agony-aunt section. I know I'd trust her advice through and through.

# 26

I was lying on my bed, fending off emails from Sadie about my 'internet presence' (or in her eyes, my lack thereof) when Suze rang. I almost did a double take looking down at the phone screen; she'd gone back to her sporadic communication since I'd visited. I sat up straight, brushing some chocolate digestive crumbs off my chest.

'Hi. You okay?'

There was a beat on the other end of the line, and I could hear the kettle boiling in the background. 'Hey Flick. Yeah, I'm fine. I do need a favour, though.'

I tried to detect the tone of her voice; did she sound more upbeat than the last time I'd seen her? I couldn't tell. 'I would immediately agree, but the last time I said yes blindly to a favour I ended up weighing out hundreds of bags of wild-flower seeds for an event.'

She laughed on the other end. 'You have to admit, those party favours were sweet. Hmm, 'Espresso Yourself' or 'Big Apple'?'

'What on earth are you on about?' Phone conversations with Suze were always like this. She never seemed to understand that I couldn't trace the tangents of the conversation.

'I'm painting my nails. 'Espresso Yourself' or 'Big Apple'?'

I thought about it for a moment. 'Erm, 'Big Apple'.'

'Excellent choice. So anyway, I have a thing. I really would go on my own, but everyone normally brings a date and I wouldn't care but I don't want to be sat next to Sad Phil –'

'Suze, I'm going to need more context.'

I heard her catch her breath. 'Sorry, I guess I'm kind of bitter about the whole 'bring a date' concept. It's stressing me out. Work is having a party, to celebrate all of the other parties we've managed to pull off. As if we need anything else to plan.'

Usually, the word party to Suze was what the word 'walk' was to Kernel. I said as much.

'Are you comparing me to a golden retriever?'

'Not intentionally, but yes. Why aren't you excited?'

Suze sighed. 'I'm not *not* excited. I'm not hugely over-excited either. It's one of those fancy events where all the branches of the company come together for a celebratory mixer. And nothing is ever in Liverpool when it could be in London. No offence to your city.'

I paused, ready to interject that *Liverpool* was my city. Something stopped me. Was I finally beginning to feel like a Londoner?

'Where is the event?' I settled on instead. London was the best place to throw a party.

'It's on the South Bank, in one of those posh hotels. Tons of food, free bar. I'll love you forever if you come with me.'

I had seen where this conversation had been headed from a mile off. 'I mean, if only to save you from sitting with

Sad Phil, of course I will. Although I kind of feel sad for Sad Phil – do we need to form a trio?'

'No, he's a pain. I left my Hobnobs in the cupboard at work and he ate every single one of them. You're a lifesaver, Flick. Thanks.'

Her voice had become muffled, and it sounded like she was balancing me in the crook between her chin and her shoulder as she poured water from the kettle. I smiled at the image. At the same time, though, Suze would *never* usually be found starting off the weekend with a cup of tea. That was my territory. She was usually out with Codie.

'It's next week, is that okay? I know this is late notice, but I've been all over the place. I was considering bailing on it completely, but I think it'll look bad if I don't show my face.'

'I'll be there, don't worry. Come and stay with me here in the house, you can meet everyone.' I couldn't *wait* for Suze and Kitty to meet, I had a feeling they were going to get on straight away. 'The only question is' – I looked at my twenties list on the wardrobe door – 'does this count as working at one of your events? If so, item ten on the list is about to be completed.'

'Oh, believe me, if I didn't have to go, I wouldn't. It definitely counts. I'll even hand-deliver some of those chocolate brownies from Leaf you love so much. That's how grateful I am. What are you doing tonight?' I could hear a teaspoon clinking against a mug. 'I've got a saddening lack of plans. Might re-watch *John Tucker Must Die.*'

'Um . . . I don't know yet. You know – if you get lonely you can just call me. Whenever. We could even sync our laptops, re-watch it together.'

'Yeah.' I could picture her waving me off. 'I appreciate that, but I know you probably have way more exciting plans than me. You don't need to pretend to be boring for my sake. Thanks for the favour, I owe you one. Enjoy your evening, sis.'

I flinched when she said goodbye and hung up, shocked at that final exchange. My sister was more abrupt, more cynical, less herself. She was also completely right; why *had* I lied and pretended that I hadn't been doing anything tonight? Teddy would be coming over any minute now, and the girls were downstairs preparing fajita ingredients and a questionable jug of sangria. It wasn't that I felt guilty for having plans, it just felt important that Suze knew that she could call me whenever she wanted. When I pictured her alone in her flat on a Friday night, I wanted to reach through the screen and hug her tight.

'Knock knock,' I heard a voice say softly, along with the sound of knuckles against my door. 'Can I come in?'

I smoothed my bedspread down, smiling. 'That depends.'

'Depends on what?' His voice echoed back through the wood.

'Whether you're going to judge how messy my bedroom is. I don't think I've sorted through my washing pile in a week. The one benefit of us fake-dating is that I don't have to tidy my room for a boy.'

I heard Teddy laugh. 'Only one benefit?'

'That and I don't have to pick your towels up off the floor.' I referenced the first ever conversation we'd had about dating each other. Or rather, pretending to date. 'Come in.'

I couldn't help that I was a bit nervous for Teddy to see my room. My stomach fluttered, reminding me of the first time I'd invited Aaron into my uni room.

'Wow.' He ducked under the beam above my door. 'I thought you were exaggerating the size of this room for the column. It was at full capacity before I even stepped in here.'

I watched him turn, taking in each corner of my room. He smiled at the candle with 'Fresh Start' written on the front of it, and at the goofy photo of me and Suze on the dresser.

'I think I'd get on with your sister.'

'I think so too.'

He finally faced me, looking mischievous. 'Okay, so you need to close your eyes.'

I frowned, suspicious. 'What kind of surprise is this?'

'Just shut up and close them, Sage.'

I did as I was told, leaning back on my hands and smiling even though I had no idea what the surprise was yet. I wasn't nervous about him being in here any more. I could hear Teddy shuffling around the room, murmuring to himself, swearing once or twice.

'If you're going to be standing in front of me in your birthday suit . . .'

He pushed me over onto my side. 'Don't project your hopes and dreams onto me. Okay, you can open them now.'

I opened my eyes.

'Ta-da!'

'*Teddy.*'

Standing in front of me was a sleek, black keyboard, the ivory keys lined up just waiting to be used. Teddy was still dressed in his suit from work and was standing behind it, looking extremely pleased with himself.

'You did not do this.'

He perched on the end of my bed. 'I did. Gumtree at its finest. Let's crack number five off this list.'

I was beyond touched that he'd thought of this. Piano was a hobby that my mum had gently forced me into when I was six, and I'd played right up until my twelfth birthday. I'd wanted to pursue it of my own accord ever since. It was like tennis; finding the right rhythm could distract you from the very worst day.

'You like it?'

I scooted along the bed and wrapped my arms around him, squeezing. 'I *love* it. You did not have to do this.'

He shrugged. 'I know I didn't. And for a second there, lugging this thing up your death stairs, I did question why I did. But I wanted to.'

I didn't take my arms away, just pulled back to look at him as he spoke. 'You know, I'm no Beethoven.'

'If you think that's going to get you out of serenading me, you're sorely mistaken.' Teddy smiled softly, gesturing to the keyboard. 'Go on.'

I pulled the keyboard in front of the bed so I could sit on the edge and play from there. I couldn't remember much from my childhood, but I think everyone who's been forced to take piano lessons – particularly in Liverpool – remembers 'Let it Be'. It only took a second of unfamiliarity before I knew where I was going with the keys. There was something really satisfying about knowing I was completing an item on my list. I couldn't see Teddy, with my eyes focused on the keys, but I could feel his presence. It was something that had happened gradually, but now, he was one of the people I searched for first in a room.

'You know, Sage, you aren't that bad.' He perched himself next to me.

'The highest compliment.'

'Well, it was a bit of a risk, providing you with an instrument. I'm relieved, to say the least.'

With my head turned to listen to him, we were now only centimetres apart. My cheeks flushed with the proximity. The lines were definitely blurring between us lately; not quite actually dating, but feeling like more than friends. Looking up at him now, and glancing down at his lips, surely he felt it too. I noticed the scar over his eyebrow again, touching it lightly with my fingers.

'How did you get this?'

Teddy smirked. 'So observant. I got it from climbing a tree with the twins when I was 10 years old.'

I pictured a 10-year-old Teddy. *Cute.* 'Did you fall out?'

'No,' he winced, 'less cool than that. Got to the top and was impaled by a branch.'

I couldn't help laughing; that was so him. We'd both moved even closer together whilst he was telling the story, if that was possible. I stared at his lips again, curved slightly in amusement as he watched me laugh. How badly would it mess everything up if I kissed him?

'Guys, *taste this.*' Kitty burst through the door at that exact moment, causing us to widen the distance between us significantly. 'What is *this?*'

She put down the jug of sangria and walked over to the keyboard. 'I haven't played the keyboard in years. Is this your doing, Stewart?'

Teddy held up his hands from where she was pointing at him. 'Guilty as charged.'

Kitty shot me a look. A look that obviously said, 'he bought you a keyboard?!', but I just shrugged and grinned at her. 'Wow, you have friends in all the right places, Flick.'

She gestured for me to scoot over so she could have a go, producing a way more impressive piece of music than I just had.

'Of course you're a piano prodigy, Kit.'

She shrugged. 'I grew up in an extremely musical household. I can play five instruments.'

Teddy's eyes narrowed. 'You know the recorder doesn't count, right?'

'Har-har.'

'You can't keep us in suspense like that. What are the five?'

'Okay' – she counted them off on her fingers – 'piano, flute, guitar, saxophone, and now I count the mixing decks as my fifth.'

'You have been holding out on us. Who just casually plays the saxophone?' I jabbed her arm, making her laugh.

'It's hardly like I could have lugged all the instruments to London. They're all waiting for me at my parents' house. Whenever my brother and I go to visit them, we have an extremely musical weekend.'

Teddy snapped his fingers. 'You're like the Von Trapps!'

'I think I'm going to pretend that you didn't just say that.' Kitty shuddered. 'I'm not sure I could pull off gingham. Or a staircase number.' She stood, grabbing the jug of sangria again. 'Anyway, I've perfected this. Just enough fruit to mask the fact that it's 99 per cent booze. Come down soon?'

I nodded and she left, satisfied with my response. Teddy wasn't as close to me as before, but he still radiated heat. 'I can't remember the last time that someone did something this nice for me.' I stroked the keyboard affectionately.

He shrugged. 'Well, I'm highly invested in the list now. I do think this might be the start of an unhealthy Gumtree obsession, though. Did you know that you can buy literally anything on that site? I almost bought a set of Russian dolls for no reason whatsoever.'

I looked up from the melody I was playing absentmindedly. 'Has anyone ever told you that you're extremely odd?'

'Once or twice.' When I glanced up at him, he was already looking at me.

'What?'

Teddy's little finger nudged mine from where it lay next to my hand on the duvet. I felt the electricity all the way down my spine.

'Sage . . .' He started to talk, and I watched him change his mind. I doubted he'd say what I wanted to hear right now. I'd already rejected him once before; he was unlikely to try again. 'How about some sangria?'

I struggled to adjust to the sudden change of pace. I was always extremely vocal about the fact that I wasn't ready to date yet. This was my doing.

'I could drink some wine.'

He nodded, standing up and breaking the atmosphere. Before the proximity disappeared completely, I squeezed his hand.

He looked at me expectantly. 'What's up?'

'Thank you.' I pointed to the keyboard. 'For this, for being here.'

He pulled me up towards him so that I was standing too and kissed the top of my head. 'You're welcome. There's nowhere else I'd rather be than in this crazy house.'

'They are kind of great, aren't they?'

Teddy smiled. 'You're *all* kind of great. Although I do have a soft spot for viral columnists.'

We headed downstairs to join the others. Sophie was stood in the kitchen with Maia, both of them murmuring quietly whilst they tossed the veggies around in a pan. Stacey was fiddling with the speakers, scrolling through her playlists and highlighting the benefits of each one to Kitty.

'It's just, the 'Fiesta' playlist suits the mood, but there are some real bops on the 'Friday' playlist.'

Kitty humoured her as she poured from the huge jug into six glasses. They were like a well-oiled machine – Sophie was busy running tortillas and salsa to the breakfast bar whilst Maia began to grate cheddar into a bowl. All four of them were playing their own part in the Friday-night dance, so that by the time we all sat down (listening to the 'Fiesta' playlist), everything was ready at once, piping hot.

I held up my sangria. 'To the start of the weekend. God knows we need it.'

Everyone echoed me, holding up their own cups of *very* alcoholic sangria. 'To the weekend,' they all repeated, begin- ning to assemble fajitas so full they looked like they might burst. Something so simple, and yet I couldn't believe I'd almost missed out on it. The thought of a parallel universe, one where I'd be tucked into a ball on the couch in my old flat in Shepherd's Bush, Aaron stirring something on the hob, seemed so alien. Not for the first time, the thought of that alternative Felicity Sage caused a lump in my throat. But not because I longed for that reality, instead it was because I felt sad for her. Teddy squeezed my hand under the table.

'You okay?' He mouthed it to me.

'I'm great.' I squeezed his hand back before reaching for another tortilla.

And I absolutely meant it.

# 27

I applied my eyeliner slowly, holding my breath and hoping for the best.

'Are you trying to look like you need the toilet?'

The wing smudged. 'Stacey! Stop making me laugh!'

'Sorry, sorry.' She held up her hands. 'I'm just trying to feel useful.'

Kitty scoffed from where she was lying on her bed, doing nothing for once. 'In the last five minutes, all I've heard you do is complain about your colleagues and tell Flick that she looks like she needs the loo.'

'Well, I mean, she did.' Stacey shrugged, going back to doing her own makeup. 'Top up?' She gestured to my Disney mug, which was precariously balanced next to me on top of an eyeshadow palette that I was borrowing from Kitty.

I took a swig of the vodka lemonade left in it. My nose wrinkled. 'I would say yes to a top up, but how much vodka is *in* this?'

'I know what you mean.' Kitty winced as she took a sip of her own. 'Who thought it was a good idea to buy supermarket-brand vodka? This tastes like lighter fuel.'

'If you drink it fast enough, you don't even notice. It just tastes like saving money.' Stacey sipped from Kitty's glass. 'You're such a wimp anyway, this is majority lemonade.'

'It's *supposed* to be majority lemonade. I do have to get up there and perform tonight, you know. It's kind of the whole point.' She undid one of her braids, fixing it and pouting at me. 'I wish you were coming.'

Kitty had one of her biggest gigs yet tonight. Apparently, the club that she was mixing for didn't often hire female DJs. She'd been hyped up all week, making us sit in the dark in the living room to hear her set. Stace had bought glow sticks for us to dance with, and by the third night we knew the beats of her set by heart. I was sad to be missing it.

'I need to be there for Suze.' I bit my lip. 'Maybe I can try and convince her to swing by with me after the dinner.'

'You know I'm only kidding. Stacey, Maia and Soph will be there to hold the fort.'

As if on cue, a light knock sounded on Kitty's door. 'Guys?'

Sophie came into the room, grinning when she saw the glitter all over the floor. 'I'd expect nothing less than this, Kitty.'

'Got to stay on brand.'

Soph perched on the bed; it was rare to see her without Maia. She fiddled with the long braid (which seemed to be made up of other, tinier, long braids) that fell over her shoulder. 'Maia had one of her exams today, and it didn't go great.'

I felt a pang of sympathy for my housemate – her career was so important to her.

'Oh shit.' Stace looked sad. 'I did wonder why I hadn't seen her tonight.'

'Yeah, she's not feeling great about it.' Sophie absentmindedly turned one of the pots of glitter over in her fingers. 'She feels awful about missing the gig tonight, but I think I just need to make her some food and let her wallow in it, you know? She'll be fine tomorrow.'

Kitty sat up. 'Don't let her worry about the gig.'

'Everyone knows I'm the loudest cheerleader anyway.' Stacey poured another vodka lemonade and handed it to Sophie. 'Give her this, will knock her right out.'

'I'm sure she'll be ecstatic.' Sophie took a sip, spluttering. 'I like your ratios, Stace – Jesus. What time is your sister arriving, Flick?'

'Any minute now. Which colour?' I held up three lipsticks.

'*Red.*' All three of them said it in unison without looking.

I applied it in the mirror, hurrying to get it done before the doorbell inevitably went. Suze was always on time. I stood, grabbing my bag. 'How do I look?'

Kitty wolf whistled. '*Ravishing* darling. Teddy would pass out.'

'For the last time –'

She finished the sentence for me. 'Yeah, yeah, nothing is going on. Blah blah blah.'

Sophie was laughing. 'Maia *does* secretly call you Fleddy.'

'Traitors, all of you.' Saved by the doorbell, I went downstairs. I passed Maia's door on the way, debating whether to knock and let her know I was thinking about her. I knew that a bad exam would have wounded her pride – rather than rub salt in the wound, I'd bring her a cup of tea and a biscuit tomorrow. I was craving an afternoon on the couch anyway;

life was hectic now in a way it hadn't been last year. For the first time, I felt like I was one of the commuters on the Tube rushing home, having somewhere to be every night after work. I'd loved being an observer of the city, but now I felt like a working cog in the huge machine.

When I reached the bottom of the stairs I yanked open the door, desperate to see my sister. 'Suze!'

She was standing on the step, hair in an elegant chignon. I squeezed her tight.

'Hello, you. You smell like alcohol. Can I have some? I need some Dutch courage for tonight and I need it *quick*.'

★★★

I stared out at the river Thames, the lights from the South Bank reflecting off the water and making it sparkle. I knew what working for a smaller company felt like, but this was a different *world*. We were in an events room at a posh hotel, our seats situated right by the glass that was separating us from the water below.

'I still can't believe that you've rented out a room here for tonight.'

Suze tapped her fingers on her leg. 'It's next level, I know. You should see the menu. I think it's lobster related.'

As much as I loved the view, that sounded gross. 'Do you think they'd –'

'I put you down for the vegetarian option, don't worry. Miles ahead of you.'

'If you're miles ahead, why doesn't this say Flick?' I pointed to the name card in front of me, which read 'Miss Felicity Sage'. I felt like I was at a wedding.

'Have you seen mine? This wasn't a nickname sort of situation.' She wrinkled her nose at her own card, which said 'Miss Susan Sage'. I sometimes forgot that Susan was even her name; she was so utterly a Suze.

I people-watched for a minute, my eyes tracking the room to get the measure of my sister's colleagues. There were a lot of middle-aged people chatting to each other, clinking glasses whilst everyone took their seats. I could see why she'd needed a date – everyone else seemed partnered up. I spotted an older man sitting apart from some of the others, his suit drowning him. He was picking his nose. A grown man, picking his nose at an event that was about to serve posh food in tiny portions.

Suze mouthed to me 'Sad Phil'. I stifled a laugh, bringing my glass to my lips.

'Tell me what some of these are again?' Suze pointed to the view.

'Okay, so that on the left is St Paul's.' I pointed to the domed roof. 'And that one is The Cheese Grater. Well, it probably isn't called that, but that's what everyone says. That one there is the Gherkin.'

My sister was grinning. 'You're a proper Londoner now, aren't you? I wouldn't have a frigging clue what any of those were.'

'Weird, I guess I do feel a bit like one.'

Her expression turned mischievous. 'Might that have anything to do with a certain someone?'

I'd tried to stop Kitty and Stace from bombarding her whilst I made her a drink back at the house, but clearly I'd been betrayed. 'It has to do with a lot of things. Whatever they've been saying to you, feel free to ignore it. I usually do.'

'Susan?' A man tapped her on the shoulder, making us both jump. 'Sorry to interrupt, but we're having an issue with the microphone.'

'On it.' She turned to me. 'We aren't done with this conversation. Be right back.'

I watched my sister as she walked across the room. She looked radiant tonight in a gold, floor length dress that shimmered when she moved. Think Blake Lively in *Gossip Girl*, the night that she first danced with Dan. I couldn't have been prouder.

★★★

Whilst I waited for her to come back, I got up and stole the opportunity to walk right next to the windows, centimetres away from smashing my nose up against the glass. I walked a bit like a crab across the room, not wanting to take my eyes off London.

'Are you planning on doing that the whole way around?'

I whipped my head around, startled that I'd been spoken to. A man in a suit was staring at me, two glasses of fizz in hand.

'Champagne?' He held one out to me. 'It might be prosecco, to be honest.'

Like I would be able to tell the difference. 'Thanks.' I accepted, taking a huge gulp.

The man – tallish, dark haired – chuckled. 'I was hoping we might cheers first.'

'Oh, sorry.' I put my hand over my mouth, embarrassed.

'I was kidding, I'm in total agreement.' He necked his own glass back too, holding up the almost empty flute in salute. 'I'm Graham.'

I blinked back. Was this man *flirting* with me?

'Felicity Sage.' I held out my hand, not wanting to instigate a kiss on the cheek. I thought of Teddy, probably sitting at home watching a crime documentary. We were six episodes into a seven-part drama – he'd better not have been watching the seventh episode without me.

'Who are you here with?' Graham gestured with his empty glass to the throngs of people milling around the room.

'I'm with my sister, Suze?'

In fact, Graham actually looked like her type. I craned my neck, trying to locate her. 'She's here somewhere . . .'

The more I looked around the room, the more evident it became that she wasn't in here.

'I know Suze. Someone you call when things go wrong and you need crisis management.'

I tried to concentrate on what he was saying, but I was getting a bit concerned. It was like a sixth sense. *Where was she?*

# 28

'I'm really sorry.' I put my glass back on one of the round tables. 'But I need to go and find her. My sister.'

Graham looked disappointed, but he quickly fixed his expression. 'Absolutely. Go and find her. If you're around later, I'm on that table over there.' He pointed to a table near the front.

I said my goodbyes and left, trying to navigate the room as quickly as I could whilst wearing these stupidly skinny heels. I would never understand how society had progressed in so many ways, and yet heels were still this uncomfortable. I longed for the bunny slippers beside my bed. I shuffled twice across the floor before I spotted the sign for the toilets, walking in and lifting the hem of my dress so that it didn't graze the floor. It might have been a beautiful building, but these were still toilets after all.

'Suze?'

A woman who was checking her reflection in the mirror shot me a look but I ignored her, listening.

'Suze?' I whispered it this time.

There was no reply, but a sniffle came from the final cubicle. I ducked my head to see what shoes I could see (when it's your sister at stake, anything is acceptable), and spotted her green heels.

'Hi Flick.' She pushed open the door to let me in. She was sitting on the toilet with the seat pulled down, mascara tracks hastily brushed across her cheeks. 'I didn't want to come and get you when you were talking to Graham.'

'You absolutely should have done.'

'Why?' Another sniff. 'He's cute. Look at you, attracting men left right and centre.'

'I can't tell you how far that is from the truth.' I crouched down so I was at her level. 'What's going on?'

Suze sighed. 'I don't even know. I was just watching everyone with their boyfriends, or their husbands, and I felt so low.'

I wanted to hug her, but the size of the cubicle didn't really lend itself to it. Suze wasn't the only blonde I knew lately who'd been comparing herself to everyone around her.

'I really thought that if I dragged myself out of bed tonight and put on this dress, I might feel like the old Suze.'

'The old Suze?'

'I don't feel like the red lipstick, artsy Suze that you always tell me I am.' She looked down to her feet. 'I don't know what's wrong with me lately, I really don't.'

'There's nothing wrong with you. It's alright to feel out of your depth sometimes.' I put my hand over hers.

She hiccupped. 'It's not just sometimes. I feel so down, all of the time. Nothing major has happened, I just can't shift this sad feeling. I'm *sad*, Flick.'

My heart broke for her. This was the first time I'd heard Suze admit to not feeling good. For my sister, this was a huge admission. It was hard to admit that you didn't know how to fix something.

'First things first, is there anything I need to go and do out there?' I pointed in the general direction of the room I'd just come from. 'Is everything sorted?'

Suze shook her head. 'It's all done. That was easy, they hadn't switched the microphone on.' She put her head in her hands. 'When I think about going back in there, it's like, I can't catch my breath. And the more I think about the fact that I can't catch my breath, the harder it is to catch it.' She put her hands on her throat.

I was pretty sure my sister was describing a panic attack.

Fresh tears filled her eyes. 'Don't tell Mum and Dad. I don't want them to have to worry, and I don't want work to know either.' Her hands were flapping around.

'Hey.' I stilled them. 'I'm not going to tell anyone anything. Just try and focus on your breathing for a second. You do not have to go back in there.'

She stared at me until the rising of her chest evened out again. Her eyes closed for a minute, and I stayed still, sensing that she needed to centre herself.

'When I googled what to do when I feel like this,' she sniffed, 'it said to focus on your senses. What you can see, hear, smell . . .'

'Oh God. We might be in this super-fancy place, but this is still a bathroom. Focus on the other four, don't smell.'

She finally laughed. 'I'm glad you're here, Flick.'

I admitted defeat, perching on the floor and trying to resist wrinkling my nose at the thought of the germs. 'Me too.'

'This is weird, right? Me needing you?'

It was, but it also felt natural. I'd been relying on her for so long that it was definitely my time to return the favour.

'Here's my plan.' I patted her leg. 'We can leave whenever you want. But if you do want to go back in there to show your face, we'll eat the posh food, listen to a speech or two, and *then* we can leave. I know exactly the place for afterwards.'

Suze squeezed my hand. 'Look at you, taking control.'

How I'd become someone that my sister could look to for direction, I had no idea.

'I learnt from the best.'

***

About an eight-minute walk away from the event space was a spot I'd found last winter, after a few work drinks when Felix and I had been too tipsy to make our way home without sobering up first. It wasn't anything fancy – a typical greasy spoon – but the fact that it was open twenty-four hours made it the perfect stop after a rough night.

'Do you not think we're going to look a bit out of place?' Suze gestured to our dresses.

'This is London. No one will bat an eyelid. Last time I was in here I was sitting in a booth next to two people dressed as Mario and Luigi.'

She raised her eyebrows. 'Fair enough.'

The rest of the night had passed by quickly. After a quick fix of Suze's make up (luckily, for the first time in my life I'd packed my bag with useful things), we'd gone back into the dining room. Graham had tried to catch my eye, which I'd avoided at all cost, much to Suze's amusement. After a reasonable amount of time, we'd slipped off, my sister saying a few goodbyes to her friends from work. You wouldn't have been able to tell that she'd been crying in the toilet cubicle an hour earlier, but I knew that was the whole point. Sometimes you couldn't tell. But that didn't mean you should stop looking.

Now, Suze slid behind a booth, reaching for the sticky menus that were always kept behind a snow globe. The first time I'd been here with Felix, I'd brought one home from the restaurant to add to my collection. It was sitting on my dresser, a tiny glass globe with windmills inside. It may have originated from Amsterdam, but it would always remind me of this place. The one holding the menus up in this particular booth was from Hawaii, a palm tree floating among gold dust posing as sand. I shook it upside down, smiling as the dust fell.

'I've never understood your obsession with those things.' Suze shook her head, turning the menu over to read the other side. 'I know we just ate, but apple pie and custard sounds *divine* right now.'

I put the snow globe back in its place. 'I just love the concept. A tiny little world laid out to see. No surprises.'

'It's a tacky glass globe, Flick.'

I shrugged. 'It is what you say it is. And I say it's a tiny little world. So, shall we split this pie that you speak of?'

'Have you ever known me to share dessert once in our whole lives?'

'Point taken.' I scanned the specials board, which had said the same thing every time I'd been here. 'My head says "Flick, there's no way you'll be able to eat blueberry crêpes", but my heart insists that I will.' I put the menu down. 'I'm up for the challenge.'

'This is why we're sisters.' Suze grinned at me. We ordered, stacking the menus back behind Hawaii.

'How gross would it be if I took off my shoes?'

I looked around. We were the only customers apart from one young woman, who was sitting at the back and typing furiously on her laptop. Suze was waiting for my verdict expectantly, hands already on the buckles of her heels.

'I think considering that I was sitting on a public toilet floor two hours ago, we might as well go the whole hog.'

I watched her groan as she released her feet from their confinement. She was brighter now, joking around about stuffing her face with apple pie, but I was still worried. We both knew we weren't done talking about everything. Her advice – to move into a houseshare, and to start my twenties list – had turned my year around. Suze was constantly caring for people, most of all me. She needed it back right now.

'What are you thinking about?' She poked me with her straw before sticking it into her lemonade.

I didn't want to take this moment of peace from her. 'Nothing really. I was wondering how Kitty's gig was going.'

'I can't believe you know an actual DJ. She's very cool, I like her.'

We sat in silence for a few moments, eating. It was definitely true that there was a separate stomach for dessert; these pancakes were going down no problem.

'Thank you for tonight, Flick.' Suze didn't look up from her pie. 'I needed you, and you were there 100 per cent.'

'That's what sisters are for.'

Her eyes welled up. 'I didn't want to burden anyone with all of this.' Her hands gestured to herself. 'Everyone seems to be doing so well – Codie, you, Mum and Dad.'

I swallowed the mouthful I was chewing, putting my fork down. 'You're doing well too, you know.'

She sniffed. 'I'm heading towards 30, and I can't seem to hold down a relationship. My gigs are unreliable and hardly make any money. I feel like I could always be *more*, you know? More successful, more attractive, more compassionate. I think that's why I was so rude to you when you started talking about your column. I was jealous.'

I was genuinely shocked by this. 'Suze, you're someone I look up to. A lot.'

She shrugged. 'How do you know if you're doing it right? Growing up, I mean.'

It was Suze speaking, but it could have been Stacey in her messy bedroom, or Teddy that first day in the park. We were all trying to figure it out.

'I don't think anyone actually knows what the hell is going on half the time.'

Suze cradled her lemonade, looking sceptical. 'You think?'

I nodded. 'I'm not trying to invalidate the way you feel, I just don't want you to think that you're alone. Life is weird, I think you just have to do what feels right for you.'

She considered what I'd said. 'Thanks, Flick. That does help.'

'And you're nowhere near 30! Let's calm down.' I squeezed her hand as she laughed.

We finished our food, chatting about mindless topics – a trick Dad had taught Kernel, and Mum's new vegetable patch. It felt good, catching up.

'So . . . Teddy.' She gave me a pointed look. 'Please tell me I get to meet him. I've heard so much about the man.'

I sighed. 'Can a platonic relationship not exist?'

'Of course it can. But I've heard the way you talk about him. And I don't talk that way about *my* friends. Plus, he got you a *keyboard*, Flick, and he made you pierogi.'

I interrupted. 'How do you know that?'

Her expression said it all.

'Oh, for God's sake. You were only talking to Stacey for two minutes.'

She waved me off, laughing. 'The point is, I think the most sentimental gift Eric ever bought me was a voucher for *his* favourite restaurant.'

'Okay, he is thoughtful. I know he is, I'm not oblivious. But I have no time to be dating. I'm not ready yet.'

'Sure you're not. You know, you just told me that everyone goes at their own pace.' Suze grinned as she wiped her mouth with a napkin. 'So where does that leave you? Oh my God. You're going to have to roll me home.'

I stabbed the last of my pancakes with my fork. 'On it.'

# 29

'You're the talk of London!' Sadie appeared by my desk, shoving some comments from Alexis's Instagram post in my face.

Felix looked up from his screen. 'Usually I'd be sarcastic here, but you actually are. All of the emails we're getting are requests for more of the column. People don't want articles about box rooms and Netflix recommendations any more. That podcast must have attracted a lot of attention.'

It was Monday morning, and my episode of *The Sunday Podcast* had been released yesterday. I'd already had texts from Stacey (with exclamation marks) about her shout out. Mum had asked how she could post a podcast on Facebook, and a couple of friends from university had commented on my Instagram, cooing over the fact that I'd met Alexis. Apparently, she was a bigger influencer than I'd realised. I scrolled through the messages again as I bit into my pain au chocolat.

'This is just the beginning.' Sadie sighed happily. 'I was thinking we could organise a live agony-aunt session . . .'

'Do I get a say in this?' I interrupted her, taking a swig of my coffee. I'd been up so late last night playing board games with everyone (an attempt to take Maia's mind off things, which she'd gladly accepted) that I'd had no time for breakfast this morning.

Felix clicked on something in the company's inbox. 'According to this email, you've really helped Marianne, from Ipswich, get over her ex-boyfriend and start to claim her life back. Oh, and this other one is from Hallie, in Cardiff. Apparently, you inspired her to go back to university to study nursing. And that's just two of about eight emails I've read *today*.'

I put down my coffee, navigating a completely unexpected lump in my throat. The column had been a major factor in me finding my place here. Thinking of it doing the same for someone else was lovely.

'I think she's going to cry.' Felix sniffed. 'I feel a bit emotional myself.'

Sadie was looking at us like we'd grown antenna. 'This is a *good* thing, people. It's what I've been saying all along. This is bigger than a small column in a – let's be honest – less than famous magazine. We've all been through rocky patches. It's a universal experience that brings us all together. Everyone wants to hear a success story, to remind them that they can find a way out of whatever it is that's getting them down.'

We both looked at Sadie.

'Damn.' Felix held out his fist for her to touch. 'That might be the most insightful thing you've said in this office, Sades.'

She flipped her hair. 'I speak for the people.'

As she walked off, Felix snickered. 'And she ruined it.'

The day passed quickly; for once, it was comforting to get back into the mundane administrative tasks that I was used to. I loved the column, but it was keeping me up at night. How could I ever look Marianne from Ipswich or Hallie from Cardiff in the eye, knowing I'd fabricated a successful relationship?

'Felicity?'

I whipped my head up from my desk, where I'd been engrossed in a different episode of Alexis's podcast whilst I worked. Sadie was right. She was *good* at what she did; her podcasts were really interesting.

'Can you come in here for a sec?' Cecilia was standing by her door, beckoning me in.

'Good luck,' Felix whispered, not making eye contact.

When I reached the office Cecilia beamed at me, gesturing to the seat in front of her. I took it, suspicious. Every time I walked in here she dropped some kind of bombshell.

'Felicity, I wanted to talk to you about a few things. I'm proud of you. I know that a lot of what we're asking from you doesn't come naturally, so I want to commend you for that. When we started this graduate scheme I had no idea what to expect, but it's surpassed my expectations and it's exactly what we needed for the magazine. We've decided to continue and take on another grad in September.'

Without even thinking I clasped my hands to my chest. 'Oh, that is such good news! I can't wait to meet them.'

'Obviously' – Cecilia wrote something down on a sticky note and stuck it to her desktop, always thinking two steps ahead – 'this means that your role will change. You'll no longer be our magazine assistant. We'd like to keep you here with us, if that's something you want too. I'd like you to have a bit of a think about what your role might evolve into. Whether it be a junior editor position or something else.'

'I don't even know what to say.' I was *so* relieved to know that come September, I'd still be here at *Influence*. And a promotion, no less. I couldn't wait to ring Mum on my lunch break. It had been hard living in London on a grad scheme wage.

'No need to say anything, just say you'll think about it.' Cecilia smiled.

'I absolutely will. Thank you.'

'And one last thing before I let you go. We're definitely going to run with the print column in June. A culmination of *The Twenties List*, if you will. In a double-page spread.'

I was taken aback. We very rarely handed out double-page spreads to new writers.

'That's . . . also amazing. I'll start thinking about what I want to write.' *Am I living in some kind of parallel universe?* I pinched the skin on my hand. Yep, it hurt. This was real.

Cecilia laughed. 'I knew you'd be shocked. I wanted to give you enough advance notice – because obviously June deadlines will be here before you know it. I can't wait to see what you come up with; make sure that you ask Felix if you need any guidance.'

I must have been looking shell-shocked, because she continued. 'You remind me of myself, Flick, when I was your age. Take every opportunity when you're offered it. That's how you move up in this industry.'

After all the late nights and hard work, it felt really good to have it all pay off. There was one more question I had to ask, as much as I didn't want to.

'And Teddy?'

Cecilia cocked her eyebrow. 'What about him?'

'Do I admit to fake-dating him? In the article, that is.'

'Heavens, no.' She started tapping on her keyboard, already letting her mind drift to the next task on her to-do list. 'I have to be honest, I kind of assumed that it wasn't fake any more.'

*Why did everyone keep saying that?*

'You must be a natural at acting, Flick. If the journalism doesn't work out, maybe try that.' She couldn't see the expression on my face, so she kept chuckling.

I left the office, already creating a mental list of who I wanted to share the news with. Mum, Teddy, the house chat. I already had some ideas about my piece for the magazine – I wanted it to be more than just an extension of the column. Especially now, after this weekend with Suze. I could see the bigger picture; how my list of mostly trivial items linked to the huge pressure that all my friends seemed to associate with being in our twenties. This was a chance for me to kick-start my career and write something meaningful. But I just couldn't shake the guilt.

★★★

I twirled spaghetti onto my fork. Teddy was grabbing an extra portion already; I'd never known anyone to eat meals so quickly.

'That's good though, right, that she's decided to go and talk to someone? This is the first step.'

Suze had called on her way home from work, letting me know that she'd been to see a GP. She'd taken a week off work to go and stay with Mum and Dad, using up her annual leave and taking some well-needed rest. A week spent in our childhood home, with Kernel as soft, furry protection and plenty of Dad's comfort food, was a good plan. When she'd called today, she'd sounded exhausted, but more positive than she had done in a while. I'd been able to hear Dad in the background, shouting that dinner was ready, Mum humming along to the radio as she set the table. It was funny how a place and the people in it could make you feel instantly safe. I smiled, looking around the kitchen. I had multiple places like that.

'I'm proud of her. I think she's been bottling it all up for a long time. It takes a lot to admit to yourself, most of all, that there's something wrong.'

Teddy leaned on the counter, shovelling pasta into his mouth. He nodded. 'It was similar with Greg. He was on a waiting list for a long time, but after he did get the call, my family decided we needed to do something to support him. Even if it was something silly or small, we used to take it in turns to go for chocolate milkshakes with him every week after his sessions. He was a little sceptical at first, I mean, we hardly spoke about the actual sessions until he was ready to. But having us there no matter what, I think it helped.'

I smiled into my bowl. I wanted to meet this family.

'So, any idea what you're going to write about?'

I'd told Teddy about the promotion and the spread in the magazine today at work, and he'd immediately grabbed his coat and taken me to 'our' sandwich shop to celebrate, toasting the news with cappuccinos.

'I've got so much I want to say, it's just figuring out the best way to say it.' I was gesturing wildly. It was funny – the column was something I'd been reticent about, but writing about this decade of life had become something I was deeply passionate about. 'I want to write what we're all thinking, but no one ever says out loud.'

Thinking about the people I was writing for made me think about Marianne and Hallie and all of the other young women who I had 'helped'. I felt my face start to crumple.

'What is it? What's wrong?' Teddy reached out, rubbing my back in slow circles. 'You seem so excited about this.'

I hiccupped, feeling more and more panicky by the second. 'I feel *awful*.'

Teddy frowned. 'About what? I don't understand.'

I explained what had happened in the office today. Felix, Sadie, the stories of the other women. And Cecilia, telling me I reminded her of her younger self.

'And I really admire Cecilia, I do, but do I want to be like her? She convinced me to create a fake relationship, feels no guilt about lying to the office . . .'

'Okay, let's take this piece by piece, shall we?' Teddy took the fork I'd been clutching, which had left angry red marks on my skin. He pushed the bowl away, turning my chair so he could clasp my hands in his.

'Cecilia is your boss. She asked you to write the column, and she was the one who asked you to include dating in

287

there. You're a 22-year-old grad, what were you going to do, refuse?'

'Well, no, but –'

'You aren't a bad person for wanting to progress in your career. I can't help but feel like most people would have done the same thing. Besides, no one got hurt, did they? The magazine is doing great, and look, we *could* have dated. It isn't that far-fetched. You were always going to start dating at some point, and the fact that it's helped those women can only be seen as a bonus.'

'But Hallie, and Marianne . . .' Fresh tears came to the surface.

'Hallie and Marianne are doing great. They said so in their emails. And listen – do you think Cecilia would be this upset, or feel this guilty?'

He had a point. 'I guess not.'

'You know I'm right. It makes you feel uncomfortable, which is a sign that you've got a conscience. I'm not worried the power has gone to your head. I promise you, most of the people who read that column would have done the same thing.'

We sat in silence for a few minutes whilst I mulled over his advice. His annoyingly good advice. All I could do now was write the best article possible, to shine a light on all the pressures that people faced as young adults. I owed it to all the people I'd lied to.

'Feeling any better?' Teddy wiped a final tear from my cheek.

I nodded, pulling my pasta bowl back towards me.

'Ah, the appetite has returned. We're back in business.' He started eating his own again, passing me the parmesan. There weren't really words to explain how thankful I was that I had him in my life.

'When you said we could have dated,' I took a breath, 'I would have, you know. If Aaron hadn't –'

Teddy gave my hand another squeeze, pulling me into him. I focused on his heartbeat against my ears, a steady, comforting beat. 'I know, Sage, I know.'

\*\*\*

## The Twenties List: Moving On is Hard to Do

*Dear Reader,*

*I'm back! Did you miss me? The weeks are truly flying by at this point.*

*When I started writing my twenties list, I chose things that seemed relatively doable, but I still had no idea how I was actually going to put them into action. Now, the list is as much a part of my life as brushing my teeth or moisturising my legs (okay, that's a lie. I rarely moisturise). I spend at least ten minutes every day sitting at my keyboard. So far, it has only produced a mixture of 'Wonderwall' and 'Yesterday', but I'll take what I can get. I've got Polaroids all over my bedroom walls, which takes me right back to university and sticking photos to every available surface. I've also finished reading my third memoir – Michelle Obama's. Highly recommend. How does one live a life so interesting that they can write a book about it? Asking for a friend.*

*So many of you have been sending questions through to our inbox, so I thought I'd take a moment to answer a few more. I can't promise that my advice will be any good, but I can promise that I'll try my best to channel my inner older sister. God knows I've relied on mine for advice over the years. We got a few questions this week that fall into a definite theme:*

**'I read *The Twenties List* religiously. I recently got out of a relationship and I'm struggling to come to terms with the fact that it's over. How do you accept and move on?'**

**'Flick, I can't stop watching *Bridget Jones* and eating Phish Food. There must be a heartbreak solution, but I can't find it. Any advice for an immediate cure?'**

**'My girlfriend moved out last week really unexpectedly. Life feels like it's gone drastically off course. How do you pick yourself back up when all you want to do is let it drag you down?'**

*I feel like I easily could have written all three of these when I was dumped. Heartbreak is the actual worst. However you spin it, it hurts to wonder what you did wrong. How many of us have woken up in the morning and instantly remembered, desperately trying to go back to sleep and return to that semi-conscious state of ignorance? It doesn't matter who you're grieving – and, despite what anyone tries to tell you otherwise, heartbreak is a form of grief – it hurts.*

*There is no magic solution to heartbreak, I don't think (I know you were probably hoping for something a bit more helpful than that). But the honest truth is that you just have to ride it out. Chocolate helps, as well as company. And like my mum used to say to me and my sister when we fell out with our friends at school, time is the biggest healer. Little by little, it will get better. One day you'll wake up and you'll realise that you don't feel like crying in the shower. You might look back months later and realise that heartbreak was one of the best things that ever happened to you. It's horrible when something so huge is completely out of your control, but we're built for resilience. One day you'll meet someone who makes everything make sense.*

*We're all in this together. Sending all my love and praying for a speedy recovery for you. Speak soon,*

*Flick x*

# 30

'You've mastered it!' Maia came into the kitchen, where I was slicing up a loaf of sourdough.

I winced. 'I would love to tell you I hadn't bought this from Tesco Express.'

She burst out laughing. 'You definitely could have got away with that. You're too honest.'

Too honest. I winced. Sure, that summed me up right now. Maia helped herself to a slice, grabbing some peanut butter from the cupboard and slathering it on. She seemed in much better spirits this week, ready to take on the legal world again.

'So, how's it going?' She directed the question at me from behind her hand, saving me from the sight of her talking with her mouth full.

'Good. I've just been working on my submission for the print issue. It's due next week.'

With my deadline looming I was cramming every spare second I had into the article. The sourdough had been an impulse buy. I needed stress carbs. During my final year exams I'd made my way through at least three loaves a week. PB&J,

Marmite, jam . . . you name it, I ate it on toast during exam week.

'How's the studying for the re-sit going?'

Maia sighed. 'I'm bricking it. I really thought I had it the first time. I wish I didn't let things like this knock me down so badly. It's probably why I prep so much.'

'It's an insane amount of stuff to remember, Maia. Your worst exam effort is probably my best.' I smiled. 'Take as much sourdough fuel as you need.'

'Thank you. I'm glad you deal with stress the same way I do.' She grabbed another slice of bread, putting it in the toaster this time. 'I do love baking bread, but can I tell the difference? Probably not. This is divine.'

She sat next to me and we worked in silence for a while. Of all my housemates, Maia was the one I liked sharing silence with the most. Stacey didn't do quiet – in her words, half of her profession relied on her having 'the gift of the gab'– and Kitty's tutoring sessions could be quite distracting. Maia was a reassuring presence.

'What angle are you aiming for? For the column?' She pointed to my screen.

'I wish I knew. I want to talk about everything I've learnt this year, but I know that's not possible. It's all kind of up for debate. Definitely can't leave out all the fun of living in a houseshare.' I grinned at her. 'And how women should lift each other up, always.'

'Well, that sounds incredible. So, what's up for debate?'

'It's just . . . Cecilia lives for the dating angle. As you know.'

I'd told the girls how I'd agonised over the dating aspect of my column, and they'd all agreed – everything else I wrote about was honest. I still wasn't sleeping well.

'Ah.' Maia looked down at her keyboard. 'You know, as much as it's a column for the magazine, it's your project. You started it from scratch before it ever became *Influence*'s property. You deserve to write what you're passionate about. It's artistic licence.'

'You know, you really are starting to sound like a lawyer.'

She seemed pleased with the comment. 'I hope so. I'd write what you just said. It sounds authentic. It sounds like Flick.'

I really, *really* wanted to sound like Flick.

'Guys?' We heard Stacey come through the front door, her voice ringing out throughout the house. 'Where are you all?'

'We're in here,' I called back. 'Kitty's upstairs deciding which hair dye to go for next.'

Maia shook her head, laughing when we heard her bellow up the stairs in the direction of Kitty's bedroom. I could hear music being turned off on the floor above, and the creak of the floorboards.

'I think I'm feeling lilac? Do you think I can pull it off?' Kitty walked in and sat on one of the bar stools, plonking a box dye in front of her.

'As long as you aren't dying Soph's hair green, I'm thrilled with whatever you choose.' Maia closed her laptop and frowned curiously. 'What is this, some kind of family meeting?'

Stace bounced into the kitchen, having dumped her stuff in her room. 'Actually . . . kind of.' She looked a little bit sheepish.

I saved my progress on the article, closing my laptop. A Carlisle family meeting meant business. The last time we'd had one had been when Kitty seriously thought she'd contracted an STI and needed our support to ring up and get her results. It had been a false alarm, but we'd all shared the burden of the fear, nonetheless.

'Okay, so.' Stace braced her hands on the counter. 'Team meeting. I have an announcement.'

Knowing Stacey, this could be something as minuscule as getting a muffin for 13p in Sainsbury's, to completely life-altering news. You never knew what you were going to get. We were all sitting in a row opposite her, waiting.

'I feel like we're on a game show or something.' Kit grabbed a peach from the fruit bowl, biting into it.

'To be fair,' Maia said as she glanced between us, 'I think we'd make a pretty good team with our combined knowledge.'

'Guys.' I could hear Stacey's foot tapping on the floor. 'I know I'm a drama queen, but this is genuinely important.'

'Sorry. You have our undivided attention.' Kitty spoke, letting a dribble of peach juice run down her chin.

'So, I've been thinking a lot about how long I've lived here, and how my life feels a bit stagnant. They've offered me a promotion at work, which means a bit more money, and –'

'*No.*' Kitty grasped it first. 'Oh my God.'

'Yeah.' Stacey's skin was flushed. 'I'm going to miss you guys so much, but I've lived here for three years now. It's time.'

We all sat there in shock for a minute before Maia broke the silence. 'Firstly, congratulations on the promotion.'

Both Kitty and I rushed in with our congratulations.

'I'm so proud of you.' Kitty smiled, her eyes watering slightly. 'Look at you go.'

'And you thought you were stuck.' I gave her a knowing look.

I'd never seen my friend glow this brightly. Stace beamed back at us. 'I know, it's crazy. This house has been with me through some of the most formative years of my life. It deserves to do the same for someone else now.'

I could tell we were all trying hard not to show how much the news had upset us.

'When?' Maia was forever practical.

'First of June. I've emailed the landlord – it's official. They're going to try and find someone to fill my spot before the end of the month.'

I heard a sniff at the end of our line of three.

'Oh *Kit*.' Stacey moved to hug her, squeezing her tight. 'I'm not leaving the city!'

'But who am I going to convince people to dye their hair crazy colours with? Who'll make lethal sangria with me?' She was full-on crying now. Kitty, who never seemed to get upset about anything. Ever.

Maia was clearly as dumbstruck as me. 'I mean, you aren't getting your hands on my hair, but I'm going to be a lawyer soon. I have very strong persuasive skills when it comes to convincing other people.'

Stacey rubbed Kitty's back. 'See? You've still got the dream team right here.'

Kitty and Stacey were different in so many ways, but it had been clear from my very first day in this house that they were as close as housemates could be.

'I'm sorry, I'm making this about me.' Kitty wiped her eyes.

'Our entire friendship, I've made most things about me.' Stacey shrugged at us. 'What? I'm self-aware as well as self-absorbed. You're allowed to take ownership of this moment. It's my parting gift to you.'

That just made Kitty cry even harder. 'I literally don't know where this has come from. I'm not usually a crier.'

'Maybe we're rubbing off on you,' I suggested. 'We'll only know for sure when you start sobbing in the shower. Bonus tip: if you turn up the pressure, there's less chance of being heard.'

'Flick, I'm on the ground floor and I heard it.'

I pulled a face at Stacey.

'It just won't be Carlisle without you.' Kitty sniffed again, reaching for the kitchen roll.

'Did we or did we not say that when Tara said she was leaving?' Stacey put her hands on her hips. 'Don't ignore me, Katherine. Did we or did we not say that?'

Her voice was small. 'We did.'

'And isn't Flick the best new housemate we could have asked for? Look, she bakes bread and everything.' She bit into a chunk of sourdough.

'I didn't —'

Maia put her hand over mine, mouthing 'Take the credit'. I stopped talking.

Kitty was nodding now, her expression brighter. 'We didn't think there could be a new Tara. And you aren't, you're our Flick.'

Maia's expression was soft. 'And Flick is exactly what we needed.' She turned to Kitty. 'We'll find another housemate like we did with Flick. It'll be fine.'

Stacey threw her head back. 'God, if I'd known you guys would react this way, I would have got a film crew in here. So, I have exactly twenty-three days left in this house before I move out. That's twenty-three days of some serious Stacey-Kitty-Maia-Felicity fun.'

'Please don't call me –'

She smirked. 'Felicity? What was that?'

I rolled my eyes. 'Okay, I'm in.'

Maia nodded. 'Me too. Bring it on.'

Kitty took the longest to respond, wiping her eyes with the kitchen roll. 'Of course I'm in. God, they don't make this stuff soft, do they? I feel like I have no skin left around my eyes.'

'That is so gross.' Stacey wrinkled her nose. Anyway, back to the twenty-three-day-plan. Instead of wallowing tonight' – she pointed at Kitty – 'we're going to kick things off by going out-out.'

I saw Maia look down at her laptop at the same time as me, and then I looked up at Stace, who was waiting expectantly for our response. She really had been a catalyst for all the positive parts of the past four months. Even when she was meddling, Stacey had brought me Teddy. She'd been a rock when I'd needed one. And now she needed us.

'Get the glitter.' I pointed to our 'glitter drawer' in the kitchen. 'We have to go full Carlisle. Kitty, no time to cry, you've got work to do.'

Stace mouthed 'Thank you' at me before pointing to Maia and then to me. 'You text Sophie. And you text Teddy. This is going to be *so* much fun.'

# 31

We were in the queue outside when I felt a tap on my shoulder. I spun around, almost bumping into Teddy's chest.

'The better half of Fleddy, present and accounted for.'

I narrowed my eyes. 'On what grounds?'

'My ability to get to Shoreditch for a night out on such short notice.'

He had a point. This had been our most spontaneous night out yet. We still had over three weeks left of Stace living in her ground-floor room, but nights like these felt limited.

I leaned in to hug Teddy. 'That's true. I respect the commitment. You can hold the title for one night and one night only.'

Kitty – who had managed to pull herself together and stop crying for long enough to do her signature glitter braids – pounced on Teddy, drawing him into a conversation about the trailer for the latest Marvel movie. I smiled as I watched them get more and more animated. They were so different; Kitty was wearing her dalmatian-print jumpsuit and giant platforms; Teddy, on the other hand, stood beside her wearing a plain black T-shirt. It didn't matter, though. They drew from each other's energy.

'You know, you never smile that way when you look at me.' Stacey nudged me and I wiped my expression clean.

'How do you know that I don't?'

She shrugged. 'Point taken, but I suspect not, regardless.'

I deliberately ignored the comment.

She held her hand out for a stamp when we reached the front of the line. 'So, what's your poison tonight?'

Teddy jumped in before I could answer. 'She keeps promising me that she'll try an Old Fashioned. Bottles it every time.'

I sighed heavily. 'He wants me to try his old-man drink.'

Maia, who had been hanging further back in the queue with Sophie, spoke. 'You know, it's actually quite a trendy drink.'

Sophie nodded. 'We had them last week at this bar in Ealing. They were the bartender's special. He did a dark chocolate version.'

I didn't need to look at Teddy to know that he was wearing a smug smile. In fact, I refused to give him the recognition that he was clearly craving. 'Fine, I'll drink one. But only because you two recommended it.'

'Sorry, what was that?' When I finally gave in and glanced back at Teddy, he had his hand cupping one ear. 'Felicity Sage was, what? Wrong? It is not, in fact, an old person's drink?'

Kitty jostled him. 'She might actually kill you.'

He smirked, hooking me in with his elbow and kissing the top of my head. 'She would never.'

301

Maia and Sophie exchanged a look that they thought I couldn't see, but I ignored that too, making my way to the bar.

When we'd finally elbowed our way through the crowds and found somewhere to sit, Teddy passed his glass over to me. 'You promised. One sip. Then I'll let it go.'

I wrinkled my nose. 'But it's *whisky.*'

'It really isn't that bad.' Sophie pointed to the glass. 'It just tastes like bitter orange peel.'

'Wow, you're really selling it to me, Soph.' I took the glass and tried not to grimace as I took a sip. She was right; I could taste the orange. The only problem was that it tasted like someone had burnt it, dipped it in lighter fluid, and blended it. I said as much.

Teddy put his hand to his chest in mock hurt. 'Don't hold back, though. I want you to be honest.'

I laughed. 'Hey, you made me try it. Don't say I didn't warn you.'

Stacey came back from the bathroom with Kitty, where they'd been for the last ten minutes. If I squinted in the semi-dark, it looked like Kitty might have been crying again. I hadn't filled Teddy in on the situation yet, so I did it quickly whilst the two of them tried to find a seat.

'Oh shit, that's big news.' Teddy looked concerned for Kitty. 'I thought she seemed a bit down.'

'Yeah, it took us all by surprise.'

'C'est la vie though, right? That's the beauty of a houseshare. Plus, I've seen the four of you in your natural habitat. You guys are going to keep in touch for a long time.'

My cheeks flushed with pleasure. I'd barely kept in touch with anyone from university and it was my biggest regret.

'And you, of course.' I nudged him. 'You're one of us now too, you know.'

He cleared his throat. 'If you'd told me to picture this a few months ago, I wouldn't have believed you. How can you go from feeling so lonely to feeling so content?' He tapped my nose lightly with his fingertip. 'It never would have happened without you.'

I was touched. 'Hey, it was you that came over to me that first night.'

'Don't kid yourself. My life here has been an adventure since you walked into it.'

He was leaning towards me, fighting to be heard over the music. It felt good to be this close to him. I made a mental note to keep my eyes on the top half of his face, crossing my fingers that he hadn't spotted my gaze wandering down to his mouth.

'Where do you guys want to go after this?' Stace was sitting on the other side of me. When I turned to chat to her, she leaned in. 'Flick, I'm telling you, you're blind if you can't see what you both want.'

It might have been the sip of whisky, but I was momentarily confused. 'I thought we were talking about tonight.'

She shook her head. 'A conversational diversion. Besides, I *am* talking about tonight. You and Teddy. It's like watching two magnets try to pry themselves away from each other.'

I stifled a laugh. 'You think?'

Stacey patted me on the cheek. 'I've dated *a lot* of people, and not one of them has ever been caught looking at me the way he always seems to be looking at you.'

***

The second bar was even busier than the first, but being part of Kitty's entourage meant you were never too far from an excuse to skip the queue. She seemed to know someone everywhere we went.

'You're extremely popular tonight. You won't even notice that I'm gone!' Stacey poked her and got a dirty look in return.

'Too soon. I'm still licking my wounds.'

Maia leaned against the bar, cradling a glass of red wine. 'Me too. My mind is processing as fast as it can –'

'Which, for you, is *very* fast.' I interjected, and she smiled.

'Fast as that is, it's struggling to compute this. The house is going to be so *quiet*.'

Stacey pulled us all in for a group hug. 'You know, the Carlisle legacy never changes. No matter where we end up going.'

'Or who we end up going there with.' Maia gave me a gentle shove towards the other end of the bar, where Teddy was ordering in the next round of drinks.

'*Yes, Maia.*' Kitty high-fived her.

'It's painful to watch.' Maia laughed. 'How far can it be to go from fake dating to real dating? They're all over each other all the time anyway.'

'We are *not*.'

All four of them, Sophie included, shot me a look.

'Wait, what's he doing?' Stace squinted in the direction of the bar. 'Who is he talking to?'

My heart dropped into my stomach. 'What?'

'Don't turn around,' Kitty instructed.

I ignored her, suddenly desperate to see whatever it was that was getting them riled up. I immediately wished I hadn't. Teddy was leaning over the bar, talking to the bartender. She was twirling her hair around her index finger, laughing at something he was saying. Why did this feel worse than when I bumped into Aaron with his new girlfriend?

'Are you okay?' Kitty steadied me. 'You look a bit pale.'

'She's doing the majority of the flirting.' Maia was dissecting the situation from behind her wine glass. 'He's just chatting. Not displaying any of the traditional male mating signals.'

'Bloody hell, Maia. We aren't watching a David Attenborough documentary.' Stace squinted again. 'I mean, this isn't ideal. I felt like we were approaching a breakthrough with Flick for a moment there.'

Teddy wasn't leaning over the bar any more, but he was still talking. He hadn't looked back at us once. My cheeks felt hot. I was jealous.

'I'm going over there.' I psyched myself up. *What else was I meant to do?* I couldn't just watch this happen. I was pretty sure – in fact, I think I'd been subconsciously pretty sure for a while now – that I had a thing for Teddy. He was my person.

'Holy shit! Really?'

Kitty swatted at Stace. 'Shut up, don't put her off the idea.'

Stacey bit her lip. 'Oh right, yeah. I'm team Fleddy, all the way. You've just got some serious balls. Or, not balls. Whatever the feminist version of that saying is. Now go over there and show us the Fleddy moment we've all been waiting for!'

'I'll go if it means you never use that phrase again.'

Kitty pouted. 'But we already bulk bought the Fleddy slogan T-shirts.'

I ignored them. Were my palms clammy? Teddy was now cupping his ear to hear what the bartender was saying more clearly. The conversation was still in full flow. Was I really going to interrupt them? I glanced behind me for a second to see all four of the others pretending that they weren't watching. None of them would be next in line for an Oscar. Maia broke character to shoot me a subtle thumbs-up.

'Teddy?'

He turned, surprised to see me for a second or two before his expression broke into a smile. 'Hey Sage. This is Hannah.'

The bartender stopped flicking her hair, wary. 'Your cocktails are there.' She gestured to the glasses on the bar top.

*Nice try.*

'Oh, thanks.' I stayed right where I was.

'And Hannah, this is Flick. The fake girlfriend I was telling you about.' He laughed as he said it, not realising the cataclysmic mistake he'd just made. He couldn't go around letting *random strangers* in on our secret. As soon as a tiny amount loosened, it could unravel completely.

'Teddy, can I speak to you for a second?' I was livid.

I waited whilst he wrapped up the conversation, barely saying bye to the bartender before I stormed off into the corner of the bar. 'Are you kidding me?'

Teddy had finally caught up to me. 'Kidding about what?'

'Telling that random girl about the column. I can't believe what I've just heard. It's not a joke, Teddy, it's my whole *career*.'

'Whoa. Firstly' – he held his hands up – 'I didn't mention anything about the column. I hadn't got to the context part yet, and I wasn't planning on it. It was a random conversation with someone at a bar. Mystery, intrigue. Nothing is more mysterious than having a fake girlfriend. And secondly, I know how hard you've worked. I know how worried you are about it. I was never going to put your career at stake, and you know that. You know me. What is going on with you? What is this really about?'

I didn't pause to think. 'We have to be more careful than that. If people find out that I've lied –'

'How would they?'

'If *Hannah* tells someone, they may then read the column and figure it out . . . why were you even talking to her anyway?'

Teddy flinched. 'Why was I – Because I'm allowed to talk to a woman at a bar. I'm single, remember, Flick?'

This wasn't quite the romantic movie-moment I'd envisaged.

'Right.' I really felt like I might be about to cry. I gritted my teeth, feeling the blow from his words in my stomach.

'This relationship,' he said with air quotes, 'is fake. Yes?'

I felt it bubbling up inside me, this feeling of frustration, of anger and sadness. I should have said yes when Teddy had asked me out that day in the staffroom. I should have let this play out the way it was meant to, instead of creating this tangled mess. It didn't help that he looked ridiculously attractive when he was irritated, either. I was in the shit. I had completely fallen for him somewhere along the way, and now we were out flirting with other people at bars and yelling at each other in room corners.

'Are you about to cry?' Teddy's tone changed and his face softened. He reached out to wipe a rogue tear from my face. 'I don't – I don't understand. Me and you, together – it's all fake, right?'

There were now only centimetres between us – our argument had changed shape into something more intense.

'I don't want it to be.' It came out quieter than I'd planned.

His thumb rubbed my cheek before he pulled my face towards his, finally closing the gap between us. Teddy smiled against my lips as he kissed me. From somewhere behind us, I heard a loud cheer that sounded suspiciously like Stacey.

He murmured against my lips. 'Pretending is overrated. I think the real thing is much, much better.'

# 32

I opened one eye. When I wasn't met with a throbbing pain, I tentatively opened my other eye. *Phew!*

I patted around next to me, trying to limit my movement. Aha. Found it. My phone screen read 10.09 a.m., a surprisingly early time for me to wake naturally after a night out. I had three messages: one from Mum, asking me to call her; one from Suze, letting me know that she'd be up for a FaceTime this evening; and one from the group chat. Stacey had written 'Wearing my Fleddy T-shirt today, and always', and the others had reacted to it with hearts. I was surprised she was awake, to be honest, after how late I'd heard them eventually get in last night. Or should I say, this morning. My phone buzzed again with another text, and I turned it over quietly before reading. I looked in Teddy's direction, but after a moment of hitched breathing, his breaths evened out again. Was it weird of me to just watch him as he slept? Probably.

'You know, what you're doing right now toes the line between cute and weird.'

I jumped out of my skin. 'Not as weird as you pretending to be asleep.'

He smiled without opening his eyes, reaching around until he found my hand, pulling me into him.

'Shut up and pretend to be asleep with me.'

I hesitated. 'Shall we talk about last night? What it means?'

A noise of protest came from Teddy. 'Later, Sage. Come sleep with me.'

I tucked myself into his side, my mind whirring too fast to even think about falling asleep again. I couldn't believe *Teddy* was lying here next to me. And why did he want to delay our conversation? What had last night actually *meant?* I thought back to my column entry about modern dating; it really was confusing. As if he could read my mind, he spoke.

'You know, I did not anticipate this when you told me to meet you in Shoreditch last night.'

'I'll be honest,' I traced my fingertips against his torso, 'neither did I.'

'I thought you were going to slap that girl.'

I reeled back, offended. 'I would never do that!'

'You were hardly welcoming.' He was laughing now. 'I've always wondered what having two girls fight over me would look like.'

'I know you're just trying to wind me up, but it really is working.'

He pulled me on top of him. 'So, you definitely don't want anything to do with me right now, then?'

I wriggled, but he had me stuck. 'Nope. Nothing.'

'I thought we were done with lies.'

The idea of not having to lie to my readers any more was a welcome bonus of last night's revelations. Suze had been right yet again; it was incredibly hard to fake falling in love with someone without it becoming the real deal. I hadn't mentioned that to Teddy yet, but I knew what I felt. He had no idea how easy it was to be around him.

'We *are* done with those. We're never faking it again.' I kissed him, laughing as he pulled me closer.

★★★

It was over an hour before we made any effort to get up for the day, basking in the miracle that neither of us were suffering from the night before.

Teddy sat up – it was still so strange to have a man in this bed – and leaned back against the headboard. 'I hope they aren't mad that we left early last night.'

I thought back to the group chat. 'Trust me, they aren't annoyed. I think they would have actually been more frustrated if I hadn't made a move.'

He shot me a sideways glance. 'Just for the record, I will always have made the first move. You shot me down first, remember?'

I put my head in my hands. 'Don't. I've cost us a lot of time and energy.'

Teddy shrugged. 'I was only kidding. I actually think things might have turned out completely different if we'd dated from the off. This has been a complete rollercoaster, but it's been fun. You have to admit.'

As much as I'd lost sleep over the whole thing, it had been fun. We'd been a team.

I flopped down onto my pillow again, sighing happily. 'There's just something about Sunday mornings, isn't there?'

Teddy was flicking through a stack of Polaroids that I was keeping on my bedside table. 'Mmm.' He was distracted, making his way through some of the photos I'd taken so far. The likelihood of making it to 100 before my twenty-third birthday was slim, but the twenties list had mileage for a whole decade. I had nothing but time.

'This one is my favourite, by far.' He held up one that we'd taken in the living room the other night, all four of us pulling faces. Maia was doing bunny ears behind Kitty's head.

I grabbed the camera. 'I bet we can take a new favourite.'

Teddy wrinkled his nose. 'I mean, my hair . . .'

'Is this you admitting to the hair gel I know you use?'

He took the camera from me. 'Let's just take the photo.'

We posed, me nestling into him, both of us smiling with the covers pulled up to our chins. When it appeared, I sat the card-sized photo on the duvet next to us, watching the film develop.

'And I also got one last night.' I leaned down the side of my bed, where the photo I'd taken in Kitty's bedroom had fallen.

Stacey was holding the camera, caught in laughter as she snapped the photo, the rest of us unaware. I was mid lipstick application, squinting, and Maia had been texting Sophie, relaxed on Kitty's bed. Kitty was the only one who had anticipated the photo opportunity, throwing up a peace sign, glitter already applied to every available inch of her body.

'That is exactly what I love about this camera.' I pointed to the photo as I added it to the pile. 'You get one chance, and it just captures you as you are. No hiding.'

'You're starting to sound more and more like a writer every day.' Teddy kissed my forehead. 'How's the article coming along?'

'It's . . . getting there.'

'You don't sound convinced.'

I sighed. 'To say Cecilia and I are butting heads over it would be an understatement. It's a work in progress.' I picked at a thread on the duvet spread. 'I want to write something honest. Cecilia is not as convinced.'

'I'm sure you'll manage to convince her. Hey, this turned out pretty good.'

The photo was now fully developed. I stared at the girl in the Polaroid. She looked happy. I was proud of her. I wanted my article to reflect that.

'Flick?' A shout came from the second floor. 'Flick, I'm sorry to interrupt, but I think you might want to come down here.' It was Kitty. Her voice sounded weird.

I shared a confused look with Teddy, and he gently pushed me towards the edge of the bed. 'Go, go. I'll be fine up here.'

'You sure?'

'Yes.' He smiled. 'Just hurry back. We have' – he checked his phone – 'thirty-seven minutes of morning left.'

I pulled my dressing gown on, dragging a brush through my hair and grabbing a piece of chewing gum from my desk.

'Coming!' I took the stairs two at a time, landing on the first floor with a flourish. My mood was almost buoyant; I was pretty sure there wasn't anything that could bring me down.

'Hi Flick.'

I glanced at the front door in horror. If looks could kill, the one that Kitty was shooting Aaron right now would finish him off.

'You okay?'

I nodded at Kitty. 'Yeah, thanks.'

She went back into Stacey's room, narrowing her eyes at my ex-boyfriend again as she left. Correction: there wasn't much that could bring me down. I stared at Aaron, standing in our doorway. Except this.

\*\*\*

I led him into the living room, feeling slightly sick at the thought of Teddy upstairs, patiently waiting for me to come back to bed. What the *hell* was going on?

Aaron made himself comfortable on the couch, taking off his jacket and leaving me no real choice but to sit next to him. 'So . . . how have you been?' he asked.

I was struggling to keep up, and it wasn't because of the gin consumption last night. 'How did you even get this address?'

He paused. 'Ah, yeah, I can see how that might look weird.'

I took in his appearance: a bit less put together than the last time I'd seen him. Not that I could make any judgements, considering my bed head.

'I called your mum. She told me that you were living here.'

Now the message made sense. Mum never usually asked me to call her so early when she knew I'd been out the night before. *Why* hadn't it occurred to me to call her back?

'Right. You called my mum.' I sat in silence for a moment. 'Why are you here again?'

I wasn't trying to be rude. Okay, maybe I was a little bit. Seeing him took me right back to all the times he'd made me feel two inches tall.

He cleared his throat. 'It's just . . .' Aaron trailed off. 'God, I don't even know how to say it.'

My eyes narrowed. 'Try.'

'I think I made a huge mistake.' His cheeks were reddening.

Had I woken up in an alternative universe? I blinked back, unsure what to say.

'I imagine this comes as quite a surprise.' He pulled a cushion from the couch, cradling it to his chest, caving in on his lanky frame.

'A bit of a surprise, yeah.' What I really wanted to say was *How dare you? How could you just forget me? How could you have decided to leave me in the dark, if it wasn't even what you really wanted? And why, for the love of all that's holy, have you decided to turn up on my doorstep now?*

I didn't say any of that. I just stared at him, dumbfounded. 'But, Sara —'

Aaron cut me off. God, I remembered how much I'd hated it when he did that. 'That was a mistake. I got carried away in my new job . . . well, in the idea of a new everything, really.'

Nice.

'And I didn't think it through.' He reached out, taking my hand in his. *What was happening?*

I looked down at our hands, folded together neatly on his lap. Once upon a time, I would have done anything to have this back. Now I just stared at our entwined fingers. There was no emotional connection there. It felt wrong. I pulled my hand back.

'Flick . . .'

'Aaron.' His name felt foreign on my lips. 'I don't understand why you thought that you could just turn up here, and –'

He cut me off again. I gritted my teeth. 'Well, Sara was listening to podcasts at work, and she passed me her phone and said, "isn't this your ex-girlfriend?" I had no idea about the magazine, or the column, but when I listened to the podcast, everything just clicked. Hearing you talk about our breakup, and going on dates. It made me feel *ill*.'

I'm pretty sure I physically recoiled. 'Me being happy made you feel sick?'

'Not you being happy. Just . . .' He ran his hands through his hair, which had grown longer and more unkempt than when I'd last seen him in Camden. 'It made me realise that us breaking up was a huge mistake.'

I tried to absorb the information. Movies had taught me that this was the big climax in a romantic storyline, where I'd start crying and take Aaron back, believing him when he said he'd never meant to hurt me. Back in January, when he'd turned up on my doorstep for the first time, I would have been fully prepared to fit that mould, dramatic background music and all. But today when I listened to what he had to say, I saw right through it.

'Do you not think it's odd that you were able to just move on from us and create this whole new life, not checking in on me once? Since you're supposedly still in love with me, that is. I *was* still in love with you for a while, and I'll be honest, I knew everything there was to know about your life.'

Aaron flinched. 'I was just in a weird headspace, and I –'

This time, I talked over him. '*You* were in a weird head-space? You left me high and dry in the middle of London, and I had to figure everything out with absolutely no warning. It's really funny to me, Aaron, that you'd turn up here after listening to the podcast and hearing that everything in my life is going *well*.'

It was a figure of speech; I didn't actually find it funny at all. He clearly didn't know what to say.

'Your mum said that you'd missed me. That they'd missed me.'

I made a mental note to have serious words with my mother.

'You want me to get back together with you because my family misses you?'

'Well, no, but do you not remember how good we were together?'

This struck a chord. I swallowed the lump in my throat. I felt so sad for that girl in Shepherd's Bush. Completely unaware that the blanket of security that she'd knitted for herself was about to be ripped from her. But without it, she wouldn't have met Kitty, or Maia, or Stace. Or – I thought of him upstairs, my skin flushing slightly – Teddy.

'We were good together, but –'

Aaron pounced on it. 'So don't you think . . .'

'Will you *stop* interrupting me, Aaron? It's so bloody irritating. The version of me that dated you doesn't exist any more. Even though it broke my heart at the time, I know that you made the right decision. I'm happy here, without you.'

I exhaled, fired up by the monologue. From the other side of the wall, I heard a tiny cheer. I could just picture Kitty and Stacey in Stacey's bedroom, trying their best to hear the conversation.

'What was that?' Aaron whipped his head around.

'Nothing.' I hid my smirk. 'So, if that's all you came here for . . .' I trailed off, hoping he'd catch my hint. I had a lot that I wanted to do today, and it began with going back upstairs and telling Teddy just how glad I was that he was in my life.

'So that's it?' Aaron was getting irate now. 'After all we've been through, that's it?'

'You mean like when you broke up with me out of nowhere?' I stood up. 'Aaron, I have such fond memories of our relationship. But I'm different now. They have to stay in the past.'

He wiped his eyes. 'It's him, isn't it? The guy you mentioned in the podcast?'

I couldn't say yes outright because it wasn't just that. 'Partly.'

'So what? Are you and him, like, together?' Aaron had his nose wrinkled in disgust. I remembered seeing him with Sara; I'd been upset, sure, but I hadn't reacted like *that*.

'I . . .' I paused. Were Teddy and I together? I wasn't sure. He'd deliberately delayed our conversation earlier, probably because he wanted to sleep, but I couldn't just pretend we'd had the conversation when we hadn't. It wasn't my decision to make alone. We were done pretending. I decided to go neutral. Besides, it was none of Aaron's business. 'He's been there for me; he's my friend.'

I heard someone clear their throat behind me. My blood ran cold.

'Right.'

When I turned, I saw Teddy standing in the doorway. He was wearing a lot more clothing than when I'd last seen him. And he didn't look pleased.

'Teddy, wait.'

He smiled. 'It's okay, Sage. You told me as soon as I met you that that's all we were going to be. I'm not sure why I let myself believe otherwise.' He moved towards the front door, not even acknowledging Aaron.

I moved fast, trying to catch him on his way out. 'Teddy, you don't understand. I just didn't want to make any assumptions –'

He put his hands on my shoulders. 'Felicity, I don't have any intention of wasting my time. I've done it before, and to be frank, my interest in doing it again is at zero. I'll see you at work tomorrow.'

He closed the door behind him, and I put my hand to my chest in shock. The door to Stacey's bedroom opened, and I could see both of them staring at me, clearly sympathetic.

I stormed back into the living room. 'Please.' I picked up Aaron's jacket, handing it to him. 'Leave.'

# 33

Teddy wasn't answering my calls. It had been a week since Aaron had come to the house, and a week since I'd last spoken to Teddy. He'd sent one text:

    I need some time.

I'd heard nothing since. And on Wednesday, when someone from the tech team had come up to the office, it hadn't been him. He was avoiding me, and I didn't blame him. Although it had been a huge misunderstanding, I could see it from his side. First, I'd told him I didn't want to date him. Then, I'd asked him to fake-date me. And then, when we'd finally got together, I'd told my ex-boyfriend that we were just friends.

'Yeah.' Kitty winced. 'When you put it like that . . .'

We were sitting on her bed drinking mugs of tea, me alternating between sitting up to take a sip and lying face down on her duvet, groaning. Stacey's rule about not wallowing had gone out the window.

'I know. He's never going to speak to me again.'

'When you say things like that you sound like Stace. Of course he's going to speak to you again. Just maybe not for a while, and maybe just as a friend.'

I groaned again. 'How have I managed to screw this up so badly?'

She shrugged. 'We all do it. I'm the queen of screwing up. The last time I was dating, I went to his parents' house and managed to let a very poorly timed 'that's what she said' joke slip out over dinner.'

When I took a sharp intake of air, she nodded. 'I know. I never heard from him again, funnily enough.'

At least she'd made a good go at trying to get me to laugh. Below us, the front door shut, and we heard the other two start talking. They'd been instructed to buy lots of chocolate from the corner shop. Oh, and biscuits. Chocolate ones.

'Guys?' Stacey's voice echoed up the stairs.

'We're in my room.'

They joined us moments later, as we budged up on the bed to make room for two more. Maia threw her tote bag down on the duvet. 'I think the checkout assistant was concerned for my health.'

I rooted inside. Chocolate cookies, chocolate buttons, and a tub of chocolate ice cream. 'Were you sent by the gods?'

'So I've been told. Scooch,' she instructed, squeezing in next to me. 'What's going on here?'

'Surely not another pity party,' Stace teased, yelping when I thumped her in response.

'Denial.' Maia pointed at me, reaching for a cookie. 'When's your draft due?'

I let my head fall back against the headboard. 'Don't remind me. I'm still in a battle with Cecilia over it all.'

'Isn't the deadline on Thursday?' Stacey tilted her head, and then clocked my expression. 'Definitely not helping. Sorry.'

'And how are *you* feeling?' Maia aimed the question at Kitty, who was scrolling through her phone. 'Nervous?' She had a date tonight, with a man she'd met on a dating app whose bio said he was 'looking for someone to share London with'.

'I'm not feeling optimistic, I'll put it that way.'

'It's always those dates that end up going well.' Stacey chewed on her nail. 'Plus, there were no shirtless photos or photos with ex-girlfriends in his bio. We're off to a good start.'

Maia scrunched up her nose. 'Do people really do that?'

'You'd be surprised by how few don't. And I have to admit, I've fallen for it a few times.' She visibly shuddered. 'Mistakes were made. Never trust someone who thinks it's normal to name their pecs.'

My phone started buzzing in my back pocket. I pulled it out.

'Ooh, is that your sister?' Kitty pounced on me, reading the screen. 'Pick it up pick it up.'

'You've only met her once. Why are you so enthusiastic?'

'It was enough,' Stacey said, nodding, 'to know that she has what it takes to be one of us.'

I did as they instructed, waiting for Suze's face to fill the screen. She wasn't looking at the camera when she appeared, instead rooting through her cupboards whilst she waited for me to pick up. She was always doing *something* whilst she was on the phone.

'Hello?'

She snapped to attention. 'Hey. I was just looking for . . .' she found an item and pulled it out, '. . . these!'

A share-pack of Doritos was dangled in front of the camera. I smiled. Although there were still duller days, my sister's spark had started to peek through again.

'Is everyone there?' She squinted, and Maia, Kitty and Stacey leaned into the shot. 'Oh, hi guys!'

They all replied, Kitty jumping right in. 'Please tell me that you're looking for a place to live in London.'

Suze laughed. 'Flick filled me in. I'm not, unfortunately. Hey, maybe you'll get someone super weird.'

'Well, we already have Flick.' Maia shrugged. 'How much worse could it get?'

I poked her.

'So, I was ringing because I thought of a solution to the Teddy problem. Or at least, a step in the right direction. I've been mulling it over.'

I set her up against the lamp on Kitty's bedside table so we could all see.

'I'm all ears.' I gestured for her to go on. It felt good that she was giving out advice again.

'Well, you're still stuck for the direction of the article, right?'

I groaned again.

'Will you shut *up*?' Stacey threw a pillow at my head. 'Go on, Suze.'

'I thought so. Right, I was thinking, a major part of this column was based on something that wasn't real.'

'Ouch.'

Suze laughed. 'I'm not wrong though, am I? So, my solution is to just base the article on the opposite. Base it on the truth.'

All four of us sat in silence.

'You're going to have to be a bit more explicit here, Suze.' Maia shook her head. 'I'd like to think I'd have at least understood, but no.'

My sister rolled her eyes, brushing her hair behind her ear and navigating the strands so that they didn't get caught in her hoop earring. 'Tell the truth. About everything. Fake dating, the column, the pressure to be the 'right' kind of 22-year-old. Just treat it like a diary. Be completely honest.'

'They do say honesty is the best policy.' Stacey looked serious for once in her life. 'I'd be way more likely to trust someone if they told me the truth. Even if it wasn't exactly what I wanted to hear.'

'What do you think?' Suze looked at me.

I had a feeling that, once again, my sister might just be right.

***

'You want to do *what*?' Cecilia blinked at me.

I repeated myself, trying to ignore the slight shake in my hands. I'd shut the door behind me when I'd entered her office, but right now, I wished I had the support of Felix.

'I just don't understand how this will do any good. This article is a real opportunity to build yourself up, Flick, not to tear yourself down. It puts everything' – she looked at me pointedly – 'at risk.'

'But it isn't just about me. It's about Marianne, and Hallie, and the other people that wrote to us to say that they'd read the column.' I bit my lip. 'Please Cecilia. I need to do this.'

She sighed. 'Is this about Theodore?'

'No.' I paused. 'Okay, it's a tiny bit about him. But it's mainly about the column, and the list. This article is meant to be about what I've learnt. I *want* to write about that.'

'Even if it doesn't go down well?' Her eyebrow was raised, challenging me.

'Even if it doesn't go down well.'

That part was admittedly the scariest bit of the whole plan. There was nothing like admitting that your dating life was a complete lie to rile up the online trolls and put your promotion in jeopardy. But not doing it and letting everyone believe the lie forever terrified me even more.

'We're really going rogue with this, you know.' Cecilia smirked. 'I knew our secret mission would come back to bite me at some point.'

Come back to bite *her?* I could tell her a story or two about getting bitten on the arse. As far as things went, it hadn't even nipped her.

I could see that she was still undecided. 'I won't mention you, or the magazine influencing my decision to fake-date Teddy. That final decision was all on me.'

She tilted her head. 'You really want to tell the truth, don't you?'

'Isn't that what journalism should be?'

Cecilia choked on a laugh. 'In an ideal world, yes. Okay, go for it. I'm giving you free rein, but full responsibility when it goes – inevitably – wrong.'

A sigh of relief escaped me. 'Thank you. I think.'

'Flick?'

I stared at her. 'Yeah?'

'You might be a stupid journalist, but no one can say that you aren't a brave one.'

'I'll keep clinging to that when the comments start to roll in.'

She laughed. 'It's not the comments I'd be worried about. Sadie and Felix are the ones I'd be fretting over.'

*Shit.* I hadn't even thought of that.

I left the office, feeling lighter than I had in a while, comforted by the thought that in a few days, the burden would be lifted.

Felix grinned at me. 'Getting put in the naughty corner?'

'Something like that.'

He pointed to a mug perched next to my keyboard. 'Made you a Malteser hot chocolate.'

'You did?' I clasped my hand to my chest. 'You angel.'

'Yeah, well, I haven't seen Teddy up here all week. Plus, you've been moping more than Noodles did when he had his bits chopped off and had to wear a cone for a week.'

'I don't love that analogy, but thanks for the hot chocolate.' I didn't elaborate. At least this time I wasn't lying; I actually *was* moping over Teddy.

'Well, you know, you've tackled heartbreak before, you'll do it again.' Felix returned to his keyboard, pulling up one of the online articles ('What Does Your Favourite Sex Position Say About You?').

I thought back to January. I *had* conquered it before, that overwhelming feeling of uncertainty. That was what I was most proud of. It wasn't dating; it was Carlisle, and my job, and the friends I'd made. It was bouncing back and realising that the thing I valued most was no longer a relationship, but my ability to be myself. *That* was what I wanted to write about for the magazine. Even if Teddy didn't want to listen, I knew I wanted to say it. I pulled up a blank page, scrapping my previous notes for the article and preparing to draft something totally new.

Felix glanced up. 'What's that?'

'It's going to be my article.'

'You're starting a fresh first draft? *Now?*'

I nodded, typing away furiously. 'I know what I want to say.'

He put his hand on my shoulder. 'RIP if you don't get it in by Thursday. Cecilia will skin you alive.'

There were so many reasons why Cecilia might skin me alive, especially if this didn't go to plan. I was surprisingly at peace with that. When I was satisfied with my initial notes, I pulled my phone from my back pocket, finding the number I wanted. I nodded to myself, deciding to take the leap, and dialled.

'Hello?' A cheerful voice answered.

'Hi, Alexis?'

'Felicity! How is it all going? I can't wait to read your article.'

'About that . . .' I inhaled deeply, crossing my fingers and toes, 'I need your help.'

★★★

### Transcript of second interview with Felicity (Flick) Sage for The Sunday Podcast

*Alexis: Hi guys! Welcome to this week's episode of* The Sunday Podcast, *an exclusive broadcast to interrupt normal programming. You might remember last month's episode with Felicity Sage, magazine assistant and writer behind* The Twenties List *feature at* Influence. *Well, she's back! Flick contacted me last week to ask if she could record another episode of the show, and of course I said yes. The crocheting episode I had planned was never going to be as juicy as this. If you've been reading Flick's column over the past few months, you'll know that her final instalment is a spread in the next issue of* Influence, *set for publication next month. This episode will be a little taste of what's to come. Hi Flick, welcome back!*

*Felicity: Thank you for having me back, I did not imagine I'd be here again so soon.*

*A: It's my pleasure. Stories like yours are what* The Sunday Podcast *is all about. So, tell us, why is it that you wanted to come back?*

F: *Here goes. \*Pauses\*. I've been feeling some guilt over the column, and the message I've been sending out to my readers. This podcast seemed like the best place to be completely transparent and set the record straight.*

A: *I'm honoured that you think that. For anyone that's listening to you for the first time, that might not have been here last month, what is your column all about?*

F: The Twenties List *started out as a personal project, completely separate from the magazine. A way for me to have fun, coming out of a long-term relationship. It started out with tiny things, like dying my hair and reading five memoirs, but then my boss caught wind of it. When I started writing* The Twenties List *professionally, it became so much more. It became a way for young people like me to connect. We've had a lot of people write in to us to share their own stories and I feel so connected to them. If you're listening, I admire you all a lot.*

A: *I know that there are a lot of those readers out there. I love that they reached out! So, what has changed since the last episode we recorded together? Are you still dating? I know there are a few listeners of the podcast who are rooting for Flick and Teddy.*

F: *That's why I'm here. I want to tell our story. Our actual story.*

A: *Ooh. \*Claps\* Do tell!*

F: When I started drafting my original list, way before it became the column, I was determined not to date. I was newly single, and I just wanted to settle into my houseshare. I wanted to focus on healing my heart. I was terrified by the concept of sharing my life with someone else again, because I felt like I'd only just got it back.

A: And then Teddy came along . . .

F: He did. But our original meet-cute was actually the week before I said it was, in a random set of tennis courts near our offices. I instantly felt this connection with Teddy, but the honest truth is that he started out as my friend. He actually asked me out, and I said no.

A: NO!

F: Quite the error in judgement on my part, but yes. The first time he featured on The Twenties List – as my friend – some of my readers mistook it for a date, and everyone was so excited that it just spiralled out of control.

A: So what actually happened with Teddy? Have you been just friends this entire time?

F: Most of the time, yes. I didn't want to let down the people who seemed so excited about the dating element to the column. Behind the scenes, Teddy and I were becoming best friends, but for the sake of the column . . .

*A: You were becoming an item. Wow, I never would have guessed that. But, did you just say 'most of the time'?*

*F: As sorry as I am about my lack of transparency with my experiences in modern dating – and I am truly sorry for that – I genuinely did start to fall for Teddy. Somewhere along the way, we really did become Flick and Teddy, even if it was obvious to everyone but us. He's the most thoughtful, sarcastic, intelligent person I know, and he has no idea how easy it is to be around him. I feel like I can be completely myself. We might not be conventional, but our story is ours.*

*A: So you're setting the record straight. Once and for all.*

*F: I struggled with the column for a long time after the dating element came into it. How could I possibly give advice to other people when I wasn't sure what was happening myself? I agonised over it, but by then it felt too late to admit it. Integrity in journalism is so important to me, even if it doesn't seem that way.*

*A: What made you decide to be honest now?*

*F: I couldn't write my final article without being honest, because what I have to say is about so much more than dating. I want people to realise that their life has more value than the sum of the people they date.*

*A: This is exactly what I like to hear. Flick, it has been so lovely to have you on the podcast again, and I'm honoured that you chose here as the place to tell your truth. We all make mistakes, and I think that it's the ability to own up to those errors that makes us who we are.*

*F: Thank you. I just want any readers of the column to know that I never intended to create an illusion of what being in your twenties is like. I wanted to tell the truth, and I promise from now on that I always will. I hope people will be able to see that when they read my upcoming piece.*

# 34

'How are you feeling?' I poured tea into Suze's mug first, and then Mum's, passing them the milk from my side of the table. We were catching up in a café not too far from my office; Suze had been to a work meeting near Liverpool Street this morning and had brought Mum along for moral support. They'd travelled first class – Mum's way of trying to make Suze's first big meeting in a while seem more exciting than daunting.

Suze paused. 'I want to say it's an easy fix, but it's not. Some days I wake up and life feels really, *really* difficult.'

Mum squeezed her hand.

'But on those days I know I can just head to Mum and Dad's and work from there. I'm done with ignoring help when it's offered.'

A couple of months ago, I could have never pictured Suze talking about her mental health so bluntly. I was unbelievably proud of her.

Mum was welling up. 'I don't know what I did to raise the two of you, but I must have done something right. Oh, it's your dad,' she got up from the table, 'he probably wants to know what I've left him in the freezer for tea. Be right back.'

Suze smirked. 'Typical Dad.'

'Classic.' I opened a packet of brown sugar. 'How has work been about everything?'

'You know, better than I expected. Obviously, not everyone gets it, but most people try. We're in such a high intensity industry; the more people I speak to about it, the more I realise that I was never on my own in the first place.'

'Isn't that the truth.' I grinned. 'You don't have a chance of ever being alone when you're stuck with us.' I gestured to Mum, who was walking back.

'He didn't know how to defrost the chilli con carne in the microwave.' She shook her head. 'So, where are the 'must see' spots around here, Flick?'

Suze shot me a look. Without warning, Mum had abandoned our birth names and started using our nicknames. It was nice. I reeled off a list of recommendations.

'Are you sure you can't come, love?' Mum patted my hand.

I wished it was realistic to take annual leave right now, but Alexis's podcast episode was about to launch, and it was going to be all hands on deck. I had to wipe my palms on my jeans at the mere thought of the chaos. I refreshed Apple Podcasts. Ten minutes to go. I was secretly pleased that Suze had brought Mum to London. I needed all of the moral support I could get too.

'She's got a date with the internet trolls, she can't come and wander with us Mum. Are you nervous?' Suze cradled her mug to her chest, sitting back in her chair. 'I won't lie, I would be.'

'*Susan.*' Oof. It was back. Mum tutted at her eldest. 'Everything is going to be alright, Flick. I just know it is.'

'I mean, of course it's going to be alright, most things usually are.' Suze looked affronted. 'I was just being realistic. This afternoon might be a bit bleak.'

'Well yes, there is that.' Mum winced. 'Sorry.'

'I'm fully aware that the next week or two of my life might be a shitshow – sorry Mum – more than fully aware. I dreamt about it last night.'

I'd woken up in a cold sweat, imagining the comments. Even worse, imagining Teddy not listening to the podcast and it all having been for nothing. Well, not nothing. My conscience was clear for the first time in a while. But I still hadn't broken the silence with Teddy; it was painful. Maia in particular was confident that he'd come around, but I wasn't convinced. He'd looked so *hurt* that morning, standing in my living room.

I downed the rest of my tea. 'Well, I better go back to the office and face the music. When Felix finds out, all hell is going to break loose.'

Mum pulled a note out of her purse. 'Get yourself a Chinese or something tonight.'

'Mum,' Suze snorted, 'a takeaway might not fix this. Also, I don't think I've ever seen anything more Northern than thinking a tenner will cover a takeaway in London.'

'I know it won't fix everything.' She crossed her arms. 'But I always find that good food helps.'

She reminded me of my housemates, who stood firm in the same belief. I kissed her on the cheek and took the money, swinging my bag over my shoulder. 'Oh, it'll definitely help. I'll be crying into my fried rice. Thanks, Mum.'

Mum pulled another note out. 'You'd better get a double portion, then.'

\*\*\*

When I walked into the office, I was ambushed. Felix dragged me by my elbow into the staffroom.

'You little minx.' Now that he had me cornered, he went back to stirring two mugs of tea. 'You completely had me fooled. I was planning your wedding in my head and everything.'

'I feel awful.'

'At first, I wanted to set Noodles on you, when she's all riled up after seeing a spider.'

'A fate worse than death, I'm sure.'

'I have the scars to prove it.' He held a mug out to me. 'I was a bit hurt when I first heard it. We're desk buddies, you know? But we both know how Cecilia can be. Plus, she did email last night about some kind of bonus because of the column, so I'm feeling forgiving today.'

I silently thanked Cecilia.

'So, where is lover boy?' Felix smirked. 'I'll forgive you completely if I can call him that from now on.'

He must have seen my face fall because he put the mug down. 'I take it things aren't going well.'

'It's a long story.' I put my own drink down – it suddenly wasn't as appealing. 'And with all of this going on, I'm kind of bored of talking about myself. Tell me about Sebastian and Noodles?'

Felix led me back to our desks, starting a long story about how he'd fallen out with Seb last night for eating the last of the hummus. As exciting as falling in love was, part of me prayed for the mundane arguments that seemed to come with time.

'It'll be alright you know. Whatever it is.'

I opened up my laptop to the column. 'I hope so. I need to take my mind off it right now. Jump from one shitstorm to the next. What's the damage, do we know yet?'

'I was just on my way to come and talk to you about that, Felicity.' Cecilia appeared behind us, her heels clacking on the floor. 'In fact,' she spoke a bit louder to the rest of our row, 'let's all gather together to review. This podcast was bound to rile people up a bit.'

Behind her, Fiona sent me an SOS signal. Sadie was trying to catch my eye, mouthing 'Teddy?!' in my direction. I already wanted to leave the office, catch the fastest Tube home, and get under my duvet. Instead, I gave myself an internal big-girl talk and gathered with everyone else.

'So obviously' – Cecilia gestured to me – '*The Twenties List* turned agony-aunt column has been one of our most popular features this year so far. A lot of new readers, and the ability to tap into a new demographic. I'm wondering how the follow-up podcast with Alexis Lastbury is going to change that. We need to be aware of what our audiences are saying, and how we need to adapt and respond. Damage control, if you will.'

A handful of the staff were staring at me. I blinked back.

'To be honest,' Felix began, pulling up the email inbox, 'it isn't that bad.'

'Define "isn't that bad".' Cecilia narrowed her eyes.

'We got a couple of emails asking whether the column was still going to be taking on dating questions, whether readers were still allowed to write in . . .'

Cecilia nodded. 'Surprisingly tame. Sadie?'

'I'm afraid things are a bit more divided on social media. A lot of our readers follow Alexis so listened to the podcast straight away.'

'And?'

Sadie wrung out her fingers, for once looking a bit scared to say anything. 'Well, some of the reviews are fine. A few people responding with their own dating horror stories, and someone saying that they were glad Flick was speaking out about the constant pressure to be dating.'

I hid my eyes behind my hands. 'Be honest. What were the bad ones?'

'I think a lot of people were quite attached to the column. And when someone they trusted ends up not being 100 per cent transparent . . .'

Cecilia marched over to the computer. 'You're dodging the question. What do the comments say?'

I went over too, both of us hovering over Sadie. The comments were less than glowing: a combination of 'What a liar', 'I can't believe the audacity of this girl' and 'This is so sad, I loved Fleddy'.

'It's not ideal.' Cecilia spoke. 'How many comments?'

Felix was checking. 'Since yesterday? One comment every few minutes or so. There's over a thousand.'

'Shit.' I covered my mouth, embarrassed. It didn't matter anyway; I couldn't imagine that I was going to get employee of the year.

'So, in terms of damage control . . .' Sadie looked to Cecilia for guidance.

'Give me a second.' She massaged her temples. 'There is no such thing as bad publicity, there is no such thing as bad publicity . . .'

As she continued to chant to herself, Felix sidled up beside me and whispered in my ear, 'She's finally cracked.'

I bit back a laugh.

'Right!' Cecilia clapped her hands together. 'Here's what we're going to do. There's a huge number of new potential readers here. Whether or not they think positive things about Felicity, they're listening. Let's jump on that. We need Felicity to speak up again. Not back down. No hiding.'

'Another column update?' Fiona offered.

'That's not a bad shout. As with most things online,' Sadie said as she kept clicking through the comments, 'this will die down.'

Felix held his phone up. 'Slight issue. Look at the newest article on *Nineteen*.'

*Nineteen* was our rival publication. My pulse skyrocketed.

'What are we supposed to be checking for?' I frantically scrolled. I knew this had been a bold move – owning up to a fake relationship instead of just letting it fade into the background – but it was still stressful to watch our hard work go up in flames.

'Look. Here.' Felix flipped his own phone around to show me, but it loaded on my screen at the same moment.

'Oh God.' Sadie put her head in her hands.

The headline read *'Influence? At What Cost?'*

No one spoke for a minute as we all read the article, condemning the magazine for allowing a false storyline to be circulated which supposedly jeopardised the state of modern journalism.

'I mean, this is just ridiculous.' Felix scoffed. 'The storyline is half true anyway! Fleddy is thriving.'

I wouldn't have said thriving, exactly, but I got his point.

'Half true or not, it's still out there now.' Cecilia was pacing back and forth now. 'Trust them to pounce on this. Vultures.'

'Have you seen the comments, though?' A girl from the marketing team, Piper, spoke. 'They're mostly defending Flick.'

We all looked. Surely enough, amidst the comments accusing me of falsifying information, there was a cluster of comments defending me. And at the helm, leading the pack, was a user named 'StaceFace'. I could have cried.

*@StaceFace14: Come on? Haven't we all felt the pressure of dating? I'd probably have done the same thing. Surely learning and growing is the point of being in your twenties.*

And in response:

*@Callmebyyourfame: Completely agree with you @Stace-Face14. If I had a pound for every time I'd made a mistake at 22, I could finally get on the housing ladder.*

*@twentyfiveandthriving: HAHA. Love that. I don't know about you guys, but a little friends-to-lovers fake dating/not-so-fake dating is top-quality content. Give me more.*

*@LianneRichardson27: It's kind of like a romance novel when you think about it. Plus, I'm learning more about myself and my own life from Flick's column than I ever have from this site. Shame on you for posting this.*

That was just the start of the comments in my favour. I made a mental note to buy a bottle of Stacey's favourite wine on the way home.

'Wow.' Cecilia smiled. 'Look at that. A corner of the internet has your back, Flick.'

My heart had been beating at double speed, just waiting for her to fire me. I breathed a cautiously hopeful half-sigh of relief at her using my nickname.

Sadie was still clicking. 'I actually think that this – publicizing Flick's journey – could be a good move for the magazine. What's the point of an experiment like *The Twenties List* if you can't go wrong somewhere, and then find your way back?'

Cecilia stood up straight. 'Okay. Let's build on this and draw up a plan of action. The print deadline for the June issue is only a couple of weeks away, and we're going to bounce back with a glorious spread about life in your twenties. The mistakes, the lessons, the pressures. Flick has it all under control. I trust her 100 per cent with this. Now, this is going to see a lot more sales than our last issue, given the situation. So everything else has to be perfect. Team, let's see some action. Support each other, ask for help if you need it. It's going to be a hard couple of weeks, but we've got this.'

Everyone jumped up, moving back to their desks and cracking on. Felix was staring at me in disbelief.

'I thought I'd be packing all my things into a cardboard box right now.'

He patted me on the back. 'I like to paint a rosy picture most of the time, but me too, my friend, me too. I don't think I've ever heard Cecilia say that she trusts anyone.'

'I don't know whether that scares me or motivates me.' I lifted the lid on my laptop, diving into the article. I was prepared to work as many hours as I needed to. This had to be perfect.

# 35

I pushed on the door, knocking slightly to let her know that I was coming in. She was sitting on her bed, folding clothes and putting them randomly into boxes.

'Staceface?'

She grinned. 'You saw it, then. I was wondering when I'd hear from you.'

'You saved my life today.'

'Well, I thought that since it was my comment that got you into this mess, it might as well be my comment that tried to get you back out of it.' She patted the space next to her. 'And God, those internet trolls just don't know when to stop, do they? Why do they call you chicken legs?'

I stretched out, pointing to my legs. 'It's because of these babies. I'm chickeny and I've learned to accept it.'

'That's growth right there.' She tucked some hair behind her ears before carrying on folding.

I joined her, starting with a pile of mini-skirts. There didn't appear to be any rhyme or reason to the packing. I could see that there was a pair of earmuffs in the same box as a bikini.

'Cecilia was ready to hit the roof about the article until she saw that comment. You really started a revolution – there's hundreds of people defending the column now.'

'Flick.' Stacey blinked at me. 'Those people are defending *you,* not the column.'

I waved her off. 'Potayto, potahto. Is there a system here?' I pointed to the stacks.

There was a moment of silence as we both looked around the room.

'I *hate* packing. Can you tell?' She sighed, falling back onto her pillows. 'What if I'm making the wrong decision? What if I'm sitting there in my new flat, scared and alone wondering why on earth I gave Carlisle up?'

I nodded. 'It's always a possibility.'

'Wow,' she laughed, 'you were a bit of a one-hit wonder with the advice.'

'You didn't let me finish.' I folded another T-shirt, taking over the packing that she'd been doing, making sure nothing was creased. 'It's always a possibility. But what if it's the best decision that you've ever made? What if you love your new place, and the parties you can throw in it, and the extra wardrobe space?'

She conceded. 'I do have a lot of clothes.'

'You're telling me?' I held up one of her T-shirts, which had the name of a popular dating app emblazoned on the front. 'Why do you even have this?'

'I have a bad habit of never throwing anything away. I think a rep gave it to me in a club.'

'Christ.' I folded it despite the bad taste, tucking it in on top of a Camp America T-shirt. Of everyone I knew, Stacey was the most influenced by fashion magazines and Instagram. And yet, things like this lurked at the back of her wardrobe. It was testament to how a person's true self was revealed bit by bit as you got to know them. I felt robbed that I'd only shared the same space as her for five months. There was still so much to learn.

'It's just scary to do something different.'

I nodded. 'When I had to move, I thought it was the end of the world.'

'And?' She blinked back at me expectantly.

'It only took me a few weeks to realise that my security blanket had actually been holding me back.'

'Huh.' Stace mulled it over. 'I'll check back in with you when the dust has settled. So, they didn't fire you, then, I assume?' She was flicking through one of her magazines now, pausing on a page about mauve colour schemes.

'No, I think I'll be alright for now. At the end of the day, it was Cecilia's idea. I was just stupid enough to execute it for her. Now all I have to do is write the best bloody article you've ever seen.'

She smiled. 'Done and done, then. Right? See, I told you this would all work out.'

'I think your exact words were, "You're in a pickle now, Flickle".'

'That was witty and you know it.' Stace sighed. 'I'm going to miss this.'

'Miss what?'

'This. Hanging out with my best friends twenty-four seven. You know, sometimes I can take a really long time to warm up to people. You've made quite the impression. I'm glad that you moved into the attic.'

I flopped back on the bed next to her. 'You don't have to tell me that. I thought you wanted me out in the beginning.'

'I did.' She was unbelievably blunt. 'But that would have been a mistake. You're a Carlisle girl.'

'Without you, who would have taught me never to use kitchen scissors to trim my split ends?'

'I literally shudder at the thought. It was like walking in on a wild animal hacking at their fur on the kitchen worktop.'

I would *definitely* miss her colourful imagination.

'So, has Theodore crept out from the woodwork yet?' She said it nonchalantly, but I could tell she really wanted to know.

'No. He still needs time, I guess.'

Stace blew out a breath. 'For *what*? It was a huge misunderstanding. One proper conversation and you'd be Flick and Teddy again. Or, sorry,' she put on a deep voice, '*Sage and Teddy*.'

I shoved her. 'You're not funny.'

'You know what I mean, though. It was a split-second conversational mistake. If anything, it showed that he was more than a rebound. You had no desire to rub your new relationship in the face of the boy who dumped you. That takes more strength than I ever have, that's for sure.'

'Should I just go round there?'

Stace nodded. 'It's probably for the best. To be honest, he's being a bit of an idiot, and sometimes guys just need our help to realise it.'

It had occurred to me multiple times that this was the obvious solution. What did I have to lose? At this point it wasn't just my love life at stake. I missed our friendship too. There were no funny internet jokes in my inbox, chosen specifically to make me laugh. No lunches in the park, or tennis after work. Life was a bit boring (aside from the whole internet scandal).

'I can practically hear those cogs turning in your brain.' Stace was packing her nail polishes into a shoebox. 'Worst case scenario, he turns you away and you've lost two trips on your Oyster card. Best case scenario, he pulls you into his flat and you have hot computer-guy sex.'

'Is that even a thing?'

'You tell me, Flick, you tell me. Now go!' She shooed me out of the room. Standing on my own in the hallway, I pondered what she'd suggested.

Stacey was right, I had nothing to lose. I grabbed my keys.

★★★

I'd been rapping on his front door for about three minutes before I decided that I'd crossed over into annoying door-to-door salesperson territory. I hit my forehead gently against the wood. His neighbour – a woman with a bag piled high with fruit and veg, wearing trainers and yoga pants – had eyed me up suspiciously on the walk to her own flat. I was officially the sad girl you see in movies practically hugging the door.

I perched on the ground. I hadn't come all this way just to give up. He might have gone to play tennis after work, or nipped to the Sainsbury's Local down the road. I knew Teddy well enough to know that he liked to avoid too much time spent in his flat. He'd come back eventually, and I was prepared to wait. I pulled up the notes app on my phone and started playing around with one of the final sections of the article. I was *this close* to being ready to submit. It was terrifying. My phone started vibrating in my hands – probably Stacey requesting an update. Not bothering to read the caller ID above my notes, I picked up straight away.

'Hello?'

'Where are you?' The voice on the other end sounded confused. It also sounded nothing like Stacey.

'*Teddy?*'

I heard him let out a short breath and could practically feel him smile through the line. 'Yeah, it's me. It's also 8 p.m. on a Monday night, and there's no way that you'd usually be anywhere but underneath your duvet eating Doritos.'

'You know me so well.' He really did. I'd been planning on curling up and doing exactly that after I'd helped Stacey with her packing. 'Wait, how do you know that I'm not?'

'I may be standing in the middle of your room.'

'How did you –'

'Stacey. She let me in.'

I imagined how funny she was finding all of this.

'So . . .' He laughed. 'Any chance you're going to tell me where you are?'

'That depends.'

'On what?'

'Whether or not you're going to see the absolute irony here.'

'Lay it on me.'

'I'm at your flat.' I paused, 'On the floor waiting for you to come home, to be exact. I've practically knocked a hole through your door.'

On the other end of the line, he started to laugh. Belly laugh. 'Sorry, that's just too hilarious. No wonder Stacey kept snorting. I thought she had a sinus issue.'

'Hilarious? This was meant to be my big apology moment.'

His voice softened. 'It was?'

'100 per cent. Does the fact that you're in my room mean that you're ready to hear it?'

'The fact that I'm in your room means that I *may* have realised I should've given you the chance to explain in the first place.'

I pulled the phone away from my ear, taking a moment to calm my breathing. 'I missed you.'

'I missed you too.' He coughed. 'Really missed you. Have been bored out of my mind, missed you.'

I savoured the moment, closing my eyes and just appreciating how nice it was to talk to him again.

'I bet the brownies at work taste nowhere near as good when you're not splitting them with me.'

I opened my eyes. 'I wouldn't go that far. I quite enjoy eating a whole brownie. Hang on. I'm peeling myself from

your floor as we speak. Prepare to witness the fastest movement across London that you've ever seen.'

'I can head towards –'

'No, honestly, I want to come home.'

'Okay, Sage. I'm not going anywhere. Be safe?'

There were so many ways to say that you cared about
someone. I swallowed the lump in my throat.

'Yeah, I will. See you soon.'

# 36

I'd never really craved superhero abilities, but right then in that moment I so badly wanted to be able to teleport back to Carlisle. I almost knocked a small child over in my haste to get off the Tube. When I finally got back to the house, Stacey met me at the door.

'I've been watching from my window. This is too funny.'

'Stop procrastinating!' I ordered, pulling my trainers off and moving past her to run up the stairs.

She pouted. 'But all this packing is taking so *long*. Hey, Flick?'

I turned, letting out a short breath. 'Yeah?'

'All jokes aside, I told you it would work itself out.' She was smiling at me, fiddling with the zip on her jacket. 'Now go get him!'

I took the stairs two at a time, landing on the attic floor with a huff. Had those stairs always been so steep? I put my hands on my knees. It hurt to inhale.

'Did you think I was going to leave? You cannot have been at my flat. No one travels across London that fast.'

I glanced up. Teddy was sitting on the edge of my bed, grinning with amusement.

'I was too! It turns out that if you use your elbows to get past people, anything is possible.'

He gestured for me to come over and sit next to him. I instinctively went to kiss him, but he stopped me, brushing my lips lightly with his thumb. 'Let's talk about this first. I don't want to start off on any more bad notes. I shouldn't have disappeared into thin air. It was immature of me. I'm sorry.'

I leaned into him, instantly comforted. We'd both made mistakes to get to this point (mine admittedly worse than his). It definitely wasn't the most conventional way to start dating, but it meant I knew that I was sure about this. I was 100 per cent in. 'It was my fault. I should have been honest with Aaron about you. I should have been honest with a lot of people. But I didn't want to taint this' – I gestured between us – 'something I value so much, with something that made me value myself so little.'

'I understand.' Teddy looked serious for a moment. 'I panicked when I heard you talk about us just being friends, especially after what had happened the night before, and because that's a million miles away from where I want us to be. I panicked because I'm scared of wasting my time; I spent too long in a relationship that wasn't going anywhere to want to do that again.'

I touched my nose against his. 'You're not wasting your time, Teddy. I'm in this for keeps. Was that not obvious when I put my career on the line?'

Teddy started laughing. 'I know. When I heard the podcast I realised how little all of that other stuff mattered.' He rested his forehead against mine. 'You called me thoughtful, sarcastic, and intelligent. Are you officially changing your three words to describe me?'

I thought back to the game, and back to that night. I was glad I'd kept it shared between us, rather than with the whole of the internet. I pulled my face away from his. 'Nah. Three words to describe you would never be enough.'

'God, I love you.' Teddy finally kissed me, but I was too frozen in shock to fully kiss him back. He laughed against my lips.

'You do? I wanted to say that first.'

He tilted my head up to kiss me again. 'Of course I do, and sorry, but tough. I've been wanting to say it for a while, and if you snooze, you lose, Sage. I can't believe I'm lucky enough to say I fell in love with my best friend.'

For a long time I'd viewed myself differently, marked by the words that Aaron had left me with. I understood now that it had never been about me.

'Are you crying?' Teddy's voice was incredulous as he swiped at the tear. 'I'm having a weird feeling of déjà vu. I have to say, this is not the reaction that I was anticipating.'

I trapped his hand against my cheek. 'I cried at the RSPCA advert the other day. It's the last few weeks; I'm like a tap.' I hugged him tight. 'I love you too, for the record.'

We lay back on my bed, staring up at the ceiling.

'I bet you're glad I came and pestered you that day at the courts.' Teddy sounded smug.

'No, that was still annoying. I was clearly trying to have a moment. Maybe we should still pretend we met in the café. I have to give it to you, it was a good story.'

'Built entirely on lies.' He pulled me on top of him. 'I would never have shared my sandwich.'

★★★

'Do you remember your first night here, Flick?' Kitty started pulling plates out of the cupboard. 'When you almost burst into tears over a takeaway?'

'Har har.' I grabbed some glasses. 'That story gets funnier every single time you tell it.'

'It was *sad*.' Maia patted me on the shoulder. 'Don't worry, Kitty got ghosted by someone she was dating last year and cried when Justin Bieber came on the radio.'

'You're not meant to tell people that, it ruins my image.' Kitty pouted. 'I was crying because that song had been playing when we . . .'

'Jesus, Kit. That should have been your first red flag.' Stacey continued pouring wine for everyone.

We were all leaning on the breakfast bar, as close as possible. Teddy had gone to pick up food from down the road, and Sophie was on her way, called upon in the group chat for an impromptu dinner party.

'One day, we're going to have to learn to cook properly.' Kitty sighed. 'Half of my bank balance goes towards poppadoms and spring rolls.'

'Maia is literally the best cook I've ever met. We just don't give her the chance to suggest it before we pull up the Deliveroo app.'

I nodded, gesturing to the hob. 'Stacey has a point. Maia made a curry the other night, and I swear I saw stars.'

'You guys just hadn't eaten anything homecooked in a while.'

'I cannot get over this place.' Kitty was now scrolling through pictures on her laptop, looking at Stacey's flat. It was small – anywhere you wanted to live alone in London tended to be – but it was going to be all hers. She beamed every time she spoke about it. It reminded me of Suze when she'd moved into her flat. I knew why I was drawn to these girls in the same way that I was drawn to my sister. They didn't judge, and they were always honest with me. We were in this together.

'When does the new girl move in?'

Kitty's face fell. 'Two days after you leave.'

'Wow. Moving on from me that fast?'

'No! The landlord suggested it. We don –'

'I'm messing with you, Kit.'

The soon to be newest member of Carlisle was a graduate, moving from Manchester (I couldn't *wait* to ask her if all my favourite haunts were still the same). As much as I was going to miss Stace, I was excited to meet her. I was collecting people's stories like stickers here in this house. My life was a patchwork quilt of all the people in it.

'Is it just me,' Stacey started, 'or is Teddy hotter now that he's had his little sulk?'

I flapped her with the tea towel. 'He could come back any minute!'

'He knows I'd say it to his face. No one messes with our Flick and gets away with it without at least a little ribbing.'

'Ignore her. She won't say a word,' Kitty said.

'Maybe I will, maybe I won't. Fleddy deserves the truth.'

I didn't even dignify it with a response.

'Are you going to talk about it in the magazine?' Kitty munched on one of the breadsticks we'd placed in the centre of the worktop.

'Probably not. I mean, that's the whole point of the article. I know what the pressure of modern dating feels like. Life is about so much more than *just* that.'

Stacey placed her hand over her heart. 'This is *so* our influence. I have to take credit. Have we ever met a Carlisle girl that we couldn't help?'

Kitty shook her head. 'Never.'

The front door opened and Sophie walked into the room, talking to Teddy with grand gestures, who was following behind, arms laden with bags of Italian food.

'Bon appétit.' He set it all on the table, leaning to kiss me on the cheek. '*Molto bella.*'

'Do you actually know how to speak Italian?'

He paused, looking sheepish. 'I googled it in the queue whilst I was waiting for the food.'

'Smooth.'

I watched him start to pull dishes out from the bags, passing them around the table.

'This is a lot of food.' Sophie laughed.

'Go big or go home, that's what I always say.' Stacey took a slice of garlic bread.

'I literally don't think you've ever said that.'

She narrowed her eyes at me. 'Who ordered fettuccine? And there's a bolognese here, and a calzone, and —'

'If you list everything you guys ordered, we'll be here all day.' Teddy laughed. 'Let's just go for it.'

Everyone followed his lead, diving in and piling up their plates. This weekend was Stace's last with us, and although everyone was tiptoeing around it, it felt like there was a finality to tonight. She was such a core member of our group. I caught her eye across the table, and she winked at me. Stace was going to be just fine; she was ready for this, to move on. It was the rest of us that were dragging our heels.

'You okay?' Teddy nudged me with his elbow. 'Do you want some of this?'

When I nodded, he put some garlic knots onto my plate.

I leaned my head on his shoulder. 'I'm glad you're here.'

'Nowhere else I'd rather be.' He kissed my forehead.

I let my gaze wander around the table again, watching everyone chatting about the stupidest of things, like the latest season of *Love Island* and a quiz Kitty had taken to see which *Brooklyn Nine-Nine* character she would be. I'd been told that university would be the best years of my life, but I wasn't convinced. Teddy squeezed my hand under the table, shovelling food into his mouth and laughing at something Sophie was saying. We were all going to be alright in the end. I just knew it.

★★★

## The Twenties List: The Final Chapter

*When I was in primary school, I remember doing an activity
on what we'd like to be when we grew up. At that point being
a ballerina was my top choice, but one dance lesson later it
was clear that wasn't going to happen. Fast forward to
secondary school and after one cookery lesson, I played
around with the idea of being a chef – I can make a mean
lasagne, but that's about it. Pretty soon after that, when people
asked what I wanted to be when I grew up, they meant it. I
was supposed to know what subjects would suit me best,
and what degree would set me up for a career that I hadn't
even decided on yet. In the playground we exchanged predic-
tions like they were playing cards: I want to be married by
25, I want to move to America, I want to travel the world.
Our childhood was built on the idea of what was going to
come after it. So it's no surprise that most of us go out into
the real world with five-year plans and long-term goals stuck
to our bathroom mirror, repeated like a mantra at every job
interview or first date.*

*My twenties list was a list that I created when part of my
five-year plan went wrong. I wanted to move to London after
graduation. Check. I wanted to get a grad job. Check. I wanted
to live with my boyfriend and be engaged by 23. Not-so check.
I saw the lack of control I had over my life as a failure, and
I panicked. I was living in a houseshare with three strangers,
with no clue what to do next. The twenties list was a way of
reclaiming some sort of plan. If you've been following my
column for* Influence, *you'll know that I've managed to*

complete most of the items on my list: I've taken enough Polaroid photos to make my room look like a shrine to my twenty-second year; I've learnt to tolerate black coffee; and I've lived in a houseshare and not only lived to tell the tale but have had the best few months of my life.

What really happened when I started writing my column was a lot more than reading five memoirs or starting to play the piano again. It went beyond anything I could have written down and aimed for. The twenties list taught me that as much as you can plan and hope for a smooth trajectory, life doesn't often offer us the luxury of things going to plan. And the moments where we feel most out of control are the moments that shape what comes next.

We spend a lot of time on our phones, scrolling through highlight reels, wondering how our lives can be so messy when other people seem so put together. Our twenties are often our first foray into life without a clear path mapped out for us, and it's so easy – I would even go as far as to say inevitable – to compare and compete. I notice myself doing it all the time. How can someone I vaguely know be getting engaged, or buying a house, when I'm struggling to pay rent? How can my ex be doing so well when I feel like I'm barely getting by? I wish I could eat brunch every morning at aesthetically pleasing cafés like that person, or travel to the other side of the world on a weekly basis like another. And on, and on, we go.

There's no point in comparison, because everything is so unpredictable. There's something so freeing about realising that there's no set template for what being 22, 25, or 30 should look like. Pacing is everything; I'm not convinced I'll find mine for a long time.

My online writing space very quickly – and, regrettably, very inauthentically – became a column to answer the modern dating woes of London and beyond. How I, Felicity Sage, became someone that people felt they could come to for honest dating advice is beyond me. I know as much about dating as I do about the London borough system.

I started this year with heartbreak, and I'm approaching the midway point with a partner who makes me feel valued, but, more importantly, makes me value myself. My experiences with modern dating made me realise how much pressure there is to find someone. Anyone. To get that sunset photo on your Instagram feed, or to have someone to spend Sunday mornings with. When actually it's more important to be able to spend Sunday morning with yourself first. In the beginning, I thought dating would be the only thing that people would be interested in reading about – that it was the only thing that made me seem interesting. I feel really sad for that girl. I love Teddy, and I love our tennis meet-cute, but no more or less than I love all of the other parts of my life. My friends, my job, my family.

It's taken me months to accept that feeling out of control is the new normal. Having control is, let's face it, a bit of a construct anyway. Whether you're sleeping in your childhood bedroom wondering what comes next, looking out of the window in your tiny city flat, or maybe even panicking because life hasn't panned out the way that you imagined it would, know that in my entirely un-expert opinion, it's all going to be alright. *You might meet a friend of a friend tomorrow, and all of a sudden that metropolitan loneliness won't seem so lonely. You might see a job advert that will change the course of your life. You might experience something entirely unexpected, and not in a good way. But time heals most things, and it'll heal that too.*

*Whoever you are, wherever you are, I'm rooting for you. Always. This decade is no longer than the others, but there's magic almost everywhere you look, if you look hard enough.*

*Signing out,*
*Felicity Sage x*

# 37

'So, if we could all raise a glass,' Cecilia said as she held up her own, 'and toast this month's issue of *Influence*. This is by far the most ambitious that we've been. As a small publication with once limited reach, these past few months should be celebrated.'

'Hear, hear!' Sadie, who had already snuck one glass of prosecco in, hiccupped.

'And it would not have been possible without every single one of you. Cheers.' Cecilia swigged the bubbly and everyone else followed her lead, excitement building at the sight of our boss chugging alcohol. One thing you realised when you got older is that adults in offices were just like kids in the cafeteria, cheering when someone spilled their lunch. Felix winked at me from across the room, miming a 'cheers'. I followed suit and we both took a gulp, united in the relief that this issue was finally on its way to being out in the world. After managing to submit my first draft of the article minutes before the deadline, the run up to today had been hectic. Not only had I been overseeing the aspects of the magazine that I always did, but I had been running through the *many* drafts of my own article and working tirelessly with Sadie to iron out the social media campaign. It was amazing to see it all come together.

Teddy squeezed me to him and whispered in my ear. 'See? I promised that everything would turn out great in the end.'

Life felt a million miles away from the scandal that had accompanied our fake relationship. I'd already had responses from the earlier readers who subscribed to the print edition of the magazine, and they were lovely. The dust had settled, and people seemed happy enough to move on.

'It appears that way,' I murmured back, taking another hefty gulp of the fizz. I could see the other guy from tech worming his way around the crowd of our employees, making a beeline for Felix. I snickered into my glass.

'So, how will you be celebrating the end of your time as *Influence*'s agony aunt?' Teddy tickled me, making me shriek.

'I'm thinking a nice long evening doing absolutely nothing.'

He smiled. 'Sounds good to me. I'll do the cooking.'

'I'll do the eating.' I pulled a face at him when he started to protest. 'You know you think you're Teddy Ramsay. Don't try and pretend otherwise.'

'It all started with the pierogi.'

'Felicity?'

I jumped at the sound of my name, engrossed in my little bubble. Cecilia was gesturing for me to come over to her, swaying slightly.

'Felicity, come here!'

Teddy shuddered. 'I don't know what it is, but honestly, she just gives me the fear. I can feel it in the pit of my stomach right now.'

I shoved him. 'Without her, I never would have dated you.'

'I think you mean fake-dated, the source of your anguish? Besides, I would have won you over eventually.'

I rolled my eyes. Cecilia was getting impatient, so I handed him my glass and wandered over. I'd been pushing the future of my job to the back of my mind; nothing had been officially signed to confirm a new role for me, and since she'd offered it, I'd completely disregarded her advice and gone rogue. I readied myself for the worst.

'Everything okay?'

'Felicity.' She pointed to her office. 'Please, come into my office for a chat.'

*Oh God.* This was actually happening. I glanced behind me and saw Teddy's eyes widening as I followed her into the office.

'So, I've been thinking.' She put her glass down on the desk, crossing her arms. Her face wasn't betraying a thing. 'About the future.'

I felt the colour drain from my face. 'Yes?'

'I've been discussing it with the powers that be, and with the finance team, who have revealed the extent of the revenue this quarter. Are you okay, Felicity? You look a bit pale.'

'I'm fine.' It was a squeak.

'I know I said I'd wait for you to decide which type of role we'd explore for you, but I believe I've drafted up the perfect position. Junior Editor *and* Columnist. It would encompass all the things you like about your current workload on the editorial side, and you would carry on as our permanent agony aunt. It's a route for the magazine that we've never tried before. For a column like that, you have to have a writer that people connect with, and I believe we've found that in you.'

A hysterical laugh bubbled its way to the surface. I clapped a hand over my mouth. 'Sorry, nervous laughter. I thought you were about to fire me.'

'*Fire you?* Why on earth would you think that?'

'Well' – I couldn't believe I was bringing this up now – 'I did kind of go rogue. I mean, I took quite a big risk.'

Cecilia looked at the floor smiling. 'That you did. But do you know what? We could all learn a thing or two about integrity from you, Flick. Speaking of being honest, I was also thinking that you might take the new grad under your wing a bit in September. Show her the ropes?'

I was speechless.

'So, what do you say to being our *Influence* agony aunt, long term?' Cecilia rapped her knuckles on the desk. 'And I promise, I won't ask you to fake-date a member of the team again.'

I wasn't sure if I was actually awake. In most of my panicked fever dreams, this wasn't how our conversation had gone. 'Well, of course I want the job.'

Cecilia clapped her hands together. 'Brilliant! We'll iron out the finer details of your job description tomorrow, but for now, let's go and top up these glasses.'

She led the way out of the office, tapping her glass for attention when we re-entered. 'Everyone, please say hello to our permanent *Influence* agony aunt.'

The team cheered, and I caught Teddy's eye across the room. He winked at me.

'I'm so excited.' Sadie grabbed my arm. 'Imagine where we can take this next. I'm thinking of a weekly Instagram takeover, and maybe a special edition feature on your favourite spots in London. And I . . .'

I tuned out, unable to believe what was happening, nodding in the right places and probably signing myself up to a whole host of things I'd later live to regret. For now, though, right in this moment, I felt completely content.

★★★

'I really like this one.' Maia held up her laptop. 'Four bedrooms, a pool, *and* a courtyard.'

I sighed. 'Imagine drinking Italian wine in an Italian courtyard.'

'Is it near gelato?' Kitty squinted at the screen. 'I need to have gelato on hand at all times. It's a matter of importance.'

We'd been crowded around Maia's laptop for the past hour, trying to find the perfect villa for our trip to Italy. It had been a spontaneous decision, spurred on by the fact that Stacey had been leaving. We said it was for the twenties list, one of the final things that I needed to tick off, but we all knew it was a way of ensuring that we had a date in the diary to spend some time together after she moved out. No one really knew what would happen when we all lived apart.

'Okay, so that's one bedroom for me and Soph,' Maia said as she counted us off on her fingers, 'one for Fleddy . . .'

I didn't even try to protest; at this point it had stuck.

'One for Stacey and Kit, and the other for Suze and Tara. This is perfect.'

Kitty started to interrupt. 'But is there –'

'It's Italy. There's ice cream everywhere.' Maia pointed at the map. 'Look, literally down the road.'

'Let's book it.' Kitty smiled, placated.

We were due to fly next week, which had caused some serious stress over the accommodation. Luckily, when you were friends with someone like Maia – who had already made it clear that she needed somewhere with Wi-Fi, for work purposes – a logical strategy was never too far out of reach.

'And you're *sure* that we shouldn't check again in case Lily wants to come?' Kitty bit her lip, anxious. Lily was the new housemate who we hadn't met yet. She was arriving any minute now, all of us waiting like a welcome committee in the kitchen.

'No. She told me that she's starting her internship on Monday. It's too last minute.' I checked again on my phone for the email. 'She did say "next time", though, so there you go – we're going to have to visit Italy twice.'

'What a hardship.' Maia poured herself some juice from the fridge. 'Okay, I'll book this.'

I couldn't believe that in a handful of days we'd all be sitting around in the sun, Suze included. She'd met Tara at Stacey's leaving party, and they'd immediately hit it off. After losing so much confidence with her social life, I was proud of her.

There was movement outside the front door, and Kitty jumped out of her skin. 'God, this is it.'

I crossed my legs. 'Wow, so this is what it's like to be on the other side of this moment. I'm not going to lie, it's equally as terrifying.'

'You two look like an interview panel, sat there like that. Act natural. Come over here,' Maia said, waving us over to the kitchen.

We did as she said, managing it just before the front door opened. There was a moment of silence, which, all credit to her, Maia tried to fill with murmurs about the villa, before the door to the kitchen moved an inch or two.

'Hello?' Another girl, about my age, wandered into the living room. I could hear muttering behind her, questions of 'where do I put this?' and 'which one is hers?'. Clearly our newest addition had parents just like mine.

'Lily, is it?' Kitty jumped up, immediately resorting back to the friendly face that I'd first bumped into when I'd arrived at Carlisle. You would never know that ten minutes before, she'd been mourning Stacey moving out of the very same room that Lily was moving into. It was funny how different things seemed with a bit of perspective.

'Yeah.' Lily popped a box of cupcakes on the living room table. 'I brought these, kind of like a housewarming gift? Even though I know you guys have lived here a long time, and it's technically me that's warming to the house, I just —'

She was babbling, pulling on her ponytail and looking extremely anxious. I remembered it well.

'I'm not about to get bogged down with the technicalities.' I grabbed a cupcake and licked off a bit of frosting. It was chocolate buttercream; I liked her already. 'These are super cute, thanks! Want me to show you your room?'

Lily nodded, thankful to have had her babbling stopped in its tracks. 'Definitely.' She tucked her hair behind her ear. 'Thank you.'

'No problem. I'm Flick, and this is Kitty and Maia.'

They both waved from where they were leaning against the worktop. Maia tilted her head. 'Welcome to Carlisle.'

As I led our newest housemate to her room, greeting her parents, I felt this warmth bubbling up inside my chest. Almost without realising it, I'd become just as much a member of this house as anyone else. And although Lily looked terrified right now, I had no doubt that in the end, she would too. It was just the way of it. A safe space, carved out in a world that could sometimes threaten to drown you. A house that reminded you that fresh starts were possible, and a group of people who believed in that too.

'So, how do you feel about takeaways?' I directed the question at Lily, who was busy setting – of all things – a tiny snow globe on the dressing table.

'I feel like I could eat.' She smiled, warming up a little bit.

I glanced around at the belongings her parents had already brought in from the car. A fluffy rug, a stack of books, a box full of coffee mugs. Soon, this room would be Lily's, not Stacey's, as my room had ceased to be Tara's when I'd moved in. On my way back into the kitchen, I closed my eyes, silently thanking the universe for bringing me here. Next week was my birthday, and I'd be turning 23. Twenty-two had been wild, full of pockets of magic and moments of joy. It had also been one of the hardest years of my life, and I'd learnt how to be resilient. I'd fallen in love, not just with Teddy, but with life again. With London, and my job, and my place in the world. I had an even better feeling about 23.

# Acknowledgements

Firstly, my biggest thank you is to Meg, for taking a chance on Flick, and on me. It's such a rare thing to have someone understand exactly what you want to do with a story, and we've been on the same page from the beginning. I'm so honoured to be your first acquisition.

Thank you to everyone on the HarperNorth team for taking Heartbreak Houseshare and turning it into a real book. It's changed my life, and I couldn't be more grateful.

I love a classic love story, but this novel is also a love letter to female friendship. Thank you to Ellie, for being the first person to set eyes on my manuscript, and for being honest about the jokes that weren't funny. I needed that. Ellen, thanks for being the best housemate and always knowing when to put the kettle on. Thank you to Beth and Rosie, who will always be my favourite part of uni. Don't tell my lecturers. To Ciara, for being my own personal agony aunt, and to Ellie and Eilís, who have made York my home, and for showing up always.

This book is dedicated to my parents, who by now, are pros at dealing with both heartbreaks and houseshares. I'm thankful every day that I don't have to go through my twenties alone. Mum, thanks for igniting my love for storytelling and for getting just as excited as I do. Dad, thanks for being a calming presence and never doubting me for a second. You're my favourite people in the world.

There's a line in the book about Flick and Suze being tied together by an invisible thread, spun by years of family parties and camping trips. I've always loved writing about sisters, mainly because I was blessed with an incredibly sassy, brilliant one. Rachel, thanks for rooting for me, I'll always root for you.

Thank you to my Mama and Grandad, the two people I wish more than anything could be here to see this book be released. Thanks for letting me write my first ever stories on your living room floor. To my Nana, for telling all your friends to buy the book, and to Martin and Ness, for being people I can always turn to.

And finally, this book is for anyone in their twenties, wondering how on earth you do this decade right. Writing Heartbreak Houseshare helped me feel a bit less lost, and I hope it might do the same for you too. We're all in this together. I've got my fingers crossed for us.

**Harper
North**

HarperNorth would like to thank the following staff and contributors for their involvement in making this book a reality:

Hannah Avery
Fionnuala Barrett
Claire Boal
Charlotte Brown
Sarah Burke
Alan Cracknell
Jonathan de Peyer
Anna Derkacz
Tom Dunstan
Kate Elton
Mick Fawcett
Simon Gerratt
Monica Green
Megan Jones

Jean-Marie Kelly
Oliver Malcolm
Alice Murphy-Pyle
Adam Murray
Genevieve Pegg
Agnes Rigou
Florence Shepherd
Angela Snowden
Katherine Stephen
Emma Sullivan
Katrina Troy
Daisy Watt
Chapman & Wilder